SCRATCH

SUE MILLARD

Jackdaw E Books, 2018

Cover and text Copyright © Susan Millard 2018

Cover design by Charlie Farrow, © Susan Millard 2018

First published in Great Britain 2018

ISBN 978-0-9573612-9-4

JACKDAW E BOOKS

Daw Bank, Greenholme, Tebay

Penrith, Cumbria

CA10 3TA

England

http://www.jackdawebooks.co.uk

Other titles by Sue Millard

Fiction:	Non-Fiction:
Against the Odds	*Hoofprints in Eden*
Coachman	*One Fell Swoop*
Dragon Bait	*Fell Facts*
The Forthright Saga	*Fell Fun*
The Twisted Stair	Poetry: *Ash Tree*

Chapter 1.

A shower of hail was dragging its skirts over the fells to rattle across my windscreen, and I chose a lower gear and let the pickup and horse-trailer crunch their own way downhill over the bouncing ice. By the calendar it was spring, but the land to either side of the unfenced road was still brown with tussocks of tawny sedge, dead dark patches of heather and the soaked wintry russet of bracken.

Robbie slouched in the passenger seat, swaying to our movement and deep in an exchange of phone texts.

"You don't need me on Monday night, do you, Mam?"

"I don't know. How many ewes are going to lamb on Monday night?" The mare in the trailer trampled briefly and went quiet again as the road levelled out. "What are you planning?"

He said, "Beth Langdale's inviting me over."

I glanced across at him: no longer my little blond baby but a tall handsome youth. Sometimes that jolted me. How could I have been a mother for more than twenty years? Inside, I was still the young woman I'd been when Madoc and I were first married.

"And who's Beth Langdale?"

"You know. We met at the Young Farmers last month. I'm sure I've mentioned her."

"You may well have done. What happened to Olivia?"

"You mean Jessica."

"Do I? I can't keep up with all your girlfriends."

He went on texting, a slight smile on his face.

The hail stopped as suddenly as it had started, and ahead of us the sun lit our farm like a spotlight. The steep grassland of Stone Side was lined with limestone walls that ran down from the face of the Scar, and the ancient long-house and its cluster of buildings sat back, settled against the hill like an old man in an armchair. I was still getting used to the idea that it was ours.

We reached the farm gate and I drove carefully over the cattle grid, trying to avoid the potholes in the steep, stony track.

"I must talk to your Da about getting a load of gravel."

Robbie said, "It isn't worth it till the weather cheers up. But if you don't put your foot down we won't make it up to the yard at all."

"You get on with your love letter and don't fuss me." I negotiated the stone gateposts without mishap and let the pickup and trailer roll to a halt at the bright end of the yard. "There. All done with kindness."

The lambing shed door rumbled open, and there was Madoc, standing in the sunshine. He was wearing a woollen hat I'd knitted for him back in our Lancashire days, so long ago that much of the dark blue had faded to grey; his wellingtons and the hems of his waterproof trousers were edged with sheep muck, and a wisp of wool hung from the zip of his jacket. Kip the sheepdog stood pressed against his leg, desperate to greet us but waiting on orders.

"Picture of the well-dressed lambing attendant!" said Robbie, with a laugh.

"What's that old saying about pots and kettles?"

I slid down from the cab and for a moment Madoc's blue, steady gaze met mine. There was always something reserved in that lean face, something that didn't go with the working clothes. He performed a solemn, ceremonial wave of greeting, as though I'd been away a month. Not too tired to play-act, then. I waved back.

Robbie dropped the ramp with a creak of springs and opened the rear gates, and I ducked in through the side door and unfastened the pony's lead rope to let her shuffle backwards out of the trailer. The sun lit up her rounded hindquarters and broad back, winter-furred in bright bay-brown. Her tail was black and long enough to tread on, her mane hung in a deep curving line and its silky forelock half covered her face. She stopped partway down the ramp – a stout little war-horse, flaring her nostrils, flickering her ears, deeply suspicious.

I saw Robbie move impatiently, and I warned him just in time, "This one's got brains. Let her use them." He backed off. I was aware of the dog crouching in anticipation and I heard Madoc gave him a low warning to stay.

I said more gently, to the mare, "It's all right, Zilla. Go steady."

She whinnied, shivering the hair across her flanks. From high in the fields my two younger ponies called back and they exchanged a flurry of excited messages which eventually convinced her the place was safe. With a slither and a clatter, she backed all the way down onto the concrete.

"Where are you going to put her?" asked Robbie. "In High Field with the others?"

"No. Tomorrow will be soon enough. She can go in the spare stable for now. Then you can have all the joy of mucking out ready for Uncle Dava's new horses."

"I'd forgotten they were coming," Robbie said. "Should've kept my big mouth shut."

Madoc waited until I'd led Zilla into the stable before he came over.

"A bay mare?" he said, leaning on the door frame. "Well, it's a change from all those black geldings."

Kip stood up against the half-door and the mare gave a warning snort, then worked off her agitation by tramping round the loose-box and shaking her head as if to show the hay-net, the sawdust bedding and the water bucket exactly who was in charge.

Robbie parked the wheelbarrow and a muck shovel beside the trailer and came to stand at the other side of the stable door. Between him and Madoc, they almost blocked the light.

"Well, Da, what d'you think? Has Mam picked a good one?"

"You tell me."

The dog stood on his hindlegs again so Robbie rubbed his ears affectionately while he considered the mare. "Well. It's mature, easy to sell on for a profit. Provided it's sound."

"Which she is," I said, slightly emphasising the word *she*. "She was too strong for the kids to ride, and much too clever for their mother."

"Other than that, it's just another neddy with short fat hairy legs."

I countered, "She's got better bone than any of the thoroughbreds."

"That's just as well – she's that solid, she practically needs pit-props."

Madoc chuckled, though the insults were hardly funny any more; well-worn and expected, like rival football chants. My Fell pony purchases demanded far more ingenuity from me than the young horses he schooled to begin their racing careers. Three-year-old thoroughbreds were Etonians, well versed in the ways of humankind. Through the early stages of their education, the bridling and mouthing and saddling and long-rein driving, I left Madoc to his own devices, and I knew he wouldn't need any help till he was ready to mount them for the first time. By contrast my Fell youngstock were aboriginals who'd never seen a house, let alone a school. Even the youngest had their own primeval independence. Relationships with them had to begin with patience, through encounters that looked like nothing from the outside, but inside were exacting and intense: "I've been sitting in the field all morning, waiting for that yearling to come to me. And, bless him, he's just walked right up and touched me!" Or: "That two-year-old still won't let me pick up his back feet! I'll be in the stable all afternoon, at this rate." Each time they placed their trust in me I was reminded that they were being more generous than I was myself. I must educate them without breaking their independent spirits, and sell them only where I believed they would be safe. And Madoc left me to do all that because he knew how much it meant to me.

"You don't usually do re-schooling," he said. "How much did you pay for her?"

He didn't usually ask. I said, "Next to nothing."

"Tell me, Siân."

"Six hundred," I said. "They threw in her saddle to clinch the deal. Mind, you could see with half an eye it didn't fit her."

"Cheap." He raised an eyebrow. "Are you sure she's registered?"

"First thing I checked. She has a Fell Pony passport that says she'll be six next month. No, I bet that saddle's been half her trouble. I'll trade it for something wider and start her again from scratch."

"Oh well. She's your risk."

"Yes, love. That's the whole point."

Chapter 2.

I knew as soon as I walked into the house that Jack was up to something. I could hear scuffling noises in the kitchen, and him laughing, and then a loud wooden thump like a brush hitting a cupboard. Cerys raised her voice in protest.

I kicked off my boots and went in, and as usual with Jack, it was like stepping into a cartoon. He held my good floor mop in both hands like a hockey stick. Cerys was still in the dark-green uniform that she wore for work at the motorway services, and she stood balanced, facing him down. When he saw me he pretended to hide the mop behind his back, but his grin widened. His curly red hair stood up as though electrified.

Cerys exclaimed, "Mam? Deal with our Jack before I strangle him!"

An orphan lamb, in a box in the warming oven of the Rayburn, bleated in response to her voice. Cerys said to it, "Oh, be quiet. I *know* you're hungry."

I said, "Get some milk for him then, and leave Jack to me. Go on."

She abandoned the situation and went to the larder where we kept the milk-replacer.

"Now then, mischief!" I said. "What have you been doing?"

"Did you know you can use soap to play ice hockey? It doesn't half go!"

"And where exactly has it gone to?"

"In the goal! Owen's scored again!"

I was still running on the adrenalin of fetching the mare home. "I'm warning you. Don't make things worse than they already are. Where's the soap?"

Cerys, coming back with the bag of powdered milk, said, "It's under the table, I think."

I told Jack, "Pick it up and put it back where it belongs. Give me that mop." He handed it to me, still smiling, and ducked under the table.

I asked Cerys, "What set him off?"

"Who ever knows what sets him off?" Cerys poured water into a feeding bottle and began to count in scoops of milk powder. "The lamb was bleating."

"His name's Gareth," Jack said, from somewhere level with my ankles.

"Whatever," said Cerys. "I came in here to see what it wanted. Next thing I know, Jack's got the mop and he's smacking the soap round the kitchen –"

We were interrupted by the soap whizzing between my feet to bounce off the cupboards along the opposite wall and I realised there were white skid marks all over the quarry tiles. I gave my bossy-mother warning cough.

"Ahem! Come out of there NOW."

"You missed it!" he said. He surfaced from under the table, one sports shoe in his hand from hitting the soap, the other foot still shod.

Cerys asked, "Aren't you ever going to grow up?"

"Is there a rule that you have to?"

I picked up the soap and put it by the sink, Jack put his trainer back on, and the lamb trampled about inside his box and bleated again. Cerys capped the milk bottle with a feeding teat and began to shake the mixture.

"It's all right," I said, "you can give that to me now. How was work today?"

"Crazy. Michael sent me over to the southbound services to fill in for somebody who'd called in sick. Well! I thought our side was pretty busy, but it was *mad* there."

"People going home from holidays, I suppose. You'll be glad when school starts again."

"Yeah. Going back for a rest." She handed me the bottle.

"Supper won't be ready for a bit, so go and get changed, eh love? Oh, and put that bag of milk away."

"Okay."

As the door shut behind her, I said to Jack, "Here. See this bottle? Feed this lamb."

"He's called Gareth," he said. "Can I have a drink?"

"Did I hear you say Please? Right now the lamb –"

"Gareth."

"All right! He *needs* a drink. He needs it much more than you do."

Cerys came back, and in a series of lithe movements made a drink of hot blackcurrant juice and a second exit.

"*She* didn't ask," Jack said in outraged tones.

"She's been at work," I pointed out. "And when she's not working, she's revising for exams. Come on now! Warm that bottle in the microwave. Half a minute at the most. Sit down quietly and feed the lamb – whatever he's called."

"Gareth." Jack put the bottle into the microwave and set the timer.

The kitchen phone rang. "Oh! Why do cold calls always come at supper-time?" I snatched it up. "HELLO!"

"Siân? It's me. Nothing wrong, is there?" The piercing voice of Hazel Wharton from Underscar, the next-door farm. "How'd it go?"

"How did what go? Sorry – the microwave's on, I can't hear you properly, wait a tick." The timer pinged and Jack took out the warmed bottle. I mouthed at him, "Shake it." Then I said to Hazel, "Sorry. The kitchen's having a small crisis."

"Your kitchen's always having a small crisis. Who is it this time?"

"It's sorted," I said. "Nothing serious. What can we do for you?"

Jack settled cross-legged with his back to the stove, pulled the cardboard box out of the warming oven and carefully lifted scrappy little Gareth into the gap between his knees. How nice it would be if he could keep that gentleness and not submerge into the bog of teenage sulking that we'd ploughed through when Robbie hit puberty.

"Did you get the pony home safely?" said Hazel's voice from the phone.

"Oh, yes, she's in the stable." A glance at the clock showed me I had forty-five minutes before Madoc and Robbie were likely to come in wanting supper. I tucked the phone between ear and shoulder so I could carry on talking while I made myself a cup of tea.

"I thought so," said Hazel. "Our Andy says you came home quite steady."

"Your old man's better than a spy satellite," I said. "Yes, it went all right."

"Excited?"

I put a teabag into my mug and poured in hot water from the Rayburn kettle. "Oh, no more than your Andy is when he buys a new tup. I'm looking forward to riding her but the problem will be finding the time, you know how it is."

Jack looked up at me. "Oh, can we ride this one? You never said."

"Hush, I'm talking to Hazel."

She said, "What I phoned for was... do you want to come to choir on Monday?"

Monday. Was anything happening on Monday? The square on the wall-chart appeared to be empty.

"You said to remind you," she went on. "I'm going with Jean but she says she'll give you a lift too. And there's room for Cerys, if it isn't beneath her to bring that voice to a village choir."

"I don't know – well, I have this feeling that there *is* something happening on Monday and I haven't written it down."

Hazel said helpfully, "The kids going back to school."

"No, I remember now. It's Robbie – he's got a date." I carried my tea to the fridge and added milk.

"Lucky boy. Who's it with?"

"Langdales' girl, what's she called, Beth."

"Langdales from The Ghyll, at the other side of Tebay? The daughter who's training to be a nurse?"

"Oh, is she? Could be."

A hissing noise drew my attention. The lamb was sucking hard at the feeding bottle and the teat had begun to collapse, but Jack was so distracted by earwigging on my conversation that he didn't seem to have noticed. I prodded him with the toe of my slipper and hissed, "Let the air back in." He did, and chuckled at the rude slurping sound it made.

Hazel asked, "Are you there? So what, if Robbie has got a date? He won't want you to hold his hand."

"Well, no, but if Robbie's going to be out then Madoc or I will have to be in the lambing shed, and Cerys is doing her A-level revision so I can't expect her to police Jack. I caught him just now playing ice hockey with the soap."

"A mere nothing," said Hazel. "Why don't you bring both of them to choir?"

I looked down at the lamb on Jack's knees, and the jeans he'd almost grown out of. He'd be bored if I dragged him along to choir, and a bored Jack was an inventive Jack. I said, "No. I don't think I have time right now. I'm really sorry."

"Ah well. Anyway, here's Andy coming in for his tea. I must dash. Perhaps we'll see you after lambing?"

"Oh yes. If not before. Bye."

Jack looked up from feeding the lamb and asked, "What's for *our* tea?"

"You've got ears like a bat. We're having Cumberland sausages."

He said, "I don't like sausages."

"Yes, you do," I said.

"Is it the ones in the fridge that Cerys brought home from work yesterday? I really don't like them when they've gone past their sell-by date."

Damn the boy and his quick eyes. "They're perfectly good sausages," I said.

"I'm thinking of becoming a vegetarian." He stroked the lamb's hard little head.

"Well then," I said, "you'll have to make do with carrots and spuds. I'm not catering for anybody's fancies tonight."

"I didn't say I was, definitely – I'm just thinking about it."

"Then think about it while you're laying the table. Pop Gareth into his box for now, and wash your hands."

He said, "Mam, I'm not a babby any more."

"You still have to wash your hands."

He lifted the lamb back into confinement and stood up, brushing crimped white hairs from his jeans onto the floor.

I pushed myself off the warmth of the Rayburn and went through the stairwell to get vegetables from the larder. At the foot of the stairs, bolted to the wall, there were the coat hooks where we kept our "tidy" jackets, and the gun cabinet with the key-box beside it, and on top of the gun cabinet a plastic carrier bag bulging with other plastic bags. I pulled one out and went into the larder, a square room with thick, plastered stone walls and a long slate bench that trapped the cold. Shelves on the walls held tinned fruit, sauces and dry goods and shop-bought marmalade; I'd hidden the last three jars of home-made strawberry jam right at the back. On the highest shelves I'd shoved away the empty jars, the spare pans, and the plastic storage boxes where we kept the farm medicines and single-use syringes. Cerys had dumped the bag of milk-powder under the bench beside the heavy paper sacks of potatoes, carrots and onions, still rough with soil from Robbie's garden at the farm we'd left in September. I shook open my plastic bag and filled it with vegetables.

When I turned round Jack was at the doorway with cutlery in his hands. I shooed him back into the kitchen, tipped the veg into the sink and began to scrub and peel the potatoes.

He dawdled over laying the table, setting each piece of cutlery very carefully in its place. I was holding my breath while I chopped onions when he said, "Ma-ammm?"

I recognised the drawn out note that meant he'd been thinking, and he was sure I'd disapprove of what he'd been thinking, but he was going to try his luck anyway.

"Mam? Will you let me ride the new pony?"

Should I draw breath to answer, and end up streaming with onion tears? – or hold it and have him pester me till I gasped for air and had to answer anyway? I turned on the tap and ran water over my hands and over the onion, which gave me time to think.

"We'll see. Let me find out what she's like, first."

"But I'm always the one who has to sit on the three-year-olds for the first time, so if I can't ride this one when it's already broken, that's not – " I saw how he stopped himself saying "not fair" and I smothered a smile. He finished instead by saying, "It doesn't make sense."

"I'll explain if you get a chopping board and come here and chop these carrots. Be careful, this knife is *sharp*. Now, it's like this. Zilla's been ridden a bit, but somewhere along the line, something's gone wrong for her, otherwise she wouldn't have been for sale. So I have to find out what's wrong, before I can put it right, okay? Now, I'm not saying you'd do anything unkind to her, but I don't want to have to filter out the things *you* might do, from things other people did to her before she came here. I don't know whether that makes any 'sense' to you."

"Oh. Then it's like – you're being a detective." He cut the top off a carrot and said, "You don't want to muck-up the crime scene."

"Yes, that's one way of putting it."

"But when you make me sit on a horse that you bought wild," he said, with a sidelong glance, "isn't that us committing a crime?"

"No! A wild one is a completely blank canvas. I try to get everything right first time, so I don't muck things up."

"But the old painters changed stuff all the time. There's that programme on telly where they x-ray them, don't they, to find out if they're fakes. D'you think Zilla's a fake?"

"No... I think she's had a bit of overpainting. But how can I tell, if you start painting more on top? I can't x-ray her to find out what's in her head! You leave her to me."

Jack sighed. "Okay. Then can I watch The Simpsons?"

His face was innocent, but I knew he was striking a bargain. I took a deep breath and began afresh on the onions.

Chapter 3.

I woke from a doze to find that the television was silently displaying three people on a sofa, laughing and talking to a man with prompt cards in his hand. The clock showed a few minutes after eleven. Robbie, curled asleep on the sofa, snored lightly. When I had sent Jack to bed an hour ago Robbie had already been asleep, so it must have been Cerys who'd muted the sound on the television. Where the curtains didn't quite fit the window I could see the flat dark of night, and the quietness of the chimney suggested the air outside was still and frosty.

Slowly I worked out what had woken me: the click of the back door closing. So, Madoc had come in from the lambing shed. I got up to switch off the television, and on my way to the kitchen I patted Robbie to wake him.

Madoc was putting on his slippers, holding the towel-rail of the Rayburn to keep his balance. There were strands of silver among his fair hair, and when he looked up at me I saw lines drawn in his face from nostril to mouth, and blue shadows under his eyes, that made him look all of his forty-eight years. Of course he was cold, and tired, and the electric light was unflattering, but there it was, plain: neither he nor I were young any more. The fact slid in under my heart the way his remoteness had in the afternoon. But, for the same reasons, now was not the time to talk about it.

I had moved the lamb in his cardboard box out of the confines of the warming oven, and Madoc stepped around it and sat, rather heavily, at the table.

"Tea?" I suggested.

"Please."

The lamb stood up and bleated for attention, but right now Madoc's needs were more important than his. I touched my palm to the aluminium flank of the Rayburn kettle and decided it wasn't anywhere near boiling, so I took it across to fill the electric one, then set the teapot at the end of the stove to warm. The pot, white china decorated with blue irises, had been a wedding present, an elegant and miraculous survivor of twenty-plus years of use. During the winter, while we lived in the mobile home and renovated the essential bits of the house, I'd painted the kitchen the same white and blue, but I was struggling to keep either the kitchen or the pot free of smuts from the old Rayburn, which we'd kept mainly because we couldn't afford to replace it. Two propane gas rings from the mobile home gave me some flexibility but nothing beat the Rayburn for heating the water, especially during the power cuts we'd endured over winter. Solid and shabby as the old stove was, it kept the heart of the house beating. I made the tea.

Robbie came into the kitchen, stretching. He twitched a chair round so he could straddle it, and rested his head on his folded arms. "I hope you told the yows I want a quiet night."

"Three new sets of twins and four singles so far," said Madoc. "They're popping them out like they were shelling peas."

"Blimey," said Robbie, and stifled a yawn.

"Any problems?" I asked Madoc.

"Not a bit. The lambs are up and sucking."

"Well if the yows all lamb that easy," said Robbie, "I should be able to sleep right through."

"Don't bank on it," said Madoc. "There were two more starting when I came in."

"Hey-ho."

"Well," I said, as reasonably as I could, "they've got to lamb sometime, so they might as well do it and get it over with. There's nothing so tiring as a lambing season that drags on for weeks."

I poured three mugs of tea and handed out chunks of fruit cake. Robbie wolfed his down between gulps of tea, but I didn't think Madoc was aware of what he was eating.

I told Robbie, "Take a flask with you when you go out. There'll be enough hot in the kettle to fill it."

"No, I'll come back in and make a drink when I need it."

"I wish you'd do as you're bloody told," Madoc said. His voice was flat and expressionless.

"If I come in I can steal some more of this cake. Is it one of Hazel's?"

"Yes."

"I thought so."

I was unsure whether it was compliment or criticism. "How can you tell?"

"I can't. I don't know why she bakes so many Christmas cakes. But Danny says she ends up giving the last ones away."

"Which Danny would that be?"

"Daniel Wharton? Lives next door? You know, Hazel's son? You can't have forgotten!"

Before I could speak again Madoc said, "She's tired. And so am I. Don't push it."

I said to Robbie, "If you've got to come in during the night, don't make a noise. If you wake me I'll hide the cake!"

Robbie laughed. "Would you like to think that one through, Mam?"

"No, I wouldn't! Have you finished your tea? Right – off with you."

"Slave driver. I may cry." But he went out into the porch, pulled on his boots, outdoor clothes and a woolly hat, and disappeared across the yard.

Gareth the lamb trampled vigorously in his box and repeated his high, demanding bleat. This time I mixed a bottle of milk and sat on a chair to feed him. He explored all round the teat with excited nibbles and butts before he took a firm hold and began to suck.

"Well, look at you," I said. And to Madoc, "This one could go out to the shed tomorrow."

"He could if we had a pen to put him in," said Madoc. "I've had to start making pens out of straw bales in the empty stable."

"Did you tell Robbie about that?"

"No." He rubbed his forehead. "Oh well."

"He'll work it out," I said. "And Jack will be quite happy if the lamb has to stay in the kitchen. He'll probably want it to keep goal for him."

"What? You're not making any sense."

"I came in at tea time and I found him playing hockey with the soap."

"Honestly, that boy!"

When Gareth the lamb finished the bottle of milk I put him down on the floor, where he tap-danced and slid by turns, while I replaced the newspapers in his box with a couple of fresh sheets and got rid of the soiled ones in the Rayburn fire. Madoc drank his tea in slow mouthfuls. With the lamb fed and boxed for the night, I sat down again at the table. There was a pause.

I took a deep breath and said, "Look, love. I've been thinking."

It was hard not to start every conversation with the slap in the face that was money. Ever since I had left Dava's stables and become a wife and mother and maid-of-all-work, my contribution to our household expenses had been simply that I didn't take a wage. We were not earning much yet from the farm and our joint bank account was usually in the red.

I said, "I'd really like to get a job – you know, off the farm. Cerys says the motorway services are looking for extra staff for the summer."

Despite his tiredness he made the effort to pay attention. But he said, "Oh, Mouse, please don't take on anything else. I'll still need you to ride exercise with Dava's horses, and before you know it there'll be the holiday cottage to look after as well as – all this." He glanced round the cluttered kitchen.

"I know it's untidy. That's why I thought... why don't we employ someone to clean the cottage, someone who really likes doing it? I could cover their pay if I worked at the services."

"It sounds convoluted," he said doubtfully.

"It pays more than the minimum wage, and that wouldn't be just the holiday season."

"But if someone can earn above minimum wage at the services, why would they work for us for less?"

"I don't know. I thought it might suit someone who only wanted a few hours... And if the kids could give me a hand in the house..."

He laughed briefly. "Well, Robbie won't, now he's working part time for Langdales."

"I didn't mean Robbie," I said.

"And Cerys won't because she's already working at the services, and then she's away to college in the autumn. And as for

Jack! Anything more complex than a spoon, he has to take it apart – imagine yourself leaving him in charge of a vacuum cleaner!"

Damn it, he was right, but I didn't have to like it.

"I'm just trying to – "

"– be helpful. I know."

That wasn't the whole truth, of course. It wasn't only the money. There was also a kind of restlessness that had got into my bones during the winter, living through the dark months in the mobile home while the builders were at work on the house; I'd become starved of daylight, cramped with cabin fever. Before we had fairly begun to benefit from moving into the house, lambing had arrived with its twenty-four-hour work, and tomorrow two young horses were due to arrive for pre-training.

I said irritably, "Well, if I'm going to stay sane, I'll have to keep buying ponies."

"I know. Have I ever said you shouldn't?"

"I thought you were cross that I bought the mare?"

"I wanted to know how much money you'd got tied up in her, that was all." There it was again.

I said, "We don't go on holiday, we don't go anywhere, we don't go out."

"I know."

"Don't keep saying that! I've got to have a challenge to work on. You made me feel like Zilla was an extra, like some kind of indulgence."

"What? When did I say that?"

"This afternoon. They pay for themselves, don't they? They chewed down all that rough stuff for you on Sweet Holme and Syke Side. And if I've got to be Mrs Mop for the holiday cottage, *I need them*. I've got to let off steam somehow!"

"Keep your hair on," he said mildly. "I won't ask you to give up your ponies. At least, if I ever do, you'll know we've really got our backs to the wall. Don't forget I'm the one who's got to live with you when the steam builds up."

"Well then." I picked up my mug, and found my hands were clumsy. "Damn it, my tea's gone cold." And catching Madoc's expression, I said, "Don't you dare laugh." We both suffered from laughter as a reaction to anger, a rogue trembling in the chest that could become painful.

"Would I?"

"Of course you would, you bastard."

He said, "Then you'd better go out and play with the new mare in the morning, hadn't you?"

"Yes. I bloody well will." I tipped the rest of my tea down the sink. "Well. How soon can we paint the walls in your damn-and-blasted cottage?"

He chuckled at my vehemence. "I don't know. I'll phone the plasterer tomorrow and find out."

"Tomorrow's Sunday," I reminded him, "and Uncle Dava's sending us some horses."

"Ah, dear..." He yawned. "Come on, Danger Mouse, time for bed."

Chapter 4.

Cold sunshine was filtering through the bedroom curtains when I woke. I became aware of the sounds and sensations that defined the morning condition of the household. Everything normal. Madoc's place beside me was empty but I could hear him downstairs rattling the ashes out of the Rayburn fire.

In the bedroom on the other side of the landing Robbie was already faintly snoring, and I wondered whether it had been a busy night in the lambing shed. There was no sound from Cerys or Jack. Downstairs there was a scrape of metal, then the back door opened and shut, meaning that Madoc had gone out to empty the stove ash-pan; the same again, reversed, when he returned. Then he started talking, and although I couldn't make out the words the pattern of his conversation told me that he'd brought Kip the sheepdog in from his overnight kennel and was talking to him. However, when I dressed and went down to the kitchen, there was no Madoc, no dog, and no lamb, only a used mug and a plate of crumbs on the draining board, and at floor level the cardboard box and two empty dishes.

Gracie the cat greeted me with a hop-and-nudge against my shin.

"Where were you last night, you dirty stop-out?" Madoc wasn't the only one who talked to animals as though they could talk back. I stroked her black fur and she rubbed round my ankles in a spike of ecstatic purring. "And don't tell me you need breakfast, because you don't."

Gracie sat at my feet and continued to purr while I made myself a cup of tea and drank it. When I put my coat on to go out she strolled into the front room to commandeer the recliner.

Outside the air was sharp, the sky was blue and clear, and there was Zilla standing at the stable door with pricked ears and a pleading whinny. When I went over she reached out to me, her whiskery muzzle searching the pockets of my jacket.

"Hey you...There are no treats in there." I ran my fingers through the long fringe of hair under her jaw. "Poor starving creature. Never mind, there's plenty of grass where you're going."

I headcollared her and led her out of the stable and up to High Field.

It was a simple enough task but my brain was working fast, partly with anticipation and partly with a taut awareness of danger. Between frost and sunshine and early morning hunger Zilla was on her toes, jigging sideways instead of walking by my shoulder, while up at the gate to High Field the geldings, Rocky and Marshal, were swinging their heads and trampling about in mute argument. First meetings were always tricky, no matter how kind the individuals' temperaments, and although Zilla would probably carry authority over them by her age and sex there was no guessing how the mix was going to react. It wasn't just the steep slope that made my heart pound.

When we reached the gate I let Zilla reach over the top bar to touch noses with the three-year-olds. Necks arched, ears pricked forward, nostrils flared. Their muzzles barely touched before they flinched away, as though even a breath might scald. I stood to one side, unable to stop myself grinning with excitement.

Rocky stepped forward and moved his head towards Zilla's shoulder, and she squealed indignantly and lashed her tail. Rocky startled, then edged closer and tried again but this time she clanged a fore hoof against the lower bars of the gate, which made both the three-year-olds shy away in a half circle. They nipped each other and swung their heads, awaiting the reactions of this tetchy duchess. She stood tensely for another half minute, then she blew a ferocious snort, shook her head, and reached down to graze.

I said, "Well, if that's all," and I opened the gate and let her into the field.

They were quiet for a few seconds as I closed the gate, then Zilla set off at a gallop and the three-year-olds scuttled after her with a noise like kettledrums. Up the slope they went, until the wall below Thorny Bank brought the three of them bucking to a halt and turned them trotting along the boundary, flouncing their black manes and tails. Zilla reached the far end of High Field, spun and led them plunging back down, giving snorts that would have done credit to a whale. When she skidded to a halt at the gate all three posed with their heads up, blowing white clouds of steam.

Rocky, the bolder one of the two boys, dared to come alongside and touch his nose to Zilla's flank. Immediately she lashed out with a hind leg, sideways and back, a lightning strike that would have broken his shoulder if he'd been standing an inch or two nearer.

"You witch," I said under my breath.

There was a pause, in which Zilla lowered her head, flattened her ears evilly and stalked in a circle. The geldings stayed at a respectful distance, so she shook herself and walked quietly away across the slope. The geldings followed a few steps behind her, and all three settled to graze.

It was over. They were a herd.

My senses widened again, from Zilla, to the field, to the rest of the farm and the countryside below. I could hear the mistle thrush singing in a pine tree near the house, and from the fell the long, bubbling call of a curlew – the moorland messenger of spring. I walked back to the house, swinging the headcollar and rope, with the blood running light through my veins.

Chapter 5.

"Da?" Robbie leaned in through the kitchen door. "There's a horsebox coming."

We were sitting with our boots off, warming ourselves with mugs of tea.

"One of Hardings'?" asked Madoc.

"Don't think so. It's dead smart, but it's not their colours." He didn't wait for a reply, but went back out towards the lambing shed.

Madoc began to pull his boots on. "You'll want to see this."

"Will I?"

He glanced up at me, smiling, so I tipped the last of my tea down the sink and by the time the horsebox inched into the yard we were both outside waiting for it. Robbie was right: it was dead smart. A coachbuilt Mercedes, painted a metallic sea-green and emblazoned on both sides with white leaping horses.

The driver opened his window a fraction and looked out at us.

"Is this Stone Side, ey?" He had a strong Liverpool accent.

"Well, if it isn't," said Madoc cheerfully, "we're living in the wrong house."

The driver picked a clipboard out of the door pocket and squinted at it: "Madoc Shawn Owen?"

"Yes," said Madoc, "One of the three." He dodged my prod at his ribs and waited, hands in pockets, with a faintly amused expression.

I said to the driver, "You've got our names mixed up there. Madoc AND Siân. 'Sharn'. That's Welsh Jane, not Irish John."

"Whatever." The driver glanced round at the farm buildings and offered Madoc the board and the pen. "Sign there."

"Unload the horses first, and let's see if they've travelled all right. After that, I'll sign anything you like."

The driver sighed, but he tossed the board onto the passenger seat and climbed out.

One horse inside the box gave a plaintive whinny, the same cry for company that Zilla had given the previous day, and I looked up towards the Scar to see how the mare and the youngsters would react. They'd heard it all right; they lifted their heads as one, and for a moment they held the pose, black and brown against the wintry green of the grass, their long manes lifting on the wind. Then they simply resumed grazing, a little herd close-knit and caring nothing for others. I've seen that happen so often. How could the Fells decide by that horse's voice that he was not important to them? What quality did it lack, that Zilla and the three-year-olds had instantly recognised in each other?

In the meantime the driver had lowered the ramp and trudged up into the horsebox to swing back the partitions. The first horse he led out was a big framed animal, his legs and tail protected by fleecy green travelling gear and his body cocooned in a padded rug. One four-year-old thoroughbred, delivered in protective wrapping. Inside it, he was such a dark brown he seemed black. He clattered down the ramp, circled the driver at the rope's end and gave a high, whistling neigh. Up in High Field the mare lifted her head again, but it was the other horse in the box who called back to him.

He had bold eyes and rather long ears, and there was a lot of intelligence in that head, perhaps too much. A prince, at the very least. And to my surprise he wasn't a gelding; he was an entire colt.

"Now then, boyo," said Madoc, as he took the horse's lead rope from the driver. "Well, you've got shoes on. That's one less job to do. Come on, there's a grand lad."

He led him to the stable where Zilla had been overnight, and as I watched the colt's long, elastic stride and swinging tail I acknowledged that Madoc had been right: this was something worth seeing. By the time I closed the stable door I'd decided that, prince or not, I liked him. I didn't have to ask how Madoc felt: I could tell by the way he stroked the horse's neck, the quiet word as he removed the headcollar and released him to explore. He waited. The colt circled the box and raised his head thoughtfully. I wondered if he could smell the mare who'd occupied it yesterday. At any rate he relaxed enough to nip a few stalks of haylage from his net and begin to chew.

The second horse the driver had brought us was a thin chestnut, protected, like the colt, with travel boots and rug. He fidgeted about at the end of his rope, looking round with long-lashed, sensitive eyes, then he stood still and whinnied. Again the Fells decided not to reply. The colt in the stable turned around and came eagerly to the door.

"Hee-y'are." The driver gave me the lead rope, and while I led the chestnut into the second stable I could hear him behind me shutting partitions and throwing the ramp back up.

When I came out, Madoc was asking, "Where are the passports?"

The driver fetched him a large brown envelope and, while Madoc checked the details, he leaned against the cab door, checking his phone. I'd seldom seen such offhandedness in a visiting driver. They were usually wiry, chirpy countrymen whom we took into the kitchen for tea and cake and sent on their way with thanks for a job well done. But this one smelled sour to me, and urban. Tattoos showed at neck and wrists. I was sure he would sneer at our half-modernised house, the second-hand cupboards and the ancient sooty Rayburn. I decided I wasn't going to invite him in.

Madoc evidently felt the same. He scribbled a signature and handed the clipboard back.

"There you are. Don't let us keep you."

The driver pocketed his phone and grumbled a wordless reply, then heaved himself up into the horsebox and started the engine. He did a three-point turn to get out of the yard, and Robbie came out of the lambing shed to observe, in a silence that bordered on criticism. Then the box went rumbling down the track through the fields, over the ringing cattle grid, and away south towards the motorway.

Madoc said, "I wonder why Dava didn't use Hardings."

The west wind blew suddenly cold. The sky came towards us thick and white and hail clattered over the slate roofs like someone emptying a bucket of gravel. We huddled against the wall to shelter and the brown horse, hearing the trample of nervous hooves in the next box, came to the door and looked to us as though to gauge what his reaction ought to be. When we didn't jump he released his tension in a couple of loud snorts and went back to the hay-net.

"That's a smart horse," I said, over the rattle of the hail. "What's he called?"

Instead of replying Madoc drew the passport out of the envelope and showed it to me, open at the pedigree. I had to read it twice before I took it in.

KING COEL (GB), Brown colt

Sire: CROWN PRINCE (GB)

(by CROWN IMPERIAL (IRE))

Dam: CARBON COPY (GB)

(by CYMRU (GB)).

King Coel was a grandson of our own stallion, Cymru. And that was very rare indeed, because Cymru had died so young.

~~~

It had been close to lunchtime on a grey midwinter day when our local vet, Stuart Thompson, arrived to examine and rasp the stallion's teeth. I had stayed in the house with Robbie who was then just a year old, too young to risk near the stables with a stroppy stallion. I was in the early stages of pregnancy with Cerys and still prone to day-long morning sickness, so the baby food I had warmed for Robbie was puréed lamb stew, bland and inoffensive like the music on the radio.

The dentistry seemed to be taking a long time and I hoped Cymru wasn't being awkward. He'd his moments, over his career as a racehorse, with Dava regularly threatening to geld him. Madoc understood him though. There was still a photograph on our dresser, taken at Aintree when they won their last steeplechase together; I was leading him to the winner's enclosure and his head was up and his ears pricked; his success had just pushed his value over a hundred thousand pounds. At that point he still belonged to Dava, who was only visible in the photo as a tweed-clad shoulder and the strap of a binocular case, but Madoc in his crimson silks was reaching down to slap Cymru's dappled grey neck, and I was looking up at him, laughing. We were a team, a happy, winning team. The photograph took me back there, every time.

But on that winter day Madoc had come in from the yard, hurrying, leaving the door open to the wind. He began to root among the papers by the telephone, pushing aside *Horse and Hound* and the *Racing Post*, looking underneath them, slapping them down again.

"What's the matter?" I asked. The stud diary fell to the floor. "What are you looking for? Stop, it, love. What's wrong?"

"For Christ's sake!" He made a fist and slammed it down on the wood. "Shut off that bloody radio."

Shocked, I reached for the switch. Madoc never swore, not unless something catastrophic had happened. I picked up the fallen diary and stood holding the big book against my body, shielding myself and Robbie. Madoc stared at me for a moment and then, as though a spotlight had been switched off, he blinked and said, "Sorry. I need the letter, the thing from the insurance company."

I went cold all over. "The renewal notice? It isn't in here, love. It'll be in your desk."

Madoc went through to the damp little room he used as an office and began to flip through papers there. I fastened Robbie into the high chair's safety harness and shut the back door.

Madoc came back with a bright card folder. He opened it and read a printed page inside. He turned it over in disbelief and read it again.

"It's expired," he said. "The insurance. It expired last month." The blankness of his face chilled me.

I said as calmly as I could, "Tell me what's happened."

"It's Cymru," he said. "He's dead."

He dropped the insurance papers on the table and sat down, slowly, like an old man. I sat too, next to Robbie in his high chair.

"He was being bloody stupid about his teeth. Stuart sedated him and we'd just finished when he collapsed. Crashed into the wall. Bang. Just like a heart attack —"

"But didn't Stuart have the antidote with him?" I asked. "I mean, vets always do, don't they? In case."

"He had it in his pocket."

"And it didn't work?"

"Jesus Christ! Of course it bloody didn't!" He clenched his fists and I could see he wanted to beat them on the table. After a moment he put his head in his hands. I didn't ask any more questions.

Robbie smacked his palms on the tray of the high chair and squealed, "Mam! Mam-mam-mam!" so I got up for the jar of purée and trapped his grasping little paws while I spooned lamb stew into his mouth. We had planned our entire future around Cymru. Madoc had sunk all his savings into buildings and house improvements, hoping the new breeding season would bring us more mares, and then with their service fees we could afford to pay the stallion's insurance premium. The mares had not come yet, not in sufficient numbers. Only now we didn't have him any more, nor any money to replace him. I scraped lamb stew off Robbie's chin to spoon it in again, desperate to satisfy and quiet him while we faced up to the death of all our plans.

Madoc said, "I should have renewed the insurance." The bitterness was live and hurting in his voice. "How can a horse die of bloody dentistry?"

~~~

We didn't find a stallion to replace Cymru. We had no money to buy or even lease anything near his quality. So Madoc had gone doggedly back to farming, because we had the land, and at least farming was something he understood; and when Dava asked us to pre-train young horses for him we went along with that because it paid, and educating thoroughbreds was where Madoc's skill lay. In some ways I thought he was actually happier putting in the foundations for young horses' careers than he had been when he was racing them, but the loss of Cymru grieved him more than he would admit.

No wonder he had wanted me to see King Coel arrive. This was not just a smart young horse: his pedigree made him family.

Madoc said, "Helen Rogers bred his dam, didn't she, out of your filly Double Jump. But it's a chap from Manchester who owns him, name of Humphrey. Dava says he's a bit of a wide boy. I mean, the chestnut next door, he's registered that as 'Zanzibar Clubman'."

I said. "God, how ugly!"

Madoc chuckled. "Pretty names don't make them run any faster." He slipped the passports back into the envelope.

The hail stopped as abruptly as it had started. The brown colt continued to pull forage from the net, and in the sudden quiet the grind of his teeth sounded loud, steady and comfortable. Outside, a low streak of sunshine lit the Scar, white with blue shadows against darker clouds.

Robbie came across the yard, shaking his hood clear of hailstones. "Anyone going to check these sheep, before it goes dark?"

"There's time yet," said Madoc.

"I wish you'd kept this building as it was last back-end, when we moved in."

"Full of old timber and rats?"

"You know what I mean! For cattle. These boxes have taken all the best space." Robbie squared up to his father, eye to eye. "I suppose now you're back into racehorses you'll be besotted as usual – both of you – never mind lambing time!"

Madoc leaned on the door post, arms folded. "At least when Uncle Dava sends us horses, you get jam on your bread-and-butter."

"That doesn't mean I've got to hang around admiring them like a big daft kid."

"Now then." I made a calming gesture, and he swallowed whatever else he'd been thinking.

"All right! Here's the key to the quad bike." Madoc tossed it to him. "Get going!"

Robbie went across the yard at a run.

The bike roared. Its tyres scrabbled over the concrete and the colt whirled to face the door, but Madoc said in a low, calm voice, "Wo-hoa, fella. Nothing to worry about," and he went back to his net of haylage.

Madoc handed me the passports. "I suppose I'd better check what the boy's actually doing."

"He's worried about the weather. Don't be too hard on him."

"I won't." He fastened his jacket, ready to set off.

"Which of you's doing the lambing shift tonight?"

"He is. I'm going to bed early to cuddle the wife."

Chapter 6.

It was raining, a westerly gale hurling water thick as sea-spray. The Easter school holiday had ended. Cerys and Jack needed waterproofs for their walk to meet the school minibus, while out in the fields the ewes and lambs crowded behind their corrugated shelters or stood in the lee of walls with their heads down, shaking water out of their ears.

I abandoned any idea of riding Zilla.

At mid-day, Madoc and Robbie came back to the house. I was putting dinner-plates into the bottom Rayburn oven to warm and as the men shed their waterproofs in the porch I heard Madoc say, "It's no good. Where are you going to buy pedigree Angus cattle at a price we can afford?"

Robbie was still taking off his leggings, and I couldn't hear his reply. He began to open the kitchen door and Kip the sheepdog poked his rain-soaked head through the gap.

I said, "Don't bring the dog in when he's all wet and dirty!"

Robbie swore, and roughly told Kip to go and lie in his basket at the end of the passageway. Oh dear. The argument must have been going on for some time. As the door swung half open, I could hear it continuing.

Madoc said, "We haven't cleared any of the loans we took to move here."

Robbie came back at him. "Well, shouldn't we be making plans? We never seem to look forward!"

"What? We moved here to give you a bigger farm to work with. If that isn't looking forward...!"

"Yeah, but we still just meander along, doing the same old things that we did at Longlands, year in, year out – except now we have to worry about owing money all the time. If it isn't the bank it's Uncle Dava or, God help us, Gwylim!" Robbie's voice twisted scornfully over the name.

"I owe a hell of a lot to Dava," said Madoc. "And it was good of Gwyl to lend us anything at all."

"Lucky old Gwyl to have that kind of spare change! What kind of desk pushing does he do, to have that much money to chuck around!"

Madoc came into the kitchen followed by Robbie, who was saying, "I wish we *were* dealing with the bank. I could make a business case to the bank! But not to you! And I can only talk to Gwylim through you!"

"Never you mind about Gwylim. We can't have cows lying out in weather like this, cutting up the ground and losing flesh. And we can't house cattle as well as the sheep. We don't have space in the buildings."

"We could put something up!"

Madoc didn't answer. We'd got a mortgage and a bridging loan from the bank to buy Stone Side while we waited for a buyer for Longlands, and they also gave us, perhaps too easily, a further loan to do the most basic upgrades to Stone Side's house – roof patching, plumbing, electricity, windows and doors. Dava had come forward with an offer to pay for planning approval and building of the all-weather gallop that we needed, plus a small exercise arena for long-reining and backing his youngsters. He had proposed a zero-interest repayment plan which Madoc took with relief, even though it came with a further contract.

Problems had arisen, though, when we realised the worker's cottage that adjoined the house needed repairs more urgently than the original building survey had suggested, and we'd decided to modernise it as a potential holiday let. The bank had reached its limit by then, so we'd been pleasantly surprised when Gwylim offered the same amount that Dava had lent us. It was unusual for him to be so forthcoming, but he'd played the part of the generous elder brother, saying simply, "Family. Pay me back when you can." We had no idea whether he would need the capital back, or when, but we needed to begin work before winter set in, so we took it.

"Wash your hands," I said, "and sit down, for heaven's sake."

Madoc didn't appear to have heard.

"You obviously have no idea," he said to Robbie. "We don't have cash to invest. I don't mean cash to convert buildings. I mean any cash. Remember there's the bridging loan to pay off as soon as the subsidy comes in. I don't know how much we'll be able to pay back to Dava and Gwylim this year – if anything. We may yet have to sell Syke Side and Sweet Holme."

"You can't sell the hayfields! That's so shortsighted!"

"I'm trying not to sell any of it."

"You wouldn't get a bid that's anywhere near what they're worth to us for hay and grazing!"

"I know that! But you'll have to forget about cows for a while."

"How long? How long is a while?"

"A couple of years, at least."

"But Mam has pedigree ponies *now* –"

"Stop it!" I said, but they were both too angry to notice.

Madoc told him, "The ponies come cheap and they don't need any more shelter than a thorn bush and a stone wall. They've already chewed down a lot of the old grass you were complaining about. They pay their way. If they didn't, they'd have to go."

I struggled not to say anything. I wished Madoc wasn't quite so ready to define what I could and couldn't do in terms of the bottom line, and to ignore the deeper needs that drove me. I was sick of everything being about money.

Robbie said, "But we have to reserve buildings for Uncle Dava's racehorses, which are a complete and utter waste of space!"

I couldn't let that go by. I said, "Dava's horses paid for your school uniforms, and your driving lessons, and Cerys's driving lessons, and a lot of stuff you've probably forgotten. It was only bad luck that we lost the best horse we ever had – and let me tell you, if we still had him, it's your cattle and sheep that would have been the sideline, not the horses." I dumped the bread on the table and followed it with a clatter of cutlery.

"All right!" said Robbie. "I know the story. We all feckin' do. How many different ways can you say *If Only*."

I didn't look at Madoc. He turned his back on Robbie and began to wash his hands at the sink.

"Dava's racehorses are helping us pay off our debts," he said, over the rushing of the water. "So long as he keeps sending them, I'll work on them. Get used to it."

"Well, you can stuff your veg garden then," said Robbie. "I'm not going to break my back digging a patch of waste ground, when I could spend the time working for Beth's family and getting a decent wage!"

"D'you know, I'm beginning to wish we'd bloody stayed at Longlands." Madoc grabbed the towel off the Rayburn, and as he dried his hands his voice rose, as though echoing all the years of disappointment. "I'd love to have bought a thoroughbred stallion and built some foaling boxes, instead of buying a bigger farm! Christ almighty, Rob, don't you realise that moving here was ALL about giving you a future?"

"Oh yes, that's right, make me feel guilty. I won't let you tie *me* down to money!"

"Fine," said Madoc, "you'll be ready to pay your own car insurance, will you? And your tax? And your rent?" He balled-up the towel and threw it at Robbie, who caught it in clenched fingers.

"All right! Just don't expect me to graft here all day earning next to nothing. If there's a job needs doing for cash off the farm, that's where I'm going." Robbie flipped the towel across his shoulder and began to wash.

"See?" said Madoc, turning away. "We all have to make compromises."

My hands shook slightly as I served out the stew. Madoc and Robbie sat down without looking at each other or at me.

I tried to eat, but the potatoes tasted of salt and the vegetables had the texture of a bath sponge. I put down my knife and fork and wiped my eyes, knowing that neither of the men would see me, entrenched as they were in their own anger.

"Is the stew all right?" My voice sounded thready.

"What?" Madoc looked up. "Yes, yes, it's fine."

Robbie just grunted, his gaze fixed on his plate.

"We've nearly used up all the onions." I cleared my throat and went on, "The ones that are left are sprouting, or else going brown and mushy."

Another silence.

I tried again. "Have you got much done this morning?"

Robbie said, "Falling over ourselves with all these ewes lambing. I wish we could stack them up until the weather improves."

"So long as the lambs are dry and sucking, they'll cope outside," said Madoc shortly.

"They're all lambing at once! What the lambing shed needs is a mezzanine floor!"

"It's like this every year, remember? Give it a week – it'll sort itself out."

I let them subside again, and in the pause I remembered that I Hazel had phoned with a message for Madoc.

"There's a dog fox going through Andy's fields every night. Hazel said she lost half a dozen hens this week."

"I know," said Robbie. "There are piles of fox shit on all the molehills. That's why I take the .22 when I walk round the fields."

"Your certificate only covers the shotgun," snapped Madoc.

"Well, the shotgun's useless at any distance. I'd have to practically shove it up the fox's arse."

"Stop it!" I was beginning to weary of the task of mediating between them. "Look, love – why don't you let him use it, if he needs to? Otherwise, you're going to have to padlock a chain through the trigger."

I got up and began to clear the table.

Madoc said to Robbie, "All right. But remember the .22's lethal at half a mile. Be careful. I don't want you killing more lambs than the fox does."

Chapter 7.

The following Sunday morning I was upstairs in Jack's bedroom, putting away washing, when I heard the staccato ring of the cattle grid and saw a white Mercedes coming up the track to the farm.

There was no mistaking the car or its driver: Madoc's brother Gwylim, hard on the heels of a phone call the previous evening. All he'd told us was that he wanted to discuss the loan, but he was driving fast, every crunch of his tyres flicking mud and gravel at his paintwork, and that didn't bode well for the coming meeting. The Merc disappeared behind the sheep shed then came growling through the gateway into the yard, and Kip began to bark; he didn't see Gwylim often enough to be sure whether he deserved a greeting or a warning.

I forced myself to be calm in spite of my apprehensions, to finish putting away the washing, to make my hands move smoothly, to stand the empty basket in its corner. With luck none of the kids would get mixed up in the argument that was looming. Robbie was away at The Ghyll for the day, helping Beth Langdale's family with the lambing, and Cerys was at Underscar singing with Katie Wharton. Jack had put on waterproofs and cycled into the village to spend the day with his school-friend Wilse Robson.

I went quietly downstairs. Kip was silent, penned at the far end of the passageway. Madoc's reluctance to talk about the phone call last night had worried me enough to attack the housework, so the kitchen this morning was tidy; the Rayburn towel was fresh and the quarry tiles shone.

If I hadn't known Gwylim for so many years I would hardly have recognised him as Madoc's brother. He'd always been short and stocky like their Uncle Dava, and although he was younger than Madoc by a couple of years his eyes and jawline were already blurred by soft living. His shoes, jacket and glasses came from the designer end of a market we didn't frequent.

I slid the kettle to the hot end of the Rayburn and reached up to the shelf for mugs.

"Do you want to sit in the front room, or in here?" I asked.

Madoc decided the matter by taking his usual chair at the table. Again, it seemed ominous to me that he didn't choose the more relaxed option. Gwylim sat deliberately at the opposite end, leaving me a choice of sides. I compromised by leaning against the Rayburn.

"How's it going?" said Gwylim. Over the years his accent had slid away from Welsh towards Liverpool Scouse and become quite different from either Madoc's or mine.

Madoc stayed silent and looked at me so I replied, "Not bad."

"Lambing all right?" He seemed determined to be affable, at least for the moment. At least to me.

"Wet," I said, "mostly – but that's nothing new."

"And it'll be sweet land on this limestone," said Gwylim, "and I suppose that's the main thing. Better than the farm you had in Lancashire. And a lot easier to get to than Afonwen."

Their father's holding in North Wales had been ancient, beautiful, and remote; its roads ran between walls close-coupled as hunting hounds, roads so narrow and twisting that we had to accept they would prevent anyone bringing mares to us by horsebox. That move away from the Owen family farm and north into Lancashire had been the first compromise Madoc had to make. When we sold, it was during a nasty period of negative equity, when the value of a farm could fall below the amount borrowed to invest in it. We'd done better than some people, but we got out of Afonwen at a loss.

The kettle, working its way up to boiling, gave a faint snakelike hiss.

"I see you've smartened up the house, ey."

"Thanks. The whole place is a lot safer than when we bought it."

I brewed a pot of tea and put the drinks down in front of the two men. Too late, I saw that I'd given Gwylim a mug with a thin rim of Rayburn soot. I wondered whether he'd notice but apparently he didn't. I took a halfway-house seat at the table.

"I do hear news of you," Gwylim said. "I catch up with Dava every now and again. One of the young horses you broke-in for him last year, it's already won a couple of small races."

"That would be Parkour," I said. "We follow them too, you know."

"Of course," he said, "of course you do. And how's that Jack-the-Lad, ey? Mister Mischief? I promised to show him how to handle a rifle."

"That's nice of you, but he's out. Maybe we should leave it till he's a bit more responsible."

"Aye well. What about Robbie? I hear he's doing a bit of contracting?"

Madoc joined in at last. Perhaps he could see which way Gwylim was trying to turn the conversation. "Robbie works part time for a couple of our neighbours. I'd hardly class that as contracting."

"It's good that he's earning, though – he'll be paying his way then, ey?"

"Of course," I said, and wondered whether I should have admitted that.

"We knock some rent off his wages," said Madoc.

"That's another plus, then. Not so much cash flowing out."

"Look, Gwylim – what's it got to do with you?"

Gwylim smiled again, but without humour, as though he had expected this. "Defensive today, aren't we?"

"And you're not? I heard Linda's divorcing you and you're worried about cash."

"Ey, you shouldn't believe every bit of gossip you pick up." He leaned back in his chair as though Madoc's challenge didn't worry him, but a vein in his throat was pulsing faster.

"Dava told me," said Madoc, "so it's hardly gossip. He said Linda's taken off with the kids. He's no reason to make that up, has he?"

Gwylim had married much later in life than Madoc and me. We'd only met Linda a few times, and after the wedding he hadn't extended any invitations to us to visit, except for the baptisms of their two girls.

"All right, all right, she's gone, yes! She's got copies of the company accounts and if she presents those figures to court, I'll be wiped out for the next ten years."

I thought Linda had been very canny to grab the most favourable set of accounts but I was sad for the girls, apparently less important than the money.

Madoc sat back and folded his arms. "I'm sorry, of course, but Linda can't be awarded what you haven't got."

Gwylim forced a laugh. "You don't suppose those figures are pukka? She got her hands on the set we quote to potential investors, the ones that say we're not only asset-heavy but we don't owe anyone a brass farthing. I've got to marshal all my liquid assets as fast as I can."

I tried to find something helpful to say. "Aren't there assessors and negotiators in divorces these days? It won't really have to go to court, will it?"

Gwylim waved my question aside. He was watching Madoc. "That's not the point, is it, ey? I lent you that money on a gentleman's agreement, no interest, no questions asked. And now I need it back."

I waited for him to say something more definite, but he didn't and I began to wonder whether he was telling the whole truth. Why did he suddenly need liquid assets? Was the divorce only a symptom of something bigger?

Madoc said, "My concern has to be feeding my own family and keeping a roof over our heads. It's damned difficult for us, to be honest. The farm hasn't broken-even, and it won't for a couple of years. The old fellow who owned it never applied for Single Farm Payment, so we had to go out and buy entitlements, and the subsidy's been delayed – and even then, between the bridging loan and the overdraft it's already spoken for."

"My heart bleeds for you, it really does." Gwylim began talking to me again. "How's your father, Siân? Shop doing all right?"

"I've no idea," I said. Dad had brought me up to believe that there was never anything to spare. "Probably not."

"But he pays for Cerys's private tuition?"

I pretended to laugh. "If you mean her singing lessons, he contributes, but that wouldn't make a dent in your loan. And don't ask about my stepfather – he hasn't got any money to chuck about."

Gwylim shrugged, and waited.

"There's still Dava," I suggested.

"Believe me," said Madoc, without taking his eyes off Gwylim, "I'd rather have borrowed from Dava in the first place. But he doesn't have all that much to spare, did you know that? When we put in the all-weather gallop, Dava paid the deposit, but Anna chipped in her own money to help pay the balance, and she was the one who said the loan had to be without interest – not Dava. So I don't think either you or I could get any more from him."

"Have you tried?" asked Gwylim.

"No, Gwyl, I haven't. You know what it's like in his business! Owners may forget to pay training fees but horses don't forget to eat, they go on needing staff to look after them, and bedding and shoeing and vet treatment, and it all has to be paid for up front. Dava has enough drain on his bank account without us."

"Well, then. If you won't ask Dava, it comes back to you," Gwylim said. "The holiday cottage is ready for use now, isn't it? That was the whole point of the loan. So you can go to the bank and mortgage it. Then it's sorted, isn't it, ey?"

"D'you think I hadn't already tried the bank, when we first decided to renovate? When we presented the idea alongside our existing mortgage, the first thing they looked at was our income, and their 'Don't Lend' alarm went right off the scale. So the bank won't stretch for us and Dava can't. They were both pretty tight on what instalments they wanted and when we had to pay them. I'm not complaining about that, because at least with them we know exactly where we stand. But when you offered to fund the renovations, you were so – what's the word I want? *Diofal...*"

He looked at me, searching. I knew what he meant. When Gwylim had given us that money he was boasting. *Look, big brother. Look what I can do. You had a wonder horse and a sparkling public career, and your life fell to bits just the same. So here's a little bit of the money I'm making – now I'm going to sit back and watch you graft.*

"Offhand," I suggested. "Cavalier."

"That's it. You were so cavalier about lending the money, zero interest and all. I didn't think you'd want anything so soon."

"I obviously haven't made this clear," said Gwylim, chopping with his hands on the table, as though in frustration. His face was flushed now and there was a sheen of sweat on his neck. "I'm not asking you for interest. I'm telling you, I need the whole sum. All of it."

"What?" I tried to pick up my mug, but my fingers didn't seem to be under my control. Tea jumped out and splashed on the table.

"But – forty thousand pounds!" Madoc protested. "It all went into the renovations. We haven't got anywhere near that much in cash."

Gwylim shrugged. "Maybe not right now. But you're sitting pretty here, aren't you? Land and buildings. I'll give you till the end of May."

"It's still impossible. We couldn't raise forty thousand in a year, let alone a few weeks."

"I've got to liquidate, so you have too."

I stood up and went for the roll of kitchen tissue to mop the table. Even that eluded my grasp, so I yanked off a handful, angry at my own clumsiness.

Madoc was saying, "No. Whoa there, Gwyl. I was thankful for that money, but you must see, we can't repay everything, just like that."

"Why not? You've had the use of it for nearly a year."

"Because you're not going to stampede me into breaking up the farm."

I came back to the remains of my tea and wiped up the spill. I sat moulding the wet tissues into a pale brown ball but I thought

Gwylim was more uncomfortable than I was. I could see that pulse in his neck, pounding, pounding.

"I'm giving you decent notice," he said, as though trying to make his demand sound reasonable. "And after all, when you needed the money I lent it to you straight away."

"You did, and I appreciated it. But you were flush then, weren't you? What's changed?" Madoc sat forward now, his attention all on Gwylim. For a moment he was a race riding jockey again, a younger, fiercer version of himself. "Why the sudden deadline? I simply don't believe this has anything to do with Linda and the girls."

Gwylim sat still, lips pursed as though he contemplated a series of replies, all of which he discarded.

He said, "I could get a court order. Ey? D'you want to go that far?"

That was when I lost all sympathy for him. A court order would mean bailiffs assessing the land and animals and machinery, tramping through our house, rummaging in the children's rooms to turn even their small comforts into cash. A mug with soot on it would never be enough revenge for that.

But Madoc raised an eyebrow at Gwylim and began to laugh. "A court order? You are going to take *me* to court? Bring it on."

"We're not going to agree, then, are we." Gwylim's chair scraped across the tiles as he stood up. He looked down at Madoc, and at me. And yet he hesitated. When he spoke again it was almost mechanical, as though someone was pulling a string in his back to make him talk. "Forty thousand, cash, by the end of May. Phone me when I can collect."

Chapter 8.

The letterbox clattered on the back door, and the post van was driving away, a ripple of red through the glass in the passageway. There were two ominous brown envelopes addressed to Mr & Mrs M Owen, but there was a white one for me alone, and the handwriting was unmistakably that of Peter Davies, my father. After a moment I dropped all three letters on the table and went back to emptying and reloading the washing machine.

Gracie the cat rubbed round my ankles, radiating the usual morning purrs.

"You can't want breakfast," I said. "What about that big fat rabbit you were eating in the garden?"

But the purrs escalated to meows and attempts to climb up my jeans, so I fed her. Then there was another pause in which the washing machine swished and rumbled and the cat crunched biscuits.

Those two brown envelopes were probably bills. I didn't want to open them. But Dad's letter was mine, and it would nag at me unless I read it. I ripped it open.

Dear Siân

I hope I've got your postcode right. I think I may have confused it with your old house in

Lancashire. Here's a tenner for that rascal Jack. It must be his birthday about now. I suppose he'll prefer cash to anything I might think of buying for him.

I went to the optician last Wednesday. Praise be to Simon – you know Simon, my assistant – for driving me to New Ferry, but it's a shame we had to shut the shop. I have ordered a proper new pair of specs and paid for them. My eyes seem to be in better nick than the rest of me. I daresay the optician wouldn't have let me go home without paying, in case I dropped dead.

With all that done, yesterday I had to go to see the Doc. I think I have convinced her that I am doing my exercises properly, but I am getting to be an opium addict, wearing these patches to kill the pains in the joints. They work, mostly, but they make me sleepy and stupid. It's a nuisance having to leave the shop in Simon's care for all these appointments, but there's no alternative. I wish I could be certain he isn't dipping his hand in the till.

When I was in New Ferry I happened across that randy postman your mother ran off with. He's got a new woman by the looks of it, all wrapped up in one of those floaty scarf things, whatever they call them – and those ugly dogskin boots. She was shaking a tin for some worthy organisation. I pretended not to see either of them.

My mother hadn't just "run off" with Richard the "randy postman" – she had in fact married him. She'd died of breast cancer ten years ago, but once again Dad seemed incapable of acknowledging the changes brought by the passage of time.

At least you still keep your own feet firmly on
the ground, even if the ground IS a hundred and fifty
miles away.

Will you be coming to see me this summer? I
know you'll remind me that you're wedded to the
farm and the nags as much as to your Welshman and
I suppose it's hard to tear yourself away from land
worth half a million, but I'd like to meet the
grandkids again – they must be so tall now that I'll
need binoculars to see their faces. Remind them that
their old Greengrocer Grandad is still alive – just. I
can still pick up the telephone, if they can bring
themselves to call. I like to know how Cerys is
getting on with her singing lessons.

tarrah well

Dad

I folded the letter and the banknote, and stuffed them back into the envelope. Like Gwylim, Dad overvalued the farm – why stick to the truth, when a bigger version made a better story! – overlooking our scrimping and saving and mortgages and Madoc's constant hard work. He simply didn't comprehend that we were land rich, but cash poor, and if we were going to benefit from the land we simply had to give it our strength and time.

Dad always tried to make me feel guilty for not visiting him often enough to make him happy. Journeys to the Wirral had always meant leaving Madoc behind to feed animals, and the long drive with three young children on increasingly busy roads had always been stressful. The visits themselves weren't often a success. I had spent part of one day helping him to unload several pallets of veg and potatoes into the rear of the shop and trying to keep all three children out of trouble; it wasn't till I'd trailed the kids across town to Mam and Richard's little terraced house that we'd got anything other than fruit to eat. Another time, when I had persuaded Dad to take a day off and meet us at Chester Zoo, the weather had been appallingly wet and I'd ended up taking the children round the Zoo by myself while he sat in grumpy solitude in the café. And the fact that I was still going over all those things meant that Dad had succeeded yet again in taking over my head. I felt a surge of irritation against all our relatives, Madoc's and mine, young and old alike.

Dad hadn't believed we could make a go of either the stud farm or farming, so when Cymru died he was openly scornful of us for having hitched our wagon to such an unreliable star. After that, all our house moves had been in search of land that was cheaper per acre, planning ahead for a bigger farm where we might make a better living and Robbie could be part of the business. Cheaper land had meant moving north, certainly, but it wasn't fair of Dad to read each move as a further retreat from him. Resentments continued to underlie all our conversations like the twinge of scar tissue after an injury.

I usually wrote straight back, bam, get it done, over with. My letters had long since become merely factual, describing what Madoc and Robbie were doing on the farm, what Cerys was singing, what scrapes Jack had got into that week. I never wrote about how I was feeling, because I remembered what the atmosphere had been like before Mam left him, all sulks and acid silences. It renewed my conviction that my marriage was none of his business, even if I had been willing to lay it out for his dissection, and I wasn't. And now Gwylim's demands were churning round my brain, and I couldn't write to him about those, either. Love? Perhaps. No kisses.

I pushed the letter into the hip pocket of my jeans, put on coat and boots and carried the sheets out to the garden. Replying would just have to wait.

The sky promised the first fine day for a week, a pale thrush-egg blue beyond the grey-green top of the Scar. If I pegged my laundry on the garden line most of the creases would blow out, and the wind would add the scent of tumbled miles of clean grass; it was a win all round over the electricity-hungry dryer. I tucked the washing basket into the porch so it couldn't blow away, and with a feeling of escape I went round the house to the barn to get half a bale of hay for the ponies.

I heard Madoc before I saw him, thumps and metallic clangs coming from the lean-to behind the dog-kennels where he kept reusable fencing materials, posts and wire and sheets of corrugated metal. He was loading fence posts into the quad bike trailer. I stopped for a moment to watch him. It wasn't often I got the chance to study my husband when he was unaware. His frame was still taut and athletic, his blond hair shone under the spring sunshine, and there was no denying it: he was still handsome.

Kip the sheepdog was standing on the bike seat, his black and white body taut with controlled excitement. He must know that the fence-posts were too big to be played with but he was unable to resist the fact that Madoc was throwing them.

When I chuckled Kip heard me, and his slanty-eyed grin and swinging tail-wag gave me away, so that Madoc looked up and paused, and stayed there looking, a fencepost poised in his hands. The tiredness of lambing and the bitterness of our debt to Gwylim had vanished; those dark-blue eyes, that I had loved for more than half my life, found mine and held me. The world took a deep breath and shimmered to a halt around us.

Then Madoc threw the post into the trailer and asked, "What's up?"

I realised the strings of the half-bale of hay were digging into my fingers. "Oh, nothing."

"Gwylim hasn't been on the phone again?"

"No," I said, and changed the hay to my other hand. "I'm just going up to feed the nags. Where's Robbie? In the shed?"

"Marking lambs and ewes so we can turn them out."

"That's all right then," I said lightly.

He winked at me and went back to pitching posts into the trailer. As I carried the hay up the field I couldn't help smiling.

~~~

My little band of Fell ponies stood up the hill, basking broadside in the sunshine; and though they looked sleepy, they weren't asleep. Zilla lifted her head and pricked her ears at me, and all three ponies came bucketing down the slope towards the gate.

I split the hay into several piles, well separated, and stood back while the inevitable skirmishes took place. When Zilla had made her choice and settled down to eat the two geldings accepted what she had left, and then it was safe for me to walk up, pass a hand over their thick fur and feel their ribs. The new grass must be growing, because they were definitely beginning to fill out.

Zilla looked rounded and solid under her shiny bay coat. I wondered if she was in fact too fat for so early in the year, and to find out I ran my fingers through the hair on her flanks.

Her hind foot whipped past my thigh in a lightning sideswipe.

I froze. When I looked down, there was a streak of mud across both legs of my jeans. It was only luck that she had missed me.

"Well!" I said to her, as mildly as I could. "You bad thing. Was *that* why you were so cheap?"

She stood tensely, not chewing, as though she expected to be punished. Her left ear stayed fixed on me, while the other twitched back and forth. I moved closer to her head and tidied her forelock in as neutral a manner as I could manage, while underneath the sweep of hair her black-outlined eyes were wary. I smoothed her neck, staying quiet and unthreatening until she allowed herself to relax. And then I walked away from her and tried to work out what she'd just told me.

Someone, somewhere, had made Zilla seriously afraid of anyone touching her flanks. And since then someone had punished her, a lot, for defending herself. She was saying that my task now was to restore her confidence.

While I thought, I went up the field to check the water was running. I must give her time to get to know me. Time would include bringing her down to the farm yard, to brush and clean her regularly, handle those lethal hooves, and saddle her to go out riding. I mustn't punish her for kicking. Building her trust and breaking the vicious cycle was going to take a while.

I stopped by the thorn bushes that the ponies used as a windbreak, and looked back down the field. The farm and the yard were laid out below me: the slate roof of the house, the untidy bushes round the garden not quite hiding the flapping sheets on the line; the buildings and the M-shaped double span of the sheep shed roof; Madoc standing on the quad bike footrests as he towed the trailer down the gravel track; Kip balancing on the rack behind him and barking. The sounds, delayed by distance, floated to me on the wind.

Our fields were not yet as tidy as Robbie demanded they should be. The previous owner as he aged had not only neglected the paperwork for subsidies but made less and less use of the land, particularly the two big meadows across the road. Syke Side and Sweet Holme had been very overgrown when we moved in, so over the winter I had pastured the ponies there to begin the work of reclamation. We would still have to clear some perennial weeds before those fields would grow good grass for hay, but at least they were usable now for sheep. That was where Madoc was going with the materials for temporary windbreaks. The fields close to the house, which were already provided with shelters, had begun to look rather bare under the pressure of the newly lambed flock, and he was preparing to move most of them across to Sweet Holme to let the grass recover.

The generations who had farmed Stone Side before us had planted knots of trees in the corners where the field walls met: evergreen Scots pines with rusty, scaly brown trunks and brushes of dark needles; ash trees grey-barked, still winter-bare and withdrawn; sycamores just showing a hint of green at their tips. A long drystone wall divided the farm from the rough fawn-coloured fell on my right, and pale tractor-ruts marked the Roman road, an ancient track that came down the fell and passed the farm gate, running south for the V in the horizon that was Tebay Gorge. The gallops that Dava had paid for were in the field next door, two all-weather strips climbing the slope, the one nearest the far wall barred with flights of hurdles.

I put my hands in my pockets and realised the letter from my father was still there, along with his ten pound note for Jack's birthday.

I had no idea what Jack might like, though he always needed jeans and tee-shirts to replace ones he'd grown out of or wrecked, and a tenner wouldn't buy anything he really wanted, certainly not anything related to his current craze to use the rifle. I thought he'd probably stash it away for purposes of his own which he wouldn't want to divulge. Perhaps I should thank Dad for an invented purchase like a new riding helmet. It was true Jack needed one.

He was the only one of our children who had much interest in horses. We had once borrowed an old Shetland for Robbie to ride, but after a couple of years he lost interest, and though Cerys had never been scared of the thoroughbreds or my Fell ponies she had preferred to walk and run on her own; while Jack blew hot and cold, sometimes keen, more often reluctant. Of course none of them had ridden any of the racehorses, because the young thoroughbreds arrived full of irresponsible energy, needing direction which our children were still too immature to give. It was Madoc and I who taught the horses to carry a rider, to canter alongside each other without spooking, to gallop competently and to jump the practice hurdles, ready to be trained in earnest by Dava.

I faced the slope again and walked on up to the lonnin which was a right of way across the face of the hill, to the limekiln above our top wall. I decided to follow it back to Underscar and see Hazel Wharton. She wouldn't mind me having a moan about the emotional pressure Dad was putting on me, and she might even have a suggestion for the imaginary birthday present for Jack. I opened the rusty old gate at the farm boundary, and walked down to Hazel's house.

Chapter 9.

When I reached the kitchen door I knocked and walked straight in. Hazel had once told me off for waiting outside in the rain for my knock to be answered, and since then only time I'd found the door locked in daylight hours was when she and Andy had gone to a funeral on the other side of the Pennines.

The Underscar kitchen ran on electricity and bottled propane, its butter-yellow and white paint unblemished by soot, its floor sparkling clean. I couldn't help comparing it to my own kitchen, where there always seemed to be breakfast crumbs on the table and scraps of horse bedding on the floor. Perhaps Hazel's kind of tidiness only descended on you when your children had grown up. Or maybe I could only achieve it if we redesigned the whole house.

Hazel made an entrance through the inner door with a heaped-full basket of bedding.

"Morning, stranger!" She was a short, broad woman, dressed in a skirt and jumper that would have suited someone my mother's age, and her voice had an edge that could command husband, children or animals at the far side of a large field. She was probably only ten years older than me, old enough to offer advice, young enough to confide in. She dumped her basket beside the washing machine, and straightened up with a sigh.

"The damn weather's been that wet and windy, I didn't dare put anything out on the line."

"Me too," I said.

"Aye, I saw you'd done some sheets." She opened the washing machine and began to drag her own sheets into an empty basket. "I thought you'd be out with that new pony of yours – making the most of the sunshine."

"I'm going to, but between lambing and the weather – "

"Aye," she said. "All the rain we've had! I do feel sorry for them people down country who've been flooded. And did you see that on the news last night, that house that fell into a sink hole?"

I shook my head. "I'm not sure I know what a sink hole is."

"You maybe haven't lived here long enough. It's what you get when limestone falls in. The water eats it away underneath, you see. Doctor's Pot, just up from your gate, that's been an awful big sink hole. This is a nasty bit of country – pitted with them, all the way to Shap. In summer you can't see a lot of them, they're all grown over with bracken and seaves – so don't you go riding across there unless you stick to the tracks." I assured her I wouldn't, and she pushed the problem aside along with the basket of damp washing, and began to stuff the next batch into the machine. "Eh! I'm all behind today, like a cow's tail."

She filled the soap dispenser and set the machine off.

"Them sheets," she said, "is off Katie's bed. She come home pissed and fell into bed and decorated the duvet. I keep telling her to lay off, but when she's out with the lasses, she won't take a blind bit of notice."

I made sympathetic noises. The day when Katie had turned eighteen had already passed into folklore: how the wild farm girl had celebrated with a round of the Penrith pubs, to which underage Cerys, and Robbie as driver, had been the only sober spectators. I said, "I do hope our Cerys won't go mad when her birthday comes."

"She won't," said Hazel, with certainty. "Got a good head on her shoulders has Cerys. She keeps our Katie right – well, as much as anyone can. Pity she wasn't with her last night."

"She did a shift at work in the afternoon and after that I think she was revising."

"Well, there you are. Disciplined."

With the washing machine beginning its next cycle, Hazel seized the basket of laundry and headed for the garden. I followed and helped to peg the sheets out on the line.

She said, "I suppose it's a blessing Katie can't pass her driving test."

I was lost for a moment. "How'd you make that out?"

"She'd be forever picked up for drink driving and we'd spend our whole lives fetching her home from the police station – that's if she hadn't broke her silly neck – or worse, put somebody in hospital. She's no more wits than a hen. She's far better off in the passenger seat."

"Just as well there's a minibus to get her to work," I said.

Hazel gave a short laugh.

"She doesn't appreciate that. Oh no. The only thing in her head at the moment is, she's going to get onto one of these television talent shows. Well, that's not going to happen, is it? And if it does, how's she going to audition in London or wherever?"

"Aren't they auditioning in Penrith in July?" I said, vaguely remembering an article in the local paper.

"Aye well, she'll do as she likes, I doubt." Hazel straightened the last billowing sheet on the line and pegged it, with an air of dismissing the topic. We went back indoors where the machine was now churning the next batch. "And how's lambing going with you?"

"Thick and fast. Madoc's putting up shelters so we can move some ewes into Syke Side."

"Aye," Hazel said. "Andy told me."

"It amazes me how Andy spends ten minutes chatting to Madoc over a wall, and between them they know everything that's being done – or *not* done – on every farm between here and Tebay."

Hazel chuckled. "My mother used to say if you sneezed in your attic at midnight, the next day someone would ask after your cold."

"On the other hand, I can guarantee that Madoc won't have asked how you are, and Andy won't have thought to mention me."

"Then it's about time us women had a catch up," said Hazel. "Let's have a brew."

She made coffee and opened the biscuit tin, and as she offered it to me she said, "I had a right good laugh in Morrisons t'other day."

There was a story coming. I chose a chocolate digestive and waited.

"I met this woman, Sally, they call her. I haven't spoken to her in years. Well, *she* hasn't spoken to *me*, more like, since that time her husband pinched my arse and I was daft enough to tell her."

I bit into the digestive and used it as a reason to avoid comment.

Hazel went on, "She tried to make out I'd asked for it! Silly piece. Anyway, there she was, stood next to me in the checkout queue. I thought she was going to walk by with her nose in the air, but no, she acted like we'd never fallen out at all. You could have knocked me down with a feather. I had to take her into Spoonfuls for a quick cuppa to get over it."

"Quick?" I asked, perhaps more ironically than I ought to have done.

"Cross my heart, it was only half an hour! Well to cut a long story short, Sally admits I was right after all, you know, about her husband and his wandering hands. She says he ran off a month later with some secretary or other. Mind, it's a bit late for her to apologise to me, isn't it! Five years on!"

I managed to laugh with her.

"Anyway," she said, "I tell her I'm sorry to hear that, and Sally says, it's all right really, because he was only gone a few months, and then he come back and settled down as if nowt had happened." She took a gulp of coffee and glanced at me meaningfully. "She didn't say why she took him back. Well I didn't ask. I'm not sure I'd have let him come back, myself. I'd never be able to trust him again. Would you?"

I could find nothing to say. My limited experience was no help. I'd gone out with a couple of boys before Madoc but they'd been just that – boys – and I pushed away the skin-prickling memory of the first stable I had worked for, and the trainer's son there whom I couldn't fight off.

"Well anyway," said Hazel, "Sally goes on with this tale, and she says hubby comes back all apologetic, and he gets a job as a manager somewhere in Carlisle, and everything's rosy for another couple of years and then he runs off again, this time with a yummy mummy and her two small kids. And he's gone a couple of months and then back he comes. And Sally lets him in *again*."

I was astonished. "She never did?"

"Oh aye!" said Hazel. "He's done it three times now! And Sally keeps taking him back! Can you believe it?"

We drank coffee and I thought about it. I couldn't say how I'd have reacted, because Madoc just wasn't the type to stray. I assumed he trusted me as much as I trusted him. I'd never needed to ask.

"Men, who'd have them!" said Hazel. "I just make sure mine gets plenty at home so he doesn't have any excuses!" She added with a laugh, "But I don't need to give you any advice there, do I, you've had more kids than I have."

I blushed, and didn't answer directly. "Maybe Sally's husband promised to change."

"Aye well," she said, with another sideways glance, "abused women always tell you that's what their husbands have said. Promises are easy made if you've no intention of keeping them."

Pie-crust promises, my mother called them. Perhaps Madoc and I should have let Gwylim go away yesterday with such a promise. Would he have believed us? How far could we could push that deadline of his, if we tried? We could say we'd made appointments at the bank and they'd been postponed. We could tell Gwylim the branch manager was a young woman who couldn't make up her mind what to do about us, or an older man who wanted advice from higher up. Except we didn't do things that way. We were too nice, too unpractised at lying.

I realised Hazel had put her cup down and was looking at me.

"Oi. You're somewhere else. What's up? You're not going to tell me your lovely hubby's run off with a secretary?"

"No. No! Nothing like that." I munched the biscuit and used it to delay my reply. "It's just money."

"Isn't it always? Anything we can do?"

I dodged away from the big problem to a smaller one.

"I got this letter from my Dad this morning, and I don't know what to write back."

"What's up with him?"

"I think the shop's getting too much for him."

"Maybe he should come and live with you."

"Good God, no!" I said, far more vehemently than I had meant to. Inviting my Dad into the house as well as dealing with Gwylim's loan was more than I could face. "Sorry – we did ask him once, but he said it would never work, him moving to a farm."

"Well, it won't hurt to write to him," Hazel said. "Make him happy, poor old thing."

"You don't know my father. Making him happy is practically impossible."

"Pop down for a visit," said Hazel, and when I pulled a face she added, "Go on. You won't be so busy between lambing and haytime. Robbie could drive you. Tell the old feller to sell up and take life easy."

I thought about it. "I don't think he can. I doubt the shop makes any money these days, not that he'd ever admit it, but I honestly don't know what he'd do without it."

"Well, that's his problem. Oh God, here's Andy," said Hazel. "No peace for the wicked." As the door opened she said loudly, "He's coming in to moan about women who spend all morning drinking coffee."

He stopped at the doorway, a solid, cap-wearing shepherd in navy overalls and well-scrubbed wellingtons.

"I see the coven's in full swing. Morning, Missis O."

"D'you want summat," asked Hazel, "or have you just come to make a nuisance of yourself?"

"I need someone with a ladylike little hand. There's a yow lambing twins, and she's not getting on wi't job. I reckon they're jumbled up." He wriggled his broad stubby fingers towards me as an explanation. "No use me riving about inside her wi' these, now is it? I could do with one of you to come and sort her out." I was flattered that he included me.

Hazel pushed back her chair and headed for the medicine cupboard. "All right, I'm coming. Siân's got enough to be doing at home without playing midwife to your bloody old Roughs."

I got to my feet ready to go, half expecting Andy to make some cheeky comment about me being here at all. He didn't, so I waited while Hazel got a fresh pair of latex gloves and some antiseptic gel, then we all went outside together and walked down the yard towards the sheep sheds. Danny was driving the tractor across to the cattle shed, with a big bale of straw on its front loader, and I could hear bellows from the young steers as they anticipated his arrival.

Hazel said to me, "Well, you'd better get on, hadn't you? Good luck with your letter writing."

"Trouble with the Rural Payments Agency?" Andy asked.

I sighed. "No. It's family stuff. But I might yet have to write to Rural Payments. Phone calls don't seem to make any impression."

"It's a bugger," he conceded. "We're all living off nowt. Reckon RPA needs to try it for a few months theirselves. Nobody else would get away with saying they might pay you sometime between New Year and Midsummer."

I realised, with a stab of guilt, that we'd actually said something very like that to Gwylim.

"Perhaps we should start paying for things in sheep instead of money," I said. We'd reached the cart track back to Stone Side. "I'd swop half a lamb for a load of firewood. You've got a good stack there. Where did you get it from?"

Andy's frosty grey eyes twinkled. "Felled those two trees just up the lonnin, that aren't there any more."

"Oh," I said. I must have walked past the stumps without even noticing.

"Nay, lass, you'd be surprised how many people have stood where you're standing, scratching their heads 'cause they can't work out what's gone."

"Like Sally," said Hazel to me, "you know, the wifey I was telling you about. I wonder how long it took her, each time, before she realised hubby wasn't just late, he wasn't coming home."

Andy said, "Dear God, have you been on about him, again?" He nudged me. "I bet she forgot to tell you the best part."

"I don't forget," said Hazel, cuffing him with the back of her hand. "I just get sidetracked."

"You do an' all. There's yon fella, going back and forrad, back and forrad…flitting between all these women…and what d'you think his job is?" His expression was consciously droll. "He looks after a recycling centre!"

Hazel's protesting slap amused me much more than his punchline. She said, "That's not the point!"

"I don't care! I think it's funny. Well, bye, Missis O. If you get short of firewood, we can tide you over." Andy spun Hazel round and pushed her, shrieking and giggling, towards the shed. "Now come along, woman, let's lamb this yow."

Chapter 10.

It was early evening and I was riding Zilla across the fields above Stone Side. Swallows zipped through the blue air, and a mistle thrush was belting-out a series of phrases from the top of the ash tree behind the house. The ewes grazed in the sunshine with lengthening shadows at their feet. The lambs had reached that joyful age where they gathered into troops to race across the newly-green pastures. One group played King of the Castle on a boulder while another bunch raced away, skipped sideways and bounced to a halt and then raced back to do it all again. The drumming of their shiny little hooves on the dry ground made me sharply aware of the approach of summer, and time going on towards the deadline when we had to give Gwylim forty thousand pounds in cash that we hadn't got.

Throughout the past week the arguments had piled up between Madoc and myself. Even though it was unlikely the bank would agree to an extension to the mortgage – even though we'd be dragged down by interest payments – he was going to talk to them because he refused to betray Robbie by selling any of the land. I had been inclined to wait till the deadline at the end of the month and see what happened – but Madoc thought Gwylim might do something desperate if we stretched his patience that far.

We hadn't told the children about the pressure we were under. They didn't need know. I knew it, though. Madoc had become so distant and preoccupied that I felt shut out, desperate not to nag, not to demand his affection. There could be no ease until he released himself from the problem he'd set himself to solve.

The holiday cottage, the cause of it all, was painted, curtained and carpeted. This afternoon I had advertised it with an online letting agency. I had scrolled through the website options that prompted me to describe what we were offering. Did it have a swimming pool? No. Did it have a jacuzzi? A barbecue area? A secure garden for children and pets? No. Did it have wifi? No. It had new mattresses on the beds, and a sofa and armchairs that I would have loved in our own house, and a heap of bills that still had to be paid. I began to fret that we had nothing to offer potential customers. I ended up writing about our "quiet rural location" and "easy access from the motorway". I set the booking fees apologetically low and tried to relieve my helpless feeling by limiting the check-in and check-out times to fit round my work with the horses.

My ride on Zilla this evening was a safety valve, but as always it had a purpose. I knew it was quite likely that the pony and I might part company at some time when I rode on the unfenced fell, and I wasn't sure I could recapture her on those hundreds of wide open acres. I had decided to pre-empt that with another step in Zilla's education. I had left her headcollar on under her bridle, and the end of its soft cotton rope was in my hand along with the reins. Now I leaned forward and tossed the rope to the ground.

And Zilla's reaction was a lightning-fast kick.

"Damn it, Zilla. What was that for?"

I leaned forward and caught up the dangling rope and again she kicked. I felt it as a thump under the saddle, no more, but for people around us on the ground that kick would be downright dangerous. It would make her unsaleable. And it would have to be sorted out.

Two fields away the brown thoroughbred, King Coel, looked over the wall-top towards us. Being an intact colt he needed to be turned out long way from Zilla, and so far I hadn't ridden her anywhere near him in case their hormones took over. The timid chestnut gelding, Zanzibar Clubman, was in his stable with a net of haylage. We'd given up using his terrible passport name and referred to him as the Ginger Ninja. On the other hand Coel's strong personality hardly needed a nickname. He was just Coel.

I arranged the rope in my hand and made the mare walk on.

What had triggered that kick on other occasions? What had triggered it now? I thought back. She had kicked when she met the three-year-old Rocky. And – oh yes – one day when I was checking the ponies' condition, I had run a hand through their fur. Maybe Zilla's hairy flank had a sensitive spot. And maybe when I'd leaned forward just now, to catch the rope, I'd let my lower leg touch that spot? I balanced myself precisely and experimented by pushing one heel back along her ribs. Instantly, Zilla kicked. Ah. I must discipline myself to avoid putting my heel there, while I found a way to desensitise her. At least the problem had the merit of being something I could probably solve on my own. I could split it into manageable chunks and deal with it. It wasn't, like Gwylim's loan, a frustration that I had to hope other people would solve.

"Walk on, honey. I promise not to tickle your ribs, okay? Walk on."

She walked on.

After a few yards I dropped the rope. By sheer luck Zilla trod on the end and brought herself to a dead stop, so I said in encouraging tones, "Clever girl," and stroked her neck.

I caught up the rope and repeated it all, sometimes swinging the loop over Zilla's head but always keeping her moving, always being careful to hold my own legs steady. Each time I dropped the rope I asked Zilla to halt. I praised her when she did it right. I watched her ears flickering to and fro as she worked out what the cue-to-halt might be: the saddle shifting on her back, the rope swinging, or its end hanging free under her nose? I could almost hear the cogs going round inside her head.

At last the moment came that I'd been waiting for, when I dropped the rope and the mare stopped before I asked. *This must be it. The rope hits the ground, I stand still.* She waited, with a little nod of her head, for my praise.

"You *very* clever girlie."

Tomorrow, in the enclosed space of the yard, I would teach her to stop without the rein cue; if that went well, I would expect her to stand ground tied while I dismounted; and after that I would walk away and expect her to wait for me. But for today what we had done was enough. I had built a new idea into Zilla's brain – and while I was doing it, I had gagged some of the worries that had been chattering at me through the week. I pointed the mare's head towards the fell gate, and we rode away to freedom.

Chapter 11.

After my ride, I found Madoc was waiting for me. He opened the gate at the end of the farm track to let us through and accompanied us back to the yard, addressing an occasional word to the mare. Halfway up the track she stopped and braced to shake her neck and then her body. It was a movement that was pure Fell pony, and riding it was like balancing on a washing machine in full spin. Winter fur flew in all directions. I laughed and spat hairs.

In the yard, I kicked my feet out of the stirrups and Madoc hooked a finger in her headcollar to hold her still while I slid from the saddle.

"How far have you been?" he asked.

"Up the Roman road, nearly as far as the track to Oddendale. She thought galloping up there was a bit exciting, but she controlled herself very well. And she's got the idea of ground tying too."

"She'll make some old lady very happy then, won't she?" said Madoc, and he pushed up the offside stirrup and pulled the leather into place with a snap.

I imagined Zilla's lightning-kick and placed it side by side with the hypothetical old lady and I thought they were, as yet, incompatible. I said, "She's not ready to go. And to be honest, I'd quite like to keep her."

"*Keep* her?" Yes, there was more than the usual emphasis in his voice.

"Why not?" I unbuckled the girth and lifted the saddle off onto my arm. I knew it was probably the wrong moment for an argument, but I seemed to be already in it. "We get on well and she isn't standing at much money on the books."

Madoc ignored the remark. "You ought to show her. There should be plenty of classes for Fells around here."

I said, "I'll show her, if you want, but I won't sell her till she's ready."

"Of course. But put her in the shop window. She could be working for us."

His use of the word "us" there annoyed me. I never told Madoc how to manage Dava's young racehorses , and until now he had extended the same courtesy to me with the ponies. Apparently that was no longer the case.

He said, "I'll put the saddle away for you. Are you going to wash her down?"

I gave him the saddle. "Yes."

"When you've turned her out, we can talk about it some more."

"There's nothing to talk about." I led the mare to the yard tap and tied her lead rope to the ring in the wall while I took off her bridle. She whickered and pushed me with her nose, hoping for food.

"Greedy madam," I said.

I glanced back and Madoc was standing looking after us, with the saddle across his forearms. I faced him, and put my hands on my hips and my chin up. We both waited, not moving. After a moment he went into the tack room with the saddle, and when he came out again he made for the house without looking back.

"Well!" I said to Zilla. "I'll cap him. I'll put such a high price on you that you'll be here for life."

I set the hosepipe going and rinsed the sweat out of Zilla's coat, careful to treat her kicking spot with respect. I felt very like kicking something myself. Madoc had come out on purpose to tell me to sell Zilla. Something must have wound him up. Had Jack been cheeky? Had he and Andy been having a mutual grumble? In that case it might have been DEFRA, or the Rural Payments Agency, or even the price of fertiliser. Or more likely, I thought with annoyance, Gwylim had been on the phone again agitating about money. The water trickled off Zilla's coat and meandered in little grey rivers towards the drain.

"Mam!" That was Jack, shouting from the back door. "Telephone!"

"You answer it."

"It's a booking for the cottage. Hurry up, Mam! They're waiting."

I turned off the tap while I answered. "I've got to put this horse out in the field. If it's the agency, tell them they can ring back in ten minutes."

"It's not the agency. It's someone asking to book direct."

Why couldn't someone as technologically competent as Jack handle a phone call?

"You've got a tongue in your head! Get the number and I'll ring back."

He vanished indoors. On the basis of that exchange I thought I could rule him out as a cause of Madoc's short temper.

I scraped most of the water off Zilla. The first of the evening midges were beginning to bite so I sprayed us both with repellent before I led her back to the field, where, predictably, she cast about for a place to roll. She went down nose first like a sinking ship, then heeled over onto her shoulder and heaved herself belly-up with her hooves waving in the air. I stayed to watch her wriggle her spine and scrub both sides of her ribs in the grass. Then she sat up, stood up, shook herself again and sauntered away with dirty marks all over her.

"Honestly," I said, "I don't know why I bother washing you."

I went back to the yard. In the tackroom I found that Madoc had put the saddle and bridle on their brackets but left the sweaty numnah and girth lying on the feed-bin. I gave an explosive sigh and took them indoors to wash.

Robbie was sitting in the kitchen, freshly showered and reeking of aftershave, and Kip sat three feet away, brown eyes fixed on the slice of pizza Robbie was chewing.

I said, more sharply than I intended, "I thought I'd fed you at supper-time!"

"Got to keep my strength up."

"What on earth for?"

"Had a row with Da." A quiet statement directed to the pizza.

"Damn. I knew there was something." I dropped the girth and saddle-cloth into the sink. "I thought maybe your uncle Gwylim had been on the phone."

"Nothing so obvious. Da wants to sell all the ewe lambs."

"All of them?" I was surprised.

"Yep."

"Even your precious Lonks?"

Robbie seemed to take my question as sympathy for his argument.

"Yes. And he won't discuss it. He just says we need the money. Why doesn't he sell some of the old ewes? We should keep the young ones as replacements. How are we going to work up a decent flock if we don't hang on to at least some of them? If we don't, then when those old ones die there'll be nothing in the flock that knows our fell, and then the fell-right won't be any use to us."

"I don't suppose he'll let it go that far," I said. But I felt a twinge of doubt. Madoc had been so grim since Gwylim's visit and his decisions had begun to look extreme. I said as hopefully as I could, "Maybe it's just that things are tight – our first year here, and that. You'll have to hope the old dears can survive another winter."

"And we need to buy another ram. A young one. Something decent. The old tup we bought with the farm is on his last legs and the other two can't serve the whole flock between them. But I suppose I'll have to argue with Da over that too."

I said slowly, "I don't think your Da's being mean on purpose."

"But he won't let me go to a tup auction with his chequebook, will he! Not if I'm looking for anything with quality. He won't pay up."

"I don't know, love, he might. Remind him that Uncle Dava says quality's always the cheapest buy. If it applies to horses, it'll apply to sheep too. And you don't need a tup till October so you've got a few months to go looking."

He said gloomily, "He won't agree."

"Do you want me to talk to him for you?"

"No!" he said, with a force that startled me. "I mean, don't, thanks all the same, Mam. Just leave it."

I sighed, recognising the family stubbornness. "All right."

"And am I free now? Interview over? I have to go and pick up Beth."

"I suppose so. Are you going anywhere interesting?"

"Just to Penrith. She's twisted my arm to watch some chick flick. Don't wait up."

"Getting serious, boy?"

"I dunno. What's serious?" He grinned suddenly. "Sheep, maybe."

"Be careful of her," I said on impulse.

He looked down at me. "What d'you take me for, Mam? We know what we're doing." He didn't quite tell me it was none of my business.

He lobbed the pizza crust to Kip, slung his jacket over his shoulder and went out.

I stood by the door with my hand on Kip's collar while the dog whined and tugged to be allowed to follow. Robbie strode across the yard, young and lithe and beautiful as the spring evening. My little blond baby. Just as stubborn as his Da.

"Drive safely," I said, under my breath. Robbie got into the blue car with a swing that was almost balletic, and zoomed away.

Chapter 12.

I picked up the scrubbing brush and set about cleaning Zilla's girth and saddle cloth. I needed to do something physical, mindless, something that didn't require care or self control, something that I could pummel to get rid of frustration.

It was such a struggle to find money to keep the farm and the family afloat. The awareness of it was a constant drag on my energy. There was a huge amount of money tied up in the land and the buildings. There were nights when I lay awake beside Madoc doing sums in my head. Property rich and cash poor. We had needed to extend the bank overdraft to pay for a recent delivery of sheep feed. Perhaps when the holiday cottage began to attract customers I wouldn't have to worry so much, but even now I was wondering how soon we could start to sell ewes and lambs, and why the government subsidy hadn't yet arrived at our new address although the payment had been promised for December the previous year. Damn the Rural Payments Agency. And doubly damn Gwylim.

And the children... What were they going to do with their futures? When we'd lived in Lancashire I had observed what happened among our hill-farming neighbours: younger sons had found jobs outside farming and the daughters worked in towns until they married into other farms. Cerys had already chosen not to be one of those. I didn't know what Jack would do, and I didn't want to control him, so long as he grew up and took charge of his own life. I just wished Robbie, who'd chosen to farm, could accept the responsibility without having to challenge Madoc all the time.

I wished too that occasionally I could keep something for myself, something lovely and funny like Zilla. The mare herself wasn't what I was worrying about, but the problems around her seemed to me to be just like all the other problems that had to be solved. I scrubbed away at the numnah, occasionally wiping my eyes with the back of my wrist and sniffling.

Eventually I was able to laugh, just a little, and tell myself this was probably due to PMT. I'd have to get on with life. Every other woman had to do it, so who was I to feel sorry for myself? I picked the wet horsehair out of the plughole, slung the numnah and girth into the washing machine, and went to the back door to brush myself off. The thrush was still singing in the ash tree, oblivious to my self-pity.

Back in the kitchen the washing machine had begun to churn, the girth buckles clanking. Now, there was that telephone enquiry to be chased up. It would be the first response to our advert with the holiday agency. Where had Jack put the phone pad? It normally hung on the kitchen wall, but the hook was empty. I was cracking up...brain gone to mush. I looked into the sitting room. Madoc was working alone at the desk, absorbed. The house was so quiet that I hadn't realised he was there.

"Where's Jack?"

"Up in his bedroom. Supposed to be doing homework, but I notice his school bag didn't go upstairs with him."

"Ah." I hadn't quite got over my weak moment in the kitchen and I didn't trust myself to talk. I went back into the hall and shouted upstairs – I could control my voice at that kind of volume. "Jack! Where's the telephone pad?"

There was a pause before he looked over the banisters.

"What?"

People seemed to be always looking down at me – Madoc, Robbie, and now Jack – I shook the thought away. "You wrote down a number for me to call back."

"Oh! Yeah, I forgot."

"Where is it?"

He shrugged, disappeared into his bedroom, came back.

I asked him, "What did you take it up there for?"

"Here, catch." He dropped the pad, fluttering. "You could have called 1471, Mam."

"And you could have left the pad in its right place."

I took it back into the kitchen.

Humphrey, he'd written. *Owner. Cottage?*

Even in Jack's uneven handwriting it was clearly *Humphrey* without an S, and there was really only one person it could be. There couldn't be two, that would be far too much of a coincidence. The owner of the two young horses, Zanzibar Clubman and King Coel... whom someone ought to go and catch and put into his stable for the night. Humphrey had phoned us once before, making an appointment to watch Madoc schooling the horses, and his voice, purring and consciously attractive, reminded me of a politician I didn't like. Then he hadn't kept the appointment, and that had annoyed Madoc. I didn't particularly want to call him, but he was paying to keep racehorses in our care, and we needed his money, so whatever he wanted to talk about, I was going to have to listen. I paused the washing machine, and went to the telephone and punched in the number Jack had written.

The connection rang half a dozen times and a male voice drawled, "If you're from Microsoft, press 1."

I paused in astonishment, and it continued, "If you're digging for data, press 2. If you're selling solar panels, press 3. Anyone who's still listening, leave a message after the tone." Beep.

I took a deep breath and began, "This is Mrs Owen..."

The line clicked, and a woman's voice came through. "Hello. Sorry, love. Chaz always lets the robot deal with callers."

"Oh," I said. Somehow I hadn't expected a woman to answer. Her voice had a gin-and-cigarettes huskiness that further disconcerted me.

"And who are you, then, love?"

"Siân Owen, in Cumbria. You phoned this evening and spoke to my son Jack."

"Oh. Yes. One of our drivers says you've got a holiday cottage, that right? How much to book for a few days?"

"Er – it depends," I said, rearranging my thoughts. Here was this woman talking about the cottage and some kind of driving business, instead of horses. Was she a personal assistant or secretary? Not likely at this hour of the evening. Perhaps Mrs Humphrey? I pushed my questions aside and tried to be businesslike. "What dates are you thinking of?"

"End of this month. The half-term week."

"Tell them it's cash," added a male voice, somewhere in the background.

I mustn't let on that it would be our very first booking. "Let me check the wall planner." I put my thumb over the mouthpiece and counted to ten while the gin-and-cigarettes relayed to the man what I'd said. Then I said brightly, "Hello? Yes. The Bank Holiday weekend is still free."

"Friday to Monday? Three nights?"

"Yes. How many people?" I poised my pencil. *Money coming in!* "Just you and your husband?"

"Hang on a tick. I better ask him. Chaz!"

That's odd, I thought. She's booking a holiday and she doesn't know how many people she's booking for?

The voice from the answerphone message spoke in my ear, fruitily resonant. "Now then, how are you doing?" Before I could reply, Chaz went on, "I'm bringing a couple of other blokes. We'll pay for five beds even if we just use four."

"There's no extra charge," I said. "Your booking is for the whole house. But I ought to point out, there are only two bedrooms – are you sure that's all right for you? It's designed for family use, really."

"The lads will fit in," said Chaz. He sounded relaxed, expansive even. "I'm treating them to a bit of off-road driving. Have you got room to park three cars?"

"That shouldn't be a problem," I said. "I expect you'll want to see your horses? They're doing well."

"Sweet," he said, but he didn't ask anything further. "While I've got you, is there anything interesting going on, that weekend?"

"What sort of thing?"

"Football. Rock concerts. Race meetings."

I thought it was odd that he hadn't asked the gin-and-cigarettes to find out before booking. But I said, "I don't know about football and rock concerts, but if you hold on, I'll have a look in my husband's racing diary."

"Do that, sweetie."

I went through to the front room, where Madoc sat at the computer desk with the bank statement and a spreadsheet. I put a hand on his shoulder and picked out the diary that I bought for him each Christmas, a small tradition dating back to our courting days. As Madoc hardly ever set foot on a racecourse now, most of the pages remained blank.

He looked up at me and lifted a questioning eyebrow.

"We've got a booking for the cottage," I said. "They're asking whether there's a race meeting that weekend."

He nodded. The tension I felt in his shoulder suggested he was still partly inside his argument with Robbie. Or with me. I didn't say anything more, just took the diary into the kitchen and picked up the phone.

"Hello, Mr Humphrey? There's a meeting at Carlisle on the Monday."

"No. We'd be going back that day. Nothing on Saturday or Sunday?"

"I can't think of anything."

"Shame," he said.

I quoted him the twenty percent deposit that Madoc and I had planned, and began to read him the bank details for electronic transfer, but at that he said, "Discount for cash, sweetie?"

I managed to resist the charms of the fruity voice. "Send the deposit and we'll get back to you."

"Okay then. Shell will send it and we can haggle over the balance when we arrive. Ciao." The line went dead.

Chapter 13.

That phone call meant the holiday cottage was starting to earn for us, even though the booking looked very lonely on the wall planner. I should go and use the computer now to mark those dates as reserved on the agency web-site. I restarted the washing machine and went into the front room, but Madoc was still sitting at the desk, and he didn't speak.

Neither of us had had ever needed earphones to do "strong and silent". I waited for so long that Kip, who had looked up hopefully, sighed and went out to the kitchen and I heard him lapping water from his bowl.

At last I asked Madoc, "Will you be there much longer?"

"Mm?" He frowned, still absorbed in whatever problem he was pursuing. Then he rubbed his eyelids.

"You should get your eyes tested," I said. It came out sounding far too sharp, so to soften it I added, "I'm beginning to think I need glasses myself."

"Well, I don't."

There it was again, that stubborn streak.

"It wouldn't kill you to go to the optician."

"I'm too busy."

"Well, give Robbie some of your jobs to do." Madoc could have a chance to ease up, if he'd only take it – but right now, in the wake of the argument with Robbie, was probably not the best time to push him.

"I can only give him so much. He can't long-rein a horse or ride exercise, can he."

"All right. Look, that phone call was a booking for Bank Holiday weekend. Can I use the computer? I'll have to mark it on the agency web-site." I felt it would be better not to mention, just then, that it was King Coel's owner coming to visit. "He contacted us direct, so we shan't have to pay anything to the agency. That makes us thirty quid up already."

"Cash or bank transfer?"

"Cash."

"Good."

"What are you working out, there?" I had to squint, too far away from the screen to read the figures.

"I'm trying to decide whether to sell the grass off some of the fields. Andy's interested in round-baling Syke Side and Sweet Holme."

"Could we still make enough hay for winter?"

"That's what I'm trying to work out. The money would tide us over. The down side is that Robbie wants to keep so many of the lambs."

"He did say something to me along those lines."

"Oh, he came running to you, did he? I told him, he isn't the one with his name on the mortgage."

"Don't be like that," I said. "Actually he didn't come running to me. I asked him if he wanted me to talk to you, and he put up the Keep Off signs." Just like Madoc was doing right now. "But isn't he right? We've got to keep some ewe lambs as replacements. They don't cost anything out on the fell, do they?"

"A bunch of crossbreds, neither one thing nor the other. And the draft ewes we bought at Penrith auction are hardly fit to go round another year."

"At least that's something you and Robbie agree on. In any case," I said, "they aren't heafed so they can't go to the fell. We'll have to breed up from the flock we took over."

"Most of the fell flock aren't worth keeping," said Madoc. "You only need to look at them! I wish we could fatten the lot and sell them, ewes, lambs, everything, and start afresh. But we can't remove all the ewes from the fell flock, so the question is how can we improve it? Robbie wants to use that Lonk-cross ram lamb."

"Well, if he did," I said, "nobody could mistake our lambs for anybody else's."

"Silly idea."

"What, mine, or Robbie's? Why don't you listen to him?"

"If Robbie made a proper case for his breed we could discuss it. But he's simply dug his toes in on the other side of the argument."

"Perhaps," I said, "we shouldn't have sold so many of the flock we had in Lancashire."

"Well, we did! It's pointless to say that now, isn't it!" He pushed himself back from the desk and said, "And Cerys has gone over to Underscar, again. Wasting her time, with exams coming up. Katie will have put some wild idea in her head."

I said, half laughing, "Is it really a problem?" I could hear Hazel's voice saying, *She's going to get onto one of these television talent shows.* Should I tell Madoc?

"It's all right for Katie," he said. "She's left school, she's earning money – but Cerys – "

"Don't be like that. Come on, love, she's got a good offer from the music college. Don't you trust her? I think you do. Hazel likes Cerys, she says she keeps Katie right."

"Cerys wouldn't listen to me if I tried."

"She would if she thought you were being reasonable." What a house full of tension tonight. I tried again for lightness. "I tell you what, love – I'll do the worrying about Cerys, and then you'll be free to worry about Jack. There's no telling what he might be picking up at school. D'you think he might be growing cannabis in the sheep-shed?"

Madoc gave an exasperated sigh. "You're not taking any of this seriously."

"I am, but honestly, cut her a bit of slack. You're making a mountain out of a molehill."

"Which of course you never do." His voice went flat, and he didn't look at me.

"What?"

"Telling me I need glasses, when what I am is bloody tired. Sick and tired, Siân! Chasing money to keep our heads above water, trying to repay this bloody loan from Gwylim. Mending walls. Fixing machinery that's past fixing. And all you can see is that I need glasses!"

"Because I worry about you! And if there's something wrong I want you to tell me."

"I do."

"But you don't. You pretend! Every time I ask if anything's the matter, you just say you're fine."

"Well, that's probably because I am fine." He looked back at his paperwork, dismissing me.

I went out of the room and slammed the door.

I put Kip on a short lead and headed up the fields to the cart track towards Underscar. The dog was full of himself, ranging eagerly from side to side and sniffing every second tuft of grass, but I was still replaying the scene in the house, and I didn't take much notice of him until he found some fresh muck and began to devour it.

"For heaven's sake, dog! Leave it alone!" He looked up at me with his ears submissively flattened, then when I relented he jumped up to lick my face. "You fool," I said, laughing, wrestling with him. "You big daft pudding. I don't want your sheep-shitty kisses. No I don't. No I don't."

I made a game of plucking the moulting winter fluff from his coat. In return he pretended to chew my hands, his strong teeth only lightly pressing on my skin, and I went on plucking until he got excited and began to play-growl. I stopped then, and perched on a through-stone in the wall, and let him settle comfortably against my leg with one paw on the toe of my boot.

The air was mild and full of the moist cool scent of new grass. Coel's dark brown back was just visible over the wall-top as he grazed in the next field. Martins and swallows swooped overhead and at the edge of the fell a curlew flew up, did a controlled stall and then glided down with a long cool bubbling song. The hawthorn bushes beside the cart track to Underscar held up fresh leaves and round bunches of buds that would soon be a froth of flowers. There were white stars of stitchwort along the hedge bottom, and at the foot of the wall a Welsh poppy hung out four spectacular yellow petals to the evening sun. It was all very soothing.

Kip looked up at me and yawned, then laid his muzzle on my knee. His trust made me ashamed.

"Poor fella. I am mean to you, aren't I?"

I knew I should do what Madoc wanted, and take Zilla to a Fell pony show. It would be safe enough to pretend she was for sale, because her lightning kick was definitely going to put people off. The trouble was, even if she suddenly became a saintly, reliable pony, and even if someone came immediately to pay for her, the money we'd get for her wouldn't fill a tenth of the hole we were in with Gwylim.

Still, by showing her, it would at least look as though I was going along with Madoc's determination to put her "in the shop window".

My reflections were interrupted then because Grace the cat materialised on the wall-top and Kip couldn't resist the temptation to pounce. She stood sideways, bushed her tail and batted him with claws like electric sparks, before she leapt away into the long grass and the dog tugged me up onto my feet.

"Pair of daft puddings," I said. The cat had vanished into the dark undergrowth of the hawthorn hedge and Kip pulled to the full stretch of the lead and play-bowed, waving his tail and waiting for her to reappear. She didn't.

A movement in the empty field caught my attention: Andy Wharton trudging along with his usual canine trio ranging about him. He was no longer wearing the cap he'd sported all winter, and the sun polished the bald spot on top of his head.

He caught sight of me and waved, and came up the slope to lean his hairy forearms on the wall. His dogs stood on their hind legs and shoved their moist black noses and white muzzles over the top stones, so Andy and I looked on while they exchanged canine formalities with Kip.

When they'd done and were back on all fours, Andy said, "I owe some thanks to your Robbie. You might pass it on."

"Oh? What's he done? I will, of course."

"He got that damn fox," said Andy. "The bugger that broke into t'henhouse and killed six of Hazel's birds. I'd been watching for it with the shotgun, but it was Robbie that got it in the end. You don't need to make a fuss, mind. Just tell him, quiet like, that I'll have a few cans of beer for him next time he comes by. I've buried the thieving bugger in the midden. Vermin."

Farm justice, I thought. "I'll tell him. How's Hazel?"

"Her knee's bothering her a bit."

"Oh, what's she done?"

"She dun't say. Twisted it, maybe? She's got an appointment with the doctor a'Tuesday. Nothing that physio won't put right – so she says, anyway."

"Does she want any shopping? I'll be going to Shap tomorrow."

"No, no thanks, she can still drive. And while she's been lame she's made a start on our accounts for't tax man, so it's an ill wind."

"I'd like to ask her something about Katie," I said. "But if she's doing the accounts I suppose I'd better not disturb her."

"Aye, she cussed me out the house half an hour ago." Clearly, it hadn't been a good day either on our farm or theirs. "She turned off telly, an' all, right sharp. In the ordinary way I'd have suggested you poke your nose round door, but tonight she might throw a pot at you."

"I won't risk it then," I said.

"Your Cerys is upstairs with our Katie, singing, I suppose you know."

"Yes."

"Peter at the pub has told them they can sing there on Bank Holiday Saturday."

"Has he? I mean – that's great."

"He's not paying them, mind, but they can put out a box for donations, so they might pick up a few bob, mightn't they?"

"Oh yes," I said. "And it's all good experience."

"Aye." He passed a thoughtful palm over his bald patch, as though assessing it for sunburn, then he admitted, "Them lasses, they make a right bonny noise, but I don't know how long Hazel's going to put up with it, not tonight anyway."

I said, "I'm sure she'll chase them if it gets too irritating."

After a moment Andy said, "I asked Madoc the other day if he'd consider selling them two big fields over the road."

I was startled. "Just the grass, surely? He didn't say anything about selling the fields."

"Aye well, no, he's gey keen to keep them, for your Robbie. And he's right at that – land's getting dearer, and they aren't making any more of it. Anyhow, it'll do that old grass good to be mown, and the rough end of it'll suit my dry cows all right. I tellt your Madoc," he said, "seeing as how my mowing is going to improve your hay for next year, I don't expect to pay so much for taking his old grass away!"

"Oh," I said, "I expect you'll sort that out between you." I smiled and tried to look confident, and wondered what else my family hadn't told me.

Andy watched Kip stand on his hindlegs at the full stretch of the lead, to sniff over the wall. "You do right to keep your dog close, when you're walking among the lambs. There's a lot of other folk should do the same."

I didn't like to point out that Andy's three dogs were pretty free-range, with no restraint other than a bit of rope for a collar. After all, it was his own field and it was safely empty of sheep.

I said, "I'm scared that if he ran further than I can whistle, he'd get onto the road."

"Aye, there's some daft young buggers drives along there and they won't care what they hit."

"I wouldn't want to lose him," I said, smoothing Kip's white ruff. "He's Robbie's really, but he's more than just a working dog, he's family."

"Aye, I can see you're right fond of him. And he's a grand sort of a dog. Is he doctored, now, or has he still got his assets?"

I swallowed a gasp of laughter, but a quick look at Andy's face convinced me the question was devoid of any innuendo. "He's all there," I said, trying for the same straightforward tone.

"You know, I wouldn't mind pups from him when yon red-and-white bitch comes in season. I'd pay you a stud fee if you let me use him."

I told myself that Andy was complimenting us, in that he admired our dog enough to offer cash for his services. "Thank you," I said. "Just let us know."

"I reckon yon bitch will come over of her own accord," said Andy with a grin. "She won't be to tell twice. A bit like your Cerys – she blushes whenever our Daniel looks at her." He winked complicitly.

"Ah...I see."

"You didn't know?"

"She hasn't mentioned it."

"Aye well, kids don't, do they." He signalled that the conversation was over by standing back from the wall, saying, "I'll let you get on. I'll stay in field, then dogs won't trouble you."

Dismissed, I completed the long circuit down Underscar's farm lane and went home by the road. The wild flowers and the grasses were thickening and it was difficult to walk on the verge so I kept to the gravelly edge of the tarmac, with Kip short-leashed against my leg to keep him safe from passing cars.

At the farm cattle-grid he suddenly tugged at the lead and began his family greeting, a wag that came from the middle of his back to fling his tail round almost to his ribs. Madoc was walking down the track to meet us.

My heart jumped. Kip looked up at me and back at Madoc, still wagging hard.

"You think he's all right, do you?"

I realised Madoc must have gone out to fetch King Coel from the field and stable him for the night. It might mean he'd recovered from his bad mood, or it might not. Silence wasn't yet the sword it had been for my father, but with Madoc it was definitely a shield, and when he didn't want to talk, I didn't seem to have the knack of making him – nobody knew that better than I did. Was I the one at fault? Or was he? The trouble was, not talking could be interpreted in far too many ways.

Madoc stopped at the gate and waited for me. Thank heavens I had Kip to provide a diversion. I let go of the lead and he bounded over to Madoc, who bent down to fuss and wrestle, almost as though he avoided watching me. How thick his hair was still. Unlike Andy, he had no bald patch.

"Hello you," I said.

He straightened up. "Better now?"

The hawthorn bushes along this field-edge had already opened some of their white blossom. Relief flooded through me like their wild, slightly dangerous scent. Perhaps there was nothing wrong. Perhaps it was, after all, just that time of the month.

"I'm all right," I said.

"Good. How was Andy?"

I hadn't realised that Madoc had observed our conversation at the wall, but it reminded me that nobody ever went unnoticed, even when the landscape looked empty. I said, "He was just pottering along with the dogs. I think he's keeping out of Hazel's way. She's nursing a gammy knee and doing the tax return."

He groaned. "Tax and VAT. That's our next big headache."

"Yeah. I didn't call in."

We walked together up the lane, almost falling back into the calm rhythm of the early days of our marriage. It was much too slow for Kip, who kept bouncing up at Madoc and making puppy noises. Madoc responded to him with growls and rough caresses, and I thought how much simpler life was if you were a dog, because people would usually make friendly noises back at you, even if they had no real content. And I thought that if Madoc really had relaxed this much, it should be easier for us to talk to each other, especially when we were walking side by side and not facing each other like a standoff.

He had once remarked that he was a fox, not a hound running with the pack. At the time it was a feeling I had shared. The trouble was, the vixen in me seemed to have forgotten how to play, and the longer I waited and the more often I failed to unlock the silence, the more complicated things were and the harder it became to say anything. I tucked my hand under Madoc's arm. He tightened his elbow to his side, but he didn't speak.

I said, "Andy tells me Cerys has taken a fancy to their Daniel, and that's why she's always going over there." It occurred to me, too late, that perhaps I shouldn't have mentioned it without asking Cerys first.

Madoc gave a faint hoot. "My sympathy's entirely with Daniel."

"You can't switch off the hormones," I said.

"But we don't need to encourage them, either. Cerys's A levels have to be her first priority."

His firmness surprised me. I'd shared half a lifetime with him but he could still knock me sideways with a few words.

I covered my dismay by saying, "Well, Cerys is old enough to know her own mind. She's almost eighteen. That's only two years younger than I was, when we got married."

Without looking at me, Madoc answered, "Cerys needs to take longer over it than you did."

For a moment I was quite unable to say anything. We had made Cerys's upbringing as different from mine as it was possible to be. She had both of us and her brothers around her and every chance of making whatever she wanted of her life. She wasn't facing a cramped future, parents divorcing, or any of the other difficult things I had been trying to hide when I met Madoc.

I stopped walking, and took my hand off his arm. "Do you think I rushed into marrying you? That I just wanted your protection?"

"No. But I do think you needed me." He rough-housed with the dog again. This time it was definitely an excuse not to look at me.

Had he been regretting our marriage all these years? It hadn't been a spur of the moment thing for either of us, but I couldn't read his emotions now and I was even less sure of my own.

Before I met him, I'd hidden things – big, important, difficult things – trying to run from the pain inside. He knew that. He had found me when I was hiding, been there to help me when I broke down on that afternoon in Chester all those years ago, when the big difficult things had burst out of me: didn't he remember how he'd held me tight, promised to marry me, given me the ring his mother had worn? Now that I needed to talk to him again, the starting point for talking about ourselves was too difficult to find. The ring was shut away in our bedroom, safe in its case, safe from the wear and tear of our daily life.

"I did need you. I still do." Did I actually say it aloud? If I did, Madoc gave no sign that he had heard.

He walked on up the lane with the dog and, after a moment, I followed him.

Chapter 14.

Charles Humphrey and his party arrived in convoy on a Friday evening at the end of May.

I was in our bedroom when I heard Kip barking at the kitchen door. I looked out of the window, and there were two four-by-fours, one black and one steel-grey, and a large, scarlet BMW Mini coming up the track from the road. I'd been anxious about our preparations for this first use of the holiday cottage, so I hurried downstairs, saying as I passed the living room door, "It's the visitors." Madoc got up out of the old reclining chair, and Kip trotted amiably out with us.

It was a black Defender that led the trio of cars into the yard, and when they eased to a halt they seemed to occupy the whole yard.

"Good lord," Madoc said. "We're going to have fun parking this lot."

"Hush, they'll hear you."

The Defender driver was in his late forties, a tall fair man running slightly to seed, like a footballer who'd broadened into a pub landlord. His passenger was a blonde, who I guessed was younger than me but looked older. She had emphatic makeup and navy fingernails, and was already brushing her windswept hair back into order.

The pub landlord flicked a glance at Madoc, then put his elbow on the open window and leaned out to focus half-humorously on me.

"Now then."

The voice was even more fruity than it had been on the phone.

"I'm Charles Humphrey. Call me Chaz. And this is Shell. How are you?"

"I'm fine, thanks." I introduced Madoc, and asked Shell if she'd had a good journey.

"Oh, it was all right," said Shell, putting away her hairbrush. "Except he's had the windows open for the whole damn trip. I've had more than my fill of fresh air."

Mr Humphrey continued to smile despite her ill-temper. I wasn't sure what else to say, but Madoc came to my rescue.

"Never, mind, Mrs Humphrey. Come on in."

Humphrey slid down from the Defender, Shell pushed her door open, and the "lads" who according to him would "fit in" got out their grey four-by-four Kia and began to unload heavy mountain rucksacks. Like him they wore jeans and checked shirts. One of them, I was sure, was the driver of the horsebox that had delivered the Ninja, back in April. Madoc assisted Shell down from the Defender, which looked like courtesy, but I got the feeling he disliked all of the visiting party. When he met my glance and raised an eyebrow, I was sure of it.

Mr Humphrey said, "Come on, Shell. Shift your arse."

I added hastily, "Yes, do come in." I pushed open the door.

"Here, you don't leave it unlocked, do you? Where are the keys?"

I picked them off the hall table and gave them to him.

Shell followed us. "Oh, so much glass. Lovely, of course, but you couldn't have a doorway like this round our way. Not without you had a high wall and electronic gates. It'd be smashed in no time."

"This used to be the main entrance to the barn," I said. "It's double glazed and it all locks, so you can be as warm and private as you like."

"Warm and private is just the job," said Charles Humphrey, so close to my shoulder that I could smell cigar smoke on his clothes. I moved away, feeling safer speaking to his wife. I made a mental note to add the words "non-smoking" to future versions of our cottage advert. "The sitting room and the kitchen are up these steps, so you get a nice view across to the fells."

"You sound like an estate agent," he said, and Shell told him, "Oh, be quiet."

I watched her black-lined gaze flit over our neutral-coloured walls and carpets, and wondered whether she wanted to change all the fabrics to hot pink or leopard print. But her questions were sharply practical. "Are there towels and sheets?"

"Of course. Just like it says on the web-site."

Madoc put down a kitbag and a suitcase in the entrance, and as he went out again the other two drivers came in, filling the space with bags and their own bulky presence. I felt Kip press against my leg. His nostrils quivered at all the new-house smells but he stayed close to me, as though for reassurance.

Shell stepped back, saying, "That dog isn't going to keep sneaking in, is it?"

"He came in because I'm here. I'll take him out in a minute." I hooked a precautionary finger into his collar, thinking: *he feels trapped. Is that because these people are strangers?* I couldn't place the other men's relationship to Charles Humphrey. Too old to be sons, too young for friends. Employees, certainly. Clean-cut, but very solid, very muscular. One had a leather jacket over his shoulder and the other, with tattoos edging out from under his shirt, seemed vaguely familiar. The word "minders" hovered. Neither of them said anything or even looked at me.

"The bedrooms and the loo are downstairs," I went on, "and the beds are made up. Oh – and there's a bottle of red in the rack here."

"A couple of glasses and early to bed," said Humphrey. "Sounds very pleasant indeed." I thought he was probably laughing at me.

I said, "Have a pleasant stay."

I had to drag Kip by the collar to get him past the minders, and I could feel a growl rumbling in there that I hadn't expected, a real growl of dislike. I didn't let him go until we were safely inside the farmhouse, with the door shut.

In the kitchen, Madoc was standing waiting for the kettle to boil.

"There are times I wonder if we did the right thing," he said, "doing up the cottage for holiday lets."

"Well, we did it," I said, "and we do need the money! We'll just have to stick at it, won't we?"

"I suppose you've noticed their Kia's blocking the gate to the schooling field. I'll have to ask them to shift it before I can work the Ninja tomorrow."

"I doubt they'll even be awake at that time of the morning," I said. "Give it a few minutes, till I've fed the dog and put him in the kennel, then I'll go and tell them. Do you want some tea?"

"No," he said. "I need a very strong coffee, and I wish Humphrey wasn't a racehorse owner."

Chapter 15.

Jack was up early on Saturday morning and came bouncing into the kitchen.

"Can I take Kip out for a walk?"

The dog got up and stretched at the word but I was instantly suspicious.

"Before breakfast?"

"Having it now, aren't I?" He got a slice of bread out of the bread bin and buttered it heavily.

"What are you up to?"

"Nothing, er, I just thought Kip might like a walk."

"He's always ready," I said. "This wouldn't have anything to do with the four-by-fours in the yard, would it?"

He answered the thought behind my question. "Can't I talk to the visitors, then? If they said Hello to me, it would be rude not to say Hello back."

He didn't so much eat his impromptu breakfast as inhale it.

"Stop rushing," I said. "Yes, you can talk to them, but they've come to see their horse and have a holiday, so you mustn't pester. Don't let Kip off, and don't let him bother the visitors."

"But if I take him out and they say, What a nice dog and what's his name, it'll be all right to tell them, won't it?"

I gave a sigh that was half laughter and half exasperation. "I don't suppose they will, not for one minute. The missis doesn't like Kip, and Kip doesn't like any of the blokes who came with her."

"Oh. All right then. But can I ask them about the shovel clipped on the Land Rover? And it's got a sign on the back, stuck on upside down. It says, 'If you can read this, roll me over'."

"I suppose they think that's funny."

"Can I use the extending lead?"

"Not your nice leather one?"

"No." He got it out of the cupboard under the sink and stood drawing the cord out and letting it reel back in, while Kip pattered about waving his tail and sneezing with excitement.

"Well, before you go anywhere, check that Robbie doesn't need him."

"But if he did need him, Kip would be out there already."

Drat the boy. "Then don't go in the exercise field when we're working the horses, especially if Mrs Humphrey's there."

Jack drawled, "Okay..." He clipped the lead onto Kip's collar, then kicked off his trainers and put on wellies and trotted out into the sunshine with the dog romping at his side.

~~~

When I went out later Grace the cat was sitting on the wall. She rose into an appreciative arch under my hand, ignoring a pair of dive-bombing swallows and the mistle thrush who chirred from the ash tree like a furious sewing-machine.

I walked up to High Field to check the water trough. Zilla whinnied when she saw me and came cantering down, bringing the three-year-olds with her. They propped to a halt and milled around me. When I didn't offer them anything to eat they wandered away again, rounded and shiny in the morning light, returning their attention to the new grass.

I could see Madoc in the exercise field, mounted on the Ninja who was standing very patiently while he talked to Charles Humphrey and Shell. Only the scarlet Mini remained in the middle of the yard, so the minders must have taken a four-by-four each. Jack was sitting on the wall-top with Kip on the long lead below, earwigging as usual.

Charles Humphrey puzzled me. He didn't fit the usual pattern of Dava's owners. Most of them were country people, knowledgeable about animals, who appreciated all the work Madoc did with their young horses. Humphrey didn't appear to fit into that category. Over the years I'd worked for one or two who begrudged the time it took to prepare their horses for public appearances; this sort expressed dismay if Dava didn't send them racing every weekend. After Humphrey's no-show at his previous appointment to watch what we did, I'd have put him firmly into the second category. However, this time he and his wife were here and showing an interest. I wondered how long they had been out there, and what questions they might be asking. Curiosity dragged me over to listen to the conversation.

I didn't make a big entrance. I leaned against the wall beside Jack, and watched Madoc as he gathered the Ninja's reins and rode quietly away from the owners. It was obvious to me how much the young horse had grown and filled out, but I wasn't sure Humphrey or Shell could see it. I was surprised, though, that Humphrey came over to me instead of discussing the horse with his wife.

He said, "Now then, how are you?"

It's curious, what qualities a voice can have. Madoc's is vibrant, Robbie's too. Cerys's singing is coloured with her warmth and sincerity. That vocal quality happens to be a true reflection of their characters. But Charles Humphrey's fruitiness reminded me of a shady politician, faking authority whether or not its owner was sincere. It made me shiver.

He leaned an arm along the wall next to me, not quite putting his hand on my shoulder. I wondered how Shell would react. She was standing back with a seen-it-all-before expression, and the heavy eye liner and mascara made her look even more disgruntled. I thought it was wiser to move away from her husband without making eye contact.

I watched Madoc and the young horse cantering away up the schooling gallop, and I said coolly, "Your horses are both looking very well."

"From what your man was saying, it sounds like I should get a Champion Hurdle out of them."

"They won't be ready for Cheltenham for a year or two. Did he really say that?"

Humphrey sucked in a breath and said with a deep chuckle, "Of course he didn't. You're going to have to get used to my jokes, aren't you!"

"Oh," I said, trying to smile back. "Sorry."

I glanced again at Shell. She didn't appear to have any interest in our conversation until Madoc finished the workout and came down to walk the Ninja past us. Then she shouted at Humphrey, "Are you done here?"

"Are we?" he asked me. Madoc was walking the Ninja up the field again, on a long rein, relaxed.

"He'll walk the horse about a bit to cool off, then he'll work the other one for you."

"Sweet. But don't you have anything to do with this?"

"Yes, I do, just not at weekends," I said.

"Hm. Like to see you ride for me sometime." I didn't like the innuendo but I tried to take no notice.

Shell grumbled, "Oh for God's sake let's go," and headed for the gate.

Humphrey made a rueful face at me. "It doesn't take much to bore her. Let's go back to the yard."

Jack slid down off the wall and Kip got up, grinning and wagging his tail.

"Mam – if Da's finished showing off, are we going back to the house? I'm hungry."

"You rushed your breakfast, didn't you! Go in then, and don't let Kip bother the lady. I shan't be long." He and the dog ran off, making a wide arc as they passed Shell.

I didn't much like being solely responsible for entertaining Humphrey, but the walk to the yard was going to be endless if I didn't talk.

I asked, "Don't you want to see your other horse working?"

"Tomorrow will do.

"They don't work on Sundays."

"Neither do I." He chuckled. "I've thrown the wife the keys to the Mini. She can have it for the rest of today. Tomorrow I'm going off-roading, so long as Henry brings the Defender back in one piece."

I gave up trying to keep his attention on the work Madoc was doing. "Which one is Henry? Did he drive the horsebox, to bring your horses here? I'm sure I've seen him before."

"No, that would have been Jamie. Bit of a sourpuss, but then I don't pay him to be entertaining." He drew on his cigar and blew a luxurious cloud of smoke. "So. What does the lady of the farm do on a fine Saturday like this?"

I ignored the purr in his voice.

"The lady of the farm," I said, "is going to catch a dirty Fell pony and give it a bath."

"Why? Are you planning to sell the dirty Fell pony?"

"There's a show, near Penrith. Tomorrow."

"Not really my thing, but I'd back you to win."

"I doubt there'll be any bookies there," I said, amused at the idea.

Shell had already gone up the cottage steps and was unlocking the door. "Don't go anywhere," she told Humphrey, and went in.

He shrugged and said, "Let's have a look at this horse, then."

I led him across the yard. Coel came straight to the door, but he tried to nip Humphrey and I raised a hand between them just in time.

"I'm sorry. He doesn't like Saturdays. He has to go out second string, on his own. He's bored," I said, "and hungry."

"He doesn't have to eat me, though – do you, you bugger!" Charles Humphrey stared hard at the horse, then dropped his cigar butt and trod it into the concrete.

"To be fair," I said, "the rest of the week we work them both together. Galloping, overtaking each other. They enjoy that. How long have you owned him?"

"Oh, not long. I took on him and Clubman around the same time. Dava arranged everything."

"I'm glad you didn't change his name."

"He was already registered, otherwise I would have." He looked down at me, quizzically. "Why? Would it have bothered you?"

I was feeling too sensitive to explain it in depth. "We used to own his grandsire. And I looked after a filly called Double Jump – and she's his grand-dam."

He shook his head, not understanding. "How'd you get Old King Cole out of that?"

"Oh," I said, "Double Jump was black, but her foal was grey so the owner called her Carbon Copy. When Carbon Copy had a foal in her turn, to Crown Prince, the owner thought it would be a good joke to register that foal as King Coel. Coal – Carbon, see?"

"Just sounds like a nursery rhyme to me," he said. "Still, there it is."

I was relieved that he didn't pursue our sentimental attachment to his horse.

He lit another cigar and leaned against the wall in the sunshine, just beyond Coel's reach. I was about to leave him there when Cerys came out of the house. She was wearing a skirt and leggings, a thin shirt and a cardigan – and even though she was carrying her guitar back-pack, her makeup and carefully shaped eyebrows said, "Danny" to me, rather than music. She looked very pretty. Charles Humphrey's attention instantly focused on her.

I said quickly, "Oh, hello, love – where are you off to?"

"I'm going to – er – to Katie's. To rehearse."

"Rehearsing. Are you," I said, and she had the grace to blush. "Well, go on and rehearse, then."

I realised that Charles Humphrey was smiling at her. She hesitated, as though the smile made it difficult for her to leave without acknowledging him.

"Good morning," he said, purring again. He looked down at me and asked, "Is this beauty another one of yours?"

For a moment I was back at Green Bank, twenty years ago and more. I was trapped in Double Jump's stable with Justin Pickering. I must hang on to the present moment – the rough stone wall under my hands, the bright sun, the mistle thrush proclaiming his territorial rights. I scolded myself for being ridiculous. I wasn't that girl any more. I wasn't. I had Madoc. I had three children and all the breadth of experience that came with them. And though Charles Humphrey might be Madoc's client, and my customer, I was damned if I was going to introduce Cerys to him.

He wasn't in the least disturbed by my silence. He said to Cerys, "You're a musician, are you?"

Cerys drew the cardigan across her breasts and folded her arms tight. "Yeah. Acoustic and vocals."

"Are you!" he said. "Got a gig coming up?"

She glanced at me, not sure how much I knew. "Yeah, we have. It's at the pub in the village. Katie and I are going to play stuff we've written."

"A songwriter as well, now there's a thing." He dug into his hip pocket, then juggled cigar and wallet to offer her a business card. "The Zanzibar Clubs," he said.

She took it, read it, turned it over.

"What time d'you open?"

"Ten thirty."

"PM?"

He laughed, richly. "Of course."

"D'you provide overnight accommodation?"

"I'd find you something convenient," he said, and smiled. *The hell you will*, I thought.

Cerys tapped the card on her thumbnail. "And how much do you pay?"

"We have an extensive clientele. You'd get great exposure."

"Then thanks all the same," she said, "but if you aren't paying, I have a prior engagement."

She offered the card back to him at arm's length and I almost laughed. This was a side of Cerys I hadn't seen before. It didn't wipe the smile off his face, though.

"Keep it," he said. "Give me a call."

Shell came down the steps from the cottage. She had changed into cream slacks and a silvery blouse, with a smart jacket over her arm, and her designer shoulder-bag had cost twice the price of their holiday.

He said, half to himself, "Here comes the thought police."

Shell let out a throaty bawl. "If you're coming with me, Chaz-Baby, come now or you'll be locked out for the day."

Without turning his head he bawled back, "I've wasted most of the morning waiting for you!" He gave me the same smile he'd just turned on Cerys, and strolled over to the car.

We watched Shell drive him away and Cerys said explosively, "It's embarrassing when old men flirt."

Charles Humphrey was probably younger than Madoc – at least in years. I said, "Is that what you thought he was doing? Flirting?"

She shrugged. "That's what *he* thought he was doing. I don't like him coming-on to me, but that makes him my bitch, doesn't it? So if I need something, I'll use him."

~~~

Madoc brought the Ninja back into the yard and we worked briskly to unsaddle the horse, wash him down and put a rug on while he dried; then Madoc saddled Coel and brought him out for his turn on the gallops.

"Where's Humphrey gone?" he asked. "He's being a right pain in the arse."

"He's gone off with his missus."

"I'm wasting my time here. He's not really interested, is he?"

"He's what Dava told you he was," I said. "A wide boy."

"Has the wife been okay about the cottage?"

"I don't know. She didn't say much. She was more bothered about getting him into the car and away from Cerys."

"Oh yes?" He heard the reservation in my voice. "What was that about, then?"

"Humphrey gave Cerys his business card."

"Why was he interested in her, for heaven's sake?"

I knew Madoc was right to be suspicious, but I said, "Singing. He said."

"Really?" He tightened Coel's girth and pulled the stirrups down ready to mount. "Surely I don't need to tell you what a crook the man is?"

"I think we can trust Cerys's good sense."

"I bet he's a randy sod when wifey isn't about. You be careful. Both of you."

Could Madoc be jealous? The two words didn't belong in the same sentence. But then, no previous racehorse owner had ever generated an atmosphere like this.

I didn't say anything, and Madoc vaulted up onto Coel and settled his feet in the stirrups.

"Are you taking the mare out today?"

"Not till you've worked Coel."

"Well, I wouldn't ride her up the fell, if I were you." Coel swung round, impatient to be out and working, but Madoc insisted on good manners and brought him back. "According to Andy the Bank Holiday brings out hordes of four-by-fours. And scramble bikes. He was talking about going after them with a shotgun! So watch your step."

This time I said, "Not a problem. I'm only going to ask Robbie to run Zilla out for practice, so she'll know what she's doing tomorrow. Then it's bath time."

"Good luck with that," he said, and allowed the colt to stride away towards his work.

Chapter 16.

When the alarm went off at dawn I was already awake. The sky was not brilliant like it had been the previous day. It was drizzly and dull. However, although Zilla was damp she was still clean, to my relief, and I managed to dress her in travelling rug and boots and tail bandage without triggering her ticklish spot.

In my head I was checking everything I could think of that might go wrong. Was her headcollar buckled properly, was she sound, did the rhythm of her hooves sound evenly on the concrete, did the soft swish of each stride confirm the boots were snugly fastened? Would she go willingly into the trailer? She put a hoof on the ramp, listened to the thump it made, and paused, until I thought of the Polo mint treats and put my hand in my pocket to rustle their wrapper. Immediately she remembered our practice and walked confidently forward. I rewarded her with a mint, tied her rope to the ring, fastened the breeching chain behind her and put up the ramp.

Robbie was sitting on the bench in the passageway, fastening the laces of his best boots, with a waterproof jacket beside him. He'd put on his formal showing clothes, a checked shirt with a brown tie, a tweed waistcoat, moleskin trousers, and a flat tweed cap.

I said, "You look very smart. Zilla's loaded, so we're only waiting for Beth, aren't we?"

"Ah," he said, straightening up. "You'd better set off on your own, and Beth and I will follow you in the car."

"But I thought she was coming here, and you were both coming with me in the pickup?"

"Her car needs a wheel-bearing. And she wants to go into Penrith, to the Saturday Market. I'm off to fetch her."

"Oh! Well, all right... but God! I hate going to shows." I managed not to add, *on my own.*

"You'll be fine! We'll only be a few minutes behind you."

"That isn't the point," I said.

"Chill, Mam. You wouldn't want to leave Zilla standing in the trailer all afternoon while we wander round the market, now would you? This is the only thing that's changed. I'll still run the mare out for you in the show class, but you'll be able to come straight home without us. "

"What you mean is, you won't have me following you round and playing gooseberry."

"Well, *you* only want me in the pickup so you've got someone to nag. *Have we got our exhibitor's number? Have we got the timetable?*"

"Tcha," I said, but he only laughed and took his coat out to the car.

I packed waterproofs and a clean set of grooming kit into the Toyota, checking essentials in my head as I did so, and Robbie drove off to fetch Beth.

I walked round the trailer, still checking. Tyres all sound, pony quietly munching hay. I reached into the back of the Toyota and put my hands on all the kit to make sure it was there. Madoc had fitted the front loader onto the tractor to muck out the lambing shed and he climbed up into the cab but he left the door open, waiting for me to set off. Our understanding had always been that he wouldn't interfere with the showing unless something went wrong. My nerves were vibrating twice as strongly as normal, though, because I was letting him think Zilla was for sale when she wasn't. Jack came out to help Madoc and persuaded Kip in the rear of the tractor cab – that waterproof really was too tight for him now – oh God, more expense.

At last I threw my hat and coat into the pickup, got into the driving seat, took a deep breath and started the engine.

I heard Zilla trample once as she found her balance, but the trailer followed me in a smooth arc to the yard gate and by the time we had travelled down the track and over the cattle grid onto the road there was no further disturbance. Now we were moving, everything was normal – the growl of the engine, an occasional clunk from the trailer-hitch and the rumble of tyres on tarmac. I was committed, so I'd better enjoy it. I switched on the radio and headed north along the unfenced, snaking fell road.

On either side there was fresh vivid grass among the young unfurling bracken, and, in wet hollows, clumps of sedges and rushes. The fell land reminded me of Hazel's comment – "a nasty bit of country" – and so I tried to detach myself from my nerves by counting how many sink-holes I could see. I lost count somewhere around thirty. Some, like Doctor's Pot, were big enough to hide a car. Yet once the bracken grew up you'd hardly see them. Hazel's advice to stick to the tracks seemed to make a lot of sense.

As I drove up the Hause the air became milky with cloud and the world closed to a wheeling fifty yard backdrop of rounded grey boulders and dark swathes of heather. I switched on the wipers and the sidelights and thought again how extraordinary this landscape was. Yet the sheep – who were by-words for silliness if you listened to urban dwellers – lived here with little effort. The Fell ponies looked as though they grew from it. And Madoc and Robbie and I survived here too, dealing with essential wildness every day. If it came to that, I had the evidence of all that, balancing behind me in the trailer.

I was well down the other side of the hill before sidelights showed in my wing mirror and Robbie's little blue car loomed out of the mist. Better late than never. He stayed there sedately and escorted us north through the long village of Shap, and between stone-walled pasturelands up the A6 towards Penrith. The anxiety began to drain out of my muscles, like the confusion of the mist becoming a steady, unemotional rain.

The show field was well sign-posted off the main road and the gateway was wide and easy. I drove in slowly, getting my bearings from little white signs that numbered the roped off show rings. I followed the ones that pointed up a short slope to where the wagons and horse trailers were parked. Robbie followed and parked beside me, and I sent him and Beth away under Beth's purple umbrella to find out how far the show classes had progressed.

I removed Zilla's haynet and fastened it to a ring outside the trailer. When I unloaded the mare she began neighing loudly to find out what other ponies were about, and swinging round to listen for answers. I left her tied there, knowing she'd be awkward until she lost interest. That gave me a few moments to look around for myself, and be curious about the people who might be showing their horses here. Enthusiasts often travelled the length of the country to find classes to show their particular breed, and there were surely plenty I'd know from magazine reports even if they didn't know me. However, with the rain still coming down hard and the wet grass ankle deep, only a hardy few spectators were standing at the ringside to watch the class being judged, and at that distance there was no-one I recognised. The horseboxes and trailers standing in rank across the field were of familiar patterns but mostly anonymous, and I didn't think I knew any of them either.

I put a waterproof sheet over Zilla's warm travel rug and I was taking off her protective boots when Robbie and Beth returned, huddled as one under the umbrella.

"Eh man," said Robbie. "I can't keep up with these pony fashions. Rugs and hoods and tail bags – who says Fells are a hardy mountain breed? They're wearing more Lycra than a long-distance cyclist."

Beth laughed and said to me, "He grumbled all the way to the tent and all the way back. Worse than my Gran."

"And look at Zilla with two rugs on," he said. "The poor ickle fing might melt because it's raining..."

I couldn't deal with his teasing at this stage of the day. "Did you find the Secretary? How long have we got before our class?"

"They told us about twenty minutes," he said. "Less now."

"Get your number then. It's in the back of the pickup."

"I'll tie it on for you," offered Beth, and whooshed the umbrella shut. Her fussing and giggling over Robbie reminded me, with a slight pang, of the can't-keep-my-hands-off stage of courtship with Madoc, and how lost I used to feel when I was away from him. When had I grown out of that?

I said sharply, "Have you two quite finished? Take her for a walk so she can have a good look round before you go in the ring."

Robbie chuckled. "Beth's already seen everything there is to see."

"Don't be a smartarse," I said. "The horse. The horse! Keep your mind on the job."

He helped me to take off Zilla's rugs and fit her show halter, then he led her away, down the alley between the horseboxes and trailers. The bath yesterday had removed the waterproofing from her coat, and without her rugs she was not pleased to be exposed to the weather and tried to turn her rump to the wind, the opposite way to the direction Robbie had chosen. He made her continue to walk, backwards so after a few yards of that she jerked her head to try and pull the halter out of his hands, and when that failed she tried to rear. I thought these were probably tricks she'd pulled on her previous owners, and further reasons for her cheapness when I bought her. I moved round the tail of the trailer to keep them both in view.

The few people they met gave them a wide berth. Robbie was very patient with her. He didn't use much of his strength, but at the same time he didn't let her go anywhere except the direction he'd chosen, and whether backwards, sideways, on four legs or on two, she would have to do what he wanted. It was inevitable that she'd give in, the only question being how long it would take. At last she walked beside him as she'd been taught at home, though her flattened ears and wrinkled nostrils still expressed total disgust.

"Well done, Robert Huw," said Beth, amused. "Look at her. She is SO cross that she couldn't have her own way."

We followed them down the bank, to the rectangle of posts and rope that formed the ring.

The other ponies were beginning to file in to be judged. It was a big class, eleven or twelve ponies, all black apart from one grey and Zilla. Beth put her purple umbrella up again. It made taut pinging noises under the rain, and brought its own little atmosphere with it, stale wet polyester and the rather shrill perfume that Beth was wearing.

Before long, even inside my waterproof, I began to shiver. Nerves had prevented me from eating much breakfast and it seemed a very long time since I had got out of bed. Worse than that, I had that dragging feeling in my belly that told of an impending period.

I said to Beth, "I don't know about you, but I need coffee, and a burger with lots of mustard. Is there a catering van?"

"Mm, it's up past the Secretary's tent," said Beth. Although her eyes never left Robbie, she read my unspoken request and said, "I'll go, if you like."

"Good lass," I said. "Here's the money. Get yourself something if you want."

She went off across the field, a brisk little figure attending, as if compelled, to the needs of others.

The steward halted the ponies at the far corner of the ring and sent the first one to do a solo trot round. I turned up my collar and pulled my hat on firmly, put my hands in my pockets and settled for a long wait. The squelch of wet turf under my boots made me wonder whether it was going to be difficult to drive off the field when I wanted to leave.

After a while someone came to stand nearby. I could smell cigar smoke; when I glanced sideways, I was rather shaken to see Charles Humphrey. His boots were dealer brogues, bright tan, the trousers khaki, and the outfit was completed by a tweed shooting coat and cap. What the devil was he doing here? I looked back quickly at the ring, hoping that he hadn't recognised me under the hat.

He had, of course.

"Now then, Siân. How are you?" The voice, again, was a deep fruity purr.

I avoided answering. "I didn't expect to see you here."

"I decided it might be amusing to drop by, and Henry here agreed." He indicated his minder, hunched against the rain in his black leather biker jacket and a Manchester United woollen hat, a lit cigarette sheltered in his cupped hand. Henry the Henchman. The chap who hadn't driven the horsebox.

I said, "I thought you were going off-roading today?"

"We're between locations. I stayed at yours to watch your hubby work my colt, and your youngest mentioned you were here."

"Then I'm amazed you found me. I have a bad sense of direction, but Jack's is the worst I've ever encountered."

"He had the show schedule in his pocket so I plugged the postcode into the sat nav and that brought us here very nicely. Are you here on your own?"

"No, Robbie's girlfriend is here too."

"Oh? Where is she, then?"

"I sent her to buy us a burger."

"I wouldn't have put you down as a burger eater. All that cholesterol."

"I'm a peasant," I said. "I'm cold and I'm hungry and if I want a burger, I'll bloody have one."

He laughed at me. "You don't really think of yourself as a peasant, do you?"

I watched the class, determined not to react.

The steward was now directing the ponies away from their walk inside the ropes and feeding them into the centre of the ring to line up. Once there, he called-up one after another to stand forward for the judge's inspection, walk away, trot back. I wondered why Jack had had the schedule in his pocket when he was riding in the tractor with Madoc, and – uneasily – what Madoc had thought about Charles Humphrey asking where I had gone.

Beside me, Humphrey lit a cigar.

"This is a slow business," he said. "Don't you think? But I suppose if you have an interest it must be riveting."

How odd it was that he knew so little. But then racing people and showing people didn't seem to mix. Come to that, Humphrey hadn't seemed all that interested yesterday – if it had been me watching Madoc ride my horse, no-one could have dragged me away in the middle of a workout – so it was hardly surprising that the nuts and bolts of conformation were a mystery to him, and breed type even more so.

I watched the judge studying Zilla. Contrary to modern showing practice he was a very hands-on man, lifting her forelock, checking her teeth, stroking her neck, feeling the quality of the long hair on her lower legs, running his palm along her flank – and at that moment, Zilla's hind hoof flashed out and back.

I gasped, "Oh! You little witch."

"Hm?" said Charles Humphrey.

"Nothing."

The judge was still upright, so I deduced Zilla's hoof had missed him – thank goodness – though it couldn't have been by much.

Robbie turned the mare and ran her out, his long stride driving her into an impressive trot. When they finished their show, to my immense relief the steward was already waving them towards the top end of the line.

"And what, exactly, is all that about?" asked Humphrey.

"The judge has placed her first," I said. "For now."

The black-clad henchman took a quick puff on his cigarette. "You mean you're in the money?"

I'd never heard him speak before and I hadn't expected him to be interested, but I said, "No money. The prizes are rosettes."

"Waste-a fucking time then."

"Shut it," said Humphrey, and added to me, "He'll learn. Now, what were you saying? Is it worth you spending a day in the rain?"

Since he appeared to be at least mildly interested I said, "A placing at a good show works the same as 'black print' in racing – it adds value when you come to sell."

"How many of your horses are you selling?"

"Three, altogether. Two boys at home."

"And they're missing the party?" said Humphrey. "What a shame. You could have improved their stud value."

"They don't have any stud value," I said, slightly scornful. "They were gelded long before I bought them."

He nodded, but Henry was startled, his cigarette arrested halfway to his mouth. "Come again?"

Humphrey didn't say anything, just examined the tip of his cigar and waited, straight-faced.

I said to Henry, "They're geldings. The vet knocked them out and removed their testicles, before they could find out what they were for."

There was a small frozen pause. Henry wiped rain off his nose with finger and thumb and avoided eye contact.

Charles Humphrey presented me with a smile that was half admiration, half amusement.

"My God, you're cool about it." He said, "Tell you what. How'd you like to come off-roading with us? Henry? She'd love it – don't you think?"

"Whatever you say, boss." Henry ground his cigarette into the grass and put his hands in his pockets.

I said, "No thanks. I'm waiting for Beth to bring me a burger, and I don't fancy a cross country drive on top of it."

"Give the burger to your son. We can go to a pub instead."

"Don't be silly."

He looked me over, a swift possessive glance as though he were judging a horse, and my heart began to beat uncomfortably fast.

"Siân," he said, purring again. His flirtatious use of my name felt manipulative, like a salesman referring to "yourself". I remembered Cerys saying, "I don't like him coming-on to me, but it makes him my bitch."

"Henry won't bother us," he continued. "He'll sit at a separate table and we can have a nice little lunch together. I promise you, it'll be delicious."

"I have the mare to look after," I said. There was a fine line between attentiveness and stalking, and I wondered which side of it Humphrey might be on. It brought back a whole range of emotions I thought I'd forgotten. Not all of them were pleasant. "And please feel free to call me Mrs Owen."

"Your son can take the mare home, surely?"

Before I could counter the idea, his smile became polite again. Beth and her purple umbrella had returned; she was carrying a parcel of rain-spotted paper napkins, from which she extracted a burger to give to me.

"I put lots of mustard on like you asked for. Here's your change." She turned a polite smile on Charles Humphrey and Henry. "Are you anyone I should know?"

"Visitors from our holiday cottage," I said.

"Oh. Okay. Hello, holiday cottage." She waggled her fingers at them both, and bit into her hot-dog.

Humphrey took a half step away, still smiling, touching a hand to the dripping brim of his cap – a greeting and a farewell in one.

"Enjoy your cholesterol. Ciao."

He walked away with Henry following, leaving a drift of cigar smoke behind him.

~~~

"Well, Mam!" said Robbie, as he untied his show number. "It hasn't been such a bad morning."

"Remind me not to work outdoors with you," I retorted. All around the field, the horseboxes and trailers shone with rain. People were sheltering inside, ponies standing patiently outside under waterproof rugs, tails to the wind, heads down. Two boxes along, the owners of a driving turnout had taken the cushions off the trap seats and put them in the wagon, and their pony was nibbling at a haynet on the leeward side of the vehicle, with a waterproof over the top of his harness.

Beth was shivering under her umbrella. I said to her, "Have you got another jacket? You'll be perished going round the market."

She shook her head. "I'm okay. That's what I'm going to buy, a new coat."

"So long as you do," I said doubtfully.

Robbie said, "I'll keep her warm, Mam. And when I said it hasn't been a bad morning I meant we were lucky – the judge could have marked Zilla a long way down for that kick. She might not have been placed at all."

"It's only ever one person's opinion," I said. I took the yellow third-place rosette off Zilla's halter and hooked it inside the pickup cab. Black print? Well, not quite.

I threw the warm rug over the mare and began to re-fit her travel boots. She stood at the far end of her rope with her head cocked in annoyance, not quite pulling to escape but letting me know she might. The moment Robbie untied her to lead her back into the trailer, she put her head down to the wet grass and began to rip up great mouthfuls as if she hadn't seen food for a week. It took all three of us, and pony nuts rattling in a feed bowl, to convince her to abandon it and load into the trailer.

Robbie said cheerfully, "I forgot – there was a woman who asked if she was for sale."

"Oh? And what did you say?"

"Da told me to ask two K. So I told her three."

"What!" I wasn't just astonished about the price he'd dared to ask. I was upset that Madoc had valued Zilla and given Robbie his orders without discussing it with me.

Robbie misunderstood my dismay. "Well, I know you don't want to sell her! Anyway, it worked. The woman went 'oof' and beetled off."

"Don't say anything to your Da."

"I'm not daft!" he said. He removed his tie and loosened his shirt collar, in recognition that his duty was completed. "Right, we'll be away now. You'll get off the field all right. Probably much better without us watching you. And there's loads of people to help if you do get stuck. But you won't. It's all downhill from here to the road."

"Yes. I hope so." I wished now that I hadn't done what Madoc wanted, bringing Zilla to the show. I felt it would have served him right if I had waltzed off in Charles Humphrey's Defender with its shovel and winch and the black-clad Henry to have a "nice little lunch". And now I would have to make up my mind whether to bottle up my anger or make a fight out of it when I got home. Or maybe I should walk over to Underscar to talk it out with Hazel. She didn't yet know me well enough to guess at the kind of emotions I was hiding, she would laugh at Humphrey's attentions the way she had at Sally and her wandering husband, and if I told her the price Madoc had put on the mare perhaps it would save me a quarrel with him.

Robbie was talking to me. "Mam? Are you listening? Beth said, Do you want anything from the market?"

I took a firm grip on my thoughts. "A pack of bacon would be useful. But only if it isn't dear."

"Of course not, that would be venison."

He hid behind Beth to escape my slap.

Chapter 17.

I was in the yard on Sunday morning when I heard the kitchen smoke alarm scream into action. I shut the stable door and sprinted across to the house to find the place full of smoke and the smell of burnt bread, and Jack standing back in awe of flames coming out of the toaster.

With the alarm screaming every other second it was impossible to talk, so I didn't waste time trying. I switched the toaster off at the wall, pitched the Rayburn towel into the sink and turned on the tap, then draped the damp towel over the toaster to quell the flames.

Cerys came scrambling downstairs in her pyjamas. When she saw I was in charge she took hold of the kitchen broom and poked its handle into the smoke alarm button.

In the silence that fell I said to Jack, "I wish you wouldn't cram crusts into the toaster! Wait till it's you that has to buy a new one!"

"Or a new house," Cerys said. She teetered barefoot to the kitchen door and started swinging it to and fro to waft the smoke out into the passageway.

Jack complained, "One day you're telling me I've got to eat up the last crusts, and the next you're telling me off for toasting them!"

"I'm telling you off for wrecking the toaster! Couldn't you see that crust was too thick?"

"No."

"Hah! He looks more like Dylan Thomas every day," Cerys observed, between swings of the door. "You know, that painting with the pout – poor little me – and my little red curls!"

"That's not fair."

I could hear door-banging and shouting from the holiday cottage next door.

I said, "Hush!" and sent Jack to the far end of the table. "If you've disturbed the visitors...Sit down and be quiet."

I cut the crust off the new loaf for myself and gave Jack and Cerys the next slices. "You'll just have to have bread instead of toast."

"Mam! Everybody wants the first crust and nobody wants the last! It's –"

"– not fair," Cerys chanted.

"That's enough!" I said.

There was a pause in which Cerys came back to the table and sat down, and Jack plastered butter onto his bread with mutinous greed. The thumps from next door had stopped, but now there were voices outside on the yard, ending with a woman shouting something about "going". A car door slammed heavily, followed by a revved engine and a crunch of hard driven tyres.

Charles Humphrey's voice shouted, "You bitch!"

Cerys looked at me, her eyebrows raised. I didn't have any explanation for the scene that had obviously taken place, but I didn't think our smoke alarm could reasonably have triggered it so I just shook my head, and reached for the butter.

Jack was busy heaping jam onto his bread, and evidently following an entirely different train of thought.

"When's Uncle Gwylim coming again?"

I tried to rearrange my thoughts, which were scampering after the departing car. "Oh God, I don't know. Sometime. Too soon."

"Oh. Don't you want to see him? He said he'd teach me to use the rifle. Da said he's a good shot. Ages ago. He won prizes."

"Explain. Why do you want to use the rifle?"

He went silent, so Cerys said, "He wants to big himself up at school."

Jack's expression made me think that his mates in the village had already called his bluff.

Cerys went on, "All he really needs is for someone to take his picture with it. Job done."

I said, "Well, it won't be me. And it had better not be you."

She stuck out the tip of her tongue and passed me the jam.

Jack said, "Why can't I?"

"Oh, for heaven's sake! You're not old enough. Eat your breakfast."

There was a knock at the open back door and Charles Humphrey looked in. He smiled, but in a strangely tight way. He was breathing hard and I had no doubt that he was very angry. I got to my feet hoping he hadn't come to take out his temper on our burnt toast and arguments.

He said without preamble, "Find out the times of trains to Manchester for me."

Not what I had expected at all.

"From the nearest station south of here," he said.

"That's Oxenholme."

"Look it up then," he said. And as an afterthought, "Please." His gaze fixed on Cerys and her pyjamas.

She said, "Jack would do it quickest," and Jack said, "Oh all right," and headed for the front room, taking his bread and jam with him.

"Get your plate!" I commanded, and he came back for it and vanished again.

Charles Humphrey said, "Can I use your phone? My wife's taken my laptop and my mobile."

That fitted with the door-slamming, the shouting and the engine-revving. I felt like applauding Shell's exit but I said, "Oh dear. What's happened to your four-by-fours?"

"I sent the boys off. They've got jobs to do. And I'm not asking you to give me a lift. I want a taxi."

"Well, we can manage that all right. Cerys, will you bring me the Yellow Pages please?"

She padded away, barefoot. Humphrey waited in the kitchen doorway, leaning his back against the hinges with his arm locked across the opening as though he wanted to control everyone going in or coming out. When she returned he held out his hand towards her but she gave the phone book to me and then slipped out of the room again without going near him.

I called after her, "Finish your breakfast."

Her voice came back from the stairs. "I'm going to get dressed."

Humphrey opened the directory and began to flip the pages, sweeping each one over with a wetted thumb so noisily that I half expected the paper to smoke under his hand. He paused with it curled back from the spine at the place he wanted, and asked me for a pen.

I gave him the one from beside the telephone, and said, "You may have quite a wait at Oxenholme – Bank Holiday services, you know how it is."

"I know," he said shortly.

I wiped the draining board. I put a dirty plate and knife into the dishwasher. I couldn't relax with this angry stranger dominating the kitchen. I was relieved when, in the front room, the printer chattered into life and Jack came back to us with a list of train times.

"Thanks," Humphrey said, with a brief nod. He looked down the list, drew lines round a couple with an air of lassoing them, and went back to the Yellow Pages.

"These taxi firms," he said. "Any recommendations?"

"We've never needed a taxi."

He punched in numbers, hard. "Hi. How soon can you get me to Oxenholme? From Stone Side Farm. Hold on a moment." He asked me: "Postcode?" I gave it and he relayed it into the phone. "How long till pickup? Is that the best you can do? Okay, okay, it'll have to do."

He put the phone down and squared his shoulders, looking at me, still with that tight, not-quite-smile.

"I have half an hour to pack."

"I must give you an invoice," I said.

"No need. Come with me now and we can sort it out."

I felt a little more equal to him this time, being on my home ground. He was at a disadvantage here, and separated from Henry and Jamie, while Madoc and Robbie were only the other side of the sheep shed. I followed him out to the cottage. He made a rapid inventory of the dining room, ignored a newspaper and a pink-top magazine that Shell must have left, and picked up cigars that went into his shirt pocket. Then he went into the bedroom, dug in his pocket for keys and unlocked the drawer of the bedside cabinet. He grunted satisfaction.

"The bitch missed my wallet. And my credit cards!"

I said, "You said you'd pay us in cash."

"I probably did. I don't suppose you take card payments, do you." He opened the wardrobe. "Give me five while I pack."

I left him and looked into the second bedroom, where Jamie and Henry had presumably slept. Everything was surprisingly tidy, the towels and the used sheets roughly folded on the nearest bed, pillows stacked naked on the other. In the kitchen, there was only a container of milk left in the fridge. The work surfaces and the cooker were clean and there were no glasses or mugs waiting to be washed. Empty wine and beer bottles had been lined up around the rubbish bin, which was full of polystyrene takeaway trays and a heavy smell of fish and chips and cigarette ends.

Charles Humphrey came out of the bedroom carrying his rucksack and his red walking jacket which he dropped onto the sofa.

"Here's your keys. You're bloody lucky she didn't take off with them too."

I pocketed them, and he paid me from a wad of twenties that felt grubby and smelled of cigars and stale beer.

"Thanks for everything," he said. "If you think she's taken anything that's yours, call me. I'll pick up straight away. Is your mobile number still the same?"

When I nodded he peeled another twenty off the wad, and held it out to me, nipped between his outstretched fingers.

"Use this for yourself. It's not for the kids or for hubby, it's for you. Buy something nice with it."

I ought to have refused it, but I didn't. I reached slowly for the note, and as I took it his fingers tightened, making the paper into a momentary connection between my hand and his – an exchange of power, like a rider demanding contact with the rein. I looked up and found him smiling at me. He let go.

"Ciao for now." He zipped the rucksack and picked up the jacket. "Right, where's that damn taxi?"

Chapter 18.

Madoc and Robbie came in for their mid-day meal in a surprisingly good humour, twitting each other and teasing the dog.

"Well," I said, "what makes you two so cheerful all of a sudden?" I glanced from one to the other, wondering whether they had reconciled their differences.

"We've marked a dozen ewes today, to sell with lambs at foot."

"And you've managed to agree about it? Wonders will never cease."

Cerys came down from studying in her bedroom. The men washed at the sink, and Robbie sent the dog to lie in his corner. When they sat at the table Madoc let Robbie do the explaining, though I could tell he was waiting to pounce on any exaggeration.

"They're old ewes with bad teeth but they've come on all right, haven't they?" said Robbie. "I've been surprised. They've done much better than they used to at Longlands."

"Mind you, we couldn't predict how they were going to perform, and it could be just luck and good weather."

"But don't you think the grass has come earlier?"

"Maybe."

"Of course it has. When did we ever think about hay-timing in June?"

"And are we?" I asked. "Thinking of hay-timing?"

"Yes," Madoc said, "we've been discussing it with Andy. The weather forecast's good till the weekend."

Robbie said, with a glance at Cerys, "Danny's going to help us mow those old meadows."

She blushed, but she went on eating without saying anything.

"Do we have to give Andy a hand in return?" I asked.

"The plan is to cut all our grass in one go, big-bale the old stuff for him, then help each other to small-bale the rest," said Madoc.

Robbie said, "There's your chance then, Cerys – you get to spend all day in the hay-shed with Danny."

"Fat chance. I've got to be in school this week."

"I thought you were on study leave?"

"Yes, for the exams. And all of them are this week."

"Well, even if we mow the grass on Wednesday," said Madoc, "we won't be baling it till Friday or Saturday. Your exams will be over by then."

"And those broken-mouthed ewes with lambs at foot," I said, "when are they going to auction?"

"First batch tomorrow," he said. "It's either Kendal in the morning or Kirkby in the afternoon."

"Andy says some of the dealers go to both. He likes Kirkby." Robbie shrugged. "It's all the same to me."

"I'd rather go to Kendal," said Madoc. "I hate hanging about half the day at home, waiting for an afternoon auction to start."

I said to Cerys, "He was just the same when he was racing. The day couldn't start early enough for him."

Cerys shuddered. "It's bad enough the exams are all in the mornings!"

Robbie said, "I don't care – I don't have to do them any more. Yay."

"It was only *one* week of your life."

"Well, Miss," said Madoc, "after your exams are over you'll be able to come with us. Come and pout at the buyers to help us sell." He added teasingly, "You'll do it much better than Robbie."

"I won't have time," she said, "and I'm not going to pout at anybody unless you pay me."

Robbie shook his head, mock-serious. "Ohh, dunno about that... I mean you never paid us when we were at Longlands, did you, Da?"

Cerys pulled a face at him. "Well, no pay, no pouting! I've put in for more hours at the services, anyway. Katie and I have to fit our practice around our work shifts. If we can only rehearse in a morning, then, me going to the auction? Not going to happen."

"What are you rehearsing for now?" I asked. But at that moment the house phone rang, and I got up to answer it. The voice at the other end, asking for me, sounded old and querulous, and all too familiar. My heart sank. "Oh! Hello, Dad. How are you? Is everything all right?"

"No, it isn't. I'm not well. Can you come down and see me?"

Oh my, I thought. *What's this? He's a hundred and fifty miles away, and we've got all this work to do.*

"You're not in hospital, are you?"

"No, not yet, but I had a couple of funny turns last week and Simon drove me to see the doctor. He says I shouldn't be lifting things."

"What else did he say?"

"I don't want to talk on the phone. I want to see you. When can you come down?"

"Is it urgent?"

"Oh no, not at all urgent, not if you don't care about your Dad's peace of mind..."

I muffled the voice against my chest and counted to ten, and Madoc asked, "What's the matter with him?"

I said, "The old bugger won't tell me. He wants me to go and see him."

"Right away?"

"I don't know! I can't go haring down there at a moment's notice. I haven't a clue what it's about." I said into the phone, "Dad, I'm sorry. I don't understand. At least tell me you're all right. Are you at home?"

"Yes, I'm at the shop. Simon's looking after things. I've got to sit and supervise him."

"Then what can I do to help?"

"Come and see me. There's some business I want you to do for me. Simon's only an employee. It's not his place. There are things I want to tell you, and I'd like to see Cerys and Robert. But don't bring Jack. I can't cope with him."

I watched Cerys clearing the table. "Cerys is sitting important exams this week, Dad."

"Is she! What about Robert?"

"He's taking sheep to the auction. And it's haytime." By now I was talking to the family as much as to my father.

"Oh! Well," he said crossly, "Come on your own, then, if that's all you can manage. Tomorrow?"

"It'll be Saturday at the earliest, Dad."

"Oh, I'm sorry to be such a drag on your busy life."

I sighed. When he was in this mood nothing suited him. Yet if he really wasn't well, that was understandable, and there was nothing I could say.

Madoc's steady look attracted my attention. "You can have the pickup," he said quietly. "While we're leading-in the hay I shan't need it."

I nodded.

"Thank you... Dad? I'll call you back when I've got something organised." I put the phone down.

For a moment I stared blankly at the wall, churning over options for the journey. I was remembering what it was like to drive long distances alone. Being baffled by road junctions where my memory from years ago didn't match new layouts. The impatient honks from cars behind when I took too long to make a judgement. My pulse began to pound just at the thought.

"Would you be able to go with me, Robbie?"

He flashed a quick glance at Madoc. "I don't think I'd better. Like you said, if we're going to cut and bale all that grass, I'll be needed here."

"Then I think I'll go by train."

"Wow, Mother! That'll be expensive."

"No, it won't, if you're not going and it's only me. A hundred and thirty-odd miles, if I avoid Liverpool. Double it – then work out the diesel the pickup's going to use. Unless you want to lend me your little car? You know, the one you brag about for being so economical on fuel?"

He said reluctantly, "Only if you bring it back by teatime."

"I can't make any promises about that," I said. "It depends entirely on what Dad's got in store for me. Just driving that far stresses me out, and that's before Dad gets started." I was feeling more and more wretched about the whole thing.

"Well, I need my car on Saturday. I'm going out with Beth."

"If that hay's not stacked, Robbie my lad, you might not be going anywhere," said Madoc with a grin. "Beth will just have to lift bales with the rest of us."

"She'll be fine with that," said Robbie. "I just don't want to be stuck without the car."

Cerys completed filling the dishwasher. "But if Mam's away and Beth AND Danny are coming – that sounds like Party Time!"

"You arrange the music," said Robbie, "and I'll bring the beer."

I looked to Madoc, at last. "Would you give me a lift to the station?"

He said easily enough, "Of course. We can't work with the hay till the dew's off. Book an early train and I'll take you to Oxenholme."

Chapter 19.

In the cool early sunshine of Saturday Madoc drove me to Oxenholme station to catch the seven-thirty to Liverpool.

"You look very smart," he said, casting a glance over my sage green jacket and coral blouse. I'd bought them from the charity-shop with Chaz Humphrey's tip. "Ready for a job interview."

"Dad will probably say I look like a tart. The skirt will be too short."

"He may not say anything. If he's as sick as he makes out, I bet he's only thinking about himself."

I knew there was a battle ahead, despite Madoc's calm assurance. I fidgeted with the engagement ring that I'd dug out of its box to be part of my armour. "I wish I didn't feel it was such a duty. I should want to go and see him, shouldn't I? He is my father, after all."

"You'll manage," he said. "Look at it this way – if he hadn't been such a grumpy old bear, you wouldn't have run away to work in racing, and you wouldn't have met me."

I sighed. "You're right – when you put it like that. I did meet a lot of people because of him."

"And then you're supposed to say, 'And you were the best of them!'"

I said, trying to make light of it, "Best of a bad lot, my darling."

"Praised with faint damns. Ah well." He returned his attention to the winding road.

When we reached the station I said, "I'll phone you when I know which train I'm going to catch, to come home."

"You know how noisy it is on the tractor – you'd do better to text Robbie – or better still, phone Underscar. Hazel will get a message to us wherever we are," said Madoc. "Any idea what time?"

"Not really. It all depends what Dad wants me to do."

"Well," he said, "someone will come for you, don't worry, even if it isn't me." He gave me a wry half-smile. "Don't fret. You're having a day out so you might as well enjoy it. But if you really have to fight your Dad, make sure you win."

"I'll try."

"Then give us a kiss, and be off." But a taxi beeped from behind us, so it was just a brief peck before he drove away.

The only seat I could find on the train was at a table where a young couple were keeping a bouncing three-year-old penned into the window corner. The surface between them was cluttered with crisp packets, chocolate biscuits, and splashes of orange juice. There was a newspaper on the empty seat. I used it to shield me against further splashes, while I smiled routinely at the parents and their little girl, and retreated into my own thoughts.

It was annoying how often Madoc was right. He was right that because I had run away from Dad's shop we were married and had the children. I knew I had a life that, for all its hardships and calculations, suited me better than I could have hoped. (And my children knew better than to throw a tantrum if they couldn't have another chocolate biscuit!) But between running away and meeting Madoc I'd seen some of the cruelties behind the glamour of racing; moneyed cynicism and greed for more money, and the casual lust that greed brought with it. I'd been shocked but I'd had to live with them – it wasn't so much that I condoned the greed, but I had to recognise the smallness of my place as a paid employee, and how little I could do to change what I didn't like. A lot of that powerlessness traced back to my parents and how I'd been taught I always had to give way to other people; "the customer is always right". (Although if the young mother and father beside me didn't take that child in hand pretty soon they would be taught the same thing by a toddler! Better not to say so, though, when we were all crammed cheek-by-jowl at the same table.)

My father had brought me up to believe I was worthless. That was why I'd put up with all the shit that I'd found myself in. Madoc might be right about it having brought me to meet him, but he was also wrong: I didn't owe my father just the good things in my life. I owed him a lot of the bad things too.

~~~

The navy and cream paint was peeling off the sign "PETER DAVIES" over the shop window, and the awning that shaded the trestle tables on the pavement outside was faded to the colour of denim. Buckets of Sweet Williams, de Caen anemones and unlikely-coloured daisies stood between baskets of plastic-wrapped summer cabbage, cucumbers, tomatoes and lettuces, and traffic-light packs of peppers.

I stepped in over the familiar chequer-tiled threshold. The room, lit by sunlight reflecting off pavement through the front windows, looked even more down-at-heel than I remembered. The shop floor felt and sounded as gritty as it had in my childhood and still smelled of damp earth; I had always wondered where the dirt came from. It couldn't all be soil from the sacks of new potatoes – marked today at their high early-summer price – yet town customers coming in from the street didn't wear work-boots caked in mud. Perhaps the dust blew in with the passing traffic.

My father was at the far end of the shop, sitting on a straight wooden chair behind the massive wooden counter and the weighing scale. The traditional grocer's coat made him a study in grey and brown.

"Hello, Dad," I said.

"You're early," he said, sounding surprised, but he didn't get up. "Have you got a kiss for your old man, then?"

I went over and gave him, as I had to Madoc, a perfunctory peck; this time, on the cheek. I recognised the smell of Old Spice – slightly faded and stale Old Spice – with an undertone of ancient tweed jacket. It took me straight back to the childhood atmosphere of conflict and I had to struggle out of it to ask, "How are you?"

"Not so good, chuck, but the doctor doesn't think I'm going to die just yet."

"Well, that's something, at any rate." I nodded to the assistant, a khaki-clad clone in his late thirties. I could only remember his first name. "Hi, Simon."

Simon nodded back. "Are you well? Kids all right?"

"Up to their armpits in hay, I expect," I said, happy for the conversation to move away from Dad's health. "The neighbours have cut their grass, and so have we, so it's all hands on deck to get it led into the barns."

"Sounds like hard work."

"It is." I thought about the sun beating on the pale, mown fields and the way they seemed to get bigger as the long day went on. I guessed Simon hadn't ever felt the weight of new-made hay, or the prickly rash that the cut stalks punched onto your forearms with each bale lifted, but he certainly couldn't know how I wished I was still at Stone Side, doing that tough mind-freeing work instead of hovering here, half-welcome, half-resented, trying to guess the mood my father was in.

I said, "So long as it doesn't come a storm, they'll bring it in all right."

Simon nodded, but my father made an irritable movement and Simon moved away to the window, where he began to rearrange the oranges.

Dad said, "I suppose I should be thankful you managed to get here at all." He raised his voice a little. "Simon, go and make us a pot of tea."

"It isn't eleven o'clock yet, Mr D."

"If it's too early," I said hurriedly, "I can wait."

"For heaven's sake let's have it now, while the shop's quiet."

I couldn't tell whether the edge in his voice was for me or for Simon – possibly both. I offered to finish the display, but Simon positioned a last orange and made a show of dusting his hands as he went through the dark doorway to the back of the shop.

There was a pause. I pulled out the old rickety stool that lived under the counter, and perched on it.

"Simon seems to know what he's doing," I observed.

"He'll do," said Dad shortly. "I have to have somebody around. Otherwise I could die and nobody would know."

"There's a cheery thought for a Saturday. You look all right here, at least for the moment. Have you got a cushion on your chair?"

"Yes, yes, I'm not making a martyr of myself. I don't trust him, mind."

"Sounds like you don't know what you want." I wondered whether Simon was the reason Dad had wanted me to travel down to see him. "One minute you think he's got his hand in the till, next thing he's the person you rely on."

"And maybe both things are true."

"You could always employ someone else."

"Someone worse, you mean. It's all right for you. You haven't got aches and pains and the doctor stuffing you up with pills that make you constipated."

"I should hope not," I said, and refused to enquire further.

He shifted position and grunted with discomfort. "Why didn't you bring any of the kids?"

"You said you didn't want Jack. And Robbie and Cerys are helping with the hay."

"I thought you said Cerys was studying for exams?"

"She finished yesterday, and a day out in the sunshine will do her the world of good."

"You mean she's too busy to visit an old fart like me."

I managed not not to snap any of the replies that came to mind.

"She's been working very hard for the exams. She deserves the break before she goes to college."

"And what exactly is she going to do when she gets to college?"

"Dad, she got a scholarship, remember? You know perfectly well she's training to be a musician."

He snorted. "She'll end up being a teacher – a primary school nanny."

"She wants to be a professional singer. And she says she's very grateful to you for the lessons." Actually Cerys hadn't said anything of the sort, but I thought it was tactful to acknowledge his contribution.

"If I'd realised it would mean her leaving home so young, I wouldn't have done it. She ought to stop with you and get a good steady job."

"I won't hang on to her the way you tried to hang on to me," I said. "You're just arguing for the sake of arguing. Stop it."

"Don't tell me what to do, miss."

I blinked. "Then don't you call me 'Miss'!"

Simon was coming back with three mugs of tea. He placed two in front of us on the counter before retreating with his own towards the window. I waited for Dad to pick up his mug before I reached for the one that was left.

"Well," I said, "you made a big thing of wanting me to visit. So here I am. Are you going to tell me why?"

"That's why. That's exactly why."

"Come again?"

"It shouldn't be a big thing to come and see me."

I thought of the arrangements I'd had to make for the journey, the early start, the lift to the station, the changes of trains. "Dad – I'm sorry, really I am, but I can't just drop everything to run down here."

"Yes, I know, you're playing with your farmyard, you're always busy. Too bloody busy for your own family."

"That's not fair. It's a long journey. You know it is, and I'm needed at home."

"Well if you have to *make* time to come and see me – !"

"I'm here, aren't I?"

"You ought to be here!" he said. "Not just blowing in once every six months!"

I said, "What?"

"You should all be here. All of you."

"You mean Madoc and the children? Oh, come on, Dad!"

"I'm telling you what your duty is."

He stopped abruptly as a grey-haired woman came in with two young children, carrying fruit and flowers chosen from the outside tables. Simon put down his mug and attended to them, and to fill the pause, I drank a mouthful of tea. I was dismayed to find it was very strong.

"Have I picked up your mug by mistake?"

"Mine's all right," he said.

I risked one more sip and put the tea back on the counter. He didn't seem to notice.

When the grandmother and the children had left with their purchases, Dad said irritably, "Well? You've had time to think. I want you here. Give me your answer."

"You're not seriously asking us to move house. That isn't going to happen, Dad. It's not fair to uproot the kids yet again."

"I want you here and that's that."

"Now listen. I'm well over a hundred miles away. The farm and the family are my job! Twenty-four-seven! It isn't something I'm doing just to fill my time." I didn't mention the horses; they were a side issue. "Where am I going to find enough hours in a day to visit you here as well?"

He said, as though making a concession, "Couldn't you commute? Once a week, perhaps."

"It isn't like you're just a couple of bus stops up the road! I'm sorry, Dad! It can't be done."

He growled, "You're a selfish little cow, you always were."

And you're a grumpy old git, I thought, but I remembered that he was old and not feeling well, so I managed not to say it.

He went on, "I'm not going into a care home, you know. Being bundled into a chair and ignored except at meal time and bed time. They rob you blind in those places and there won't be enough money to bury me when I'm gone."

I said, trying for lightness, "You used to say you wouldn't care if you were doubled up and stuffed in a dustbin." He just looked mulish. "Why don't you come and live..." I knew it should be, *"live with us"* but the words stuck in my mouth – "nearer to us? I've asked you before. Plenty of people move house when they retire."

"What? No! Imagine me moving at my time of life."

"Why would that matter?"

He put his mug down with a clatter. "I know you think *I* don't matter! That's what you've been saying all along, however cleverly you dress it up. If you'd cared you'd have stopped at home when your mother left. But oh no, you had to run off, because you were all grown up and going to make your fortune with horses. That didn't exactly work out well, did it?"

Goaded, I forgot my good intentions.

"It worked out just fine," I snapped, "because I got married to Madoc! And I'll tell you something else – when our kids go out into the world, they'll only need to make one journey to come back to visit us! They won't have to make one trip to see their mother and another to see their father, like I did!"

"Wait till it happens. You'll be lucky if they want to see you at all!"

I was about to snap at him again when Simon came over, his trainers crunching on the gritty floor. "Have you finished?"

"What do you mean, have I finished?" said my Dad. "I haven't bloody started."

"Your tea," Simon said unemotionally. When I sat back and threw up my hands he remarked to me, "Your Dad's had a cob on all this week, so I wouldn't get too worked up if I were you. I'll wash them mugs."

He carried them away to the kitchen.

"I'm sorry," I said stiffly to Dad.

He grunted. "So you should be."

"You'll have to sort something out," I said. "There's only you to consider down here, but at our end there's me, and Madoc, and the kids, and the farm, and the livestock..." I waited for him to process the idea, but he went on sitting in silence until I felt I had to speak again or stop breathing. "Well then! If you won't discuss it sensibly, let's talk about something else, shall we? What's this thing you asked me here to do, that Simon can't?"

He shifted on his cushion and drew a deep breath, which reminded me he'd always liked playing for dramatic effect.

"Go upstairs," he said, "and get the concertina file that's on the table by my armchair. Look in the W section. I want you to take the big envelope and lodge all the papers with my solicitor."

"Dad! Your solicitor's in Chester!"

"D'you think I don't know that?"

"You could just as easily post them," I said. "If they're that important, you could use registered post."

"I want you to take them, and nobody else. Is it too much trouble for you to catch a bus to Chester? It will mean you don't have to spend the day with me, after all."

"Oh, for God's sake, Dad! All right!"

Chapter 20.

I was angry with Dad. Now I had to catch a bus to Chester, walk to the solicitors' office on the west side of the city, then slog back to the station for a train to Liverpool and my connection back to Oxenholme. Was the old devil just power playing or was there something else going on? He hadn't even told me what was supposed to be wrong with him.

On the bus I looked at the envelope of documents I was carrying. Like everything else of Dad's it was second-hand so the flap was torn and not stuck down to hide the contents: a peek inside showed a couple of letters, a booklet, and a stiff heavy paper which seemed new – a standard form with a heading in black Gothic lettering, and handwritten contents. *Last Will and Testament.* I should have guessed.

Was I on trust not to read it? Dad hadn't said so. But if he hadn't wanted me to read all these papers he could easily have posted them. I stared out of the window while I thought.

Suburban houses went jerking past. Street corners, fields, hedges and trees. It must be twenty years since I last travelled this road. Madoc had been driving that rusty, nippy little MG that he loved so much. We were both still living at Dava's stables and preparing to marry and move to Afonwen.

I didn't expect much from my father's will. He'd been dismissive enough for me not to get up any hopes. But he'd made no effort to seal the envelope he'd put it in, and he could so easily have taped or stapled it shut, and if he really hadn't wanted me to read the documents he'd have sent them by a Royal Mail service and not called me down from Cumbria to be his post-boy. There had been hints in his conversation this morning: *There won't be enough money to bury me when I'm gone.* I knew him well enough to understand the slyness. His ill health was bothering him and he knew he ought to warn me how much or how little I could expect from him, but he couldn't do it face to face. Trusting me with the unsealed will was an easy way out.

So I read it.

I saw at once that I wasn't going to inherit much: whatever was in Dad's bank account, plus the two-up, two-down house with the shop in its front room – except I wouldn't get the full value of that because there were two letters from a building society detailing a recent mortgage on the property. He had nothing else.

The stiff coloured booklet, I found, was about a local retirement home. He'd drawn a big angry cross on its cover and towards the back he'd circled a sentence, *If your assets including your property are above £23,250 you will be expected to pay for your own care.* That would definitely mean selling the shop. He must have been in a very bad temper to have missed the next section which said, *If your capital is below £14,250 you will be entitled to maximum support.* Of course it presupposed that Dad would agree to go there.

The rest of that bus ride was uncomfortable. I was ashamed of having read his will, but there was nothing in any of the papers to chase away the worries about Gwylim calling in his loan on Stone Side Cottage. Nothing that could ease my resentments or make me feel any better. All I could do was to refold the papers and put them away.

Dad and I were alike in too many respects. We never talked about what hurt us most deeply. He couldn't admit that he had so little to leave me, for the same reasons he couldn't talk about the memory of my mother without denigrating her, because if he did he would have to consider whether he was, himself, a failure. And if he hadn't told me what was wrong with him, that was because I hadn't bothered to ask. It made me crosser than ever.

~~~

The centre of Chester was crowded. So many strangers, in families or singly, young and old, wandering or changing direction, walking, running, flowing and turning like leaves in water without so much as a glance at anyone else. I paused to get my bearings. Cities were hard work for me, and I had to find the bulk of the Cathedral to kick-start my sense of direction. I realised then, with relief, that only the details had changed: there might be different shop windows and signs, new wide pavements protected by bollards, and areas pedestrianised where I had been used to dodging traffic, but much of the city's framework was still the same as it had been twenty years ago.

I made my way to the Cross. Everyone I passed seemed better dressed than I was, but I had no way of knowing whether they in turn thought my second-hand clothes looked smart, casual or simply ridiculous. I got mixed up with a party of girls who were giggling and zig-zagging their way down Watergate Street. They were wearing tight colourful tops and short skirts, and flat ballerina pumps. Their legs were fake-tanned, their eyebrows tweezed and pencilled into unlikely arcs and their eyes heavily made up, but their faces were flushed with honest excitement and youth. I stepped out of their way feeling old and dowdy, and almost at once I was surrounded by a noisy bunch of young men in suits, who caused me a moment of panic. I escaped them all by climbing steps to the upper walkway of the Row.

Up there, in a haven of shadow occupied by occasional slow-moving window-shoppers, my footsteps rang hollow on wooden floors, and I managed to slacken my pace, to think calmly and accept that my urgency was mostly of my own making. There were two more things my father's summons had given me. One was the unwelcome realisation that he really couldn't be independent much longer. The other was, astonishingly, a relief: the fact that once I'd delivered the will to Dad's solicitors, what I did with the rest of the day would be entirely up to me. If the morning's upsets happened to culminate in the office being shut, well, I'd have to post Dad's documents after all, but it wouldn't really matter; attempting to deliver the will was my only responsibility for the day. It wouldn't even matter what time I decided to leave Chester. My printout from the railway web-site showed there were trains to Liverpool every fifteen minutes. If necessary, there were buses. There were even taxis. So I could use the rest of the day as a breathing space. And hadn't Madoc said I might as well enjoy it? Madoc was always right, wasn't he? So I damn well would.

I progressed steadily along the Row from window to window, thinking of myself as a rustic Cinderella let loose in the city. At one corner I passed a very chic hairdresser's; on the next, there was a bridal-wear shop; then a window displaying lingerie and swimwear to support big-busted women, while the shops next to it, in a grouping that seemed like a cruel joke, sold antiques and custom upholstery. There was a café and grill with sizzling lunchtime scents of food, but the prices made me stifle my hunger and move on.

I reached the Custom House, where the Row ended, so I had to go down again to street level, to the hot, dusty sunshine and the endless grumble of cars on the ring road, and wait with a little crowd of people for the traffic lights to let us cross over towards the city wall.

When I found the solicitors' office in the side-street of Grey Friars, to my relief its door was open, and in Reception there was a businesslike young woman who accepted the envelope for "our Mr

Sanderson" and gave me a chit for it. I was in and out within minutes. And that, it seemed, was that.

Except it wasn't.

I stepped out of the office into hot air tingling with sound – the multi-voiced roar of a crowd watching a sporting event. It carried me straight back to the time I'd spent taking horses to the races, when racing had been my life, and Madoc's life. I didn't have to think about it, I knew, that it was race day. Down there on the Roodee, a few hundred yards away, there were horses galloping, ridden by wiry jockeys in protective helmets and paper-thin boots, who crouched in colourful silks over those horses' withers and swung arms and bodies and whips to keep the rhythm of the sprint going to the line. I stood there on the pavement outside the solicitors' office, and lost myself in the roar till it reached its climax and then sank, as it always did, into a mixture of satisfaction and regret.

I squared my shoulders. I'd delivered my Dad's pathetic documents. I'd done what he wanted, no matter how cross it made me. But now I deserved to have some fun.

I set off at a brisk walk towards the racecourse.

~~~

The Wall above the Roodee was crowded, busier than I'd ever seen it. The street was closed to traffic, and all along it people stood three and four deep looking down onto more crowds, all anticipating the next burst of horses and colours.

People. All those people.

I would not, could not ever, dare to push into a close crowd of strangers. But if I didn't dare, the only option would be to stand where I was, at the edge of the pavement. I would be held back from everything that I knew must be down there on the manicured grass of the racecourse – the white rails, the sunbursts of flowers, the brilliant colours and, above all, the horses. Everything there would be familiar, the preliminary ring and the saddling pens, the paddock, the weighing-room, the jockeys' silks, the white tents and the red-brick stands, and in the enclosures the men sporting Panama hats and smart suits, the women in designer dresses.

I wanted to enjoy the beauty of fast horses, smell the sweat, hear the squeak of boots on racing saddles, feel the ground tremble and see the turf fly as hooves thundered past. I wanted to be carried away by speed.

I must get onto the course.

To my right, at the high black and gold railings of the Tattersall's gate, attendants checked ticket holders' badges before letting them in to the stands. I couldn't afford those prices. I was very hungry by now, but if I just paid for Open Course admission I could afford to stop by a catering van, and carry my food out into the country to eat while I stood at the rails of the track. Among the slovenly smartness of the 'cheap end' my second-hand clothes would fit right in.

A couple in the crowd near the Wall moved away, casual watchers I supposed, caught by the brief dazzle of the race and now, with the finish over, released back into everyday life. As I stepped aside to let them go by a voice purred in my ear, "Now then, Mrs Siân. How are you?"

I swung round almost into the arms of Charles Humphrey.

"My God," I said.

He laughed. "Never that!"

He was conventionally smart in a light grey suit, the jacket a little too small and unfastened to reveal a bulge of blue shirt and tie, with a matching slip of cloth in the top pocket. Race glasses in a shiny leather case hung from his shoulder and behind him were the two henchmen, buttoned into dark suits that looked too stiff to permit free movement.

Humphrey asked, "Are you here for the racing?"

"No – I was delivering some documents for my father. I didn't realise it was race day."

"I find that hard to believe," he said. "And where are the family?"

"They're at home. It's haytime."

"Aha. Footloose and fancy free. Tell me – have you had lunch? No? Then come and join me. I've got a table in the racecourse restaurant."

I should have said that Robbie was with me, or any of the children. I could have snubbed him completely by saying I had a train to catch. But I can never make lies sound convincing. As it was, the buzz and promise of the racing had got hold of me, and I couldn't for the life of me walk away from it.

He saw me hesitating.

"Let me treat you. I guarantee, it won't be burgers."

I laughed then. "All right."

His glance flickered over me like a metal detector, and his smile broadened, so that I was conscious again of the shortness of my skirt and the deep vee of my blouse, and for just a moment I wondered whether I was being reckless. But I was hungry. And I was committed.

He put his hand in his pocket and brought out a tangle of pasteboard badges and string tags. "Isn't it lucky," he said, "that I've got a spare ticket?"

~~~

He took me by the elbow and piloted me through the gates, and across the terraces of Tattersall's enclosure, with his two minders following a couple of paces to the rear. His hand was hot on the light fabric of my jacket. Would it be rude to draw my arm away? But it was his money that had paid for the jacket.

I said, "I've never been here on a race day. I used to be a stable lass. But they would never have let me in wearing my yard boots and jodhpurs. I'd have attracted several large men saying stop-here-at-the-gate-please-miss."

"Would you?" he said, without much interest. "I come here a lot. I've got two fillies running on the Flat, and this is handy."

"Oh, have you?" It was the first time he'd ever volunteered any information about himself, and I was surprised. "I thought you only had National Hunt horses."

"The two that are with you? No."

"It won't be long before they're ready and we'll send them back to Dava."

"It makes no odds if they stay with you for a while."

Again, that wasn't what I expected. "Thank you. That's a kind thought."

"Not really. You don't charge as much as Dava." He gave my arm a little shake, and when I glanced up at him in surprise, he said, "Lighten up."

Was he laughing at me again? Even when he smiled, his eyes told a different story.

At the far edge of Tattersall's we reached the most expensive enclosure, the County Stand. His badges seem to open all gates. And perhaps because of the stiff-suited presence of the henchmen, other racegoers only gave us one glance before stepping aside.

He stopped to talk to a stout red-faced man in a tight expensive suit who was accompanied by a couple of women in high heels, thin dresses and thick make-up. They reminded each other with extreme hilarity about nights out and parties and people I had never heard of, while the minders put on sunglasses and became even more impersonal, and Humphrey let go of my elbow long enough to light a cigar. He seemed ready to gossip forever. I waited, trying not to get too close to anyone and hoping my stomach wouldn't rumble, and while I stood back from the conversation I caught glances between the women that were slightly disturbing. Neither of them asked Humphrey where Shell had got to, nor who I was. I felt my cheeks reddening at the speculations that would be rampaging through their heads. Perhaps I ought to walk away. I could; his admission badge tied to my shoulder-bag would allow me to go wherever I wanted on the course. But Humphrey topped a surge of conversation with a joke of his own, and before I had made up my mind he was saying, "Ciao," and had taken me by the elbow again, walking me across the turf of the race track itself to the paddocks and buildings in the centre of the course.

On the far side he almost bumped into a crisply-tailored elderly gentleman who raised his stick, either in self defence or in greeting, it was hard to tell which.

"Oh! Hullo, Humphrey." He took in the presence of the henchmen without flinching but he lifted his trilby to me. "Who's the young lady you've captured?"

I hadn't been complimented as a "young lady" for quite some years, and again it was embarrassing to be seen as Charles Humphrey's property, but at least the challenge meant that he introduced me properly.

"This is Siân Owen." He laid a hand on my shoulder. The hand with the lit cigar. I stood very still. "Siân, this is Arthur Whalley."

"Hello. My husband," I said deliberately, "is breaking-in two young hurdlers for Mr Humphrey."

Whalley didn't miss a beat. He replied, "Pleased to meet you, my dear. And your name is Owen? Now, that's a name to conjure with. You're not one of Dava's relatives, are you?"

"I'm married to Madoc. His nephew."

"Well, well! Are you now? I remember him as a damn good jockey." He gave me a shrewd though kindly glance, and when I reddened and looked away he shifted his attention to Charles Humphrey. "You know, I've been friends with Dava for a long time, a very long time. I sold him a nice colt once – a grey – must be twenty years back. We'd won the Chester Vase with it the year before." He looked enquiringly at me. "What was that colt called now, you'll remember it, my dear, the name escapes me?"

The crowd went on bobbing past us. I said, "Cymru?"

"What's that? Yes, it might well have been. He was sired by that long distance horse, the one that Dava was so keen on. What was it called, Banner, something like that? Never mind! How did the colt do for him?"

My mouth had gone dry. Whalley's knowledge must go deep, beyond the foundations of my marriage, and I realised that for all his pretence at memory loss, he was gently reminding me which family I belonged to.

I said, "Dava had a good season with him, and Madoc bought him for stud."

"Ah! And how did that go?"

Best to stick with simple statements that needed no explanation.

"The horse died," I said.

"What a shame." Whalley brought out that commonest of farming cliches: "Still, these things happen. I'm sure you coped."

Coping is what you do when there are no other choices. I forced my mouth to smile now, as I had then, and I was grateful when Whalley smiled back, so that I didn't give away how dearly Madoc wanted the colt who was Cymru's grandson, the horse Dava had put in our care to learn to race on behalf of Charles Humphrey.

"I must say, Humphrey, I'm surprised at you applying to move the Hamilton filly to France," Whalley said, "My boy was rather shocked you gave him so little notice, you know? Not really the thing." He prepared to walk on. "But it's nice to have met you, my dear. Give my regards to Dava. And to your husband, of course." He lifted the trilby again, nodded to Humphrey, and he and the stick tapped briskly away.

As we walked on, Humphrey observed, "He's not fit for much any more. His son has the trainer's licence now." He seemed unaware there had been any criticism of either me or himself in Whalley's conversation. "Anyway – I promised you lunch, and here's the restaurant. Let's go in."

I was off balance and very hungry and I could hear Cerys's voice in my head saying, *When I want something I'll use him.* So I went in.

Chapter 21.

In the restaurant large TV screens were relaying the action from the course. It had a sunny glass wall overlooking the parade ring, and it seemed to be full of people, including the hen party I'd met in Watergate Street – people with flushed faces, rowdily eating and drinking. The diners' standard of dress was mixed, and only my comfortable shoes might have given away the fact that I was a horsewoman rather than a punter.

Again, Humphrey's badges worked magic: there was a lunch reservation, and we were shown to places on the cool side of the room. I was well aware that he'd only invited me on the spur of the moment, and most likely because he'd already bought the race day and lunch as a package and so my meal wasn't going to cost him anything more. He nodded at the henchmen to sit behind him nearer to the door and said, smiling, "I'd rather look at you than at them."

I suppose if he hadn't turned up when he did, I might have just watched the races for half an hour from the Wall above the course and never dredged up the nerve to buy an entrance ticket; I'd have caught an early train back to Liverpool and felt regretful but satisfyingly puritanical. All the same, it gave me a pleasant sense of privilege to be treated as myself, for once, rather than a wife or a mother or a wayward child.

I keep a strong enough hold on my wits to sit, like the henchmen, facing outwards. Racing was a big world, far bigger than the pony show circuit, a world in which everyone, not only the professionals, travelled long distances to meetings. I had been uncomfortable talking to Arthur Whalley, and there might well be other people here who'd know me and Madoc and Dava and Cymru, and some of them I wouldn't want to meet. I had to spot those before they spotted me.

The waiter brought us huge menus on which every dish sounded delicious, with prices that would normally be way out of my range.

Humphrey said, "The sea bass is good here. Is that okay for you?"

I nodded. "And white chocolate cheesecake to follow."

I handed the menu back to the waiter and Humphrey ordered a bottle of Sauvignon blanc, this time not consulting me.

While we waited, he asked, "Tell me – what did you buy with the money I gave you? When my soon-to-be ex stranded me at your holiday cottage?"

"A bucketful of black pudding," I said. I wasn't going to admit he had bought the clothes I was wearing.

"Oh! I'm disappointed. I told you to spend it on yourself."

"I don't have to do everything I'm told."

The hen party by the window had fitted each other with printed crimson sashes and huddled round the bride-to-be. Humphrey observed their secretive, giggling conversation the way he might observe cattle grazing in a field. The huddle broke suddenly into shrieks of laughter.

I said, "I saw them on the way here, maybe an hour ago. They've got a bit lively since then."

"They'll have smuggled-in their own vodka," he said, unconcerned.

I laughed. "There aren't many hiding places in clothes like that."

"It used to happen a lot in my first club in Manchester. The cleaners used to find the empties, flat half bottles usually."

"Did you ban it?"

"No, of course not. I told my manager to undercut local prices. The customers soon realised that smuggling-in booze actually cost them more than buying ours. We sold a lot more after that."

The wine came and the waiter went through the little ritual of letting Humphrey – not me – taste a sample, before pouring two glasses and leaving us the bottle.

Humphrey raised his glass to me. "To unexpected meetings."

I mumbled, "Meetings," and sipped the wine. It was fresh flavoured, almost acid. I put the glass down. "I just don't get why drinking so much equates to fun. It must be a city thing."

"I bet there's just as much drinking out in the country," he said. "Lonely old men with dustbins full of beer cans."

The waiter came to serve our sea bass which was, as Humphrey had predicted, very good. He ate with a neatness and concentration that surprised and repelled me almost as much as the greed I had expected. The sun shifted round to us and brightened the blue daisies in the table decoration. The hen party by the window grew noisier. I drank my way down the glass of wine, curbed my impatience to go out and watch the horses, and tried to think of something innocuous to talk about, while Humphrey seemed satisfied to watch the TV screens relaying another race. The waiter removed our empty plates and served dessert.

I asked, "Your chestnut horse – why did you call him after the club?"

He stared at me. "You ask the strangest questions."

"I'm only making conversation," I said. I felt my cheeks burning, and that seemed to amuse him. "You offered my daughter the chance to sing there. It would be odd if I didn't want to know more about it."

He said, "All right then. I opened my first club in Manchester five years ago – that's the one I'd have suggested, if she'd agreed to sing. But – she didn't. Her loss. The second one's in Liverpool, and I just opened another in Leeds. And I've got an outdoor centre in the Yorkshire Dales. So I name my horses to give the businesses publicity. I'd have liked the brown colt to run under a Zanzibar name and not Old King Coel, but I think I told you, he was already registered."

I nodded without speaking. Humphrey knew how to manipulate people – I would have bet that even the outdoor centre had bonus uses, like taking the edge off the physicality of men like Jamie and Henry, the way you would turn dogs loose in a paddock to bond them into a powerful, dangerous pack. I didn't want him to guess at our interest in King Coel.

Humphrey reached for the Sauvignon and gestured towards my glass. I shook my head. The sweetness of the cheesecake was certainly making me thirsty, but I was already a little light-headed.

"No?" he said. "That's a shame."

He put the bottle aside, however, and took another precise forkful of his *millefeuille*.

Henry and Jamie had finished eating and were sitting now like bookends, scanning half the room each. Their jug of water was still half full, and as there was no sign of our waiter I got up, took my empty glass across and held it out to them. They both looked to Humphrey and then, as though given an order, Jamie pushed the jug within my reach.

I filled my glass and drank. The water was sweetly cold, with tiny remnants of ice cubes floating in it. I drank the whole glassful.

I filled the glass again and carried it back to the table, but I didn't sit down. I was impatient to get outdoors and close to the horses. Humphrey was exceptional among the owners I'd known. Nightclub owner, racehorse owner and who knew what else, he'd bought himself a package to enjoy an afternoon's racing, yet here he was sitting in the restaurant, backed by his muscle-men and watching everything at second-hand via TV screens.

He shaded his eyes against the sun to look up at me. I reached for the table decoration, pulled out one of the blue daisies and faced the flower towards him.

"My Dad sells these in his shop. Do you know, they aren't naturally blue? He says the florists stand white flowers in dye to make them colour up and sell better."

"Does that matter?" he asked.

"Of course it does." I dropped the flower into the glass and set it by his empty plate. "I'm going to watch the horses now. Thanks for lunch, and, you know, ciao."

~~~

The heat and noise and sunshine and the smell of trodden grass swamped me in a huge, anonymous embrace. Forget Chaz Humphrey. Forget Gwylim's time bomb ticking. Forget my father and his sad little manipulations. The wine was still tingling in my veins. I was going make the most of this afternoon, while I had the chance.

I walked to the far end of the paddock and found a gap between the racegoers to watch the horses parade for the next race. No-one took any notice of me; they were studying racecards, glancing at the runners being led round, looking down again to mark numbers and check form. I sneaked a look at my neighbour's card which was folded back at the page for the race, and saw it was going to be a fast five-furlong sprint. A dark bay horse came striding by. Number three. Its physique was heavier than the lean long-distance shape I was used to in Dava's hurdlers and steeplechasers. It held its head low, almost as though it was sleepwalking, but its bulk was all muscle and it had the taut belly of an athlete.

Chaz Humphrey's voice said in my ear, "You should have waited for me." Henry and Jamie were at his shoulders, their eyes once more expressionless behind sunglasses.

"You seemed to have settled down for the afternoon." I had to pitch my voice against the background hum of the course, and no doubt it came out more strongly than I intended. "I was missing the racing."

"I'd have escorted you, if you'd just asked," he said. I looked up at him, but he was watching the horses. He glanced at his racecard, then flapped it shut in dissatisfaction. "Twelve runners... these sprints are a lottery. And they're over before you know it. I think I'll drop the fillies at the end of the season."

"Sell them, you mean?"

"Sell, lease, whatever," he said, with an air of being surprised that I needed to ask. "Gordon will find someone who wants them."

"Poor creatures."

"Why?" His expression suggested he was just being perverse now, seeing how far he could push me. "He tells me there are plenty of nice women who 'rescue' racehorses."

"They may be nice all right, but it takes a lot of skill to make a rescue turn out well. Your fillies may not be that lucky."

"You'd prefer them to go to France as steaks?"

"I didn't say that! But why not? So long as they're dead before they travel, it might be the best end of them."

"You really are quite a bitch," he said, with a note of admiration in his voice.

"I'm a peasant," I said. "Remember?"

The jockeys came out from the weighing room in a little flood of colour. The lads walking the horses brought them in from the outside track onto the grass in the centre where they met their owners and trainers. The jockeys were legged-up onto tiny saddles and the mounted horses resumed the parade, heading now for the gate towards the course. Humphrey folded his arms and watched.

"Pick me a winner, then, peasant lady. Is this grey thing nice enough for you?"

The dappled horse jigged past with its rider and its handler, and I said, "If you like rocking-horses. But this one looks more like a winner, to me." The dark bay horse was coming towards us again, the jockey in green silks with white cross-belts.

"Slipknot," he said, consulting his racecard. "Anything else catch your eye?"

"Not so far."

"Okay then. Let's go and find a bookie and I'll split whatever we win. Deal?"

I chuckled, thinking he wasn't serious. "If you want to waste your money."

"Deal," he said.

He set off though the crowd, and I followed him because, once again, as if by magic, space appeared around us and the henchmen, and this time he was going the right way for me, passing the bookies' stands lining the track, going away from the winning post and towards the start. He didn't hesitate at any of the pitches until he reached O'Reilly's, right at the far end, where a sinewy man with bloodhound eyes nodded unemotionally at him.

Humphrey brought out his wallet. "Afternoon, Dermot. Now, Siân, what's your horse's name?"

Dermot's list of runners and odds showed that Slipknot was favourite, at five to two. I had to raise my voice above the loudspeakers naming the horses and the jockeys.

"Slipknot," I said. "But it's awful short odds."

Dermot intervened. "Lady, I'm not here to give money away. You want to back it at longer odds, look around and see if you can find 'em." He took a bet from another punter, while Humphrey stood watching me, the cash ready in his hand. The runners were beginning to canter out, past the big television screen and the loudspeakers strident with the commentator's voice, and away towards the starting stalls, and I realised that the longer I hesitated, the less time I'd have to find a good place to watch the race.

I said quickly, "Slipknot. Number three."

"Three," Dermot repeated, as he took and checked the notes. "A hundred to win."

I said to Humphrey, "Don't you mean fifty pounds each way?" and he said, "No. Dermot knows what I mean."

He insisted I took the ticket.

He turned as though he meant to go back to the County Stand, obviously expecting that his betting slip in my pocket would bind me to follow him, but I didn't want to. I'd already been made to feel out of place among the smart people, in my charity shop jacket and blouse, so I didn't want the County Stand. What I craved was closeness to the horses – to hear their breathing and their thundering footfalls and feel their energy through the ground under my feet. I slipped round his minders and set off at a fast walk in the opposite direction.

I was free of him, but only for a short while. When he caught me up he was panting. "Where the hell are you going?"

"The start, of course," I said.

"Among the picnic-eaters?"

"I want a place by the rails."

"You won't get one unless we come with you." The minders were at his shoulders, still breathing easily. I didn't answer, just went on walking, and let that betting slip drag him along with me.

Five furlongs is no distance at all to a horse, but we couldn't cover it on foot before the race started, not even with Jamie and Henry to clear our way. The last of the runners were already being loaded into the stalls. The doors crashed open and the crowd began to yell, and I darted into the first gap I could see at the rail. Humphrey and the minders crammed in behind me.

The twelve horses came galloping, tight to the curve, a wave of muscle panting and straining, and as their hooves battered the ground my chest hummed in sympathy. Then the fluttering rainbow colours were past and gone and racing down the straight.

The press of bodies – the bare-armed woman to my left, the fat man sweating through his suit, Humphrey and his henchmen – was suddenly too much for me. I pushed the woman aside and wriggled away from the rails into less crowded space.

The crowd had already roared for the finish and the commentator was giving out the result: Slipknot had won by half a length.

Humphrey caught me up again. He said, "You should bet more often. I'd put my money where your mouth is, any day."

I ignored the innuendo, and offered him his ticket. He wouldn't take it.

"It's yours, peasant lady. Let's go and laugh at all the losers."

He put a hand on my elbow again and walked me back to O'Reilly's stand. Henry and Jamie waited at one side, their dark glasses concealing where they were really looking, while Dermot counted the notes with a quick shuffling movement from one fist to the other.

Fifties! Seven of them! Humphrey pushed them into my hand and closed my fingers over them. His hand was softer than I expected, hot and sweaty.

"There you are. If it hadn't been for you, I'd have wasted my cash on the rocking-horse."

I had a sudden, mad idea. The deadline for repaying Gwylim was getting closer, and maybe this ruthlessly generous gambler might see a solution I'd missed.

I said over the crowd noise, "No," and I put the money back into his hand. "Give me a loan instead."

Chapter 22.

"What a curious proposal." After a moment he took the notes and folded them away. "A loan?"

"Yes. Can we go somewhere a bit quieter, and talk about it?"

There was a glint in his eyes that I couldn't immediately identify. Calculation, yes, I expected that. But what else? Humour, amusement, triumph? Yes. Triumph. I'd given him, voluntarily, something that he'd expected to have to work for, and it wasn't the money. I'd made a mistake and I didn't know where.

I said, hastily, "Strictly business, of course."

He said, "We'll see."

He took my elbow and began to escort me through the racegoers, past the bookies' pitches, back towards the restaurant. And then I saw someone coming towards us, someone whose good clothes and stocky figure had become much too familiar in the last couple of months. And he'd spotted us. My brother-in-law, Gwylim.

"Oh God," I said, half jokingly. "Kill me now."

"What?" Humphrey looked around the crowd to find out what had alarmed me. When he saw Gwylim he chuckled and said, "Oh, is that all?"

I wasn't sure how he felt about Gwylim's approach until Jamie and Henry closed up behind us and he let go of my arm and gave them a soothing hand signal. The way he waited made me think of a fencer deliberately lowering his guard to taunt an inferior opponent.

"Well, hello there," he said.

"Hello there yourself." The resentment in Gwylim's tone confirmed my impression that Charles Humphrey was the boss. "Don't you ever lose the watchdogs?"

"No."

Gwylim glanced at me and muttered, "What the hell are you doing here?"

I didn't know how to answer him. Humphrey answered for me. "Say what you have to say and move on."

There was an uncomfortable pause in which Humphrey and his men stood facing Gwylim, bound together by the tensions between them, while the business of the racecourse surged on round us, taking no more notice than an incoming tide.

Gwylim's attention seemed to be split between Humphrey and me, as though he couldn't decide what to say to either of us in front of the other. "Maybe now isn't the time."

Humphrey nodded. "And maybe you're right. Trickle away before you embarrass yourself."

But it cost Gwylim a lot to back down with me watching. He said with a scowl, "Why are you talking to this bastard?"

I glanced at Humphrey who chuckled, drew out a pack of cigars, selected one and began to remove the cellophane.

I said as lightly as I could, "I've been to see my father. He wanted me to do some business for him in town, and Mr Humphrey and I just happened to bump into one another."

"Yeah, right. Let me give you some advice – if you have to tell a lie, at least make it a good one. "

"I've no idea what you're talking about."

"Watch your step. He makes out he's friendly, but don't kid yourself."

"Gwyl, boy," drawled Humphrey, "shut up and go away."

Gwylim said to me, "You'll think you can get something for nothing but all you'll get is bullshit. Whatever the setup is, it stinks."

I couldn't make out whether he was attacking Humphrey or me, or perhaps both of us for different reasons. "There is no setup."

Gwylim made a scornful noise. "With Chaz-baby there's always a setup. But you wouldn't know about that, would you! You're too bloody perfect to be true."

Humphrey was lighting his cigar, and without looking up from the task, he said, "Get lost, Gwyl, before your mouth gets you into trouble."

"Oh, we'll see about that. We'll just bloody see." Gwylim turned and began to walk back the way he'd come.

Humphrey spoke over his shoulder. "Henry. Jamie." He tipped his head meaningly towards Gwylim.

They reacted as though they'd been programmed. They didn't speak, or make any disturbance that would attract attention. They stepped round Humphrey and me and I doubt Gwylim even heard them coming. They simply caught him up, pinned him by the arms and walked him away.

I watched them go in disbelief.

"Mr Humphrey –"

"No, no. I told you. Chaz."

"I don't understand this," I said. "You know Gwyl is my husband's brother? He annoys the hell out of me, but what's he done to you? And what are they going to do to him?"

He drew on his cigar. "They won't kill him."

The sheer callousness of that knocked the breath out of me. I could hardly feel my feet.

People passed us by – so many people smiling in the sunshine, so many voices, and smells of fast food and flowers and crushed grass, and litter covering the tarmac. It overwhelmed me, but I had to try and hold on to it. It was the only way I could keep control. Charles Humphrey had spent an hour or more charming me with the civilised mask of the racecourse, and now with a few words he'd stripped it bare and I was faced by a world I'd once lived in, a frightening world run by people whose money could hire tough young men to do their fighting. I realised then that I'd been wrong to play on his apparent interest, and I couldn't see where the gamble was going to take me.

I said shakily, "I think I'd better go."

"Oh," said Humphrey. "Do you really have to?" He sounded genuinely concerned. If I hadn't just witnessed how cold he could be, I might have been convinced.

"I have a train to catch."

"Of course you have. I'll drive you to the station – after all, you proposed we do business, and I think you might prefer to discuss it in private."

Chapter 23.

Humphrey's grip of my arm was much firmer this time. As he steered me through the crowds towards the main gate he made a phone call: "Henry. I'm taking Mrs Owen to the station. Look after Dermot and get over to Manchester by eight o'clock." He didn't wait for an answer and he didn't mention Gwylim, but I thought I saw connections. Dermot O'Reilly, bookmaker. Gwylim, desperate for money.

Humphrey didn't say anything more but he kept a hand on me until we reached the car park where the sun was shimmering on the steel and glass of the ranked cars. In the middle was the watchdogs' Kia standing next to his black Land Rover Defender. He opened the passenger door and a wave of tobacco-laced heat flowed out from the high cab.

He said shortly, "Hop in."

The passenger seat looked safe enough; the seats were designed for stability and protection during cross country driving, with a wide bulkhead between them. I might be able to survive a brief journey without him touching me again. I got in and he shut the door for me.

"Just take me to City Road," I said as he lumped himself into the driver's seat. "I'll catch a train through to Lime Street."

He started the engine, rearranged his jacket and mopped his face.

"I'll take you to Liverpool," he said. "We'll need half an hour for this *tête-à-tête*." He switched on the climate control and drove rapidly through the lanes of parked cars. Twin blasts of air began to chill the sweat on my skin. Half an hour. I drew my jacket closely over my blouse and pulled my skirt down, and fastened my safety belt in more senses than one.

He took the through-traffic route for the M53 and as soon as we were moving freely he pressed switches to lower both front windows, replacing the cold air-con with a warm, blustery incoming breeze. He threw out the stub of his cigar and lit another, and then he drove with his right elbow on the sill, his left hand doing most of the steering. He was still sweating.

We left the city and accelerated up the slip road of the motorway, and the speed and the traffic tightened the enclosure around us. Tick, tick, tick, the indicator swinging us out into the lanes of cars. He didn't attempt any conversation at all until the Defender built up speed and the wind and tyre noise began to buffet my ears. I reached for the switch to raise the window and he said, "Leave it," in a tone that startled me. I drew my hand back.

"That's more like it." He seemed pleased. "Now, what would you like to talk about? Horses?"

I shook my head.

"You've got quite an emotional investment in the beasts, one way and another. I wonder what it's worth to you."

I put my hands under my thighs and held tightly to the leather seat. Borrowing money from Charles Humphrey didn't seem like such a good idea.

The motorway was lined by hedges thick with summer leaf. Hip-high grasses, mown silage fields already greening with aftermath. Electricity pylons. Trees, more grasses. He passed other vehicles with a careless swerve and a tick, tick of the indicator.

White chevrons between the carriageways, concrete gantries spanning the road with mid-blue signs – ahead – above us – gone in a flash.

He changed lanes, tick, tick, slowed for the exit slip road to the Clatterbridge roundabout, and worked through the traffic-lights and the streets into Birkenhead until we reached the approach to the Tunnel entrance.

"You're quiet," he said. And when I didn't answer, he continued, "If you want this loan, you really need to talk to me."

"I'm not sure I do."

"You surprise me." He chuckled. It was not a reassuring sound.

At the toll point he reached out of the window and paid, then made himself comfortable again and drove down into the Tunnel towards Liverpool. The cars in the lanes alongside, all travelling at the same steady uniform speed, under the cold, artificial lighting, produced an effect that was hypnotic and rather disturbing.

"Do you know the old story," he said conversationally, "about the millionaire at the dinner party? He asks the woman next to him if she'll go to bed with him for a diamond necklace. She says 'Ooh, yes!' so he says, 'All right then. Will you do it for a fiver?' And then she gets angry and says, 'No! What do you think I am!' So he says, 'You've already told me what you are. All we're doing now is negotiating.'" He chuckled again and threw out the stub of the cigar. "Negotiating is something your brother-in-law is not good at."

"I know."

"Of course you do."

I wondered what he was driving at. "But you don't have to hurt him for it."

"Why not? You must have wanted to hit him yourself, lots of times. You're a very physical woman."

His use of the word *physical* took us back into dangerous territory. I tugged the hem of my skirt down and tried to be offhand.

"I'm not, really."

"Oh yes," he said, and the purr came back into his voice. "Very physical. I thought there was a bit of a spark between us over lunch. Hm?"

"No comment," I said.

"There's something hellishly sexy, you know, about a woman who knows you fancy her and pretends she doesn't. And you're flattered, all right. Otherwise you'd have slapped my face."

There were cars in front of us, either side and behind us. It would be too dangerous to hit him. All I could do was to sit deeper into the defence of the seat, the way a spider clenches itself when you blow on it. Humphrey glanced at me and went on talking in the same careless, conversational tone.

"It's an amusing little circle. Gwyl owes me money, and your husband owes him."

"I don't follow what you're saying." I thought the best way to save my position was not to give anything away. "What does he owe you for?"

He said, "You're not really that unobservant. You must have realised that Gwyl's not a very good gambler. He's been dabbling in all kinds of business and he's made a mess of them all, which is why he's been up to Cumbria more than once to put the squeeze on you. So – what if I took the pressure off him? Wouldn't your life be a whole lot easier?"

"I don't know. How much does he owe you?"

"Oh, his house and that fancy Merc and a lot of other shit. But that's not the point. Listen. I know how much *you* owe *him*. Just so you don't misunderstand me – I'm the one who can make him forget it."

When I didn't reply, he said, "Come on, Siân. This is an adult game. Think it through, complete the circle. You please me, I'll scrap the rules and we'll all be quits. That is what you had in mind, isn't it, when you talked about a loan?"

I stared through the windscreen. Exhaust fumes came buffeting through the open window. And the road sloped down, down, inside the rounded Tunnel walls, as though we were sliding into the guts of a snake.

"We could have a lot of fun together," he said. "You're a grown woman, not a naïve little virgin. You know how to take precautions. There wouldn't be any repercussions for either of us."

I blushed scarlet. "Don't be so bloody crass."

"Practical," he corrected me. "I pay for what I want. And I promise, you'll love it. You aren't going to suffer a fate worse than death."

I didn't look at him. I could smell the cigars, the sweat, the aftershave, the dry-cleaning fluid in his suit and the washing powder in the blue shirt straining across his abdomen. The road reached its lowest point and ran level under the Mersey. I closed the window and this time Humphrey didn't comment.

I thought, it didn't matter how much he flattered me, how beholden he made me feel, or how huge the debt he would write off. If I buckled now, it wasn't just Madoc I'd betray. I'd spent too many years regaining my integrity, re-learning to value and respect myself, to sell it all now.

"Nothing's going to happen," I said.

"I intend to be the best you've ever had."

My body's revulsion was instant and compelling. "You can intend all you like. I'll still say No."

"Would you?" he said, still conversational, still purring. "Well, there'll be consequences. I gave Gwyl to the boys, didn't I?"

I understood then why he'd done it, to let me see how Jamie and Henry were his to command. He didn't care about people as people but he knew exactly how to push their buttons to his own advantage. Which of my family would he throw to his watchdogs? If it wasn't me, would it be Jack? Cerys? Robbie? Even Madoc might not be able to stand up against them. I didn't want to imagine what they could do.

He seemed to take my appalled silence as acquiescence. He said, "You see? If you get yourself into the right frame of mind, everything else is quite easy."

The road began to rise again towards the yellow afternoon daylight of the Tunnel exit. My mind scrambled for answers. I was very scared of the risks I was running, and the risks to my family. Humphrey bullied the Defender through the tangle of traffic and parked, ignoring all protocols, in the station taxi rank in Lord Nelson Street. I released my seat-belt, and he turned in his seat and looked across at me. I put my shoulder-bag on my lap, shortening my grip on the straps in case I needed to punch him with it.

I'd forgotten that he didn't work like that.

"Take a few days. Think it over. I'm going to." He smiled. "Fantasising is half the fun."

I took a steadying breath and forced myself to smile back, while I reached cautiously for the door handle. "Then let me tell you about my fantasy."

He unclipped the seat-belt and leaned closer, intent on my face. "Go on."

"I'm wearing long leather boots. You're handcuffed to the bed."

My voice shook and he licked his lips as though he could taste victory. "Interesting."

"And I have got... a pair of nutcrackers." Without waiting to see his reaction, I jumped out of the Defender and ran.

Chapter 24.

The train was crowded, and I had to stand. I managed to send a text to Madoc telling him when I would reach Oxenholme, and when I didn't get a reply my anxiety went skyward till I remembered he'd told me to text Robbie or Hazel. I sent messages to both of them, trying to control my shaking fingers and the suggestions of autocorrect. The train was pulling out of Preston station before Robbie texted back, "Okay, we'll meet you."

I spent the journey home trying to make sense of the day. I found a seat, but I couldn't rest easy. When Humphrey had pressed Gwylim for his money, Gwylim must have given away how much we owed him. Humphrey knew Dava, and all our family links. He had stayed in our holiday cottage – ostensibly so he could see his horses working – and while he was there he'd learned far too much about our children and the precarious hold Madoc and I had on our home and livelihood. He had collected the information and waited for his chance to use it.

I was desperate to get home to Madoc, to safety, to the only rock solid certainty I had. But how much could I tell him about today? I untied the racecourse badge and dropped it on the floor; it was part of a package I could not have afforded and I wanted comfort from Madoc, not interrogation. I checked my watch a dozen times, willing the train to go faster.

Humphrey had handed Gwylim over to Henry and Jamie as a lesson: *Please me, or trouble will follow.* What had they done to him? They knew where I lived. They could recognise Jack and Robbie and Cerys. Dear God, what might they do to us, if Humphrey didn't get his way? Ten minutes before we arrived at Oxenholme I was on my feet and waiting at the nearest door, watching the slow wheeling of a sky that had grown dirty, with all the day's sunshine flattened to the horizon by cloud.

It was Hazel Wharton who was waiting at the station. Not Madoc, whom I needed most.

"The men are still leading in the bales off the last field, before the rain comes. I've not been much use today, with my knee, so here I am."

I thanked her and got into the passenger seat of the van, and she drove off up the hill and took the shortcut that led onto the Grayrigg road.

"Look at them thunderclouds!" She gestured towards the windscreen and the billowing sky.

I mumbled a reply.

She asked, "How did you get on with your Dad?"

I had a struggle to think back past midday. The friction between Dad and me had lit a fuse that I should have damped straight away, but I hadn't, I'd let it burn on, and it had taken me straight into the powder-keg that was Charles Humphrey. I said as flippantly as I could, "Oh, Dad and I had a stand up fight. The only reason he's still alive is because he doesn't have any money to leave to me."

"Oh! You don't mean all that. Or do you? I worry sometimes." Hazel glanced sideways at me and quickly back at the road to swerve round a pothole. She said, "Most of the time you're all good and quiet and then suddenly, Boom!"

"It's stress," I said. "That's why I always need a horse to work with. If I haven't, other people really have to look out."

She chuckled uncertainly and changed the subject. Under the flood tide of her chatter the encounter with Humphrey gnawed again at my mind. I desperately wanted Madoc's arms around me, but how could I tell him why I needed him? It had been my fault. I'd put myself in this position. How could I keep the kids safe? But how could I explain my anxiety without telling anyone the real reasons?

Spots of water as big as coins began to spatter the windscreen and Hazel turned the wipers on full pelt. "I hope they got the last of that hay put away."

~~~

"There can't be anyone still out in this," said Hazel as we drove up the farm road to Underscar, in the full rush and clatter of the storm. "They'll be in our kitchen. I told Andy to fetch everybody in after they'd finished. And don't fret about cooking tonight. Your lot can eat with us, and welcome."

I hadn't even thought about that. I said guiltily, "You're a star. Thank you."

The sloping yard was running with water. Our pickup and tractor were parked next to Andy's, close to the house, and Hazel pulled up as near as she could, but we were half blinded by rain just in the dash from the van to the kitchen door.

Inside – a shock like walking into a nightclub – the room was dim and noisy. Candlelight shone on worktops and cooker. A fiddle tune bounced and skipped merrily, pursued by stamping feet and laughter. The central table had been moved right over to the wall and Cerys was sitting on one end of it playing her violin, with Katie at the other playing her guitar. Danny sat between them using his phone to illuminate the music stand and being told when to turn pages. In the crowded twilight space between the players and the worktops Andy was tramping in time to the music with a can of beer in his hand, followed by Jack and Madoc, also with cans, and in the centre of the room Robbie and Beth danced close together, trying to keep clear of the other three. There was just room for Hazel and me to cram inside and stand against the door out of the way.

"Well!" said Hazel, at the end of the tune. "I suppose I don't need to ask if you're enjoying yourselves. But what are you doing, Andy Wharton, giving beer to young Jack there!"

"It's nobbut light ale," he said. "We couldn't make tea, the electric's gone off."

Hazel sniffed, and tried the light switch before she was convinced. Madoc slipped past her and jumped up to sit on the worktop beside me.

"Time for me to sit out. My legs are tired."

He took two cans from Andy. He smelled of new hay, sunshine and sweat.

"What's all this about your legs being tired?" I asked.

He was busy opening the cans. "I can't dance like the kids do, not any more."

"It's news to me that you can dance at all," I said. He laughed and handed me a beer. I hadn't seen him in party mood for a very long time. In the candlelight I was struck afresh by how handsome he was and how beautifully athletic. And it was a shock to realise how long it had been since he looked so happy.

There was a flash outside and a prolonged rumble of thunder. In the gloom on the other side of the room, Katie started a lazy finger-picking intro on the guitar. For a few bars, nobody took much notice, but then Cerys began to sing, and her golden voice quieted us all.

I recognised the ballad. It was one that had played endlessly on the radio in the months before Cerys's birth; it had been the backing track to the death of Cymru and all the changes which the horse's death had brought about, and it still carried painful memories. I stood leaning against Madoc and wondering whether the song stung him too. His thigh in its worn denim was hot under my palm. I felt at that moment that my body knew his so well, I would recognise him blindfold. I would not let us be separated by manipulative Charles Humphrey, nor by desperate beaten-up Gwylim or my defeatist grey father.

Cerys sang with her eyes shut but the power of emotion beat in her voice. Who could have guessed that she, the quiet one of the family, could know and share such strength of feeling? Had she learned, when still unborn, all that the song meant to me? Or was she singing it for Danny? Circles. Birth and ageing and death and mating, the generations going on. In Robbie's protection of Beth, in Cerys's attention to her music, even in Jack's fledgeling gawkiness, I could see something of Madoc, something that linked us all together, something lovely and balanced that all three of our children had inherited from him – and this, this family, was what I had put in danger. This was what I now had to lie to protect. I couldn't tell what Madoc was feeling, but when he put his arm around my shoulders, in turn I slipped my arm around his waist, and I wanted him so much I felt hollow.

Chapter 25.

We ate supper at Underscar in the candles' wavering glow, to an accompaniment of rain, the ten of us so closely crammed in round Hazel's kitchen table that we could have eaten off each other's forks. When we'd finished Cerys and Katie stacked the dishwasher with the dirty plates and cutlery, then Robbie headed off, on Beth's invitation, to her family's house to shower and change before going to a party in Penrith.

Not long after that the electricity came back on, and we all sat up, groaning and blinking in the too-bright light.

"What a rough-looking lot we are," said Hazel with a deprecatory chuckle. "Honestly, I don't know where the muck comes from."

"It's just haytime dust," said Andy. "Nothing a bath won't fix." He got up and went round the candles, wetting his fingers and snuffing each flame into smoke.

Jack rubbed his face and gave a jaw-cracking yawn, so I dragged myself to attention. "Come on, let's get you home. You too, Cerys."

I expected them to complain, but I think they were more tired than I was. They'd both caught the sun on their faces and arms; a difficulty of having redheads in the family. I foresaw a week of Jack peeling sunburned skin at every idle moment. I thanked Hazel and Andy, and we hurried out through the rain, except for Cerys, who prolonged a reluctant goodnight with Danny in the kitchen porch.

"You drive," said Madoc, going to the passenger side of the pickup. "I've had one too many." He opened the door and fended off the dog's delighted greetings.

"He hasn't been in here all day, has he?" I asked.

"No," said Madoc, "I just put him in here while we had tea." He slid into the passenger seat and Kip settled in the footwell at his feet.

I said, "Jack? Call Cerys, or she'll be there all night."

He wound down his window and shouted, "Put him down or we're going without you!"

Madoc chuckled and closed his eyes, and a moment later Cerys got into the back seat, shaking the rain off her hair and telling Jack to shut up.

When we reached home, Madoc shivered back into wakefulness.

"I'll take the dog for a leg-lift," he said, "and check the horses." He pulled on a jacket from the porch and vanished into the dusk, leaving me to shepherd Cerys and Jack into the kitchen. The house was stuffy with the heat of the Rayburn so I left the back door open to the air and the sound of falling rain.

"Shower," I said to Jack, "and bedtime."

He began out of habit to say, "Why me," but he didn't carry it through, and instead plodded off upstairs. Cerys ran water into the kitchen bowl and began scrubbing her fingernails.

"Thank goodness that's the hay done with," she said, wincing. "My hands are really sore."

"Didn't Da give you gloves to wear?"

"Yes, Mam, he did, but they still had seams."

"There's some hand cream in the drawer, next to you."

She dried her hands and sat with me at the table, slowly rubbing the cream into her fingers.

"Well," I said, "has it been a good day? Working with Danny?"

She blushed. "Mam! Every time we got a trailer unloaded and a chance to stop, his Mam would send Jack to 'help', or else she'd come herself to ask us some silly question. We didn't have a moment's peace!"

"You poor frustrated thing. You know it'll be worse when you go off to college."

She sighed. "I don't know. I want to spread my wings, to fly – to sing – and I don't know if Danny can fit in with that. I don't even know if I can...sorry if that sounds confused."

I got up to fuel the Rayburn, and patted her shoulder as I went by. "You're very lucky to have a talent to give you those wings. Don't waste them, unless you're sure Danny is always going to be the absolute centre of your existence."

She looked up at me unhappily. "I should be able to say he is, shouldn't I? Like Da is for you. But I want to earn a living as a singer and that means late nights and late getting up, and he's a morning person like Da. I'm going to have to travel a lot, and that won't suit him either. He's like Robbie, he wants roots, and that means staying at home and farming. He's fun and I want to go out with him and that, but if he asked me to marry him I think he'd want me to stay at home, and then I'd have to run. Is that awful of me?"

"No, it isn't," I said. "There'll be plenty of time for marrying and settling down." I rattled the Rayburn ash-handle and loaded the firebox with fuel. "I wasn't the same person at twenty-one that I was at eighteen, even without going to college."

"Did you mind, about that? That you didn't go to college?" She perched sideways on the chair, biting at a piece of rough skin beside her thumbnail. "I would."

"Yes. I minded a lot, at the time." I shut the firebox, and put the coal-hod back in its corner. "But I mostly wanted to get away from home, because living over the shop with your Grandad wasn't a lot of laughs. So I ran away to work with racehorses, just because I saw an advert for a stable wanting staff." I sat down again, using the movement to avoid talking about the time I'd spent at Green Bank, the months I always had to push away in my mind. There were scenes, like today's with Charles Humphrey, that I never wanted to describe to Cerys. "One of the horses I looked after got moved to Uncle Dava's stables so I decided to go with her, and that's how I met your Da. And that's why I'm here now, putting up with you and the other two rascals."

She chuckled, but then remarked, "If you *had* gone to college, Mam, you wouldn't have met Da, and we would have been...simply not. That's a scary thought."

"Yes."

Jack shouted down the stairs, "Bathroom's empty!"

"Oh bliss," she said, and got up to go. "I'll have a shower and then I'm just going to die for twelve hours." She gave me a small smile. "Everything we choose to do really matters, doesn't it, Mam."

"Yes," I said. "Yes, it does. And sometimes the things we choose not to, as well."

As she passed me she dropped a kiss on my hair and said, "Goodnight, Mam. I love you."

~~~

I went to the porch door to look out. There was no car outside the holiday cottage so I assumed the couple who were staying had gone somewhere for a meal. The rain had stopped and the air was fresh and full of the scent of hay and the honeysuckle in the garden. I leaned against the door-post, waiting for Madoc, watching the sky beyond the fell where indigo clouds still showed a flush of sunset; beautiful, impossibly calm.

Twenty to ten. Such a long day for all of us. It felt much later.

Madoc came walking up the yard, accompanied by a couple of four-legged shadows: Kip and Gracie, the dog soaked and shaking himself, the cat giving him a wide berth. Gracie came in, dismissed the biscuits remaining in her dish and sat by the Rayburn, licking her paws, while Madoc collected a tin of dog food from the cupboard in the porch and took Kip to the outdoor kennel for the night.

He came back wiping his face.

"The midges are biting," he said. "Little devils."

"Horses all right?"

"Zilla's twitching a bit, but the youngsters are just grazing. Coel is watching the night, but as for the Ninja, he's lying down in his box, next thing to asleep."

"Quite a change from when he first came here. D'you want a cup of tea or anything?"

"No, thanks." He kicked off his boots and brushed hayseeds off his socks onto the tiles. He grinned at me, anticipating a reprimand. "I'm making a mess, aren't I?"

"I don't care." I desperately wanted the strength of him holding me. I said, "Giz a cuddle," and tried not to sound pathetic.

"I need a shower," he said.

"I still don't care. *Cwtch*."

"Come here then." I walked to him and leaned my head on his shoulder, breathing in that heady smell of fresh air, sweat and hay, while he rubbed my back and waited for me to relax. At last he said, "What's up, Mouse? Is your Dad very poorly?"

"No," I said. It was hard to think back that far. "He sent me to take his will to the solicitors. I read it. I knew I shouldn't, but I think he wanted me to."

He murmured agreement. "What was in it?"

"Well, it won't be any use me bumping-off the old bugger for his money."

That made him chuckle, but he asked, "Are you disappointed?"

"I don't know. I haven't had time to think about it."

"No? You've had all day." He leaned back to look at me. "You smell of tobacco."

I should have told him then about Gwylim, and the obscenity that was Charles Humphrey's proposition. But I needed to escape it, not spend the night digging myself in deeper. I needed Madoc not to be worried, not to be angry. I wanted him to go on being happy, at least for a little while. And while it lasted I wanted to make love to him, to taste salt sweat in his kisses and get so drunk on pleasure that it would blot out everything else.

I reached up to stroke the gold stubble on his chin and said, "I'll tell you about it tomorrow." Then I pushed my fingers through his hair, and when his arms tightened around me I kissed him, slowly, lingeringly. "Come on, take me to bed. Now. Please."

Chapter 26.

When I woke the next morning, I was alone in bed. Madoc had opened the curtains to the sunshine but otherwise left me to sleep. Now the clock was showing nine a.m., which was shockingly late because the holidaymakers were due to leave at ten and the cottage would need cleaning and the bed-linen changed.

I got up quickly, and began to dress. I could hear the tractor and muck-spreader clanking up and down Scar Pasture, but there were no clues from inside the house to tell me what Jack and Cerys were doing. Through the bedroom window I could see the tractor, throwing mottled stripes of brown across the pale green of the newly-mown field. Robbie was driving. Madoc was out there too, riding King Coel at a canter up the exercise strip. I wished he had woken me up. I'd have liked to be out there with him. He perched balanced over the horse's shoulders, and although I could see Coel wanted to gallop, Madoc was applying tactful little checks through the reins, telling him he wasn't to go flat out: he had to learn to save his energy for later. Coel was not listening. He lifted his head and bounced and fought, a river of dark-brown muscle rocking with resentment.

I pulled on a clean tee-shirt, and put my phone and my penknife into my jeans pockets, but I stayed at the window to watch Madoc ride Coel up the final, steepest slope of the exercise strip. As I watched, the horse lowered his head and stopped fighting. He got his haunches properly under him and settled at last to a good, consistent stride and maintained it right to the top of the hill. I saw Madoc relax his hands on the reins, a signal all our horses understood as "job done". The two handsome creatures had achieved harmony, if only for half a minute.

"Well done you," I murmured. I reflected that the colt might well turn out like his grandsire Cymru – determined to run all his races from the front.

Robbie reached the top of Scar Pasture, where he disengaged the spreader and made a wide swing to come back down. I was just about to leave the window when he re-engaged the spreader and Coel whipped round and bolted.

I saw Madoc fall. I waited, expecting him to get up and chase the horse.

He didn't.

I ran through the house. Down the stairs two at a time. Boots on. Out through the garden to the exercise field. Coel steamed past me at full gallop, his reins trailing, but I let him go because I had to run, run, the other way, towards the place where Madoc had fallen. The tractor and muckspreader were still clanking down towards the gate, churning out a miasma of sheep muck. I cursed Robbie. Couldn't he see what had happened? My breath burned my throat and my heart hammered but I put my head down and ran and kept on running up the long, endlessly rising slope.

Madoc was still down when I reached him, a bad sign. He'd propped himself up on one elbow, the other arm raised as if to protect himself. Maybe he thought I would trip over him. He looked very white and his mouth was set in a way that told me more than a scream.

I went down on my knees beside him, panting, unable to do more than look him over. There was something I didn't like about the way he guarded his right leg. He unfastened the buckle of his chinstrap, one-handed, and dumped the helmet on the grass.

When I could speak, I asked, "Your knee?"

"My ankle. It isn't hurting yet." Again he held up a hand, fending me off from touching it. "Everything else is all right."

"Hospital job," I said, digging out my phone. "I'll call an ambulance."

"Don't be daft, it won't be able to drive up here. Get Robbie."

"What – "

"Tell him to fetch the pickup. Listen! He's stopped the spreader. Stand up and wave."

I stood up and waved.

King Coel was travelling the lower part of the field at a lively trot and Robbie must have spotted him because he swung down off the tractor and jumped over the wall. As he landed Coel broke into a gallop away from him and came thundering up the hill and Robbie put his hands on his hips and watched him with obvious exasperation. He'd no chance of catching the horse, but I thought he hadn't realised what had happened to Madoc so I gave up waving and called him on the phone. He answered straight away.

"What's up?"

"Can you bring the pickup to where I am now? Your Da's hurt his leg."

Behind me Madoc said, "Tell him to go to the tackroom and bring a couple of horse bandages. And some rolled up towels."

I relayed that to Robbie.

"Right. Towels. Bandages," he said, and made for the yard at a run.

"God bless him." I sat down by Madoc. "Should I call 999 now?"

"No," he said. "Stabilise the ankle – help me into the pickup – drive me to A & E."

"It'll take half an hour to get to Kendal – longer if they send us down to Lancaster. Can you stand that? If we called an ambulance, the paramedics would at least have painkillers."

"I told you, it isn't hurting. I know it's going to, but I don't need them yet."

"I'm only going to do that if you're sure..."

"I've had enough racecourse injuries to know. You can get me to A & E before an ambulance would even reach us here and I'll be all right so long as we get moving straight away." He shifted his weight on his elbows, and sat up. "Where's the horse?"

"Only you..." I began, in exasperation.

"We can't have him cavorting about when Robbie comes with the pickup."

"I'll catch him," I said. "In a minute."

"Catch him now. That's a lot of money running about loose. If Robbie doesn't shut the gate –"

He shifted again, and I said, "Don't you move."

He managed a short laugh. "Like I have an option."

I stood up to look for Coel. He'd trotted round the field again and was cantering back up the exercise strip at much the same pace Madoc had been trying to achieve when the two were still united. Up in High Field, Zilla and the three-year-olds stood alert and watching but he didn't seem to have noticed them. He looked slightly lost, like an adolescent so absorbed in the mechanics of free-running that he couldn't remember at what point he'd outstripped his mates or, indeed, where he'd got to. When he saw me stand up he pricked his ears and came trotting towards me.

I knelt down again beside Madoc. "It's all right. He's on his way back."

"Don't sit down, for goodness' sake. Catch him!"

I stayed on one knee. I could feel the hoofbeats through the turf as the big horse came up the slope and I knew by the quick tempo that he was still in a mood in which a human 'predator stare' might set him off again, so I didn't face him. I felt and heard the hooves slow to a walk. And when he came to investigate these two strangely recumbent humans I kept my head down and, as I hoped, he came right to me.

"There's a lad, now," I said, and while he stood over us, breathing hard, I quietly reached up and got hold of the long, trailing loop of his reins.

Madoc lay back. "I'll be damned."

"Eejit," I said. "You know I'm a specialist at this sort of thing."

"Take him back to the yard, then. You can wear my helmet. Go on, jump on."

"Pfft! Optimist." I'd never been able to vault onto a thoroughbred and I wasn't going to try it now. Madoc tried to laugh. I stood up slowly, and moved the colt away from him.

He said, "What the hell's keeping Robbie? I want this leg seen to before it starts to swell."

"I can see him – he's coming now. Don't worry. We'll get the horse put away soon enough."

"I'll need him to help me into the pickup – but you drive, d'you hear me? You drive. I want to get to A & E in one piece."

"In a manner of speaking," I said.

~~~

On Monday morning the alarm shrilled us awake. I left Madoc to dress while I hurried to get the kids off to school. I'd spent the night reliving scenes from yesterday, seeing Madoc fall, kneeling on the turf beside him then struggling to match Robbie's physical strength as we eased him into the pickup to go to hospital.

Madoc had sat sideways with his leg on the seat, and Robbie had ridden in the back with him, half sitting and half kneeling, ready to support him. I'd wanted to hurry but, knowing that every twist in the road would hurt Madoc, I'd tried to drive as delicately as possible. I didn't always manage it, and by the time we reached Kendal Madoc had become grimly silent.

The hospital sent us on to Lancaster and Robbie, who knew the city far better than I did, navigated me to the Infirmary.

I found a wheelchair for Madoc and Robbie pushed him into A & E while I parked the pickup. Madoc bore with not being allowed to eat or drink until the medical staff were sure he wouldn't need a general anaesthetic. He'd been given painkilling injections and wheeled away to the X-ray department and we had waited, talking very little. Links to the messiness of outside life were absent, no smells and none of the background atmosphere that would have defined it as a workplace or a home, so that each fresh sound of footsteps, every rumble of a travelling bed, had brought a hope that Madoc might reappear. I phoned Cerys to tell her what was going on. Robbie texted to and fro with Beth. Occasionally we, in turn, were updated with news from the medical staff. Madoc had fractured his fibula, but the displacement of the broken ends was very slight so they were debating whether they needed to keep him in for stabilising surgery.

"Lucky it's Sunday morning," Robbie had said, philosophically. "I wouldn't like to queue here on a Saturday night."

We had gone on waiting. I had read the notices and the wall signs, over and over, and grown more and more wound-up with worry and helplessness and the sheer boredom of being in a system over which we had no control. No wonder hospitals stuck those warnings everywhere, about them not tolerating abuse of the staff. Not everyone had Madoc's sweet nature. I didn't.

I had begun to feel hungry but I knew I couldn't eat anything. Robbie had brought me anonymous brown drinks from corridor machines, from which I would take a couple of sips before abandoning them. Nothing changed.

Madoc had finally been discharged wielding a pair of crutches, the seam of his jeans split up to mid-thigh to accommodate a cast on his leg from knee to toes. The doctor explained, with an ironical expression, that although a cast wasn't the only option for treating this fracture, he'd learned over decades of dealing with farmers and horse people that it was the only way to force them to take the rest their bones needed. Madoc wasn't amused.

There were blue shadows under his eyes that I hadn't seen since lambing time. He must have been hungry, too, but he didn't want the sandwich I'd bought.

"If I eat now, I'll throw up on the way home. I can eat later – let's face it, there won't be much else I can do."

So I brought the pickup to the door and drove carefully home.

Cerys, who'd never had to face the kind of injury that Madoc used to risk every time he went racing, turned white when she saw him, and hid in the larder for twenty minutes before coming out wet-eyed but composed. Jack had been full of questions, after which he'd been determined to make cheese-on-toast for everybody. I'd let him. He'd managed it this time without setting the toaster on fire or blistering himself on the Rayburn.

Madoc had spent the late afternoon and evening in the recliner, getting up every hour or so, either to hobble into the kitchen and work out what painkillers he could take, or go to the loo. I'd had to be tactful about his impatience with himself. He hitched himself up the stairs one step at a time, breathing in a tight, controlled manner that resisted help.

"I've done this before," he said. "I can do it again. I don't have to be looked after."

And Jack, our lobster-coloured impromptu chef, had gone to muck-out and feed Charles Humphrey's horses – sketchily, but he'd done it, and again without being asked.

That night it had been uncomfortable to share our bed with a plaster cast. But better, far better, than not having Madoc there at all.

Now the kitchen filled with its usual morning clamour – Jack bickering with Cerys over the last of the strawberry jam, Robbie monopolising the butter dish for his third slice of toast. Madoc appeared late, in a pair of baggy red knee-length shorts I had forgotten he possessed. He was still remembering how to manoeuvre himself on crutches and painkillers, and he was impatient with Kip for getting in his way. I moved two chairs into a position where he could sit at the table with his leg up.

The kids seemed rowdier than usual – Jack in particular. Perhaps they were testing exactly how much Madoc was prepared to let them get away with, while he wasn't physically their superior. At any rate, I found myself being sharp with them.

"Hurry up with your breakfast. I'm not going to drive you to school if you miss the bus. Cerys, are you going in today?"

"Not sure I need to. Can we look at the application form for my student loan?"

I thought of all the jobs that had to be done, which Robbie and I had been trying to divide between us since Madoc's fall.

"For heaven's sake! Can't you get advice about that at school?"

"Oh. Yes, I suppose so."

Madoc was halfway to installing himself on the chairs when he stopped, listening. "Whose phone is that, chirping?"

"Not mine," Cerys said. Jack let go of the jam and she swiped it.

"It's mine," I said. "Over there on the charger. Robbie?"

He disconnected it and handed it to me across the table. When I opened it there were four text messages waiting, all from the same number – they weren't flagged with a name and I thought for a moment they were spam. But the contents were intensely personal.

Today at 02:10: Just got in. Lying here alone.

Today at 02:11: Anticipating our next meeting.

Today at 02:12: Hope you weren't serious about those nutcrackers.

Today at 07:33: Asleep, sweetiepie?

Charles Humphrey. Dear God. I'd forgotten he had my number. I pushed the phone into my pocket and got up. Kip danced round me and I trod on him.

"Oh, get out from under my *feet*, dog!"

He yelped. There was a moment of complete silence at the table.

Madoc got his cast settled across the chairs. He said, "What is it, Mouse? Your Dad?"

"No." I couldn't explain with the kids listening. "Sorry. My head's bursting. I need fresh air."

The silence followed me out.

The yard was still in shadow, the weather cloudy grey, ordinary. The smell of the muck Robbie had been spreading on

Sunday was much more noticeable and the quietness felt sinister until I realised I couldn't hear the slight bee-like hum of the motorway. Perhaps the wind had shifted.

The swallows too had changed tactics with the weather, flying low over the fields and barely clearing the walls before zipping into the stables with beakfuls of flies. There were hungry twitterings from each nest as they arrived and when they left they swooped threateningly over Gracie the cat, who was sitting in the barn doorway on a scatter of spilt haylage.

She rolled over when she saw me, then came and rubbed round my ankles, perhaps hoping for an easier breakfast than swallows.

"I haven't got anything," I said. "Go in the house and pester someone else." The Ninja and King Coel both whinnied at me, like the baby swallows twittering at their parents. I muttered, "Shut up."

I woke the phone and replied to Humphrey's message:

Leave. Me. Alone.

I went into the tackroom to weigh out feed for the two horses. His horses. His big, sensitive, and very expensive horses. The ironies were not lost on me. Coel and the Ninja both belonged to this man who was harassing me. Coel, in spite of the bloodlines we coveted, had put Madoc in A & E. It crossed my mind how easy it would be to retaliate against Humphrey through the horses – to underfeed or neglect or abuse them while I had them at my mercy. But I couldn't do that. I would still treat them kindly because that was what we did, Madoc and I, that was who we were, just as galloping was what these racehorses did. Our natures wouldn't change. And it wasn't the horses' fault they had a shitty owner.

Through the dry swish of oats into the feed buckets I heard the phone chirp again. I put down the scoop with a clatter and read the message.

Today at 07:35: Call me and we can talk it over.

There shouldn't be anything to talk about.

I wrote: No.

I carried the plastic buckets out and hooked them over the stable half-doors. Coel reached over at once and began eating. Shuffle, nudge, crunch. He flattened his ears wickedly at the Ninja, and the Ninja, though in a separate box and perfectly safe from attack, flinched and held back until I reversed the bucket and hooked it on the inside of his door. Only then did he begin eating. I supposed he felt safe once he could no longer see Coel's aggression. For the same reason, I ought to block Humphrey's phone number. But would that actually make me any safer? I didn't know. I was too flustered to remember where on my phone I would find the command.

Today at 07:40: You've been on my mind all weekend.

He'd been entirely absent from mine.

Both stables smelled of ammonia. Jack had done his best yesterday, but two big boxes, on his own, had been a stretch too far. I knew Robbie would help me give them a thorough cleaning and fresh bedding, but with it being Monday we ought to be sorting lambs and ewes for Tuesday's auction, while prices were still good. I didn't know whether I'd have time to exercise the horses as well. If I didn't they would need some forage to keep them occupied – thank goodness there were four nets of sweet-smelling haylage lying in the barn, plump and ready to be used. I couldn't for the life of me remember who'd filled them. Jack, last night? Cerys? If only the thoroughbreds could be just turned out and forgotten for twenty-three out of twenty-four hours, like my Fell ponies. But that wasn't what Charles Humphrey was paying us to do.

I carried two nets to the stables, dumped one outside Coel's stable and took the other to the Ninja. The young horse was mildly surprised because I was doing everything the opposite way to our usual routine, giving a hay-net along with his oats; ordinarily we'd let the horses digest their breakfast so we could exercise them later with no bulk in their stomachs to obstruct their breathing. However, he allowed me to back him away from his feed and duck in under his nose to tie the net up to the wall ring. I sneaked out, leaving him cautiously eating, and went along to Coel's stable.

The colt pulled faces at me, so I paused before I opened his door, judging by his flattened ears that he was less than pleased at me interrupting his breakfast. The phone chirped again. I stepped back out of his reach to read what the message said.

Today at 07:44: Coming up to Appleby this weekend for the Fair. Let's meet.

Today at 07:45: Staying at your local. I'll find us somewhere private.

Humphrey was crowding me now. Not just suggestions, but an actual time, an actual place, and much too close to home. Why was he stalking me? Why was the simple word 'No' something he chose not to understand? And why did it feel as though it was my fault? I couldn't think straight any more.

Robbie came out of the house porch with his long, easy stride, carrying the Rayburn ash-pan and followed by our ever-busy sheepdog. They went across the yard to the ash heap. That stride, an echo of his father's, brought a lump to my throat. How could I ever say 'Yes' to anyone but Madoc?

I wrote again: No.

Today at 07:47: I expect to see you. All of you. Saturday. Remember that.

No. No more. No more demands.

I wrote: Fuck off.

Today at 07:48: Wow.

Today at 07:49: Bitch.

Today at 07:49: Lesbian.

I finally lost it. I wrote: Fuck off as far as you can and when you get there fuck off some more. And I sent it.

Jack burst out of the house laughing, pursued by Cerys. He had his school rucksack over his shoulder and he was flourishing her pink handbag, dancing, running away. She chased him through the yard gate and I heard the crunch of their running feet punctuate the quiet morning and dwindle down the track towards the road. Robbie came back with the empty ash-pan and the dog and went into the house. And the damned phone chirped yet again.

Today at 07:50: Your bro in law is still alive.

Today at 07:51: Henry knows where you live.

A mother swallow flew almost into my face. She hung shrieking for a second in the air in front of me, and I seemed to have all the time in the world to study the black intensity of her eyes, her crimson mask, her navy neck ring, her soft pinkish cream belly and her tiny, curled-wire feet, while all the time her young, in the mud nest in the stable roof, were calling to her. When she saw me she instantly switched her purpose from flying into the stable to flying out. I watched her body react. The streamers of her tail widened into a vee, spanned by an arc of white-spotted feathers, then her wings described fragile aerodynamic curves and she looped away over the roof and disappeared.

Chapter 27.

I helped Robbie and Kip to bring in the sheep and mark the ewes and lambs for auction – anything to keep the thoughts at bay. I suggested Madoc should stay on the recliner in the front room to nurse his leg and the stiffness from his fall. He refused, swallowed painkillers and came out to watch us. I was relieved that he showed enough self-preservation to stay on the other side of the wall.

The ewes and lambs complained at various pitches about being confined in the pens, and Kip prowled round outside them, panting in the sultry afternoon heat. Robbie was checking the ewes' teeth and udders before deciding which ones could go to auction with their lambs the following day. It made for a lot of shouted discussion with Madoc and even more complicated marking and penning, so when my phone rang my first reaction was to throttle it. I thought, with a rush of adrenalin, *If it's that bastard Humphrey again, I'll block him.* But to my relief, this time the number was named. It was a call from Dava.

"Hello!" I said, raising my voice above those of the lambs. "How are you doing?"

The familiar growl replied, "I'd do a lot better if you'd answer your house phone. And why isn't Madoc answering his mobile?"

"He's got a broken leg," I said.

"Oh very funny," he said. "Get him, I need to talk to him."

It had never been much use doing small talk with Dava and he had only become more impatient with age, so I didn't try to explain.

I said, "One moment please," in my sweetest telephone voice. I threw the spray marker to Robbie and walked over to Madoc. "I seem to be on switchboard duty. It's Dava, for you. I told him about your leg but he thought I was joking."

"What a man..." He took the phone. "Now then, Dava. What's up? No – I'm not. What do you mean, why not? I've damaged my ankle, didn't Siân tell you? That damn colt dropped me, and I'm in plaster for three weeks. What? Yes, the horses are fine, but they're not likely to do much work now, are they! Yes, it is, but she's managing."

"Thanks a bunch," I said ironically.

"What's that?" Madoc was listening again, and he looked away across the gallops to avoid my eye. Such an amused expression grew on his face that I wondered what else Dava could be saying. "Well, now there's a thing. I never thought to check... No. No, we'll be expecting him. Bye."

He gave me back the phone.

"The Ninja," he said, "is going back to Dava."

That would have been normal, if it hadn't been the exact opposite of what Charles Humphrey had said to me on Saturday. He'd specifically said both horses would stay with us – so this might be his way of hitting back for the morning's rebuff. And I was afraid it might only be a first strike, with more to come.

"Just the Ninja? What about Coel?"

"He's staying, at least for a while."

"How odd. Why aren't they both going?"

"He didn't say. You know what Dava's like." I could see Madoc was bursting with suppressed excitement. I didn't trust it, because it might have been due to painkillers, but when I raised my eyebrows and invited him to explain, he just grinned at me.

"All right," I said, irritably. "Keep your damn secrets. I've got news for you, though – I'm not working those horses today. When we finish sorting the sheep, I'll bring the Ninja in and turn Coel out, and then I'm going to ride Zilla."

"Okay then. You do that," he said, and hobbled away towards the house.

~~~

At last I was free to walk up to High Field. I called Zilla and she came bouncing and skidding to the gate.

"You look a right scruff," I said, as I fitted her headcollar. She was coated in dry mud and her answer was to shake herself, with a noise like someone beating a hearthrug, and cover me in a film of dust.

The two geldings were grazing and made no effort to join us. Coel, on his own in the lower field, lifted his head to watch. When we got down to the yard Madoc was outdoors again, waiting for me. Zilla snorted at his crutches, but when he held one out to her she smelled it carefully, thought about it, advanced to smell the other one, and from then on behaved as though he had always used them.

"She's a clever little brat, isn't she?" he observed. "What are you going to do? School her? Get that kick sorted out?"

Docile field work would not be enough to rid me of the demon that was Charles Humphrey.

"I'm going up the gallops," I said. "Is that okay with you?"

"Why not? Since I shan't have a chance to use them."

I tied Zilla outside the tack-room and began to brush her over. Madoc shifted his right crutch into his left hand and began to scratch her withers with his fingers. She cocked her head, half closed her eyes and stretched her nose into the likeness of a tapir.

I chuckled. "Ooh, she likes that."

I saddled and bridled the mare and rode at a walk to the gate of the exercise field, and Madoc hobbled alongside us and let us in.

"Keep away from Coel while you're warming up. We don't want him to get excited and try to jump the wall."

I began by schooling Zilla in big circles. She trotted obediently but, judging by the energy she was generating and the way she kept flicking her ears back and forth, I thought there might be a storm brewing so I pointed her towards the gentle rise of the gallop. She shook out her mane, tucked her chin naughtily into her chest, and powered up the hill with such a rapid trot that I had to stand in the stirrups above her pumping shoulders the way I did with the galloping thoroughbreds. She and I were both conscious of Coel matching her in the next field, cantering to keep up with her trot. We reached the wall of the trackway from Underscar and Coel wheeled and bucked and galloped away across his field, so for safety I turned Zilla in the opposite direction. She could still hear him though, and showed her excitement by blowing snorts that a whale would have been proud of.

"You witch," I said, laughing.

Coel trotted a circle and came to an alert halt, close to the wall, watching us. He whinnied once, then trotted away up the slope with his head and tail in the air, and Zilla, distracted by him, was definitely speculating about playful misbehaviour and only listening to me with a fraction of her brain. I managed to restrain her to a walk as I rode to the bottom of the field.

A mad idea took hold of me and I said to Madoc, "I've got to give her something more to think about. I'll ride her over the hurdles."

"What? You haven't jumped her at all yet, have you?"

We would never start a novice thoroughbred over hurdles on his own. We would work as a team, methodically, not taking risks. But I said, "She's clever. She'll be fine."

"Has *anyone* jumped her? That you know of?"

"I've no idea, but I'm going to find out."

He looked up at me, shading his eyes, without saying anything. His fall had given him time to think, and I wondered if he'd been analysing the past forty-eight hours – how little I'd told him about my Saturday away; my need for him that night; my trembling fury over the texts on my phone in the morning. I couldn't guess what connections he had made. Still, there were times he knew me better than I did myself, and this was one of them.

"Let's see what happens, then," he said. He hobbled after me to the exercise strip, where the five flights of mini-hurdles stood at right angles to the long stone wall climbing to the foot of the Scar. I was relieved to see there was a grin on his face. "Stay in the centre. And shorten your leathers."

"Yes boss," I said, wondering what he found so amusing.

I trotted Zilla round, trying to ride her in a smooth curve onto a line that would bring her parallel to the wall and facing the hurdles. She began to sidle and pull at the bit because this was something new and exciting and she wanted to go again into that mischievous ground eating trot, but I knew that trotting would make it much harder for her to jump them properly so I insisted she changed gait to a canter. Her head went down in protest, and her back came up – I knew if she could put her head between her knees and buck properly she would launch me clear off. I set my own knees into the saddle and urged her towards the first hurdle.

She catapulted into a rapid gallop and Madoc shouted, "Keep her straight!"

No need to tell me. I'd found out early on that Zilla could turn on a sixpence, and if she slung me off at this speed I would probably demolish the wall.

Due entirely to her judgement and not to mine, she met the hurdle just right. She bucketed over it, took one stride, then gave a damn-this-is-fun kick-back and set off up the slope full pelt.

I heard a whoop from Madoc, behind me. She went belting on up the hill with her black mane whipping my face, grunting with effort. She jumped hurdle two.

I shrieked, "Good girl!"

Three. Four. Five. She devoured each flight like a chocoholic in an Easter egg factory. At the top of the gallop I eased my hands on the reins. On that signal, Coel or the Ninja would have slowed, smoothly, to a well mannered canter, but not Zilla. She bronked sideways up the hill, swinging her head and snorting. She was enormously pleased with herself.

"You little *git*," I said, between gasps. "Where did all that come from!"

Carefully, sitting out her lurches and startles and attempts to buck, I persuaded her back down to where Madoc was standing propped on his crutches and laughing. I had to ride a circle round him to keep him safe from her prancing hooves.

"Better now?" he called.

"Yes."

He swivelled on his good leg to watch us. "I see what you mean about not selling her. She makes Coel look an easy ride. Do you need to go round again?"

"No. So long as I know she's got it, I can use it any time."

He watched me, still grinning, and I was on enough of a high not to care why.

Chapter 28.

In the morning, Robbie and I loaded the marked sheep into Andy Wharton's trailer and he got into the Peugeot to follow Andy down the motorway to the auction.

"Why aren't you going in the pickup with him?" I asked him.

"I want to stop off at Beth's on the way back. Her Gran's died and she's a bit upset."

"Aw... I see. Why don't you drop in and see her on the way down?"

"No, she's been on night shift, she'll be asleep till this afternoon."

Robbie was still away when Hardings' smallest horsebox rolled into our yard, steered by its stoutest and most cheerful driver. Our Jack was in the passenger side of the cab – window down, tie slackened, school bags crammed on his knee.

"I was just getting off the minibus, Mam. I saw Paul waiting to come in here. He didn't mind giving me a lift – did you, Paul?"

"Oooh, I dunno, mate." The driver drew in air sharply, shaking his head. "You better hadn't tell my boss. He says he'll skin me if I pick up hitch-hikers. Specially ginger ones."

Jack made a rude noise at him. "It's just up our track, that doesn't count as hitch-hiking." He opened the door and jumped down.

"Take your things indoors," I said, "and get changed, while we sort out these horses."

"Right you are, Mam." He was already sauntering towards the house, blazer over one arm, rucksack slung across the other shoulder, sports bag scraping the concrete. He ought to be dwarfed by all his belongings flapping around him but he seemed to have grown an inch in every direction since he left in the morning. He drifted to a halt at the doorway to let Madoc come out.

"He's turning into a fine lad," said Paul.

"Yes," I said slowly. "Isn't he."

"I like your new place," he observed. "How long have you been here?"

"September last year," I said.

"Doing the place up? It's going to be nice. Now, where d'you want me?"

I pointed, and Paul drove steadily across the yard. Both horses came to their doors to look out.

I waited for Madoc to join me. He was becoming careless of the limitations of his elbow-crutches, moving quickly on them, sometimes too quickly for my peace of mind. This time he was trying to hold the Ninja's passport as well as manage the crutches.

"I'll take it," I said, and he released it with a sigh of pure frustration.

Paul had got down from the cab and stood watching him, hands on hips. "Eh, get them shorts! What you been doing to yourself now?"

"Fell off a nag," said Madoc.

"Which one? The one I'm taking away, eh?"

"No, the one we're keeping."

Paul laughed. "What are you like! You'd do better to stick with wheels and engines."

I offered him a cup of tea. "Given the weather, I expect you'd prefer a beer, but you've got a long way to drive home."

"Yeah, tea will be fine, thanks."

I gave the passport to him and went indoors. Jack came thundering downstairs and splashily made himself a drink of squash, and when I took the mugs out into the yard he followed.

Madoc had set his back comfortably against the sunny stable wall, the crutches hanging from his elbows. I handed tea to him and to Paul and said, "I would have thought it made more sense to take both horses back to Dava – not just one."

"I was just saying the same thing to yer man here," Paul agreed, "but the boss said to fetch one, so that's what I'll do."

I caught that amused look on Madoc's face again. I said, with some annoyance, "You *fox*. I swear you know more about this than you're letting on."

"Me?"

"You. So don't fob me off!"

Madoc began to chuckle and his mug of tea developed waves so he leaned forward and lowered the tide line by drinking. He was still smiling when he came back up, like a diver surfacing, enriched by strange sightings and the promise of treasure.

"Did you realise," he said, "that King Coel doesn't belong to Chaz Humphrey?"

"What!"

"Humphrey's only leased him. The colt still belongs to Helen Rogers, and they're in the middle of an argument about the contract."

He explained to Paul, "We've known Helen forever. She bred Coel and she bred his dam. She's as nice a woman as I've ever met."

I punched his arm. "What about me, husband dear!"

Madoc leaned away from me, still chuckling. "I'd put money on Helen being the reason the colt's still entire and not a gelding."

"I knew it had to be sentiment on somebody's part," said Paul. He finished his tea and stood the mug on the windowsill. "If you don't mind, I'll clean my horsebox before we get the other horse loaded."

Jack put his glass beside Paul's mug and said, "I'll fetch the wheelbarrow," and ran off towards the midden while Paul lowered the side ramp of the box.

"So that's what you've been grinning about," I said to Madoc. I wasn't sure whether to be annoyed or not, but the words came out sounding accusatory.

He said simply, "Dava told me. I couldn't believe it myself. But there it is."

I shook my head at him and went into the stable for the Ninja. That skinny chestnut who'd arrived six or seven weeks ago, so timid that he had to be tied up before we could give him even the simplest attention, had become a young athlete, his body round with muscle and his stance confident, even arrogant. I fitted his headcollar and took the folded rug from over the door and swung it across his back. While I was fastening the straps, Jack came back with the muck barrow and the shavings fork. I heard Paul thank him.

"You're welcome," Jack replied solemnly. I hid behind the horse's neck so he wouldn't see me chuckling. He asked, "Da – when the Ninja's gone, d'you want me to muck-out the stable? Can I use the pressure-washer?"

"So long as you don't mess about." Madoc was still leaning comfortably against the wall. "What's brought this on?"

"Well, if I do it, will you teach me to use the rifle? I mean you can't do much else right now so it'll stop you getting bored."

I peered round the stable door to see whether Madoc was managing to keep a straight face.

He said sternly, "Behave, then. Don't wreck the pressure washer."

The new adolescent Jack didn't rush about yelling with delight at his answer. He parked the wheelbarrow next to the horsebox ramp, ran up into the empty stall and began to sift out patches of muck and wet shavings into the barrow. My earlier impression had been right; the youngest of our brood was standing an inch taller this afternoon than he had the previous day.

Paul watched for a moment, then let him get on with it. He strolled back to the stable door and said, "Your kids have nice manners. You should be proud of them."

"Thanks," I said. "We are."

Madoc chuckled. "Make the most of it. I think the teenage monster phase is about due."

"Aye, and that sunburn's a bugger, an' all."

When Jack had cleaned the horsebox I brought the Ninja out and led him clomp-clomping up the rubber-matted ramp and into the stall. I gave him a last mint before I left him.

"Be a good lad, now."

Paul shut the partition and let Jack help to throw the ramp up and clip it shut.

"See you again," he called, and drove off.

Jack trundled into the stable with the half-full barrow, and Madoc listened for a moment to the thud of manure being tossed into it and said thoughtfully, "He's being unusually helpful. I didn't tell you yesterday, but I've seen him riding your mare on the gallops. I assume you didn't know?"

"Not a clue. I told him not to!" I called to Jack. "Have you been riding Zilla?"

The shavings fork paused and Jack's voice from the stable said, "What?"

I repeated, "On the gallops. Your Da says you've been riding Zilla."

He reappeared in the doorway.

"Well... Yeah, I have, a bit. I didn't realise he was watching."

"That's not the point. She needs fixing."

"But she's been here weeks. And she's great to ride. Like a jet-propelled sofa."

"How about the kicking, though? Done anything about that?"

"Um," he said. "I think I should get on with mucking-out."

"I think so too!" When he'd gone I said to Madoc, "So that's why Zilla was so excited about the hurdles yesterday. She'd done it all before – with him."

"Looked like it to me," he agreed. He pushed himself upright and hobbled on his crutches towards King Coel's door. The colt didn't seem at all upset by the disappearance of his stable companion. No whinnying. No circling and stopping to listen. Perhaps he hadn't realised that the Ninja was not coming back.

Madoc stood there considering him. He might well have held a grudge about his injury but instead he said, mildly enough, "He's got real potential, this colt."

"Is that a hint that I should be exercising him?"

"No. Well, we ought to keep him ticking over, of course."

"Okay," I said. "Do you really think Helen has kept him entire on purpose?"

"I wonder. She was fond of his dam and his grand-dam. And maybe Dava's had some say in it. You know how he felt about Baner Wen, and Cymru." He left it at that, but I understood all the things he didn't say. Coel was a descendant of horses we had all loved – Dava, Helen, Madoc and I.

I asked, "Does he know what Helen wants to do with the colt? I mean, when Charles Humphrey's lease expires?" I felt my face flush at mentioning Humphrey's name so I kept my gaze steadily fixed on the horse and hoped Madoc wouldn't notice.

"I don't know. But I wouldn't call Humphrey a dedicated National Hunt owner, would you?" I murmured agreement and he added, "There must be some reason why Coel's not going straight into training. Not that I mind, of course. I'm more interested in what Helen's going to do with him afterwards."

"That's looking a long way ahead. Three years, maybe more."

There was a pause, in which I stared at the big brown colt and my thoughts ran yet again through the limitations of our finances. What with the bank, and Gwylim, and Charles Humphrey, we certainly couldn't pay to lease King Coel from Helen. But I understood completely why Madoc longed to do it.

Chapter 29.

Anxiety is a constant struggle between exhaustion and sleeplessness. To beat it down some people throw hysterics, some overeat and some drink alcohol, but the only thing I'd ever found that silenced anxiety was to choose risk and control it. That was why I worked so much with unschooled or half-wild ponies. I often frightened myself silly in the process but each time I came home in one piece I was riding a high that carried me through the day and dropped me into dreamless sleep at night. In one form or another it had been a survival strategy for the whole of my married life. Riding the young racehorses worked too, to an extent, but as I had never been able to vault onto a sixteen-hand high thoroughbred, the need for someone else to give me a leg-up rather damped the spontaneity.

Now, with Madoc sidelined by his injury, I was going to be kept away from my Fell ponies by the farm work, and yet the threat of Charles Humphrey turning up at the weekend gathered steadily like a storm cloud over my thoughts.

On Wednesday afternoon I grocery-shopped, to prepare for sheep clipping the following day. The weather forecast was bad but we had to go ahead because the commercial shearing unit was booked up every day for the next fortnight on other farms and if we cancelled, we'd go to the tail of the queue. So Robbie, Daniel and Jack gathered the sheep off the fell early in the day, before the west wind could bring the rain which would make their fleeces impossible to clip. Cerys and I bedded-out the big shed with straw to house the flock overnight, and filled the racks with hay. Between us we also put everything ready to deal with the shorn fleeces: two trestle tables near the doorway, the Wool Board's labels and record card and a couple of black pens all safe in a plastic box; a wool needle and a hank of the eight-foot-long strings we would need to sew shut the 'wool sheets' of woven polypropylene, which presently hung empty at shoulder height from the shed wall like greasy giant pillow-cases.

Thursday brought heavy downpours that turned on and off like a tap, but the sheep were indoors and dry and ready to be clipped. Daniel and his mates Jonty and Simon arrived at 8am with a pickup and trailer. While they were unloading the shearing unit and setting it up, I turned King Coel out into the pasture, where he reared and did handsprings, as though for sheer joy at feeling the rain on his skin. In High Field Zilla saw him and threw up her head at his display, and she and the two geldings burst up the slope at a gallop, bounding and kicking out at each other in equally ferocious good humour. When they'd finished warming themselves up they all had a good shake, presented their tails to the wind, and settled down to grazing.

Back in the shed, Daniel, Cerys and Robbie were diverting the lambs out of the flock into holding pens. The lambs scrambled about or tried to jump back through the bars, and bleated endlessly for their mothers, who bleated endlessly back. It took a while before we were ready to go. Normally Madoc would have helped to catch the ewes for the shearers but today I suggested that he and his mending leg might be safer in the kitchen.

"What am I going to do with myself in there?" he complained.

"Well, there's three pounds of new potatoes and two pounds of carrots to chop. Put them in a couple of pans with some water. And there's tomatoes and a lettuce to wash for lunch."

"Oh."

"But mind, you don't need to start cooking anything."

He said, "Did you remember to get the beef out of the larder?"

As an attempt to take charge it was pathetic. I answered briskly, "It was in the oven before breakfast. But the dishwasher needs to be emptied before you put the dirty pots in."

He stood discontentedly, watching Robbie and Jonty sweep the concrete of the pen where the clippers were going to work.

"Go on," I said, pushing him. "Just give in for once!"

He sighed and swung away on his crutches towards the house. The buzz of the clipping machines began, the day's long counterpoint to the voices of the sheep.

Robbie and Simon caught and delivered the first two ewes to Jonty and Daniel, who up-ended the sheep into a sitting position at their feet. With the electric clippers they cleaned off the short wool from the ewe's belly, then rapidly peeled her fleece off one side from neck to rump, rolled her onto the opposite haunch and peeled off the other side. Old ewes like ours were generally patient during the operation, as though they'd learned from previous years that it was quicker not to fight. Cerys sprayed the farm's blue "pop" on their shoulder before the shearers released them, skinny and white and smeared with colour, to bunch with the other clipped ewes and resume bleating for their lambs.

Throughout the morning I was busy collecting and rolling the wool. I worked at the trestle tables to spread each shorn fleece, pick off straws and muck, flip-in the edges, roll it inside out and tie it with a band of wool twisted from the neck-end. We packed the fleeces into the wool sheets, and about half past ten I stopped work, which the lads read as a signal to finish clipping the ewe they had at their feet; they wiped the sweat off their faces and unfurled their backs, knowing that I was going indoors to make tea.

It had started to rain again. When I came back with the teapot, milk and mugs, Cerys helped me to catch up with the pile of fleeces that had accumulated, and Robbie, who was fanatical about packing our wool sheets right for the haulier, jumped into the open wool sheet to tread the rolled fleeces down tight. When he'd finished the sheet was so hard and full it was almost box-shaped and I needed both him and Daniel to hold its edges together while I used the wool needle and string to stitch it shut. The packed sheet was so heavy it took two lads armed with wool hooks to carry it to the stack beside the door. I tied on the identity labels, pushing them inside the sewn edge of the sheet, and wrote the sheet number on our farm card. Then when we'd finished our tea we returned to the back-breaking work of catching and clipping more ewes, and rolling and packing more fleeces.

The sheep voices, high and low, ran all morning like a river, only lessening a little at mid-day when we turned out the clipped ewes to find their the lambs, who looked as big inside their thick fleeces as their stark-white and angular mothers.

When I went into the kitchen I caught Madoc with the Rayburn oven open, balancing on his good leg with the cast pushed out behind him, as he tried to lift out the sizzling roast. I stopped him, and chased him out to the shed to roll fleeces for ten minutes while I finished preparing the meal. The big stove had made the kitchen very stuffy and hot, but we ate with the windows and doors open to catch a breeze; the beef and carrots tasted good and it seemed I had guessed correctly that the clipping crew liked white bread; so on the whole, it was a satisfactory meal. That was important. Food was part of the crew's reward. Cash payments were quickly spent, but I knew from twenty years of clipping-times that the meals we gave the men were far more memorable than the money.

All afternoon it went on raining. We had a tea-break when Jack came home from school, then with Cerys helping me to roll fleeces and Jack doing the marking we were able to work through the last of the flock. Jack got himself and his old clothes dabbled with so much blue he looked like an Ancient Briton. Afterwards Cerys went indoors to wash and change while Robbie helped Danny, Jonty and Simon to pack away the shearing unit ready to travel to their next day's booking.

"We'll send you an invoice," they said, and thanked me for lunch.

Robbie unfastened Kip's leash from the rails of the end pen, and took him indoors. And I trudged out to the exercise field to catch King Coel and stable him for the night.

I called him, but he had decided by then that he couldn't care less about coming in to shelter. Instead he pranced away at a slow, springy trot, making me walk in the rain all the way up to the top of the pasture to catch him. Zilla, in High Field, stood with her chin on the wall, watching as I led him all the way back. He wasn't in the least disturbed by the profanities I muttered, at the waywardness of colts, and the miserableness of the weather, and how bloody tired I was.

Fortunately Jack had gone from the sheep shed to the stables and by the time I brought the colt in he'd not only filled two water buckets and tied up a big net stuffed with haylage, he was reading the feed list that Madoc had chalked on the tack-room blackboard. I let him weigh out King Coel's evening meal and give it to him, and then, at last, we were done.

When we came into the kitchen again the heat of the Rayburn, that had been so oppressive during the day, was very welcome. Jack leaned over the hotplate and shook his wet head so the rain dripped and sizzled, and I didn't have the energy to tell him off.

I could hear Madoc talking in the front room, perhaps using his mobile phone. There was a long, listening pause, and when Madoc spoke again his voice sounded curt and uncompromising. I wondered who had called and what they wanted. Not even cold-callers got spoken to in that tone. Dava? Unlikely. Gwylim? Possibly. Or maybe Charles Humphrey? My heart pushed its all-too-familiar thud into my ears. I shut the door.

I checked the fire in the Rayburn, and Jack took the towel off the rail and rubbed his head dry.

"Get washed," I said. "Look at the colour of your hands – you're making that towel filthy."

"What's for tea?"

"It doesn't matter!" I said irritably. "Wash!"

He moved to the sink, and slathered hand cleanser over his blue patches. Robbie came downstairs wearing clean clothes, carrying his trainers and smelling of toothpaste and aftershave.

"You got in before Cerys, then."

"Just."

"Where are you off to this evening?"

"I'm going to Beth's again," he said. "She's a bit down. She's taking a few days off work, till the funeral's over."

"When is it?"

"Monday next week."

"Will you go?"

He bent to lace his trainers. "I'll see how she feels. If she wants me to, then yeah, I will."

"D'you want tea now? There's carrots and beef left from lunch time."

Jack looked up from peeling his sunburn. "Errgh! Mam!"

Robbie said, "Oi! They were good enough for us!"

"Can we do chips in the oven, then, and peas? And can I make gravy? With those granule thingies?"

I was tired, so I said, "Anything. If it'll keep you quiet."

Madoc came hobbling from the front room. His face was very still, and he looked directly at me, paying no attention to Jack or Robbie.

"Have you got a minute?"

My heart beat faster. I said rapidly, "Robbie. Get the peas and the oven chips out of the freezer. Jack, you talked yourself into a job. And lay the table."

Neither of the boys said anything. Perhaps they had picked up the sudden intensity in the atmosphere. I followed Madoc. He'd muted the TV news, and the screen showed a talking head; then a shot of a politician walking up steps to board a plane; then the talking head again.

"Come here, Danger Mouse. Sit down." He lowered himself carefully onto the sofa and parked the crutches. I sat beside him and Kip got up from behind the recliner and came to lie on my feet. "That was Gwylim on the phone."

Well! Gwylim must be all right, then, so Humphrey's text about him had been less sinister than I'd imagined.

"What's he been saying?"

"I thought you might know."

"Oh for heaven's sake! Why would *I* have any idea..." I reined in my temper and said more moderately, "You sounded annoyed with him."

"I was, bloody annoyed. He said he saw you with Charles Humphrey at the races. Then he asked me whether I knew. I said Yes, of course I did – even though I didn't." He looked into my face, and I went cold. His eyes were sharp with anger. "He tried to imply you'd gone to Chester races to meet Humphrey. By design."

I tried to laugh, and stopped. I felt physically sick.

"That's not true."

"Of course it isn't! He can be a nasty insinuating little rat, that brother of mine."

The relief made me light-headed. But Madoc was still angry, and he was still watching me.

"He also says Humphrey beat him up and you stood by and let him."

"I didn't 'stand by'. Humphrey told his 'boys' to take him away – and I did say something, but he told me not to worry, they wouldn't kill him!"

"They didn't," said Madoc, "more's the pity. He's got a black eye and some bruises and he's lost a tooth, but he'll be fit again before I am. What's hurting him most is having to replace those designer glasses! But the point is, you didn't tell me about any of it. What else haven't you told me?"

My heart began to thud again, and I didn't answer.

He said, "Come on, Mouse, I'm confused. Gwyl said he saw Humphrey on the racecourse giving you money. "

It dawned on me that Humphrey had followed a tried-and-tested pattern, throughout. At first, when he gave me that twenty-pound note after his stay in the cottage, I'd thought it had been simply a tip, but I could see now that he'd been working out whether I could be bought. The lunch had been the next step; the hundred-pound bet that I'd thought so extravagant had been his clinching move, and the proposition he'd made on the way to the station would have come anyway, only I'd made the bargain unbelievably easy for him by talking about a loan. His technique seemed very obvious now and I was too ashamed of my stupidity to admit it to Madoc.

He said, "Come on. What happened? Why were you even there?"

"Dad asked me to take his will to the solicitors, and they're in Chester. I didn't know it was a race day. I just fancied having a look."

"You didn't mention it."

"I did mean to tell you – but then you had your fall, and we've been all ends up... "

Madoc had always had a trick of staying quiet and waiting for me to talk myself out. He had learned that it worked on me. He said nothing, and I felt I had to go on.

"I ran into Humphrey completely by accident. I met other people you'd have recognised, like Mr Whalley. There's nothing sinister about that. But you know what Humphrey's like."

"Yes," he said. "I warned you about him."

"I know you did," I admitted. "Well, I picked a horse in the five furlong sprint so Humphrey backed it. And then when it won, he gave me some of his winnings. He insisted. But I gave it back." I mustn't reveal the nail in the centre of the pattern and the agonising twist that Humphrey had given it. "If that's what Gwylim saw... well, Humphrey likes to make people dance. He was showing off, proving his power. Should I have taken his money? It was three hundred and fifty pounds, but that's peanuts compared to what we owe Gwylim."

I stopped because my mouth was dry. I could hear the boys in the kitchen arguing over which tray to use for the oven chips. Madoc sat still, waiting. I stared at the politician's face on the television, mouthing in silence. I must stay in control of my own mute button, to keep back the worst of the truth.

I said, "Humphrey likes to play with people. All the time he's finding out your weak points, so he can pressure you to – to do what he wants." I had to avoid telling Madoc about the choice Humphrey had given me: either I abandoned any pretence at self-respect, and wiped out our debt; or I refused him, and maybe we would lose the farm. Whichever choice I had made, I would have hurt Madoc.

I said breathlessly, "There's something I bet Gwylim hasn't told you – the money he's hounding us for, it's nothing to do with business, like he tries to make out. It's a debt to Charles Humphrey."

Madoc snorted, without humour. "That's about the only thing that makes any sense. Maybe that's why Gwyl's making such a thing about wanting cash. My God, if we tried to draw out as much he wants, the bank would think we were money laundering."

I said, "How much do you think we can pay back?"

"I think we could scrape up eight thousand."

I was speechless.

"I can't put a firm figure on it, not until I've talked to Dava, and the bank. What I *have* told Gwyl, is that if he insists on cash he can damn-well come and collect it."

I had serious doubts that eight thousand would satisfy Charles Humphrey, when Gwylim owed him the value of a house and a Mercedes. He would rather complete his "amusing little circle".

"When's Gwylim coming?"

"Sunday," Madoc said. "If the bank can't let us have cash at such short notice he's going to have to make do with a cheque. I expect Humphrey knows exactly how much we owe to Gwyl."

Henry knows where you live. I paused, probably for too long, before I said, "Yes."

Madoc nodded. I thought he guessed more than I had told him. If he had pushed me just a fraction more I would have howled out the rest of the story to him, but if he did have any inkling of what was happening in my head, he didn't talk about it. He just did what he always did with difficult animals, he stayed still and relaxed and let me work it out for myself.

~~~

I should have fallen into bed that night too exhausted to dream, but not even all that hard physical activity could stop my mind working. In the early hours Madoc shook me awake.

"Mouse... come on, wake up..."

I rolled away from him, still tangled in nightmare. Black suits. Sunglasses. Tattooed hands holding my wrists. Madoc switched on the bedside lamp.

"For heaven's sake, what were you dreaming about?"

"I don't know," I said.

The black suits had shut me in a lift that rose inexorably towards a place which, in the manner of dreams, I already knew was decorated with tiger and leopardskin patterns, everything smoke tinged and grubby. There had been a dog howling somewhere, very miserable and lonely.

I tried to run away down a dark corridor, ankle-breaking with empty food trays and beer cans, but my legs were too leaden to run and Jamie and Henry had caught me. That must have been when I'd begun to fight.

I mumbled, "Did I wake you up?"

"You kicked me," said my husband.

I tried to pull my scrambled brain together. "Did I hurt your leg?"

"I'll live," he said, and I knew I had. I touched my forehead to his shoulder in apology.

"I'm sorry. I'll go downstairs and sleep on the recliner."

"That's the last thing I need," he said, and put his arm round me.

I didn't argue. I cuddled up listening to the steady beating of his heart and I fell asleep, and this time I didn't dream.

Chapter 30.

At breakfast I said, "I'd better exercise the colt this morning. I can't keep on putting him out in the field just to stuff his face with grass."

Madoc carefully positioned the kitchen chairs and slid into his seat at the table.

"Well, at least that's something to make Dava happy."

"Oh? Did you phone him? What did he say about the money?"

"He'll let us postpone our next payment to him. I'll have to sort it out with the bank online."

I relaxed a little. "And Coel?"

"That isn't so simple. Helen Rogers is still arguing about something in the lease arrangement with your mate Humphrey. Dava didn't tell me what and I'm not prepared to guess."

"Humphrey's not my mate," I said. I put bread into the toaster, and pressed the handle down with rather too much force. I went to the kitchen door and shouted up the stairs. "Jack! Get a wiggle on! The bus will be here!"

Robbie came in at the back door with Kip, bending down with a firm grip on the dog's collar.

"I don't know what's up with this silly bugger today," he said, when he got the door shut. The dog coughed and shook himself. "Talk about selectively deaf! I've had to just-about drag him all the way back up the lane."

Kip sniffed the biscuits on the cat's dish but decided not to bother and padded back, his claws clicking over the tiles, to wait at the door he'd just come in by. Robbie sat down at the table and reached for cereal and milk, and Jack's footsteps thudded across the bathroom floor above our heads. I plucked the toast out of the toaster, stacked it on a plate on the table, and put in some more bread. When Jack came downstairs with a flurry of bags the dog looked round but didn't greet him, just resumed his tense vigil.

"He's fretting after something out there," I said, and added to Jack, "You're running late."

"Couldn't sleep," he grumbled. "I was only just dropping off when the alarm went."

"Were you too hot in bed?"

"No, Kip kept howling – didn't you, mutt? You must have heard him."

Madoc said, "I didn't."

"He woke me up lots of times," Jack said. He stood at the table, piling marmalade on toast.

I said, "I heard him in my dreams. I wonder if there's a bitch in season somewhere."

"Could be Andy's, at Underscar," said Robbie.

Jack disagreed. "He could smell one miles away. She could be anywhere between here and Tebay." He folded the toast and stuffed it into his mouth.

I said sharply, "Don't drip marmalade down your clean shirt!"

He picked up his bags and made for the door. Robbie got up just in time to prevent Kip sneaking out with him, and there was a brief scrum in the porch before Robbie bundled the dog back inside and the door shut. Kip sighed deeply and lay on the mat, shuddering.

Madoc too drew a deep breath, as though Jack's departure had made something easier to say.

"Your Uncle Gwylim's coming tomorrow."

Robbie groaned. "What's he want this time?"

"A repayment on his loan."

"Oh great. Just when we're starting to see some money coming in."

"Well, it's better he asks for it now than when there's nothing coming in."

"We're sitting on three hundred thousand pounds' worth of land and still struggling to make ends meet. It's ridiculous."

"You forget," said Madoc, "that the bank and Dava and Gwylim own nearly half of it."

I brought the second lot of toast to the table and said, "And that isn't as simple as it sounds, either."

"Let's not go into that right now." Madoc glanced at me and back to Robbie. "We're paying Gwylim cash, ready money. It's going to be delivered to the bank this morning, so someone will have to collect it."

Robbie said, "I was going to mend walls today."

Madoc made an exasperated noise. "For heaven's sake, man! I'd pick it up myself if I could drive! The walls can wait for half a day."

"I'm not putting myself out for bloody Gwylim."

I said, "So that would mean me going, wouldn't it? Robbie. Look at me. I'm half your size. Are you seriously suggesting I should carry thousands in cash around Penrith, on my own?"

"It's hardly the Wild West. Stick it in your bag and forget it and nobody will look at you twice."

Madoc laid his hand emphatically on the table and said, "It's Appleby Fair week, boy. If Andy's stories are true, half the villains of the north of England are up here. You'll go with your Mam."

"She'll want to go round the supermarket first, though, won't she! I hate grocery shopping."

I said, "Don't be silly. We'll have to be back by four, because I've got to let the visitors into the holiday cottage." I foresaw further protests – Robbie complaining about Gwylim, asking why we had to pay so much money all at once, being angry because his plans for the farm were being frustrated. I would allow all those complaints once we were in the pickup on the way to the bank. I would listen and even sympathise – but first I had to get him to go with me.

I looked directly at him. "Please, Robbie."

Madoc and I both waited, and after a moment he said, "Oh, all right."

~~~

We shopped. We collected the money. I was appalled at how little space those fifty-pound notes took up. About a third of the thickness of a ream of printer paper and nowhere near as wide. And apart from Robbie grumbling all the way to Penrith and all the way round the supermarket and all the way back, nothing happened. Nothing at all.

~~~

When we got home, Jack had just arrived from school and wanted to go out with the rifle. Cerys was getting ready for a singing gig with Katie at the George. Madoc locked the money into the desk, then took his crutches and set off with Jack for Thorny Bank. Robbie washed and changed and drove off to see Beth. Just an ordinary evening of pandemonium.

I stayed in the kitchen and made supper. I kept an ear open for the cottage visitors, who turned out to be two couples, each arriving in their own cars and excited about their first trip to Appleby Fair. They deposited their bags, took the door keys and drove away all in one car to have a pub meal on their way to the Hill.

Madoc went to bed early. The way the cast and crutches forced him to change his movement tired him more than he would admit. I was tired too, but I stayed up, lying on the recliner and only half attending to a chat show on the television. I was fretting about the likelihood of Charles Humphrey turning up, and Cerys and Katie perhaps running into him.

I must have dozed off, but around midnight I was roused by the sound of a car in the yard. It might have been our visitors returning, but I heard Cerys's voice in hushed conversation and giggles outside the back door so I gathered Daniel must have brought her home. I let them have ten minutes before I went into the kitchen and turned on the lights and ran water noisily into the kettle.

Cerys came in not long after, looking flushed and pretty and slightly tipsy, and outside the car started up and drove away.

"Evening," I said. "D'you want a drink before you go to bed?"

"Not really," she said. "I don't fancy putting coffee on top of lager and crisps."

"How'd it go tonight?"

"Okay. There were a lot of strangers in – people who'd been up to Appleby for the day, and people who are going tomorrow." She leaned casually against the worktop as though she meant to say more, and I was afraid of what it might be. "Mam, do you remember that man who stayed here with his wife, a couple of weeks back? The one who wanted me to sing at his night club? He seems to be staying at the pub."

So I'd been right. "Well, that's better than him staying here."

"I know. He's a creep. He's brought his bouncers with him again. They were talking about where to go driving tomorrow. People got a bit fed up with them, to be honest. I don't expect pub customers to be a perfect audience, but they kept opening maps and arguing. And of course they stayed right to the end of the gig, till we were packing up. Then he came over and asked if we'd lost his business card. He made out he was disappointed we hadn't called."

My mouth felt dry. I said, "I'm glad you didn't."

"Katie was all for it. She was like, 'It would be good publicity,' and 'You said you'd make use of him.' But it just smelled bad, d'you know what I mean? He didn't offer anything that I can't do for myself. I told him that. And he kept coming back – like a belch after eating kippers – and then he started telling me to give you a message – 'play or pay' – as if it was some sort of joke."

I was speechless for a moment and then furiously angry. "The cheek of him."

"And he said you could expect to see him here – tomorrow, or Sunday – sorry, I'm not sure which."

I went cold. How could I protect Cerys from this without terrifying her? It was all very well for me to block Humphrey from phoning me, but it was no protection for the rest of my family. I couldn't think of anything to say.

She said, "Mam, what's going on? There's always blokes who make random remarks at our gigs, but this is *weird*. Why does he need bouncers around him all the time? I'm glad Daniel was there to back me up."

"So am I," I said fervently.

"Well? What's it about?"

"I'd rather not start to explain at this time of night."

She looked at me, unsatisfied, but I didn't dare tell her any more.

"I'm not convinced Mr Humphrey's going to come here," I said, "but Uncle Gwylim certainly is. It won't be pretty. If he does, can you take off with Katie?"

She sighed. "Does it have to be Katie?"

"Not necessarily."

"It's just, she isn't talking to me."

"Because of the night club offer?"

"Not just that. I told her I'm going to audition for BBC Open Mike – "

"Oh!" I said. "Wow."

"And I'm going to do it without her. She didn't like that. So... would it be okay for me just to be out?"

"Yes."

"About the auditions – Danny says he'll give me a lift up to Penrith. If it's all right with you..."

"Yes, of course. And wow again."

"We'll see," she said. "It isn't till next week. But he'll be clipping at Wolstenholme's tomorrow, so I could give him a hand." She yawned, unselfconscious and elegant as a marmalade cat. "Well, I'd better go to bed, or I'll fall asleep tomorrow and Danny will stitch me inside a wool sheet."

Chapter 31.

At breakfast, both Madoc and I were tired and quiet. I'd lain awake worrying about how impossible it was to protect Cerys, now and in the future, from Charles Humphrey and his kind; worrying about Robbie being angry over the money we'd drawn out for Gwylim; worrying about Gwylim's likely reactions when he discovered the sum wasn't as much as he needed. It hadn't helped that Kip had spent the night howling. Madoc had got up and shut the window, but I could still hear, faintly, the yearning voice in the kennel up the yard.

Robbie dealt with the Rayburn for me and emptied the ash, then persuaded Kip into the quad-bike trailer and set off with the intention of checking the sheep and mending the wall gaps he hadn't done the previous day because we went to collect the cash from the bank. Cerys phoned Danny and stacked the dishwasher and waited for him to pick her up in the car.

I stuffed clothes into the washing machine. I set it off.

I fed Coel and rode him round every field that didn't have sheep in; twice; I turned him out to graze.

The holiday cottage visitors went off to Appleby again.

When I reached the mid-point of the morning, hanging out Jack's washing, Hazel came limping in through the garden gate.

"Hi," she said, raising her shepherd's crook to me in salute. "I decided my knee needed a walk."

"Good, I'll make us a brew."

"That sounds grand. Tell me if I'm holding you back, though."

"No," I said, "I'm ready for a break."

I unfolded a couple of the picnic chairs we kept in the porch, and when I came back with our tea Hazel had dragged the chairs up the bank to the top of the garden, and set them on the rough grass where the elder bush and the honeysuckle tumbled together over the wall. I could hear Madoc shouting to Robbie, somewhere on the other side of the buildings. I couldn't quite make out what he was saying.

"The flowers smell so lovely," Hazel said. "I couldn't resist."

I handed her a mug of tea, and we sat down. "I'm not going to apologise for the state of the grass. Robbie used to mow our lawn when we lived at Longlands, but he hasn't done it here."

"Ah, he's got a girlfriend these days," she said comfortably. "Why don't you put your ponies in here? They'll soon chew it down."

"They'll chew the washing too, knowing them!"

"Well, sheep, then."

"I'll suggest it to Madoc." We watched Jack's school shirts and trousers bellying-out on the washing-line, and I asked cautiously, "How's Katie?"

Hazel prodded the grass with her crook. "I think she's a bit miffed with your Cerys, to be honest."

"Oh dear," I said. "Cerys thought she might be."

"A chap offered them a chance to sing, in Manchester or somewhere, and Cerys turned it down."

"Yes. I heard."

"Your Cerys told this man she wanted a contract to show to you and Madoc. And he told her not to be so naïve. Or rather, 'That isn't the way things are done.'"

"That's him all over."

"Oh, you know him? Katie was keen on the idea. Said it would be good exposure, or something."

"Yes," I said bitterly. "He's very good at offering people imaginary rewards."

"Your lass has got all her buttons on," said Hazel, "so she said no. Katie isn't very suited."

"Oh dear." I didn't know whether to be proud of my daughter's integrity or ashamed of my own lack of it. It shook me to realise how fast she had got the measure of Chaz Humphrey, when I hadn't been able to stand up to him myself. But that was a road I didn't want to go down.

We sat among the scent of the honeysuckle and the less agreeable cat-pee smell of the elder bushes, looking out over the green farmland to the hazy outlines of the Howgill Fells.

After a while Hazel said, "I think you can see even further than we do from our spot. You're that bit higher."

"I love this view," I said, "but it does mean we're open to the weather. I hadn't realised till we moved here how strong that southwest wind can be."

"Aye, but your house is end on to it, so you won't get it so bad as we do, we face right into it. And you've got buildings on the other side to shelter you if the weather comes off the fell." She paused, and added, "Your fields across the road have fogged-up nicely, haven't they, since the rain."

"Yes. And the hay smells good."

"It hasn't heated up at all?"

"Nothing out of the ordinary. Madoc was thankful for your help with it."

"Aye, nae bother." Another pause.

Hazel said, "Has Andy been over to talk with Madoc about them fields? Syke Side and Sweet Holme?"

"No," I said, surprised. "Why?"

"Andy wanted to buy them before the farm come up for sale, but t'awd fella wouldn't split them off."

"Oh," I said. "I see. But one of the reasons we came here was to have more meadowland. So Robbie could make a living."

She nodded. "Then I doubt he wouldn't be very pleased if you sold them to us."

"I'm afraid not."

"Aye well."

We finished our tea, and Hazel got up to go. "I'd best be off. Andy and me are going down to the Farmers' Market after lunch. Josie Langdale is dragging her husband along. I said we'd meet them at the chocolate factory for a cup of tea, just as a break from the funeral arrangements. Will you be going? It's at church, Monday afternoon. We could give you a lift if you want."

I took Hazel's empty mug. "I don't think so. But Robbie says he's going."

"Ah, that's nice. He's still sweet on their lass then, eh?"

"Looks like it."

Madoc limped out of the house door onto the grass and called to us, "Have you seen the dog, at all?"

Hazel chuckled. "Him and me, we've got one pair of working pins between us. I never knew your hubby had such good legs – at any rate, the one that isn't in a cast. He should wear shorts more often."

I didn't comment. I shouted back to Madoc, "I thought the dog was with Robbie."

"He was, but Robbie says he's sloped off. I swear there must be a bitch in season."

Hazel screeched, without visible effort, "It'll be ours. Andy was going to bring her, anyway."

"I'll send Robbie over for him."

"Aye, right you are."

He shuffled round on his crutches and went back through the house.

"If she does have pups," said Hazel, "if you want one, just say."

~~~

Hazel had gone home. The postman arrived with a letter from my father but I clenched my teeth and resolved to wait at least a day before I opened it.

Jack was helping me to shell hard boiled eggs for lunch, and Madoc was washing his hands at the sink when Robbie came bursting in.

I asked him, "Did you find the dog? Was he at Underscar?"

"Oh aye, I *found* the dog all right."

I heard the heavy emphasis in his voice. "What's happened? Where is he?"

"Lying at the farm gate, on the grass."

"What on earth have you left him there for?" asked Madoc.

"He's dead." Robbie showed us his hands, which were grimed and bloody. He said angrily, "A car must have hit him."

"Oh my God." I dropped the half shelled egg back into the pan of water.

Beside me, Jack was scarlet-faced. Not long ago, he would have wept, but now he was doing his best to hold his emotions in check. He said jerkily, "Why didn't they stop?"

"They dumped him," said Robbie. "What a waste of a damn good dog."

Jack said, "He's got a collar and a tag. They should have brought him back here. They must have known where he lives."

Henry knows.

I felt sick. I scrambled to the yard door, pushing Robbie aside. "Mind out!"

I leaned on the hot green paint of the porch windowsill and retched into the drain. The sun made me feel worse. The water dried on my fingers. Indoors, I heard the boys shouting at each other.

"So where is he now?"

"In the quad trailer."

"You can't leave him there!"

"He's past caring, poor bugger."

Henry knows where you live.

Madoc had followed me out from the kitchen. He was standing there, leaning on his crutches, waiting. I couldn't meet his eyes.

He said, "Mouse? What's the matter?"

"The dog," I said.

"I know, it's a shame, but it shouldn't hit you this hard."

He was right. I wasn't the girl who'd wept in Double Jump's stable twenty-odd years ago. Many thoroughbreds and ponies had come and gone since then, cats and dogs had been loved in their lifetimes, and lost in old age and cried over and fondly remembered. Cymru had died still young, and that had nearly ruined us. But this felt different. The timing of it felt deliberate, a punishment for being who I was, and it took me back through all those years to the dark place where I'd been before Madoc appeared in my life.

I retched again.

He said, "It was an accident, love."

"It isn't – it's because Chaz Humphrey's staying at the George."

"What's that got to do with the poor bloody dog?"

"Him and his minders. They did it." Robbie had parked the bike the other side of the pickup and I could just see Kip's white-plumed tail lying limp in the trailer. "They killed him. I know they did."

"We don't know that. Robbie should just have kept the dog under better control, that's all."

"It's not all. It's not! If they can kill the dog, who's to say they won't get at the kids, and the farm, and us!"

"Stop it. The boys can hear you." He put his arm round my shoulders, letting the crutch hang from his elbow, and led me clumsily away across the yard. "How on earth can Charles Humphrey have anything to do with this?"

I found a tissue in my jeans pocket and shakily wiped my mouth. "He just has."

"Siân!" When he used my name he was exasperated. "The dog went off on his own, and some car driver will have hit him. They panicked and drove away – instead of coming to us like any reasonable person – but there's no reason to drag Humphrey into it, none at all."

"Don't be cross with me."

"I'm not cross with you, Mouse, but talk sense."

"I am! Oh, he wouldn't do it himself but he's got Jamie and Henry, and they're killers."

"They've certainly made Gwylim desperate for money, but why would Humphrey send them to kill our dog?"

I wiped my mouth again, unable to face answering.

After a moment he said, "Siân? Has he threatened you? Or the kids? For heaven's sake, tell me."

I pressed my back against the stones of the barn, trying to control my voice. "He wants me to sleep with him."

Madoc was still, as though he couldn't believe it. Then, I could see, he began to fit things together. He remembered things I'd told him. He remembered me coming home from Chester, wanting him, but not telling him why.

He placed his hands against the stonework either side of me, his body and his arms and the crutches like an encircling wall. He had every right to be furious, and I couldn't meet his eyes.

"Go on. Let's get this over with once and for all."

"He said if I did, he'd take the pressure off Gwylim for the money. He told me I should be flattered because Gwylim owed him such a lot."

"What a bloody insult. I don't care how much Gwylim owes him. Why the hell is he trying to buy you?"

"How would I know? When he stayed in the cottage he gave me a tip and I took it. We don't refuse when racehorse owners 'drop', do we? Then he did me a favour, getting me in to the races – and yes, I know – *there's no such thing as a free lunch* – I was polite to him, that's all. It was all public so I thought it didn't matter. Not till he gave me a lift back to Liverpool."

"You got into his car?" He let out a sigh of disbelief. "You don't half take some risks, Mouse."

"We were discussing money. He said he could help us."

"This is something else you didn't tell me," he said.

I looked up then. I was afraid. If I said the wrong thing now, he would never trust me again.

"I know. He was blackmailing me. But whatever answer I gave him, it was going to hurt you. Whatever I did, you'd be angry."

"I'm never angry with *you*, don't you know that by now? But didn't you realise what he was after? You aren't usually slow on the uptake."

I put my forehead on his chest.

"I never gave it a thought," I said into his shirt. "I never think of myself as available. I'm married to you."

"Eh," he said, on an indrawn breath, "you innocent."

He wrapped his arms around me, crutches and all.

My biggest fear had, after all, been imaginary. Madoc was still there. Yes, I was afraid of Humphrey and worried about the children and grieved by the death of the dog, but I still had my husband on my side. He squeezed me tightly, and I relished the feeling until I realised the vibration in his chest meant that my defender was actually trying not to laugh.

I punched him and said, "Shut up!"

"I'm not – "

"Liar."

"Yes. Look, I don't know whether to laugh or cry or punch something. But I'm not angry with *you*." He slackened his hold a little and said, "Have you been bottling this up since you went to Chester? No wonder you've been so odd. Why didn't you tell me? For all I knew, it could have been the farm, or the money, or Gwylim – you wouldn't tell me. I wondered if it was me."

I looked up at him. "Never."

"I kept waiting, you see, and you wouldn't explain. And with me being stuck, like this..." He looked down, at the cast and crutches. "When I can't get on with things – well, I've been sitting about and doing far too much thinking. It's such a relief to be told it isn't anything I've done. I hope you told Shit-face where to go."

"Eventually. I kept thinking it was my fault."

"You didn't! Really?"

I muttered, "The whole proposition sounded so silly, I didn't think you'd believe me."

"You utter spanner. You've got such a blind spot about what you're worth," he said, gently shaking me. "Of course I believe you. You drive me daft with the way you keep secrets, but you don't lie."

"Keeping this secret felt like lying."

"That's why it drives me daft. Mind, I never did buy Gwylim's story about you knocking-off Charles Humphrey – you'd be insane to let yourself be seen with him, especially on a racecourse where we know so many people."

"I never thought of that. Oh, I can't tell whether I'm sane or not, any more." I took out my phone and spun clumsily through Humphrey's bedroom texts. "I suppose I'd better let you read these."

Madoc took the phone. He frowned at the screen and tilted it away from the sun, and read the messages with growing distaste, right down to my final raging reply. Then he sighed and slid the phone back into my jeans and put his arms round me again.

He said in my ear, "You're some woman, Danger Mouse. I'm not going to bloody share you. Ever."

Chapter 32.

Gwylim arrived in the early afternoon. He walked straight into the kitchen, knocking loudly as he came, not waiting for any invitation. I thought he had lost weight. The designer jacket had gone; he wore crumpled dark trousers, an olive-coloured shirt and no tie, and his glasses, this time, had photochromic lenses of a shape was no longer fashionable. There was a yellowing bruise down his jaw. Everything else about him, his stance and his movement, seemed to have stiffened to the point of being brittle. I didn't think he would unbend far enough to sit down, so I didn't suggest it. I held onto the rail of the Rayburn and stared at him and, behind me, I heard Madoc push back the chair he'd been sitting on. Its feet scraped across the floor tiles and I heard the squeak of his shoe soles and the click of his crutches as he came to my side.

"Well," he said, assessing Gwylim. "You don't look too bad, after all."

"No thanks to anybody here." The missing tooth gave a slight lisp to his speech. "Let's get on, ey? You know what I've come for."

"Yes, bad luck to it. Siân, you know where the money is – would you bring it – please?" Madoc spoke lightly enough, but when I walked past them towards the front room I felt the air might take fire from the antagonism tingling between them.

I unlocked the desk, and reached into the little drawer for the banded bundles of cash. Eight thousand pounds. Too little for

Gwylim, too much for us. I accepted that with the pressure he was under it was only fair to start paying him back, but that stack of notes represented a year of our work, everything we'd earned from lambing and clipping and dosing the sheep, cleaning the holiday cottage, and feeding and mucking-out and educating horses. Giving so much to Gwylim, all in one go, was almost too much for my temper. I picked a used envelope out of the bin beside the desk and put the notes inside so I didn't have to look at them again. There was a receipt that Madoc had printed last night for Gwylim to sign. I folded it and put it in the envelope and went back into the kitchen.

Gwylim held out his hand. I ignored him and gave the envelope to Madoc.

There was a pause that crackled with resentment, before Madoc in his turn gave the envelope to Gwylim.

"Eight thousand," he said. "Count it."

"Eight! I told you how much I needed – is this really the best you can do?"

I drew a fast, angry breath, but Madoc laid a restraining hand on my arm and I subsided.

"This..." Gwylim backhanded the envelope dismissively. "It's as much use as a handbrake on Niagara Falls."

Madoc explained, as patiently as though he was talking Jack through his rifle safety protocol. "We're paying the bank. We're paying Dava. We'll pay you. You'll get it all back the same as they will. But it takes time, in farming. You know that. And right now, what's in that envelope is all we've got to give you."

Gwylim said, "The business needs five times as much as this."

"I don't doubt that," said Madoc, "but no way is it a business deal, so don't pretend it is."

"You have no idea."

245

"I know a lot more than you think." Madoc's voice was polite, but cold. "Siân – I printed a receipt – did you find it?"

"In the envelope," I said.

"Right. Gwyl, count the notes, and sign for them."

"You don't trust me."

"Neither of us do," I said. "You can take it or leave it."

Madoc laid a pen on the table for him and there was a wary pause before Gwylim counted the money and signed the receipt.

"Don't lose that," he said. "You won't get it twice."

I snapped, "I could say the same about the money."

"Then find the rest, and quick, or things are going to get ugly."

Madoc said, "We've all got to watch our step. You most of all, eh?"

There was another pause.

Gwylim said, "Well, I've got a meeting to go to." He picked up the envelope, and went out.

"Don't thank us, will you," I said under my breath. Madoc put a hand on my arm, but I shook him off and followed Gwylim into the yard. No shiny white Merc today – that was probably locked up behind one of Charles Humphrey's night clubs. He was getting into a Vauxhall, barely larger than Robbie's Peugeot and even more ancient than our pickup. It had once been a dark beetle green but had been parked outdoors for so long it was dull and faded. I should have felt sorry for him, but I didn't. As he drove out of the yard I shouted after him, "Stupid, bastard, bloody *man*!"

There was the click of Madoc's crutches behind me again. I looked round and he was standing in the porch trying not to laugh, but it looked painful, as though laughter was the only thing that stopped him shouting his frustration the way I was shouting mine.

"I thought you were going to wallop him," he said.

"I wish I had."

"Glad you didn't. On the whole."

"Still wish I had." From across the yard Zilla whinnied and put her head over the stable door. "What's that mare doing, indoors?"

"Jack brought her down from High Field – about the same time as Robbie came home from Langdale's. I think you were hoovering upstairs. He said you'd told him to work with the geldings, but he had to bring her in because she was making a nuisance of herself."

"I'd forgotten." The conversation I'd had with Jack seemed ages ago – on the far side of Gwylim taking our year's profit, and before me telling Madoc about Humphrey's proposition. "I thought Robbie went to see Beth?"

"She came back with him. They've gone into the garden to bury the dog."

I moved involuntarily towards the door but Madoc stopped me.

"Don't go upsetting him. Leave him be. Now – after all that, I need a cup of tea and two paracetamol. And *you* need to go out and ride."

"You don't mean Coel?" I said. I was in entirely the wrong mood to handle the colt. He was too valuable and too easy to damage. I couldn't take any risks with him.

"Don't be daft," Madoc said. "Ride Zilla. She's there, for heaven's sake." He prodded me with his crutch. "Go on. Take her up the fell and get lost."

~~~

I slapped the saddle and bridle onto the mare, quickly, not caring if I unsettled her. If I'd tried to drive the pickup in this state I'd get done for reckless driving. There was far too much going on in my head.

We had scraped our bank account down to rock bottom to give Gwylim that money, our whole year's income had been swallowed up, and yet because Gwylim was being hounded by Charles Humphrey we would still need to pay more, more, more.

"Bloody Gwylim," I muttered.

Robbie was grieving for more than just the loss of his dog. He'd grafted alongside us all year yet now he had nothing to show for it except a second-hand car that he couldn't afford to tax. He'd fumed about it all the way to Penrith and back yesterday, and I couldn't blame him. He had every right to feel humiliated and angry and, although he didn't say it, no longer worthy of Beth. All that was down to Charles Humphrey.

Madoc had tried so hard to be the voice of reason. He wasn't convinced that Humphrey had arranged to kill poor Kip. Madoc still wanted King Coel, and we hadn't yet been able to talk to Helen about the lease and what might happen at the end of it, but we knew that Humphrey lay like a snake behind everything we did.

And Humphrey had threatened my family because I refused to sell myself.

"Bloody Humphrey."

And my father's letter still needed answering. I couldn't remember where I'd left it. Not that it mattered. If I hadn't gone to Chester with his last will-and-bloody-testament, I wouldn't have been hip-deep in all this shit.

My head was under pressure, and the only safety valve I had was Zilla.

"Bloody *money*."

I untied her lead rope and fastened it with a bowline, like a lanyard around her neck, then I rammed my helmet on, snapped the chinstrap tight and vaulted into the saddle.

She sidled out of the yard relatively demurely while I found my stirrups. Down the farm track she began to flatten her ears at the sheep and dart her head wickedly towards any that lingered between us and the gate onto the fell, but she knew that messing about would only delay her fun, so at the gate she controlled herself while I opened it and rode through and shut it. We crossed the tarmac of the Shap road and headed south on the firm turf of the fell. She began to shudder and prance and coil herself sideways, longing to gallop and checking again, waiting for my signal.

Zilla was the only thing I had that was tough enough, lawless enough, to outrun my demons.

"Bloody *farming*. Bloody *men*."

I crouched over her neck, screamed in her ear and let her go.

~~~

No-one could have stopped us. My need to run became hers. The ragged mane whipping my arms became mine. The pistoning legs and the pump of breath in each galloping stride became ours. Hooves beat the dry turf, clattered on stones, swished over rushes, splattered through ruts. Heads to the wind, facing the sun, we swooped down the ancient trackway, surfing the waves and troughs of the fell together, one wild creature that swam, and danced, and flew. No need to think, only to revel in our own strength and speed and freedom.

We galloped for nearly a mile. Then the fell wall that accompanied the Roman road put out an arm at a right angle ahead of us, and although the old way went straight on, it was barred by a gate and became submerged in the bright green of tamed fields.

We veered away through a swathe of sun-browned rushes, and I let Zilla find her own balance and ease down to canter, trot and walk in her own time. We were both panting heavily. Where the reins had chafed her neck there was a streak of white lather and the fur down her shoulders was curled and damp. My own body was trickling with sweat.

She came to a halt and I let her stand, panting.

The wind tempered the sunshine. It carried the tuneless hum of the motorway and from somewhere across the fields to the west the smell of cut grass, the buzz of a forage harvester and the boom and rattle of silage trailers. High above us a curlew trailed a long, bubbling whistle as he glided down on stiff-curved wings. I shifted my helmet to unstick the lining from my forehead while the sweat dried.

Zilla quietly began to walk. I let her put her head down and pick her own way, round swallow-holes in the underlying rock and a rectangle of ruined walls that might once have been a building or simply an enclosure to hold sheep for clipping. Occasionally she quivered her skin to get rid of flies, but it was too hot for the midges to bother us, and too early for the biting clegs. Even with the reins almost slack we were still in tune so when she picked up a trot a couple of times I just went along with it and didn't attempt to check her. More often she reached lazily down and snatched a bite of grass. She brushed through a patch of bracken onto a hidden lawn and startled a group of rabbits who rushed to dive down holes; she blew a quick snort after them and steadily walked on. We struck a track angling away north and in a few minutes that brought us alongside the droning, anonymous motorway, so I let her follow the fence down to the bridge over the Shap road.

During the walk the demons in my brain, that had been knocked silent by the gallop, began to chatter again. Gwylim had been going to a meeting. Had that been with Charles Humphrey? I didn't know what else he could have meant. What would happen when he handed over our money and it was nowhere near as much as he owed?

It occurred to me, quite suddenly, that Gwylim might not even go as far as handing it over. He might just cut his losses – pocket the cash and vanish. In either case, where was Humphrey going to look for his repayment?

Walking was all very well, but that level of worry needed much more action.

On the other side of the road there was a stretch of short grass leading up towards the back of the Scar. I asked Zilla to canter and we rocked our way up the slope until the going began to be pocked with little swallow-holes and the turf narrowed to a sheep-trod through bracken as high as my stirrups. Zilla gave her opinion that we ought to slow down, and we rustled through the tall ferns at a walk until the trod met the high section of the Roman road. I wasn't ready to go home yet but when she scrambled into its sandy-pale ruts, she headed downhill towards Stone Side.

The farm lay sunning itself. The sheep pressed sideways, panting, into the slim afternoon shadows of walls, and the ash trees, pines and hawthorns stood in clumps of black and green against the grey-whiteness of the limekiln at Thorny Bank. In High Field the three-year-old geldings were playing side by side, each trying to bite the other's knees, and lower down, King Coel swished his tail and strolled idly towards his gate.

It was a joy to feel how intelligently Zilla worked her way along the track, zigzagging around exposed boulders, taking to the grass to avoid stony stretches. There was a long muddy stripe edged with head-high bracken, where fresh four-by-four tyre-marks had overlaid the studded tracks of a quad bike and the older, blurred vees of tractor treads. Zilla stitched the edge of it with her unshod hoofprints.

Suddenly she leapt sideways, so fast that she almost unseated me.

I caught my balance and said, "Hey, hey, steady mare."

She stared intently down the track at something invisible in the bracken a couple of hundred yards ahead, her body tensed ready to spin round and bolt back up the fell. She wasn't usually given to fearing panthers behind every rock but she stood now with her head up, ears as stiff as horns, giving long vibrating snorts of alarm. Whatever had spooked her enough to consider running away from home and companionship had to be taken seriously.

I smoothed her damp neck and urged her forward, believing that she would trust me. And, against her better judgement, she did. We advanced down the slope towards Doctor's Pot with her quivering and blowing her anxiety every couple of steps.

"Come on, you're all right. I bet it's only a sheep."

And then I saw it too. In the deep conical hollow of Doctor's Pot, a car was lying on its side where there had never been a car before. It was black, spattered with mud, two filthy nearside wheels horizontal above the bracken. It had gouged a long, curving white scar across one of the boulders. There was a slogan on the back door, IF YOU CAN READ THIS, ROLL ME OVER.

Charles Humphrey's Land Rover Defender. So much for his boasted cross-country skills. Ha bloody ha.

The windscreen was crazed with radiating cracks, and the window on the passenger side, where I'd been sitting when he propositioned me, was open to the sky. He must have had to struggle over the gear lever and the seat to heave himself out. I enjoyed the thought of his pub-landlord bulk having to squeeze through the little window frame. Served him right.

Even as I rejoiced over it, I realised there were no footprints or scuff-marks in the mud on the door panel. Nobody had got out that way. But he couldn't still be in there. Surely not. The Defender was built so strongly that a simple roll-over couldn't have hurt him.

"Hello!" I shouted.

Zilla snorted and fidgeted but I shortened the reins and rode her further round the edge of the Pot so I could look down through the windscreen.

There was definitely a man in the driving seat. Because of the angle at which the Defender had come to rest, he was lying slumped against the driver's side door and his left arm had fallen across to hide his face. The sun shone on his heavy torso but the mesh of cracks in the glass made it hard to see any details except that he was wearing a long-sleeved checked shirt.

"Hello?"

Of course, it might not be Charles Humphrey in there. He might have lent the Defender to Henry or Jamie, or some other muscle-for-brains that he employed. But whoever it was, he wasn't responding, and even if he was my worst enemy, I couldn't just leave him there and do nothing.

Zilla was still uneasy, so I rode her away onto a little grassy space just above the track before I dismounted. I looped the reins round the stirrup and undid the bowline in the lead rope and dropped it to the ground, and she put her head down and started to graze in an affronted fashion as though the grass had something to do with her previous scare. When I was sure she'd stay, I left her there and ran over to Doctor's Pot.

I began to climb down. Black flies and little pale moths flickered between me and the crazed windscreen, among the stink of bog-sludge, hot rubber and metal, the stale, sickening cigar-smoke from the cab, and the sourness of bracken. The crushed stems were slippery and twice I stumbled on broken rock hidden beneath them.

I didn't have to go further than the Defender's bonnet to confirm that it really was Charles Humphrey in there. His head was resting in the angle between roof and door with his body against the door pillar. His eyes were closed and his face was pale. There was blood seeping through the shoulder of his shirt.

I thought, in a moment of vindictive delight: *how very convenient it would be if he was dead.*

Chapter 33.

He wasn't dead, of course. He was still breathing.

I didn't know whether to be relieved or disappointed. Before I had time to think about it I heard the squelch and splash of approaching tyres powered by a big diesel engine, and I scrambled back up to the track to see a very dirty-looking Kia, bouncing towards me heart-stoppingly fast through that muddy stripe up the hill. Zilla wheeled uncertainly around her trailing rope. The Kia didn't seem to be slowing. Jamie was driving, with Henry in the passenger seat, and he saw me but he didn't brake and I was forced to back into the bracken out of his way.

When he spotted the Defender in the sink-hole he stamped so hard on the pedal that the bog-splattered tyres dug trenches. He got out twenty yards down the hill, leaving the Kia so close to the opposite bank that the passenger door wouldn't open and Henry had to scramble out through the driver's side before he could follow him up the track towards me. Their boots and jeans were plastered with wet mud. Henry's leather jacket and Jamie's white singlet and the tattoos on his bulky arms were smeared with it. What shocked me, after their rampaging arrival, was the fact that they were laughing. They strolled past me to Doctor's Pot and put their hands in their pockets and gloated.

"Made a right mess of it, hasn't he?"

"Belter! In sight of the finish line, like."

"Serves him bloodywell right for leaving us stuck up there."

"Bet he's gorra face like a pound o' smacked tripe." Henry lit a cigarette. They were breaking the law just by driving the four-by-fours on the fell, and I supposed for them that only increased the enjoyment.

"Wonder where he's got to." Jamie glanced around, almost idly, and it was only then that he saw past my clothes and my riding helmet and realised who I was. "Well look who's here!"

Henry stared at me and took a drag at his cigarette. I didn't like the speculative expression on his face, still less the laugh that Jamie gave.

"It's his farm rat. Hey, where's the man? Shagged-out in the bracken?"

It was no more than casual offensiveness but for a moment I was speechless. Had they really no idea what had happened? I said, "He's in the car."

They glanced at each other and shrugged.

I couldn't even begin to explain. "Just bloody look, will you."

Jamie started to clamber down into the sink-hole, not hurrying. Henry watched him, drawing on his cigarette. "He bet us a hundred he could beat us across country, the scone-head."

Jamie reached the place where I'd stood a few minutes earlier, and peered into the cab of the overturned Defender. Almost at once he stood up and shouted, "Give uz a hand."

"Swerve that," said Henry.

"Come here, you pillock, and gerra shift on. He's been shot."

That was what I'd been afraid of.

Henry took a last drag before he threw away the cigarette and picked his way into Doctor's Pot. Jamie climbed the bull-bar on the front of the Defender, walked across the flat side of the wing and reached down to open the passenger door. He stood aside when Henry joined him, and propped the door with both hands for Henry to drop into the cab.

They weren't laughing any more. They were grim and physical. There wasn't enough space for them both to get in, and the door wouldn't stay open for them to lift Humphrey.

Words burst out of them like bullets.

"Push him up to me."

"I'm trying, you tattooed pudden. You're not helping."

"Christ, he's a dead weight." Jamie changed hands on the door and realised I was still there. "What you lookin' at, eh, farm rat! Go on, bail. Take yer feckin' horse and get out the way." He said to Henry, "This mingin' door keeps falling shut. Cover your head – I'm goin' to kick the windscreen in."

He let the door drop with a bang. Henry beat urgently on the inside of the roof and, behind me, Zilla snorted her alarm.

Jamie heaved the door open again in a fury. Henry said something and he replied, "Yeah, yeah, all right." Perhaps Humphrey was coming round.

A bitch voice in my head was saying: *You want Humphrey out and gone. Remember he told you, "I'll scrap the rules and we'll all be quits." Well, look at him now. He can only get out with your help. Twist the knife now and you'll be quits all right.*

I unclipped Zilla's rope. Drew the reins over her head to keep her ground-tied. Climbed down, with the rope, into the Pot and up the hot metal of the Defender's bull-bar, and onto the muddied paintwork of the front wing.

Jamie snapped, "Bugger off."

He had grey eyes, narrowed with concentration, and he smelled of bog-mould and sweat. I thought if he hadn't been propping the door open he'd have hit me. He had his own ways of dealing with everything. He wasn't going to pay any attention to me unless I made him.

I tossed the trigger-clip end of the rope so the weight swung it through the windowframe. Caught it. Levelled the two ends.

"What the fuck are you doing?"

"Watch me," I said. I hauled back on the rope so the weight of the door lifted off his hands. It was heavier than I expected, but not unmanageable. "I'll hold it here. You can both lift him."

I could see Humphrey was definitely conscious now but Jamie didn't move. "Yeah, right, like I'm going to take orders from a farm rat."

"Well, I could just leave you to it, but then I'd have to call 999."

Humphrey mumbled something and Henry answered him.

Jamie moved in a burst of frustrated energy, stepped across to the other side of the frame, knelt and reached down inside the open doorway. It took some struggling and rough handling before he and Henry got Humphrey out of his seat. Humphrey could barely hold himself upright so they perched him, groaning, on the rear panel of the Defender. As soon as they had lifted his legs out of the doorway, I unlooped the rope and let the door fall shut.

Looking down at him I said, "There now. We're quits."

He cradled his left elbow with his right hand and muttered something I couldn't catch. The wet, red patch was spreading down his shoulder. An inch or two lower, I thought, and he would never have bothered me again.

"Take him to hospital," I said. "Try A & E at Lancaster."

Henry said, "Aright then, who shot him?"

"How should I know?" But it occurred to me for the first time that whoever it was might still be around, and the idea made my shoulderblades itch.

"You know, all right," Jamie said. "You're lucky we haven't got time to get it out of you."

I thought it might be time to leave. I climbed down and caught Zilla, and mounted and let her drift in a circle while I found my offside stirrup and scanned the fell and our fields for anyone moving who shouldn't be. I couldn't see anyone. I turned Zilla back towards Doctor's Pot, and the Defender, where Jamie was leaning Charles Humphrey against Henry.

"Hang onto him. I'm gonna back the car up."

He jumped down and scrambled out through the bracken to get the Kia.

I sat waiting on Zilla, feeling as though I was escorting difficult guests to the door. The bitch voice suggested I could wave them off. *Goodbye! It's been a great afternoon. Next time I'll ask the police to join us.* But caution won over sarcasm.

The Kia reversed up to the edge of Doctor's Pot. Jamie helped Henry to lift my enemy down and into the back seat, then he gunned the engine and drove away.

Chapter 34.

I rode quietly back to the farm.

Madoc, Robbie and Beth, Andy Wharton and Hazel, were standing chatting in yard, with Hazel's tatty Astra parked next to Robbie's Peugeot. There was a strong smell of newly cut grass. I rode over and dismounted next to them, and Madoc looked curiously at me.

"What's up?"

I said, "There's a four-by-four on its side in Doctor's Pot."

"Good heavens," said Hazel. Andy gave an unsympathetic grunt.

"I thought I heard something coming down the track just now," said Robbie. "I assumed it was the gamekeeper, I don't know why."

"It wasn't the gamekeeper," I said.

"I bloody hate off-roaders," said Andy. "Hate them. Riving and ripping up tracks wherever they go. And he must have been an idiot to drive into the Pot."

Hazel patted his arm. "Madoc can charge him plenty to get towed out."

Madoc waited a moment, working out the possible implications, before he asked, "Do they need any help?"

I said, "There's nobody actually in it."

"Whoever it was, he'd no business to be up there," Andy said. "I've no sympathy."

I agreed. "He's gone now, anyway." Madoc and I exchanged a look.

After a moment he said, "Andy's come to tell us about the dog."

Hazel said, "Aye, it's a shame. It looks like it was just one of those things, though. And no-one's to blame really, unless it's our Daniel."

I felt as though I was slightly drunk and being tossed in a blanket. Andy must have seen that, because he said to Hazel, "For heaven's sake, woman. Start at the beginning."

"All right, all right! Now. You remember Andy and me were going for tea and cakes at the chocolate factory?" She glanced at Beth and added, "With your Mam and Dad? Well Ted Parker –"

Beth chipped-in, "Our next door neighbour."

"Yes – well we were just going in when Ted came over to say he'd seen a dog hit by a car on our road yesterday. He said he didn't have time to come all the way up to the farm but he'd picked it up and left it at your gate, because he thought it was yours, so would we tell you? I'm ever so sorry." Her kind, plain face was scrunched up with worry.

Kip's death had been driven out of my mind by the shooting on the fell and the uneasy thought that someone might be out there with a gun. I struggled to respond to what Hazel was telling me.

"It's not your fault."

"Well it *is* our fault in a way, because it was our Danny that let our bitch get out. You can't blame the dogs for doing what comes naturally. The two of them were running about loose, and Ted says the car in front just didn't stop in time."

"You mean it didn't stop at all," said Robbie.

"Aye. Visitors." Andy was pronouncing sentence again. "I asked Ted if he took the car's number, but he said not, because with all the traffic going to the gipsy Fair and the Farmers' Market, he thought he'd better try and catch our bitch afore something else happened. Of course, she give him the slip and come home, so we didn't know owt about it until Ted come up and telt us."

It was all too much to take in. I managed to say, "Poor Kip."

"Well, look on the bright side, at least he died happy! And if our bitch holds, you can have a pup out of her. I said as much t'other day, didn't I? You can have your pick."

"Yes. Er – thank you."

"You're very welcome. Any road, you know what's what now, so we'll be off." He said to Robbie and Madoc, "You tell us if you're going to need a dog in the next few weeks – me and Danny'll be glad to come and give you a hand."

That broke up our conversation. Andy and Hazel got into their van, waved and drove away, and I led Zilla towards her tying place. Robbie and Beth and Madoc came across the yard with me.

"So what's all this about Doctor's Pot?" asked Robbie. "What's been going on?"

I put up the stirrups, ready to unsaddle. "Well. That four-by-four is Charles Humphrey's Defender."

"Ah," said Madoc. "I thought you were being a bit cagey about it."

Robbie asked, "The man who owns King Coel?"

Madoc didn't correct him. "The man Gwylim owes a lot of money."

Robbie made the connection, and laughed unsympathetically. "Well! In that case, I'm with Andy. It couldn't have happened to a nicer bloke."

At one level, I agreed with him, but there were other worries. "Have you seen anything odd this afternoon? Any of you?"

Madoc shook his head.

Beth said, "We were in the garden burying the dog. And Robbie decided to mow the grass."

"So you didn't hear anything?"

"Like what?" asked Madoc.

"Like a rifle shot?"

He met my look and raised his eyebrows. "Are you saying someone's been shot?"

I unbuckled Zilla's girth and let it swing. Madoc caught the loose end with his crutch and lifted it across the saddle for me and I slid the saddle off Zilla's damp back. "It's Charles Humphrey. He's only wounded, but that's probably how the car ended up in Doctor's Pot."

"Well now," said Madoc, with a pleased expression. "I wonder who else was out on the fell?"

"I saw his two henchmen – the one with tattoos, and the one with the leather jacket."

"What were they doing up there?"

"Racing across country for a bet." I put the saddle on a feed bin in the tackroom and came back to remove Zilla's bridle. She gave me the usual peremptory push with her nose and started rubbing her sweaty face on me "Give over, mare... I don't think they realised what had happened till they found the car. They took him off to hospital – no, I don't know where, and I don't care. As far as I'm concerned they can bandage him with strips of his own shirt."

"If I ever see the bastard again he'll regret it." Madoc looked at me and I nodded fiercely.

Beth said, "I didn't like him either, and I only met him the once."

"Oh yes, at the show." I remembered she was training to be a nurse. "If they take him to hospital will the staff have to call the police? I mean, because he's been shot?"

Beth said, "His wound would be their first concern, but then if he says he doesn't want the police involved..." She paused, and Madoc completed the sentence.

"Then it won't happen."

She said at once, "Actually that's when it gets complicated – between medical ethics and the law. The doctor will have to report that it's a gunshot wound, and if he thinks other people might be at risk too, he can override the patient's wishes. Still, I'm glad it's not me having to make the call."

"The thing that's really worrying me," I said, "is that Humphrey must have been shot actually from here – somewhere on the farm. Are you sure you didn't hear anything?"

Robbie said, "Not a chance, with that old mower running. And being at the other side of the house, you can't see the fell at all."

Madoc said thoughtfully, "Where's our Jack, does anybody know?"

We all looked at one another. I said, "I told him to go up to High Field and do some work with the three-year-olds."

"Did he actually do it?" asked Robbie.

"He must have done. That's why he brought Zilla down and put her in the stable," said Madoc. "She was getting in the way. But did he go out again when he'd finished – say, to see Wilse in the village?"

"I don't think so," I said. "Wilse's mum and dad were taking him shopping. Jack wanted him to come here but I told him I couldn't do with both of them underfoot – not with Gwylim coming."

"Then where the hell is he?"

"Well – he wasn't in High Field when I was coming home – I could see the two geldings and he wasn't with them. So I don't know where he's got to. You don't suppose..." I couldn't finish the sentence.

"I'll take the quad round the fields," said Robbie, "and see if I can find him. Coming, Beth?"

She followed him into the house. I said to Madoc, "If there's someone wandering about round here with a rifle..."

"It's not 'someone' though, is it? We hardly need two guesses who it might be. If it's Gwylim I can't believe he would have hung around. He'd be too scared Humphrey's bully boys might catch him."

"But it's not like Jack to go missing."

Robbie came across the yard, walking with purpose, and called to Madoc.

"The gun cabinet's unlocked!"

"Is the rifle there?"

"No, that's what I'm telling you!"

"What about the ammunition?"

"The open box has gone – it had half a dozen in it. I'll have something to say to Jack when I lay hands on him! Silly little git."

Madoc let out a dissatisfied breath. "I thought I told you to be careful about the combination."

"You're the one who's been letting Jack use the gun!"

"Let's find him before we jump to any conclusions. If he *has* got the rifle, unload it."

I said, "Go easy on him."

"Aye right," said Robbie. "We'll see about that." He went back through the house.

I was struggling with several worries at once now. Jack missing, the rifle missing, Humphrey shot, perhaps by Gwylim. I had helped to get Humphrey out of the Defender for all the wrong reasons. But wouldn't any passing walker, any decent person, have done the same? I had no idea where Jamie and Henry had gone with him, or what they were going to do.

"I should have called 999 as soon as I found Humphrey in the car. But his henchmen turned up."

"It can't have been Jack who potted him," said Madoc. "He couldn't hit anything moving, not even something as big as a Land Rover."

"And where is he? It's not like him to go missing."

We heard the quad bike rumble away across the field, the trailer rattling behind. Zilla pushed me with her nose and I fended her off.

"I'd better turn this mare out," I said. "You don't need to come with us."

Madoc pulled a face. "I can't just hang about. This cast's driving me daft."

He hitched along with determination beside me as I led her up towards High Field. Robbie and Beth on the quad bike were buzzing up the gallop towards the Scar.

I said, "They might take your cast off when you see the consultant next week. Give you a moon-boot, maybe, one of those things with velcro straps."

"Can't happen soon enough." He broke off and said, "What's going on up there?"

The bike was still running, but stationary, on the cart track in Thorny Bank. Beth and Robbie had got down and were hurrying forward.

My phone rang, and I answered it.

"We've found him," said Robbie's voice. Madoc glanced towards me, then back to the distant bike where Robbie and Beth had got Jack to his feet and were helping him into the trailer. "I've got the rifle. Beth's going to sit with him while we come down." He rang off before I could reply.

Chapter 35.

By the time Madoc and I got back to the house, the quad bike and trailer were parked in the yard and Beth was in the kitchen pouring hot water from the Rayburn kettle into one of my mixing bowls. Beyond her Jack was seated at the kitchen table with the washing up bowl in front of him. I went over to look at him.

"Now, love, what have you been doing to yourself?" His face was very white against his red hair and there was a cut on his cheek.

Madoc asked, half-joking, "You haven't shot yourself, have you?"

"Serve him right if he had," said Robbie.

"Let him speak for himself. But you didn't ask if you could take the gun, did you?"

"I thought you wouldn't let me, not on my own."

"No, because you're an utter pillock," said Robbie.

Beth ignored him and asked me for cotton wool and disinfectant to clean Jack's face. I patted his shoulder and went through to the larder, past the gun cabinet with the door still ajar. The rifle was back in there. Whose fingerprints were on it? Jack's, Robbie's, Beth's – and Gwylim's? I thought he'd probably shot Charles Humphrey, but I couldn't be sure – after all, yesterday I'd been certain that

Humphrey was to blame for Kip's death, and I'd been wrong. I shut the door. My hands felt unsteady.

I collected cotton wool, sticking plasters and antiseptic and a pair of latex gloves for Beth. In the kitchen I shooed Madoc and Robbie back so I could take a better look at Jack's face. His right cheek was dirty, there was a cut across his left cheekbone and his eye was half-closed. Then Beth came over with the bowl and a steamy smell of phenol.

"Sit quiet," I said to him. "Here's the expert. Have you hurt yourself anywhere else?"

He was silent for a moment, as though running in internal scan, while she deftly cleaned his face. "I've scraped my elbow." He lifted his right arm and waited for Beth to attend to it.

"That doesn't look too serious," I said. "I'm more bothered about your head. What d'you think, Beth?"

She gave him a dry piece of cotton wool to hold over the cut, and finally replaced that with a large plaster. "There you go. I don't think it needs stitches, but you're going to have a cracker of a black eye. Your mates will be very impressed."

He managed to chuckle.

"How are you feeling now?" I asked, and Beth added with greater precision, "Have you got a headache?"

"No. My face is sore."

"Sleepy?" she asked, watching him intently.

"No."

"Good." She stripped off the gloves and said to me, "He probably doesn't need to go to A & E, but if he starts feeling sick, or dizzy, or passing out, whizz him down there *toot sweet*."

I nodded. "D'you want a cup of tea?" I asked him.

"Yeah..." Slowly. "Okay."

"Anybody else? I know I bloody need one. Madoc?"

He sat at the table opposite Jack and stowed his crutches. "Yes. Please."

"Beth?"

She was tipping disinfectant down the sink. "No thanks." She squeezed out the cotton wool and dropped it into the coal scuttle.

"Robbie?"

"No," he said impatiently. "Look, are we agreed that he's not broken? Can we stop wasting time on him now?"

"Oh, do shut up," I said.

Beth took Robbie's arm and steered him towards the back door. "Come on," she said over his protests. "I've had enough drama for one day, and so have you." They walked away down the yard.

Madoc sat watching Jack. "You know we've got to ask. What exactly were you doing out there this afternoon?"

"Nothing much." He kept his head down. It might have been shock, or guilt about taking the rifle, or a combination of the two. I couldn't tell. "I had to catch Zilla, cos she kept pushing me and Mam wanted me to work with Rocky."

"But that didn't take all afternoon, now did it?" Jack moved his head slightly without looking up. I brought the mugs of tea, and Madoc asked, "What did you want with the rifle?"

Jack lifted a shoulder. "I dunno. I just fancied doing some target practice, on my own."

"You didn't fire at anything in particular?"

"I didn't fire at anything at all. Why?"

"Because somebody's been badly hurt," said Madoc, "and we need to tell the police."

This time Jack's fingers fidgeted on the washing up bowl. "I don't think I saw anything."

Madoc glanced at me. This was unusually evasive language from Jack. "Are you sure? What can you remember? Robbie coming to get you?"

Jack looked up this time, evidently relieved at the change of approach. "Yeah. I heard the quad bike, and then Robbie was there with Beth."

"All right. Now, let's get to the bottom of this," said Madoc, and Jack squirmed. "Come on. You went up to Thorny Bank? To the usual place?"

"Yeah."

"What else?"

"Well..." He paused and turned his head away. "Uncle Gwylim turned up."

Madoc and I looked at each other, and he went on, "I was loading the rifle, and he hit me."

I inspected the side of his bruised and plastered face and I began to say, "Poor lamb." But Madoc had no time to spare for sympathy.

"I thought he'd left. Do you have any idea why he hit you?" Jack didn't answer, but Madoc pointed out, "This is serious stuff and we can't ignore it. You realise, you might have to explain all this to a policeman?" Jack lifted his head and stared at him. "Right. Let's go through it again, carefully. What were you doing? Where were you standing?"

"Where we always stand, facing up the bank towards the old red bucket."

"Go on. Where was Gwylim?"

"He came from Underscar."

"In his car? Or walking?"

"I didn't see the car. He might have walked up the track. But I didn't see him till he was right next to me. I was feeding the bullets in, and he was just *there*. I said Hello and he grabbed the gun by the barrel and pulled it out of my hands."

It was the utter astonishment on Jack's face that convinced me he was telling the truth. He swallowed before he spoke again. "He had a rifle too. A big one with a scope. Then he hit me."

"With the rifle!" Madoc exclaimed.

"No, he backhanded me." Jack moved his hand towards the plaster on his cheek, but thought better of touching it.

"Thank goodness for that," I said. The idea of someone of Gwylim's weight attacking a twelve-year-old boy made my guts clench. Not to mention the terrifying potential of two guns.

"I fell down and I think I hit my face on something." Jack went silent again and I made a *wait now* gesture to Madoc. This wasn't a defiant silence; it was Jack running back in his mind through what had happened.

"Were you out completely?" I asked, putting my hand on his arm.

At last he said, "I don't know. Maybe for a little bit but how can you tell? It's like when you ask us at breakfast whether we slept well – if we've been asleep we don't have any idea, do we? I did stay lying down, 'cos I thought if I got up he might hit me again. He hadn't gone very far, he was over by the wall where the thorn bushes are. He'd got both the rifles."

I asked, "Why on earth?"

"He wouldn't leave Jack with a gun and turn his back on him," said Madoc. "Would you?"

"Ah."

"He was watching something on the fell," said Jack. "Was there a car out there? I thought I heard an engine."

"Yes."

"He shot at it."

"Our rifle? Or his?"

"I'm not sure. His, I think. Yes, because I saw the scope. He fired twice, and there was a crashing noise and he kind of jumped, like a football manager when there's a goal. He picked up our rifle and started to run back towards the gate so I lay down quick and pretended I was still out." He paused, fidgeting with the bowl in front of him. "I was afraid if he saw I was awake he might hit me again."

I would have put my arm around him, but I sensed he didn't want physical comfort so much as to know that we believed him. Thoughts were falling into place inside my head like dominoes toppling, each one setting off a further reaction. When Gwylim had left this kitchen, with our money in his pocket, he'd very likely known Humphrey would be off-roading on the fell, and been able to predict where and when. After he left our house it would have been simple to drive round by Underscar, take the car up the track as far as the limekiln gate, and walk across Thorny Bank to the fell wall. He'd have had a clear view of the Roman road, and of Humphrey driving the four-by-four down it. I remembered Gwylim's drab shirt, and the self-effacing green car. Had they been chosen as camouflage? If so, he'd been plotting this for some time – only he couldn't have expected to find our Jack standing between him and his target, with a rifle in his hands.

What made me angry was the fact that he must have seen Jack long before Jack saw him. He must have had plenty of time to think about changing his plans. He had an envelope full of our money. If he'd spoken to Jack, not hit him, just gone away, he could have given the money to Charles Humphrey. He could have abandoned every single thing he'd planned. But he hadn't. He'd swiped Jack out of his path and gone straight on.

Jack said, "Well, he came back, running, so I lay down quick and shut my eyes. He stopped next to me and I heard him say, 'Oh fuck it' – sorry Mam, but he did – then he dropped the rifle on the grass and off he went."

I let out a breath of relief. "That must have been a nasty moment."

"I was scared." Jack looked uncertainly at me, and then at Madoc. "Who was he shooting at?"

"Charles Humphrey," I said, "driving his Defender. The man who sent us King Coel."

"But why?"

"It's about money," said Madoc. He glanced at me.

"Mostly," I added. "It's complicated."

Jack asked, "Are you going to tell the police?"

"No," I said.

Madoc's eyebrows went up. "Oh yes we are."

Chapter 36.

"I'm not telling them anything about Charles Humphrey."

Madoc looked at me thoughtfully, and said, "That would be risky."

"Will they think I shot him?" asked Jack. He was beginning to shiver.

"I'm quite sure you didn't," I said, "and the police won't think you did, of course they won't."

"The bullets alone will rule you out," Madoc said. "Gwylim's always preferred a heavier rifle, with a longer range and better accuracy. Most likely a .243. But when they find out you were using the rifle by yourself, they'll confiscate it."

"So we don't tell them any more than we have to," I said, "about any of it."

Jack sat very quiet and Madoc's mouth tightened.

"We can't have my brother thinking he can use a rifle to sort out his life. We've got to report what happened, so we at least start out on the right side of the law. And that means you, Mouse."

"Why me!"

"Because you've been in the thick of it and I haven't."

Jack yawned; the after-effect of shock, I supposed.

"Go and have a lie-down on the sofa, love."

Madoc said, "I'll keep an eye on him. You just pick up the phone to the police."

"I don't want to be hustled by a stranger I can't see."

"Write everything down before you start, then."

We followed Jack into the front room. Madoc sat in the recliner, as though his presence would hold me to the task. I sat at the desk in the corner trying to make notes, while Jack moved restlessly on the sofa. Whenever I lifted my head from writing Madoc turned to look at me and I had to go on. I started with the times, the places, the checkable facts, and what Jack had said, but the notes were a mess and my handwriting was worse. I knew my prints would be all over the Defender and I'd have to explain them. I was creating a spider-web that didn't entirely make sense. What worried me was the spider that lay beyond the notes.

There was a clatter outside the back door and I jumped.

"What was that?"

Madoc suggested, "Someone knocked over a bucket?"

"But we're the only ones home." We looked at each other, listening, thinking. "Gwylim?" I whispered.

"It better hadn't be." Madoc got up, taking his crutch almost as an afterthought.

I followed, tense, as he made his way into the kitchen. Then quite suddenly he relaxed.

"Panic over."

A broom had fallen across the doorway and lay at an angle on the mop bucket, and just beyond it in the passageway the cat crouched, intent on a young bird, brown with a spotted cream breast. Madoc picked up the broom and restored it to its place. The chick fluttered onto the boot-rack and Gracie inched closer with her whiskers bushed for the kill.

"It's one of the mistle thrush babies," I said.

I went into the passageway to forestall the cat. The parent birds were chirring furiously from somewhere up the yard and the chick saw me as another threat and flapped away as far as the windowsill. Having got that far he sat panting, too overwhelmed to struggle any further. I gently closed both hands on him. He was dumpy and solid and hot, like a little feathery beefburger, and as I picked him up his beak opened to a yellow gape and let out a cry like two stones being hit together. I carried him out past the cat and up into the garden.

The grass that Robbie had mown was already crisping in the sunshine, its warm scent mixed with honeysuckle and elder. Between their intoxicating assault and the emotions of the past couple of hours, I was almost as confused as the bird. I freed him to scramble into the hedge, and when Gracie jumped onto the wall beside me I caught her up, carried her back into the kitchen and shut the door.

Madoc was in the front room when I walked in with the cat in my arms.

"Have you put the bird somewhere she can't reach?"

"For the moment," I said. "Shut the door, or she'll try again."

He shut it. I put the cat down and she began to wash, as though I had offended her. Jack lay asleep with a cushion tucked under his head. His hands were grubby, as always. It was strange to see them slack and devoid of mischief.

"Do you think Gwylim might come back?" I asked. "Jack's a witness to what he did."

"He may believe he knocked him out."

"But he must know Jack saw him with the rifle. What if he does turn up? We haven't got Kip now to warn us anyone's about."

"You can't sit here dithering at the least noise. We tell the police – I don't think this qualifies for a 999 call any more, but you could try 101."

I pulled a face. "There was an article in the paper about calling 101. It sounded like you can spend ten minutes on hold – and if the police are still dealing with the Fair I bet it will be a lot longer!"

"Well I do think it's better for you to report it than me. They must have a web site, a form or something. Use that, if you really don't like the idea of phoning. And right now I'm going to take a little walk round, to check there's no-one lurking who shouldn't be."

I was appalled at the thought of him setting off on guard duty on crutches. What if he came face to face with Gwylim, or Charles Humphrey's henchmen? I said, "Take the rifle with you."

He was still for a moment, looking at me. "That isn't the answer." He picked up the other crutch, and went out.

I stood there irresolute. *What if, what if, what if.*

Jack was still asleep, a slight frown on his face. His colour was back to normal, apart from the bruising that loomed dark under his skin. I made another cup of tea to put off having to spend ten minutes with the phone. I would probably get so nervous on hold to 101 that I'd be a babbling wreck. I took my tea into the front room and sat down at the computer.

I found the web site for Cumbria Constabulary, and a long, pale blue form headed Contact Us: Report a Crime.

It said: It may take up to 12 hours for us to respond. Call 999 if the crime is being committed now, if the offender is nearby, or if you or other people are injured or in danger.

Well, I thought, Madoc was right: the crime wasn't being committed. It was over and done with. The offenders – Gwylim and Jamie and Henry and Charles Humphrey – were not nearby; they were all miles away, probably out of the county. I flexed my fingers and began to type in the form.

It asked: Did the incident happen outside the Cumbria area? That seemed a convoluted way of asking, but I supposed it was computer logic, and the answer was easy enough. I left it as No.

Is the incident in progress? No.

Does someone require medical attention or is someone in possible danger at the moment?

I tried the *Yes* option, and got a pop-up message that said tersely, "Call 999." I thought about it. Jack was safe enough. The worst casualty, Charles Humphrey, had been taken away nearly two hours ago so if he wasn't receiving medical attention by now, he hadn't trained his watchdogs properly – and frankly, I didn't care if he was in danger. I returned the form answer to *No*.

I answered *No* to further questions about fraud, inappropriate web content, and noise from licensed premises. That brought me to "Incident Details."

Violence. It was part of the same option as Sexual Assault. The two terms, bracketed so starkly together, made me wonder for a moment whether the things in my spider notes had actually happened; still more the things I had refused to write down. I would have been very comforted at that point by a face to face meeting with a detective, preferably television-style, in plain clothes with the requisite young assistant. The ideal types always seemed to turn up without having to be called, knowing the background to what had happened so they didn't need explanations, and they asked clever questions without ever taking any notes of the replies. The best I would get in the real world was probably a uniformed constable with a radio clipped to his shoulder. On the whole I supposed it was more effective to fill in the form.

I began to type from my notes, hitting the keys too hard and having to backspace mistakes. Every so often I scrolled up and down the form looking for other, easier things to fill in, like text boxes asking for the time and date and the exact place where "the incident" had happened. There were boxes for my name, gender and date of birth (why?), our telephone number and an email address for the police to get in touch with us. I filled them all in, putting off "Incident Details" until there were no other excuses.

Should I explain what business Gwylim had come to discuss? I might have to, eventually, when someone came to ask detailed questions, but was it relevant right now? Probably not. I typed that he'd been to see us, and added the time he'd arrived. I wrote that although he told us he was going on to a meeting he had actually doubled back to the farm, and Jack had met him in the fields carrying a rifle.

I paused there and got up to look over the back of the sofa. Jack had shifted his position, but the bruise on his face was still uppermost. I sat down again at the computer and reported that Gwylim had knocked Jack down and taken at least one shot over the boundary wall.

And I'd been miles away, galloping Zilla on that wild hyper-drive across the fell.

It was an uncomfortable thought, but I supposed it didn't matter to anyone but me. For this report I only needed a boring, ordinary phrase. *I was out riding.* That should do.

I struggled to describe how I'd found Charles Humphrey wounded. The heavy pub-landlord torso. The bloodstained shirt. I stared at my spider-web, and back at the screen. If I wrote too much about him, would I end up telling the police that he'd propositioned me? How he'd held our debt over us to blackmail me? Of course, that would be – what was the phrase – corroborative evidence that Gwylim owed him money. But there had been no witnesses to anything Humphrey had said to me. Despite his hands on my body at the races, and the moments when he'd offered me money, in public he'd been very careful never to step over the mark; he'd never made any suggestive remarks in front of anyone who might take my side, and all the pressure he'd brought to bear on me had been through the situation we found ourselves in, all in private, just my word against his. Thank God Madoc had trusted me. And the text messages on my phone would be evidence – if it ever came to that. But would they think I was complicit in the shooting on that account?

It was all too complicated. I wrote: *I found a man shot and wounded in his car.* I said that we all knew him as Charles Humphrey. I would have added his address, but I didn't seem to have it, not even a postcode for his booking of our holiday cottage. I did remember 'Zanzibar', the night-club name he'd given to his horses, and I put in what I could remember of the Defender's number plate; the police would be able to check that for themselves.

I remembered how I had stood on the wing of the Defender, high on the adrenalin of my gallop, exulting as Humphrey was hauled out from under my feet. But I hesitated to put that into the serene blue of the on-screen form. I wrote instead that two of Humphrey's employees had taken him to hospital. I explained that Gwylim owed him money and we thought Gwylim had shot him because of that.

I read through what I had typed and added the last address we had for Gwylim, which was the house he and Linda had shared. I had no idea of the registration on his little green car.

It seemed a bald and inadequate report of the day's events. But if I were to start putting in more details I wouldn't know where to stop, and attempted murder and assault were surely hair-raising enough on their own without adding sexual harassment and blackmail.

I sent the form. A standard email response came back as confirmation. Almost immediately the kitchen phone rang and I hurried to answer it. Surely that couldn't be the police, not so quickly?

"Hi, Mam," said Cerys's voice, and relief washed over me like a wave. "We're at the chip-shop. D'you want us to get tea?"

"I love you. Fish and chips all round, please."

"How many shall I get? Is Robbie home or has he gone to Beth's?"

"They're still here, I think." I counted: Madoc, Robbie, Beth. I knew Jack shouldn't eat too much after being knocked out – it was part of the caution I'd absorbed when Madoc was still racing – so I thought he and I had better share a portion. "Four, on top of whatever you're getting."

"Okay. The chip-shop's mad busy but the fryers are going like the clappers, so we shouldn't be too long."

"I'll put some plates to warm," I said.

I had just collected an armful of crockery when the phone rang again.

"Madoc?" said a female voice. Not Cerys this time. "Madoc, is that you? It's Linda."

Gwylim's wife hadn't phoned us since Christmas so after today's events her call seemed too much of a coincidence. "This is Siân," I said. "What's up?"

"I'm tearing my hair out here," she snapped. "Has Gwylim been to see you today?"

"Ohh yes," I said, and carefully balanced the plates on the Rayburn lid. "He was here all right."

"Any idea where he went after that?"

"No. We didn't exactly part on friendly terms."

She made an exasperated noise. "He was supposed to be taking the girls to the teatime film at Showcase – it's Emma's birthday.

They've been dressed up and ready to go for ages and he hasn't arrived. I would have taken them, but this was supposed to be his treat, so we waited and waited, and it'll be too late now, the film will have started. It's the first time they'll have seen him since we moved, and they're so disappointed. I could strangle him."

I said, "Me too."

She was too annoyed to hear the nuances in my tone. "I've phoned everybody else I could think of, but nobody's seen him. Or nobody's willing to tell me. And now Emma's upset in case it's something *she's* done... I'm fed up to the back teeth with him."

I said, "You and me both," and bent down to open the warming oven for the plates.

"He'll say he hasn't forgotten. He'd never admit it. But he'll have found something more interesting to do, and that's the same thing. He'll live to regret it, you know. Letting her down like this. Still, that's him all over. All talk and no walk."

I shut the oven door, thinking how intently Gwylim must have been planning his ambush of Charles Humphrey. "Did he tell you why he was coming to see us?"

"Oh, no! He's never told me anything if he can help it. But he's got a mobile, so he could have let me know you'd held him up!"

"Linda, we didn't 'hold him up', not at all. He came to see Madoc for some money, and the moment he got it, he was off!"

"Then where's he gone to?"

"Heavens above, Linda, how am I supposed to know?"

It only silenced her for a moment. "He came to you for money? What for?"

I thought, *You nosy cow!* But it occurred to me that she might not know what she was asking. I began to pick cutlery out of the dishwasher. "Sorry. I didn't catch that."

She said, "Why was he asking you for money? I thought I knew all his bank accounts. What's going on?"

"Well... he gave Madoc a loan last year to convert the holiday cottage, and he wanted it all back. Didn't you know?"

"No. I remember he lent Madoc something and he was pretty pleased with himself. Some kind of family score, was it?" She made a thoughtful noise. "Awkward for us if he's running short now. How much did he lend Madoc? Did you pay it all back?"

I began laying the knives and forks on the table. "I don't think that's any of your business."

"Well, pardon me, but with the rent for this flat, we're hand to mouth here! Until the divorce settlement goes through." I could hear one of her children trying to attract her attention, in a bored, persistent voice. "I don't care about *him* any more, but – well, you know – the money matters, for the children's sake."

Mine too, I thought. "Linda. Listen to me. Did you know Gwylim's got a gun?"

"A gun? Oh, you mean his rifle? He's always had one, since before were married."

I said, as clearly as I could, "Did you know he had it with him, today?"

"Really?" She sounded genuinely puzzled. "Whatever for?"

"He knocked our Jack down, and then he shot somebody."

"What!"

"Jack's got the bruises to prove it. Honestly, Linda, if he hasn't come for the girls today I think you've had a lucky escape. I wouldn't let them go anywhere with him."

"That doesn't sound right," she said, doubtfully. "He's never raised a finger to them."

"He owes a lot of money to some very unpleasant people and he's upset them badly today. They'll be looking for him. What if they catch up with him when he's got the children?"

She drew an audible breath, and I could hear the girls bickering in the background.

She said, "Emma – Holly – hush. We'll have pizza and ice cream – " The connection went quiet and I pictured her silencing the handset while she decided what to say to them. After a minute her voice came back. "Now go and choose a DVD, okay? Siân – do you really think he's in trouble?"

"He's got bigger problems than your divorce."

She made a small noise as though I'd hurt her.

"I'm sorry," I said. "I should have called to warn you, but we're still a bit shaken up. It only happened this afternoon."

"No. I mean yes. But I can't let him visit us now, can I!"

"No." If Madoc's guess was right, Gwylim wouldn't turn up on her doorstep, or ours, any time soon, but if he did, who knew what might happen? "We've told the police – they haven't come back to us yet, but you realise they might want to see you."

"Oh! I don't care about that. They can come any time."

I heard a car outside in the yard, and doors banging. Cerys entered the kitchen with a carrier bag of paper parcels that trailed a steamy smell of fish, chips and vinegar. She was followed by Daniel, Robbie and Beth, and Madoc who was calling them to wash and sit down.

"I've got to go, Linda, sorry. The kids have come home."

Jack appeared from the front room with a face like a thundery sunrise and there was a gasp and then a babble of exclamations on all sides. Teatime was obviously going to be a re-run of filling-in the police form, only this time with audience participation.

I said to Linda, "Tell Emma, Happy Birthday – I know I didn't send a card, but – "

"Everything's been shit recently. Yeah, tell me about it."

"I'm sorry. Take care of those girls."

Chapter 37.

Our quartet of holiday visitors left, and Cerys came to help me do the changeover in the cottage.

"Did they ever get to the Horse Fair? " she asked, as we stripped the double bed. "I wonder what they made of it."

"I don't know," I said. "They asked if it was always 'like that'. Well, I only know what I've heard, so I just said, Probably. But they wrote in the house book that they'll 'definitely come again' – so it can't have been that bad."

We pulled the pillows out of their pillowcases and I drew off the bottom sheet and smoothed the mattress cover, while Cerys began to unfasten the poppers on the duvet.

"We went up to the Hill last night," she said. "Danny thought I might like the music. But it was rammed with people and we didn't know where the good singers and players were meeting. I suppose you have to be friends with them, or someone who knows them. Nobody we asked had any idea where to find them. And a lot of the visitors were rat-arsed anyway. I didn't feel very safe, so we came away."

"I know what you mean." I bundled the discarded bedding and we began to fit the fresh set. Clean pillowcases. A new bottom sheet. Toning, soothing shades of grey and blue, matching the painted walls – in complete contrast to our own scatty, uncoordinated household. "Where else did you go, then? You were late back."

Cerys was fastening the poppers on the clean duvet, and she kept her eyes on the work and didn't answer. Her face was pink.

"Aha," I said. "I see."

"You don't, Mam. Not always." She lifted the duvet and shook it into place. "Are you going to take that lot to wash? I'll start hoovering."

I took the hint, the towels and the bedding, and left her to it.

Across the yard, Madoc was limping determinedly up and down the level concrete with just one crutch, carrying the other in the unoccupied hand as though for insurance.

"Is Jack indoors?" I asked.

"No, but he's all right." Madoc eased up, as if simply walking was harder work than he would admit.

"Is he? Where?"

"In the garden."

I dumped the bedding in the kitchen and went through the house to the front room to look. Jack was up the top of the garden near the grave that Robbie had dug that afternoon. He was awake and wandering to and fro but he didn't look 'all right' to me; he was twisting something between his hands that might have been Kip's lead. I went back to put the sheets in the washing machine before I looked again.

He was still pacing.

I called, "D'you want a biscuit?" Silly question, really, but anything would do to get his attention.

When he didn't answer I went up the garden myself and put a hand on his shoulder. I almost said, "Don't..." but Cerys's brush-off still sounded in my head and I stopped, remembering how often the times when I grieved over loss and hurt had been cut short by someone comforting me, saying, 'don't cry,' 'be strong' or 'never mind' – telling me to stop doing whatever might relieve my feelings. I had hated such selfishness, and now here I was, almost doing it to Jack.

So instead I said, "How's your cheek now?"

"Sore."

"Let me see."

He shut his eyes and turned his face to the sun. There were tear-tracks across the black bruises but I didn't think it was the injury that had made him cry.

"Is it better than it was?"

"Sort of. I used some of that cream you gave me."

"Good. You know you can stop off school tomorrow, if you still don't feel well."

He coiled the dog's lead round his hand while he thought. "No, I'll be all right." And with a flash of Madoc's self-deprecating humour he glanced at me and added, "Can't wait to see Wilse's face when he clocks this lot."

"Then I'd better write a note for you to show your teachers," I joked, "or they'll be calling Social Services to take you into care."

"I think Social Services are a myth," he said, making a fist around the coiled leather. "Like God and heaven and stuff."

"Dear me," I said. "I know it's Sunday but that's a big thought for you, isn't it?"

He was quiet for a minute. His hands were still. Then he muttered, "Wilse says animals don't go to heaven."

"Does he," I said, and drew a deep breath while I considered. "Well, if it's any help – I don't think any of us do. That's just my opinion, mind. But if heaven's a myth then we can't go there, can we? Animals won't go there and neither do we. I think we just go back to being part of the earth. All of us together."

"Then why do we bother with funerals and things? I mean, Robbie's going to church tomorrow for Beth's Gran's funeral, and he never goes to church, none of us do."

It was a question I had never asked, and it made me realise how much Jack had been rattled by yesterday's events. I said at last, "It's good for everybody to say goodbye together. The church is a proper place to do that. Beth's family loved their Gran so they want to say goodbye to her, and Robbie's going along because he loves Beth."

Jack took the coiled lead off his hand and began to fidget with the spring-clip. "Even though he thinks God isn't real? That's stupid, if nobody's up there listening."

"You don't have to be rude about it. If you don't say goodbye, you can't go on with life, not properly. It doesn't matter whether you believe there's a man in the sky listening to you – or a woman, come to that. You still need to say goodbye to the person you knew. Or do something that means goodbye. They give it a fancy name these days – closure."

He was quiet for so long that I thought I'd better change the subject. "Now, what about that biscuit..."

He ignored the suggestion. "Where did Robbie put the shovel? After – you know – " He indicated the mounded earth on Kip's grave.

"I don't know. In the shed at the bottom of the garden, I expect. Why?"

"I'm going to bury Kip's lead," he said. "Next to him."

"Oh? But you might want to keep it. You weren't here yesterday when Andy and Hazel came. They said their bitch is probably going to have puppies – Kip's puppies – and if she does, they've promised we can have one."

His eyes began to glisten with tears. "Have they?" His voice wavered towards falsetto, but he swallowed hard and said, "That's nice. But I think I'll still bury this. Because a new puppy will be different, won't it? So it will need a different lead."

"Yes," I said, "it will."

~~~

A window slid open at the back of the cottage, letting out the whine of vacuuming, and over it Cerys began to sing her daily exercises, sweet and methodical and resilient. I walked back down the garden, wiping my eyes.

Madoc had come into the kitchen and was filling a glass with water. He said, "All this sitting about in a cast, it's no good. I've put weight on. I'm going to be careful for a while."

"You? Being careful?" I pulled a sheet of kitchen towel off the roll, and blew my nose. "You're in the wrong job for that."

"I meant, careful about what I eat and drink."

"I know what you meant," I said. "I was trying to tease you, for heaven's sake!"

He considered me over the rim of the glass. "Are you okay?"

"I've been talking to Jack. He's upset about Kip."

"Well, that's natural enough. He'll get over it. Did you tell him about Andy offering us a puppy?"

I dropped the tissue into the coal scuttle.

"Yes."

"Well, that should have cheered him up."

"A bit," I said, without mentioning the conversation we'd had. Let Jack conduct his little ceremony in peace. "How's your ankle?"

"It's not bad at all. I know how a bone should feel when it's mending, and it's all right. They'd better take this cast off next week though." He drank the rest of the water, and put the glass on the draining board. "I need to start riding Coel again, before I turn into the Michelin Man."

"You wouldn't! But you'd never fit that cast in the stirrup."

"I can ride him without stirrups," he said, making for the door.

"You will not! You'll do yourself an injury and be back where you started."

He laughed at my vehemence. "Tomorrow – cast or no cast, I'm going to get back in the saddle."

~~~

We finished cleaning the cottage. The keys were back on their hook in the kitchen and Cerys was upstairs in her bedroom, still singing. Madoc had gone into the garden and was steadying himself with a hand against the drystone wall while he tried to do squat exercises. Jack was copying him with a seriousness that succeeded in being both athletic and mocking, but soon as he saw me he began scooping handfuls of cut grass and throwing them at Madoc, and the gymnasium atmosphere vanished.

Madoc limped back to the house. "I phoned Dava, by the way. I was wondering what he wants us to do with King Coel, if Humphrey's not interested in the lease any more."

My anxiety level jumped a notch. "Humphrey! Pfft. I hope he's in hospital with tubes up every orifice."

"With any luck."

I tried to keep calm by making tea. Madoc, again, drank water. Jack gulped down a mug of squash then, seeing Gracie strolling into the sunlight of the open doorway, scooped her up and carried her, purring, back into the garden.

"Not much wrong with him now," said Madoc. "Thank goodness."

"I don't know. We've all had a rough time, and I think he came off worst."

We sat at the kitchen table and Madoc said, "Helen Rogers hasn't said what she wants to do with Coel, but Dava's going to ask. I checked whether he'd heard anything about Humphrey or Gwylim, but he hasn't."

The reminder that Gwylim or Jamie or Henry might be round the next corner tore at my nerves, but there was very little we could do about it. Madoc and I hadn't needed to talk again about our firearms. I realised that although we did have a rifle and a shotgun at our disposal they were not only illegal for self defence, but actually no use in practical terms. We had a farm to run, and they would get in the way of our work. We couldn't carry such a long-barrelled weapon when we were schooling horses, sorting sheep or mending walls; it was unlikely to be at hand if attackers came already armed, and then reaching for it could be an invitation to get shot. Better to keep the things locked up. All I could do was hope that neither Gwylim, Jamie nor Henry would appear.

I drank more tea.

Madoc said, "Dava's got another couple of youngsters lined up for us, just as soon as I'm fit to work with them."

"Good. Then you'd better take care of that ankle."

"I told you, I'll get back in trim – and that means riding again as soon as possible."

"Oh all right, I give in," I said. "What about the colt? Are we still being paid for him?"

"Yes, the money's there all right. But you remember Charles Humphrey's other horse – Zanzibar whatever-he-was?"

"The Ninja?"

"Yes. Dava's not very amused – Humphrey's taken him away from Claybrooke."

Knowing Dava's temper, I could well imagine that the loss of a client would have triggered volumes of colourful language. However, we both knew that racehorses were often transferred from one trainer to another on an owner's whim, so such incidents were usually more gossip than serious news.

"He said he was going to send the Ninja to France. That Mercedes horsebox came to take him away."

"Driven by Jamie and his tattoos?"

"I didn't ask. What is odd though – according to Dava – is that Arthur Whalley's son Gordon had the exact same thing happen with one of Humphrey's Flat racing fillies. The Merc came and collected her, too."

"I heard that at Chester," I said, "so it's true – but I thought there was a lot of paperwork before you can race or train overseas?"

"Oh, there is. And fees. I think Humphrey must have more money than he knows what to do with. But I don't think the filly ever reached a racing stable over there. She was back at Whalley's the following week."

"That's weird. Did the two horses travel together?"

He sipped water. "I don't think so. The Ninja didn't leave Dava's till Thursday just gone."

We puzzled over it, but there was no obvious reason for such capriciousness.

"What did Dava say about Coel?" I asked.

"Well, there's something odd there too. Apparently Helen had put a couple of unusual clauses in her lease. One said that King Coel has to be trained by Dava – which Dava was perfectly happy with, of course. The other said that the colt couldn't be taken out of the UK for any reason without Helen's written agreement – not just a Racing Clearance Notification. I've no idea why she wrote that in, because Dava doesn't run his horses abroad, he never has, but he was quite clear that's what it said, because Humphrey recently asked Helen to change it. He said he'd overlooked the clause when he signed. They argued over it for a week but she wouldn't agree, and in the end he cancelled the whole thing."

"I'm surprised a contract carried that much weight with him," I said.

"It's all very curious. Anyway, that was the reason Coel stayed here when the Ninja went back to Dava. Helen will probably owe Humphrey some sort of refund, but that's not Dava's concern, of course. He was more interested in King Coel as a potential stallion after his racing career's over."

Knowing Dava had a lifetime's obsession with that line of horses, I groaned. "Not another competition between you."

"No. I thought the same, but no. He just reminded me that the colt is Helen's property again and she might be open to suggestions. And he's right – I'd really like to talk to her, if I thought we could keep these loans under control. Only, right now, Gwylim and Charles Humphrey are very big flies in the ointment."

"And we're nowhere near sorting them out. Have you told Dava what's happened?"

"Mm. He didn't care about Humphrey, but he's really worried about where Gwylim's got to." He gave a short laugh. "Maybe he's buzzed off to France too."

I put down my mug. Contacts had begun to fire in my brain, memories clicking into place – Humphrey talking during lunch at the races, watching the drunken hen party, knowing how customers smuggled-in their own drink to avoid buying at the bar – Humphrey ordering the manager of his nightclub to undercut the prices in the local pubs so that smuggling wasn't worth people's trouble. What he hadn't given away in that conversation was the source of his supplies.

"France," I said thoughtfully.

Madoc looked at me with a puzzled expression. "It was a joke, love. Gwylim's no more likely to be in France than I am."

"Of course not, but I was thinking about what Dava said. Humphrey moved the Ninja to France, didn't he? And his filly that was with Gordon Whalley – she went to France. One horse at a time. It seems pointless, and inefficient. But what if it isn't about the horses?" I said. "What if the important thing is the horsebox, and where it goes?"

Chapter 38.

In the morning Madoc put on breeches instead of shorts, and after a breakfast of unbuttered toast and black coffee he began hopping round the porch, choosing a boot for his left leg and dragging a dark-green sock over the toes poking out of the cast on his right.

I watched him, hands on hips. "You're hell-bent on riding that colt, then?" He straightened up and looked at me, and the look said he was determined to get back to taking normal everyday risks. Well, I knew how he felt. I said, "Okay. I'll bring Zilla down from High Field."

"You don't need to."

"I'm going to. I'll see you in the yard."

By the time I'd caught the mare and brought her in, Madoc had gone into Coel's stable and haltered the colt. He had managed to lead him out onto the concrete of the yard, tie him to the wall-ring and brush him. Now he had the exercise saddle over his arm and was trying to saddle up. Coel, who didn't like the little clicking noises the crutch made, was pivoting at the full length of his rope, swinging first one way and then the other like a windscreen wiper.

Madoc was normally as patient with the animals as he was with me, but he wasn't patient with himself and I could see this wasn't going to end well unless I stepped in. I said, "If you really want to ride – "

"Yes, I do."

"You're getting him all wound up. Back off for a minute and let me help."

There was a tense pause before he nodded.

"Let me go and saddle Zilla," I said. "Give him time to calm down."

Madoc limped away and slid the saddle onto the stable half-door. That was as close as he was going to get to thanking me.

Zilla's bay coat was hard and brassy in the sunshine. Coel's was silky and dark, like a black stocking drawn over a tanned leg. I saddled both horses, smoothed Coel's neck to reassure him and went into the tack room for our riding helmets.

"I'll get the mounting-block," I said to Madoc, "and you can hop on from there."

I knew he hated being dependent on me, but he fastened the helmet chin-strap and gave another silent nod. We'd both learned long ago that the only practical way to behave with the horses was to be patient, and it was clear that if we upset the big colt any more Madoc wouldn't get onto his back at all today. However by the time I took Coel's reins and led him to the mounting block he had calmed down enough to stand quietly, and Madoc vaulted into the saddle without fuss.

Coel wanted to get moving straight away but I murmured, "Whoa now, big lad," and checked him. I said to Madoc, "D'you want to lengthen your leathers? Get yourself comfortable. I won't let him go till you're right."

I carried on chatting to the colt while Madoc concentrated on adjusting the offside stirrup. He pulled faces over it because the cast had fixed his ankle at a right angle and when he bent his knee it caught the tendons behind. He had to lengthen the stirrup-leather several times before he managed to get his woolly-socked toes onto the tread of the iron.

"We'll have to go for the old fashioned hunting look," he said. He adjusted the length of his nearside leather to match, and took up the reins.

I said, "Don't you try anything fancy. Remember you've only got your big toe in that stirrup."

"Yes Miss. One hour's walking, at the double." I replied with my severe bossy-mother cough, and he managed to chuckle. "All right – one hour's quick march."

I could tell from his movements, as much as the tone of his voice, that his good humour had returned – just from being up there on the colt's back. What was the name of that Greek in classical myth who had regained his strength every time he touched the earth? I couldn't remember, but we were both like him, only with horses. Put us in the saddle and we felt like gods. And a little crazy. I checked both horses' girths, fastened my helmet and mounted Zilla.

We walked sedately out of the yard, Coel's shod hooves clicking on the concrete, Zilla's unshod ones clopping like an axe on wood. Madoc and I both knew perfectly well that Coel could read the mare's movements. Zilla wasn't feeling at all inclined to flirt – if anything, rather the reverse – but I kept her a yard or two away from his side where that kick of hers couldn't touch him.

When we reached the exercise field, Madoc held Coel back and waited for me to open the gate from Zilla's back. She wheeled and swung in easy response to my aids and he said to her, "Well, aren't you a clever little Dobbin? You keep going like that and you might be for sale after all. Eh?" He half-smiled at me as he rode through, knowing the response he'd get.

"Not a chance."

Zilla and I shut the gate and we began a relaxed walk round the field. No clipping and clopping now, just the steady thud of hooves and the faintest swishing through the strong green grass. The grazing sheep and lambs paid us little attention and got out of our way reluctantly, like old ladies browsing in a market. Coel pricked his ears and made a purring sound with his nostrils. A bit of mane stuck up from Zilla's neck like a black punk haircut.

Half way up the first slope I glanced over at Madoc. "How's your leg?"

"It's all right for now, but I'm itching for this cast to come off."

"It beats me how you mend so fast."

"I always have. Luckily."

We reached the top of the field and turned across the slope, the tall colt downhill of the short sturdy mare, putting Madoc and me at eye level with each other. Both horses were walking energetically and I would have been tempted to move on into a trot if it hadn't been for the need to keep things steady for Madoc. He knew that perfectly well so when Zilla picked up my impatience and began to jog, he chuckled.

"This is the quietest thing we've done for days, d'you realise?"

"Yes."

I'd had another bad night, half sleeping and half waking as I went over and over the things I'd written on the police form, fearing I might have revealed my resentment against Charles Humphrey. I wished I could be as resilient as the rest of my family seemed to be. Robbie had been out in the fields first thing, replenishing the creep-feeders for the lambs, and immediately after breakfast he'd taken the quad bike to Underscar to help Danny and Andy sort sheep for auction. Jack had decided he was fit to go to school so I wrote a note to explain his multi-coloured eye to the staff, who might well be more critical than his mate Wilse. Cerys, who was catching the same bus on her way to a driving lesson and a rehearsal with her singing teacher, had promised to look after him.

We still hadn't heard where Gwylim might be, with the year's profit that he'd taken from us. What had he actually done with it? And what was he going to do next?

Madoc asked, "Did you phone the police, yesterday?"

"Not exactly."

"Then what, exactly?"

"Well, if it isn't an emergency, there's a form you can fill in, online. So that's what I did."

"Surely they should have been buzzing round by now!"

"The form does say it might take twelve hours for them to respond."

"Really! Maybe I ought to phone them when we get back to the yard. If Humphrey made it to hospital alive, Gwylim would be safer in a police station."

"Frankly, love, Gwylim's safety isn't at the top of my priorities." I leaned forward to smack a horsefly on Zilla's neck, and she swished her heavy tail. Coel read the swish as a warning that she might kick, and flung up his head. I said, "Don't you dare, you witch!"

"I suppose we'll have to wait for the police to find him."

I drew an impatient breath. "Like we'll just have to wait to find a way through this coming winter – without that money."

"It won't be all that bad," he said. "There'll be more young horses from Dava – and the Rural Payments Agency should transfer the farm subsidy into the bank today or tomorrow."

"I'll believe that when I see it."

"Besides, there is one good thing about this business with Gwylim..."

"What? He swiped this year's profits and half killed our Jack, and there's something good in that? You'd better tell me what it is, because I can't see it!"

"He won't come back here. He knows he's burnt his boats by hitting Jack – if he turned up we'd flatten him. But we've still got thirty-two thousand pounds of his invested in the holiday cottage."

"And I bet Charles Humphrey still wants it all," I said, "hospital or no hospital."

We carried on walking the horses round the fields and the sun climbed higher. The Defender in Doctor's Pot had begun to shimmer with heat.

"It must be nearly eleven o'clock," Madoc said. "Robbie should be back with Danny any time. We'd best go in."

"I thought he was going to the funeral."

"I asked him to sort some lambs first, for Kendal tomorrow. It won't take long if Danny brings his dog. With us having missed a couple of weeks, there are plenty fit to go, and we needn't worry about having too many for the trailer – Beth's father has offered to come for them in their wagon."

"That was generous," I said, surprised.

Madoc grinned. "I think Robbie is getting on rather well at The Ghyll."

We rode down to the gate where, despite the distractions of the horseflies, Zilla neatly sidled, turned, wheeled, sidled the other way while I did the opening and shutting. As we walked the horses into the yard we heard the clang of the cattle grid, followed by car tyres crunching up the track.

"That'll be Danny now," Madoc said over his shoulder.

"That doesn't sound like a quad bike. Might be the postman. It might even be the police." Coel halted by his stable door and waited, so I said to Madoc, "Let me hold him while you get down."

"I don't need help to jump off, you know."

"It's not the jump, it's the landing," I said.

I kicked my feet out of the stirrups, but before I could dismount a steel-grey Kia drove into the yard. I recognised it at once, Charles Humphrey's spare muscle-mobile. It passed the back door of the house and swerved to a stop facing us, and Jamie and Henry stepped out.

They had a wooden baseball bat apiece, heavy and black-handled, a maker's name printed across the thick end. They moved towards us, one each side of the car, massively threatening. Henry was black-clad as before, Jamie in a white vest and jeans. I saw the muscles slide under his tattoos as he swung his bat, confident, leisurely, like a player repeating the feel of a stroke.

The world congealed into slow motion.

Madoc looked at me, his face full of concern. "Get out of this, if you can."

"Too late," I said. No matter how handy Zilla was at opening gates, the henchmen would be quicker and I didn't want to be cornered.

Jamie shouldered the bat and addressed us.

"Thought we might find yez at home." His voice was neutral. Not gloating, not aggressive. Almost as though he didn't care, as though he and Henry could deal with any resistance a little hill farm might produce. "Anybody else around?"

I thought, *Robbie's due back any time. Him and Danny, they're not street-wise. They're both big lads but if they walk in on us now they won't have any clue about the danger.* I willed Madoc not to give Jamie any hint of that.

He answered steadily, "What you see is what you get. If you've come for the boss's car, you're going to need our tractor to drag it out."

"We're not bothered, ey," said Jamie. "We've just come to have a talk to yez. About money."

"I haven't the faintest idea what you're on about."

"Oh, I think you have. Your brother tried to do a runner but when we turned him over his pockets was empty." This was bad news. "So we've come to collect. Seeing as the boss knows the money was coming from you."

Coel's saddle creaked as Madoc shifted his weight. "We paid Gwylim on Saturday."

"Oh you did." Jamie nodded, still expressionless. "Yeah, right."

"We did," Madoc repeated. "There's nothing left. If Gwylim didn't pay Humphrey, that's not our problem." He didn't mention how little of the loan we had repaid.

Henry growled, "You're like your feckin' brother, trying to get clever with us." I didn't think for a moment that he'd second-guessed Madoc, but it was clear that no matter what we told him he wouldn't believe us, and that in itself was paralysing.

"It's no good being clever, ey. It didn't work for your brother," Jamie said, "and it won't work for you, neether." He swung the bat again, lazily, this time with the low forward sweep of a golfer, and he watched it swish past Coel's clean, slender legs, and looked up at Madoc. "Nice horse you've got there. Pity if it got hurt, eh?"

In my mind's eye I saw the bone of Coel's foreleg shatter, and Madoc thrown onto the concrete at Jamie's feet. Both horses shifted nervously and Coel pressed his flank against Zilla as if for reassurance, pushing Madoc's stirrup hard into my calf. I gasped and Madoc turned the colt in a circle to get him away from me. Jamie just waited.

Madoc brought Coel round to face him and said in level tones, "This horse belongs to Charles Humphrey."

Another lie, of course, but told with an appearance of calm that I couldn't hope to match, so that Jamie's glance flickered across at Henry and I saw that they weren't sure.

"What will he do if you damage it?" Madoc said, pushing at that moment of doubt. Henry reached into his back pocket and brought out his phone, and Madoc added, "Go ahead. I bet there's a policeman sitting right by his bedside to take your call."

Jamie moved in closer and said quite quietly, "Then we'll have to forget about the horse, won't we?"

I remembered the first time he'd stood on our yard – he'd been driving the Mercedes horsebox with the Ninja and King Coel aboard. I remembered his sullenness, his disdain for the job he was doing. He wasn't sullen now. He was in his element, and his enjoyment of it was very frightening. He lifted the bat and tapped it, only lightly, against Madoc's woollen-socked cast. And for the first time ever, I heard him laugh.

"Ask me how many of Gwyl's bones we broke. Go on, ask me."

I drew a shocked breath. These men hadn't come to collect money. They'd come here to hurt, to get a kick out of physical power. That was why they worked for Charles Humphrey. He gave them the opportunities and let them go. My whole body prickled with fear and my legs tightened around Zilla's ribs. I felt her shiver in response.

Madoc's mouth was set in a grim line but he said, "I'll ask Gwyl when I see him."

"Na." Jamie was still smiling. "You won't. You won't see him again."

I thought, *They've murdered him.* I let out my breath with a shudder. Then there was a growl of quad-bike engines on the farm track, and Robbie and Danny drove into the yard.

They were standing up on the treads, the way they often did when travelling fast, but they eased the throttle when they saw the horses. Danny's red-and-white dog jumped down from the rack behind him and began investigating the yard.

Robbie dismounted and took a couple of steps towards us before he realised the oddness of the scene and hesitated. I thought, *His head's still full of shepherding. He doesn't know how dangerous these men are.* Jamie made no immediate threat with his weapon. He exchanged looks with Henry, recalculating the odds, and Henry put his phone away.

Robbie asked, "What's all this then?"

"Bit of friendly business, like."

"Friendly?" said Robbie, disbelieving.

The dog trotted towards the horses. Coel snorted and began to toss his head and press up against Zilla, and she swished her tail at him so that he rebounded. Madoc gentled him with a stroke down the neck. He couldn't dismount from Coel without jarring his ankle, and anyway, on the ground he certainly couldn't stand up to Jamie or Henry. Safer to stay on the horse. I let Zilla twist in a circle. Danny shouted at the dog. It took no notice, and sniffed with deep concentration at the rear wheel of the Kia.

"Da?" said Robbie. "What's going on?"

The dog lifted a leg and drenched the wheel in a yellow stream of urine, and Henry strode across and kicked it.

The dog yelped. Danny turned on Henry. "Here! What's the matter with you?"

"Feckin' inbred yokels with yer pissing dogs."

Robbie said, "Move your car off our yard and it won't get pissed on."

Don't, Robbie. You don't know what these men did to Gwylim. Don't take them on.

306

"Gonna make uz, are yer?" Jamie squared up to him. "Come on then. Come on."

He had turned his back to me. The bat rose.

Robbie and Madoc and Danny and me and the horses –

Zilla was already shuddering with my fright and anger and when I launched her forward she went straight for Jamie and barged him over. I smacked my heel into the spot on her flank that made her kick. *Get him, you witch.* Her hooves rang like hammers. I felt her body bunch and hump under me, a thousand pounds of muscular energy. She caught Jamie two solid thumps with her hind feet and the baseball bat bounced across the concrete and Robbie seized it.

Zilla's plunge had driven Coel up onto his hind legs, forefeet striking out with Madoc doubled-up, his shoulder on the colt's neck. Henry ducked backwards from the steel-shod hooves crashing down and Danny shoulder-charged him into the side of the Kia. Jamie was still picking himself off the ground as Zilla came round full circle, her ears flattened, stamping her front feet with murderous intent. He scrambled away, one hand fumbling for the driver's door, the other wrapped about his ribs. Coel, half mad with excitement, reared again as Henry tore open the passenger door.

The engine burst into life. Zilla twisted and bucked and kicked and I heard Robbie shout, "Look out, Mam!"

Then there was a thud and a lurch and I was vaguely aware of flying before the yard thumped the breath out of me and my helmet hit concrete with a crack.

~~~

I don't think I was out for more than a few seconds. I was on my back, gasping, the engine of the Kia roaring above me. I thought, *This is it,* but even as I thought it, the shadow passed over and the sun beat on my face. Somebody hammered on the Kia's bodywork then there was a burst of glass breaking, and a yell of triumph from

Robbie. Gears clunked, the tyres screwed round and bit and screeched away.

Coel's shoes clattered dangerously close but this time I had the wits to roll aside, groaning at the bruised feeling through my shoulder and back.

I forced myself to sit up. The yard reassembled itself. Stone walls, concrete, Danny's dog, Coel's black restless hooves. The tyres went rattling off down the track and over the cattle grid. Leaving. Thank God.

I could see now that Madoc had the colt under control. Robbie and Danny came back into the yard swaggering like cockerels, Robbie with the baseball bat on his shoulder and Danny calling the dog who seemed to think it had all been a game. Madoc dismounted from Coel and I heard him grunt with pain but a moment later he was beside me, dragging me to my feet.

"You idiot! What did you think you were doing?"

I snapped, "I was frightened!"

"You frightened *me*, you spanner! They drove straight at you." Then he took me in a mighty bear hug, my helmet half-choking me. "I thought they'd killed you."

"No such luck." I fumbled to unclip my chin-strap. "Where's Zilla? Robbie – put that stupid bat down and find your Da's crutch."

"Damn the crutch," said Madoc, still gripping my shoulders.

I took off my helmet. There was a massive dent in the back of its pale brown shell. "I'm going to need a new hat."

"I'm more worried about the head inside it," said Madoc. He gave my shoulder a little squeeze and let me go. "We need to see to your mare."

I had no memory of what Zilla had done after I fell. I turned shakily to look for her. She was standing by her tying place, waiting for me, obedient to her reins trailing on the concrete, but there was a long red split in her brown hide and blood trickling down her hind leg. I limped towards her and she laid back her ears at me.

"Whoa now, my poor lassie."

"The car caught her across the arse," Robbie said. "So I put the bat through its rear window." He handed Madoc his crutch and led Coel away and propped the bat against the stable wall.

Madoc asked, "Anyone got a phone handy? Call 999."

I said, "But – "

"No more buts!" he said. "You're hurt. The mare's hurt. And Gwylim's hurt. He could be dead. If we'd called 999 the first time round, instead of using that stupid online form, all this wouldn't have happened."

I flushed, but he was right. There was nothing I could say.

"We've pussyfooted around this far too long. Put the mare in the stable," he said, "and call the police."

Chapter 39.

Danny called the police.

I gathered up Zilla's reins to lead her into the empty stable, and she followed me with a reluctance that reminded me of Jack groaning, "Why me..." I couldn't make a fuss about it because I knew just how she felt. Awkwardly, being careful of my own injuries and hers, I took off her saddle and bridle. By the time I'd put them away in the tackroom I was close to crying, wishing I hadn't put the mare into a fight she didn't understand. We were both shocked by the messages coming from our bodies – uncertain whether our sensations were pain, afraid they were going to be. She had no idea that she had saved us all from a beating. She only knew it hurt. When I went back to the stable with a handful of oats in a bucket, she gave me her usual whicker and a greedy shove with her nose, but her tolerance only stretched so far: even with oats to distract her, she wasn't going to let me get near the wound on her quarters. I wasn't in a fit state to argue. I telephoned for the vet.

A police car turned up with two constables, a lad in his twenties and a slightly older woman, who made quick assessments and radioed at once for a Detective Inspector. While we waited for him the vet arrived. He was a kindly, bearded chap who introduced himself as Chris. I brought Zilla out of the stable but she showed the whites of her eyes and his friendly advances produced only snorting and head-tossing. She wouldn't let him anywhere near her wound.

"I see," he said. "We're not going to make much sense of you without sedation, are we, little lady?"

He went back to his car for a syringe. I cupped a hand over her eye so she wouldn't see him coming with the injection, and he was so deft at sliding the needle into her neck that she barely noticed. Within a few moments her eyelids began to droop, and when her ears pointed groggily sideways he put on latex gloves and began to clip away the hair around her wound.

"I don't think I'll stitch this," he said, as he cleaned it. "The injury itself isn't deep, more of a bruise that's burst the skin, but the muscles move a lot in this area so stitches would just tear out and make things worse."

"Will she be lame?" I asked.

"Oh she'll be sore for a while, who wouldn't be! But I don't think she'll be lame long-term."

"What about scarring?"

"It's surprising how well skin will grow back in if you give it the chance. With the coats these Fell ponies have, you'll probably be hard pushed to see it for most of the year." He carried on working, talking half to me, half to the mare. "You'll have to keep her stabled for a while until the wound heals."

"We can manage that," I said. "It'll do her waistline good to be off the grass."

"I wish more people realised that," he said. "My next call's for a native pony. It's in a field of lush spring grass and it's grazing twenty-four hours a day. And guess what?"

"Laminitis," I said. "Oh dear."

"Exactly. The pony's so lame it can't move. We get at least one call every day, this time of year, and the owners are always so surprised. How are your youngsters doing?"

"Ponies or people?"

"You know whose side I'm on," he said with a wry smile. Zilla stood, half slumbering, letting him fix an adhesive dressing over her wound.

"The three-year-olds are just fine," I said. "They keep each other moving."

"Excellent." He placed a protective net cover over the dressing. "All the same, I hope that police car isn't symptomatic of anything wrong with the kids."

I conveyed a No without trying to shake my head. "It's a long story, and you've got a laminitic pony waiting for you."

He chuckled. "I'll look out for a headline in the newspaper. There now, little lady, I've finished tormenting you." He stripped off the gloves and gave her neck an encouraging stroke. "She's a tough little mare. If the car had hit that thoroughbred you've got next door – well, with him being nearly a foot taller the impact would have smashed his tibia, and I'd be loading the humane killer. She's been very lucky. Now, can you re-do this dressing tomorrow, and I'll come and look at her again on Wednesday?"

He left me with various gels and adhesive dressings and a spare net cover, and sped off to deal with the laminitis case. Outside, the young policeman had taken charge of the baseball bat, and the woman constable was sweeping up the broken glass from the Kia's rear window. I crept indoors to make myself a cup of tea and felt at least twice my age.

Detective Inspector Lewthwaite arrived – a tall, lean man in his mid-forties. My head was too overloaded by then to follow how he organised the enquiry, but he seemed to me to tackle its complexities with unhurried composure. He cleared our kitchen table to use for interviews, and kept Madoc and Danny and Robbie busy making statements. He and his colleagues seemed secure and steady and, if not precisely kind to us, at least determined to find out as much as they could to catch 'the perpetrators'. But they didn't make any guesses, and nobody mentioned my use of the non-emergency reporting form or echoed Madoc's opinion that it had been the wrong way to report the shooting; they only dealt with what actually happened, not what might have happened if I'd made a better choice. I supposed if everyone made better choices all the time, the police might never be needed.

Robbie phoned Beth to explain that he wouldn't be coming to pick her up for her Gran's funeral; he would barely have time to wash and change his clothes before meeting her at the church.

Forensics came next, with two big white vans emblazoned CRIME SCENE INVESTIGATION. We were all fingerprinted – apparently so that any evidence on the Defender, the Kia and the baseball bat could be identified. Lewthwaite directed one team onto the fell, to cordon off Doctor's Pot, and the other to Thorny Bank to find the location from which Gwylim had taken his shots at Charles Humphrey. And everything remained routine, stolid, controlled.

When the female officer sat me down at the kitchen table in my turn, and cautioned me, I couldn't think of anything to say. She led me through the day in detail: Robbie working at Underscar, Cerys and Jack away on the school bus, Madoc's determination to exercise King Coel. I had made up my mind to answer her questions accurately, to show how much I was in control. I wanted to be the sheepdog and not the sheep, but when I got to the arrival of the two henchmen with their baseball bats, my shakiness returned. I found myself babbling and mixing up my words as I repeated their threats and their boast that they had beaten Gwylim, and that Danny's dog had triggered Jamie to turn on Robbie.

She said, "Take your time. What did they do?"

"I don't know. They were making Zilla nervous, and she started kicking."

"That's your horse?"

"Yes. Horses kick to defend themselves," I said, and hoped my blush didn't make me look guilty.

The officer looked at me steadily and made a note. I went on, "She made them back off all right – and Coel started rearing, so when Robbie and Danny waded in as well, they decided they'd had enough."

For every note she made there was another question. "What did you think they'd come for? They weren't local, were they?"

I tried to explain about the money problems, until I realised I was beginning to repeat myself and the officer led me back to re-check what I'd said. It irked me that she referred to Charles Humphrey as a "victim" – although the word did make it easier for me to admit I'd helped get him out of the Defender. She asked me several times how well I knew him and I wondered whether she guessed there were things I wasn't saying. However, after we'd covered the same ground again and my answers were basically the same, she brought the interview to a close – for the time being – saying that once Jack arrived home from school I'd need to sit in while they interviewed him, too.

I was very hungry by then and began randomly buttering bread and opening mayonnaise and tinned tuna as a way of escaping the padded-cell feeling of police investigation. We ate – at least I did – in a fog of distraction. Robbie, washed and shaved and handsome in his only suit, grabbed a sandwich and left for the Langdale funeral.

I didn't get any immediate sense of what the police thought was going on. Someone had told Madoc that since neither Gwylim or Humphrey lived in Cumbria, our information would be shared and compared with other police forces. I gathered that Charles

Humphrey's gunshot wound had been reported by A & E in Lancaster, though it hadn't been married-up with my online report until the middle of the morning. I worried then in case Humphrey was well enough to send his bully-boys to have another "talk" to us about money. I could only hope he wasn't, and that nobody would think of pre-empting his orders.

It wasn't until mid afternoon that the investigating officers withdrew for a time, and Madoc and I were able to sit down and take stock, on our own.

"The school minibus will be back in an hour," I said. "How much do we tell Jack and Cerys? I don't want to terrify them completely."

"Enough to keep them wary, I suppose." He managed a chuckle, though his eyes were shadowed with fatigue. "Robbie will tell them everything, even if we don't."

"I'm worried about them going to school tomorrow. I know it's got that new perimeter fence but I don't think it's much of a barrier for the kind of people Charles Humphrey employs."

"Talk to them when they come in."

The fall from Zilla was catching up with me and I was aching all over. I made tea for both of us, and we shared the sofa and gave ourselves up to an exhausted silence.

~~~

The phone rang. I jolted awake and Madoc groaned. I got to my feet, muttering, "If that's a cold caller..."

It wasn't. It was the owner of King Coel, Helen Rogers.

"Siân!" she said. "How nice to talk to you again. How is life treating you?"

"Life," I said, "is pretty bloody complicated, but you don't need me to tell you that."

"Oh! I don't know...I think life being complicated is what keeps me going! Simplicity would be so boring, don't you think?"

I said, "I'd quite like a week or two of simplicity then, just for a rest," and she laughed.

Helen must be in her sixties now, because she had been in her mid-forties when I first met her, with a son the same age as Robbie – but she still had the same determined Lancashire voice, full of humour and good sense.

"Do you want to talk to Madoc?" I asked.

"Actually – I don't know. Can you and I have a chat first? If you've got time, with all your offspring? I've had an idea and I'd like to hear your thoughts."

"Okay. The kids won't be back from school just yet." I tucked the phone under my ear while I doused yet another teabag in a mug of hot water.

"It's about that horse of mine," she said. "Coel." I made an encouraging noise and she continued, "You know I leased him to that chap Humphrey? Well! A right prick he turned out to be. You must have heard about it?"

"I don't know the whole story," I said cautiously.

"Oh! We had a right falling-out over the contract." She repeated what Madoc had told me, about Humphrey contesting the clause preventing Coel from travelling abroad. "And the police are after him too!"

"Yes. They've been here today."

"Have they, indeed! Did they tell you about that smart horsebox of his, with all that fancy coachbuilding? There's a story going round that it was designed with secret compartments to bring drugs over from the Continent."

"Really!" Click, click, click. Facts were joining together despite my fuzzy head. "So that's why he kept sending horses to France and back. I thought it might have been booze, you know, for the night clubs."

"Well, drugs is what I heard – so much easier to hide – and he'd make a lot more money out of that, wouldn't he? Anyway, the police have impounded the horsebox and I've heard the Criminal Assets people are rubbing their hands, so I expect the story will be in the papers before long. Thank goodness I didn't sell Coel or he might have been impounded too, poor thing. And how is he? Coel, I mean, not the prick."

The Rayburn lid was hot under my palms. I shook off my vindictive pleasure at Charles Humphrey finally getting his come-uppance, and I tried to concentrate on Helen's question. "The colt's fine – though I ought to tell you, him and my mare between them, they nearly killed a couple of Humphrey's minions this morning."

"From what I've seen of Humphrey's minions, it's only a pity they didn't succeed," she said.

I agreed. I was relieved she didn't ask what the minions had been doing on the farm in the first place, and I also thought it was wiser not to pass on the vet's comment about the damage they might have done if they'd driven the Kia into Coel.

"The thing is," she said, "Coel's the only horse we've got left. We had Carbon Copy put down last winter."

"I'm so sorry," I murmured. I eased my shoulders, which had stiffened a lot while I dozed, and I changed the phone to the other ear.

"That's why I wanted to talk to you and Madoc. We didn't manage to breed a filly out of her, just the colt. Now, call me a sentimental old woman if you like, but I want to see that line carry on – and I expect you understand, because you were fond of Double Jump, weren't you? I'd like to keep Coel as a stallion. But I can't do it here at Raby, it's too small and we don't have the facilities, and both John and I are too old to up-sticks and start running a stud. I did talk to Chris about it – I think you'll remember my son?"

"Yes," I said. Kind, reliable Chris, who had turned up with Helen's old Bedford wagon to collect me and Double Jump from Green Bank all those years ago. He had transported us to Dava's stables, a journey that had taken me to Madoc and changed the whole direction of my life. Chris was probably married now with kids and wouldn't even remember me. I drank some more tea.

"He's managing our farm," Helen said, "but he won't have my horses there, he says he can't be bothered because the land at Ormskirk is far better suited to arable and he doesn't have to worry about fencing-in the cabbages and barley and stuff. He's right, of course, but it means the place is a non-starter for Coel. You see what I'm getting at."

I guessed, so I said, "I know Madoc would really like to own King Coel, but I'm afraid we can't afford to buy him."

"No, no, I'm not trying to sell him!" She sounded amused. "Heavens, that would quite spoil my fun! No, I want him to go into training first. Now, I talked to Dava, so I know Madoc's been sidelined – how is his his ankle?"

"Itchy," I said. "He's mad to get the cast off it. Still, Coel was ready to go before that happened. We'll be sad – but it was only your dispute about the lease that kept him here, wasn't it?"

"Yes. I'm going to run him in my own colours now and forget all that leasing nonsense. Now then. The thing is, at the end of next season, I'll need somewhere for Coel to spend the summer. Somewhere with good green grass, that can handle a colt. Would you and Madoc have him back?"

I found my hands were shaking so much that I had to put my tea down.

"I'll have to ask..." I felt my voice tremble. "I'll have to ask Madoc. But I'm absolutely sure he'll say yes."

"Then do. Let me know your rates. And – would you and Madoc be interested in a partnership in King Coel? Not immediately, but whenever Dava thinks the colt should retire. I mean, your farm would be ideal as a stud. What do you think? Can you plan that far ahead? It might be four years or more."

I didn't interrupt her. After the weekend I'd spent, struggling with murderous greed and cruelty, this small kindness was overwhelming. I could hardly speak. I carried the phone through to the front room and shook Madoc awake. He took one startled look at my face and asked, "What's the matter?"

"It's Helen," I said. "Helen Rogers."

"What's happened?"

I tried to laugh as I gave him the phone, but my voice wouldn't work. It was generosity that had finally broken me down; a little blue-sky gift of happiness. I could hear Helen saying, "Siân? Siân? Are you still there?"

"Helen, it's me, Madoc. Whatever have you said to her? She's sitting here crying her eyes out."

Chapter 40.

I kept Jack at home the next day. "Stay close to the house where I can see you."

"Why?"

"Because!" It was a perfectly sensible question, but I'd been trying not to think about it. "Because – what if those blokes turn up again? You've still got a black eye from what Gwylim did. I'm feeling rough, your Da's feeling rough, and Zilla's as lame as a crow. I don't want to add you to the list of casualties."

"You let Robbie go off on his own."

"He's at The Ghyll working with Bob Langdale. And he's bigger than you are."

"Can't I go out and work with Rocky?" he asked. "You let Cerys go to Underscar."

"Cerys will be safe there. She'll be with Danny," I said, "and Hazel and Andy."

"I do promise to be careful, Mam."

"You? Careful? You can go into the yard, or the garden. If you're lucky, school will forget to give you any homework."

"This is worse than being grounded," he grumbled, "and I haven't done anything to make it worthwhile."

~~~

That afternoon DI Lewthwaite visited us again. I didn't hear him until he knocked at the back door and when I let him in there was something guarded about his manner, a disinclination to look me in the eye. It chilled me. I guessed at once that Gwylim was dead.

I called Madoc. I remember him coming into the kitchen with his crutch and listening to the Inspector, then passing a hand wearily over his face. I was reminded of the day, so long ago, when he'd stumbled into that other farm kitchen with the news of a death. I was glad that Jack was upstairs.

"I hoped this wouldn't happen," Madoc said to Lewthwaite. "Are you sure it's him?"

"They ID-ed him from a receipt in his jacket pocket, for dental work. He'd had a tooth removed last week."

"Yes."

"You knew about that?" asked Lewthwaite.

Madoc glanced at me before he said, "He told me he'd had a run-in with a couple of Charles Humphrey's boys at Chester races."

"That fits," said Lewthwaite. "I'm afraid we'll have to arrange a formal identification – and I'm sorry, but your sister-in-law says she'd prefer not to do it. She asked if you would. We can't insist, of course."

Madoc took a deep breath and said, "If I have to."

"Thank you. But I imagine you can't drive at the moment. Will you need transport? He'll be taken to Oldham, to the police mortuary at the hospital."

I said, "Robbie will drive you there, surely."

Madoc nodded, but his mind was elsewhere.

"And where did it happen – exactly? I'd like to know."

"Ancoats. In a supermarket car park. It looks like they tipped him over the wall and drove away."

Madoc sat down at the kitchen table. "I suppose that's what you'd call ironic," he said. "What with his taste for designer clothes and glasses. A bloody car park."

"There's no good place to find a body," said Lewthwaite gently. "I'm very sorry for your loss."

"They bragged about killing him. I want them caught. Have you arrested Charles Humphrey? He's the one who's behind all this."

"It wouldn't surprise me," Lewthwaite said, "but it's not my case, and not my manor. A Chief Super from Manchester's in charge now, first because it's a murder, and second because it happened on his patch. We'll get them, whoever they are."

"I damn well hope so."

"We're likely to make several more arrests over the next few days. From what you've told us, Humphrey's in the frame all right, but to begin with Manchester thought it was a mugging that had gone wrong. Your brother had no money on him and no credit cards."

I must have made a sound, and Lewthwaite glanced at me.

"We'd just given Gwyl a lot of cash."

Madoc said, "The two goons told us his pockets were empty. They said he'd cheated them, as though that was another reason for beating him up."

"You wouldn't expect that sort to tell you the truth."

Madoc's anger was cold now and bitter, and my own emotions were very mixed. When Gwylim had come here he'd decided that shooting was the only way to deal with Charles Humphrey, so he'd treated Jack as though he was a fly to be swatted out of his way. Now he'd been swatted in his turn. I hoped Jack couldn't hear us, from his bedroom. I must stop thinking about Gwylim. The unknown and unimaginable details of his death mustn't get in the way of keeping our own family safe.

"It's beginning to look as though your brother's death is part of a much bigger picture." Lewthwaite was talking to Madoc, not me. "I know that won't be much comfort."

"You're right, it isn't."

I said, "The muscles who threw their weight about yesterday won't have been the only ones Charles Humphrey employed. I don't want any more of them turning up."

"Of course you don't." I was relieved the DI understood my concern. He said, "We could move you away, to a temporary address."

"Seriously?" said Madoc. He sounded sceptical. "How long would that be for?"

Lewthwaite drew a breath. "In all honesty, I couldn't say."

"Moving away might work for somebody in an office, but you can't just shut down a farm, it's a living thing, not a box."

"I see that, but perhaps your neighbours could cover for you? How do you manage for holidays?"

I couldn't imagine Andy or Danny dealing with the horses. King Coel could go back to Dava, of course, but Zilla? She needed ongoing vet care and she was quite liable to kick unknown handlers out of her stable.

Madoc said, "We can't afford holidays right now, and our neighbours have their own farm to look after."

"All right. Just remember that moving is an option if things escalate." Lewthwaite looked at me again. "Would you feel better if we could improve your security?"

I said, "Deadbolts on the doors, you mean? Locks on the windows?"

"Yes. I know Manchester are arranging things like that for your sister-in-law. We can give you a Home Link alarm. If any villains turn up, you activate the alarm, you bolt the doors and wait for us."

I considered the suggestion. Those were practical steps that we could take towards peace of mind, and although I knew we were so far from a police station that they might be only sticking plaster, I was grateful.

"Yes." I turned away to check the Rayburn kettle. "I think I'll make a cup of tea now. Anybody else want one?"

"Not for me, thanks. The recovery truck's coming for that four-by-four, and I want to be there when they move it." Lewthwaite took a step towards the door. "Someone will be in touch with you later, about identifying your brother. We'll arrange for a Family Liaison Officer to support you too." He repeated, "I'm very sorry for your loss, Mr Owen. Don't you get up, now. I'll see myself out." He left as quietly as he had arrived.

The kettle boiled, and I made two mugs of tea and brought them to the table.

Madoc said, "Bloody hell. It goes on and on."

"I know. Here's your tea, love."

"It's the cure for everything, isn't it? Cup of tea and a slice of bloody cake."

"Except I haven't got any cake," I said. "Sorry."

~~~

The following day, Robbie drove Madoc to Oldham in the pickup. While they were away, a brown-haired young man arrived in a little silver Golf. *What now?* I thought irritably. *Is this an insurance man? A loss adjuster?* He hurried to our door to get out of the rain, clutching a file of papers.

"Iwan Bradley," he said, holding out an ID card on a lanyard round his neck. "Police Family Liaison Officer."

He offered his hand, so I shook it, regretting my antagonism. His clasp was straightforward and I hesitated only a moment before letting him and his untidy paperwork into the house.

"Family Liaison?" I asked him. "What's all that about?"

"Whatever you want it to be. Think of me as your new best friend. There are going to be times in the next few weeks when you'll need me."

I reached, out of habit, for the kettle. "Cup of tea?" I asked.

~~~

When Madoc and Robbie came home from identifying Gwylim's body, neither of them wanted to talk about it. I asked questions, but all Madoc would say was, "They made a mess of him." And Robbie swopped the pickup keys for his own keys and drove off to The Ghyll, and the comfort of Beth.

~~~

I hadn't realised how disruptive a criminal investigation could be. The crime novels I'd read seemed to close swiftly after the murderer was unmasked, and they skipped over the winding-up procedural details. In real life the process was like the mills of God. Even in this case where 'who dunnit' wasn't really a mystery, it looked as though the business of arresting and charging suspects and bringing them to trial was going to take weeks, perhaps months.

The most tiring aspect of it all, to me, was the fact that we weren't in charge of what was happening. Investigation seemed to swallow most of our energy, our minds and our time. When I wasn't being interviewed or sitting with Jack while he was interviewed, I was thinking about what had happened and how it fitted with what was happening now, or what might be happening some time in the future. Things that had happened here had been downgraded to a side-show compared to the murder enquiry. The police still dealt with us, but they were preoccupied now with gathering evidence about Gwylim's death, rather than about Gwylim shooting Charles Humphrey, and they had changed their focus on the wrecked Defender, treating it now as a possible conveyor for drugs rather than as the scene of a violent crime. Living with these multiple investigations was like being inside a kaleidoscope – the events were jumbled over and over, with only the police able to see enough of the detail to make coherent stories from the patterns.

The deadbolts were fitted to our doors and windows, and the alarm devices arrived on lanyards so we could carry them about with us. Perhaps later, once there were arrests, we might find it possible to settle back into the old, unthinking peace.

~~~

I took Madoc to the hospital to have his cast removed. The nurse who dealt with him looked thoughtfully at its battered edges, but he had the grace to nod and thank her without making excuses, and I didn't talk about any of the unusual activities he'd put it through. They gave him a removable moon boot to wear, and he handed the crutches over and hobbled back to the pickup with the support of his horn handled shepherd's crook.

~~~

Iwan Bradley was still calling in daily, driving up from Manchester to bring news of how the investigations were going. He re-phrased the official terms and helped us to understand what was happening both in Cumbria and in Greater Manchester.

At the same time he managed to offer a degree of support to each of us without being patronising – something that Robbie, in particular, would have disliked intensely.

"If you want to ask questions about any of the cases – the assaults here, the murder in Manchester, anything at all – if you've got any worries, just ask me. Doing it through me lets you record what's bothering you, but it doesn't take up time that police officers need to spend pursuing actual enquiries."

He asked us whether we wanted to make 'victim personal statements' about how we felt. Madoc and Robbie turned down his offer without discussion – and anyway, Robbie escaped from the farm for most of that week by working at The Ghyll. Cerys retreated to her bedroom, and singing. Iwan didn't press either of them to talk to him.

He was less confrontational than either plain-clothes or uniformed police, quick to back off if there was any resistance on our part and leaving everything optional. I discovered that he had Welsh parents, which perhaps explained why his presence was comforting.

He went to Jack's school to talk to the Head about security on the school premises, and to explore the possibility of Jack staying at home for extended periods if things became too stressful. When Jack arrived home at the end of the school day, they stood together at the door of Zilla's stable and talked for an hour or more before they came back to the house.

Robbie and Cerys and Madoc were all in the kitchen and when Jack went straight upstairs with his school bag I didn't think much about it. I half expected Iwan to stay and chat over his customary cup of tea. Instead he asked me, "Can you spare a moment, before I go?"

I glanced at Madoc, aware that I was spending noticeable amounts of time with Iwan, but he raised no objection. We walked slowly across the yard, and Iwan talked.

"Your older kids sound as though they've found their own ways of coping," he said, "so I don't want to bang on about it in front of them, but Jack's still finding it difficult to come to terms with what's been going on."

"Yes."

"He might not want to talk about it to you or your husband. Don't worry about that. If he needs to blow off steam, I've told him I'm the person to call on."

"You'll have an uphill task," I said. "None of us confide very easily, I'm afraid."

"I'll make it as easy for him as I can. The thing is, I can document what he tells me, and these family statements often help the court to decide whether suspects are given bail or not."

"Really?"

He chuckled. "Oh yes. And believe me – there's no doubt the court's going to be busy. It won't be long now."

Chapter 41.

I woke in the night hearing voices on the landing. Cerys, haloed by the landing light, was looking in round the bedroom door.

"Mam? It's Jack."

"What's the matter with him?" I mumbled.

"I don't know. He won't talk to me."

Madoc half-woke, frowning, his eyes still shut. I laid a hand on his arm. "I'll go."

I reached for my dressing-gown and slipped out of bed. Robbie and Cerys stood on the landing, looking tousled and confused in their night clothes.

"He was shouting," said Robbie.

"He must have been dreaming." I could hear Jack making a strange noise like hiccups. "Go back to bed."

Cerys asked, "Do you want – "

"Both of you," I said, and went into Jack's bedroom.

I didn't put the light on. The glow from the landing seemed enough, less intrusive. Inside the bedroom I slid my feet along the carpet rather than stepping – you never knew what you'd find on the floor in Jack's room, anything from crisps to books to anonymous chunks of plastic – but I made it to his bedside and sat down without mishap.

His breathing had a hitch in it and I sensed that if I wasn't there he would be crying, like the small boy he had been only a few months ago.

"Hey," I said, "what's brought this on?" He burrowed into the pillow and didn't speak. I rested my hand on his shoulder for a little while in silence. "Were you having a bad dream?"

After a moment he turned onto his back and sniffled. I found a tissue in my pocket and gave it to him, and he sat up and blew his nose.

I told him, "Robbie and Cerys woke me up because you were shouting. Must have been quite a dream."

He spoke over the tissue. His voice was harsh, like someone with a bad cold. "I was up on Thorny Bank. Uncle Gwylim was punching me and then two men came and got hold of the rifles and started hitting him. There was blood running down the field." His tone wavered upwards, but he swallowed and said with more control, "I asked Iwan today – about what really happened to Uncle Gwylim. He didn't want to tell me but I said I had to know because Da and Robbie aren't talking about it."

I patted his arm and sighed. "No wonder you had a nightmare."

"Gwylim was trying to kill Charles Humphrey, wasn't he? When he hit me." Another pause. He said, "I keep thinking about it. What if I'd stood up again? If I could have stopped him shooting, they might both have been safe."

"He'd got it into his head that the gun was the only way out of his problems. He was going to shoot Humphrey, whatever it took – so it was always going to be nasty."

"But I should have tried." he said. "I feel like I'm a coward. Robbie put up a fight – "

I interrupted by giving his shoulders a little squeeze. "That isn't a fair comparison. There were four of us when those men came. You were on your own, and Gwylim might have hurt you very badly."

"But what if..."

Madoc looked round the door, and asked quietly, "All right?" and I felt the reaction in Jack's body as he shut down whatever else he was going to say. I could have thumped them both.

"Go and make a pot of tea," I said. "Enough for all of us, not too strong. I'll sit with him till he goes back to sleep."

I did just that, but though Jack drank the tea the conversation had ended. I had to go back to bed and worry about it until, some time in the early hours, I too fell asleep.

~~~

In the morning it was raining, summer rain, steady and grey. We were all tired and I didn't wake Jack. When the school minibus driver tooted her horn at the road-end I let her go on tooting and after she drove away I phoned the school office again to say Jack wouldn't be in.

Madoc put on a light waterproof and went out to exercise Coel. Robbie mucked out the two stables, popped into the kitchen to say he was spending the day at The Ghyll, and left.

Cerys retreated to her room, where she did vocal warm-ups and began to practise an aria she was learning. I didn't recognise the language, and she sang it in loud, unpredictable bursts which sounded very aggressive. I could have wished for more peaceful household music but I let her get on with it and went out to the stables, where the yard was troubled only by the twitter-filled comings and goings of the swallows through the rain.

Zilla was healing well physically, but the tedium of being kept indoors for her own good was proving a trial for her temper. I gave her a hay-net to munch so she could take out her irritation on it while I re-dressed her wound. I had developed a knack for removing the dressing, to achieve just the right angle of pull – and even then I was careful to tuck myself closely into her flank, in case she objected to the feel of the adhesive being unstuck. Otherwise she might kick me through the wall into Coel's stable.

When I'd finished I took the used dressings back to the house and disposed of them in the Rayburn fire. Upstairs, Cerys continued to repeat phrases of her music. Jack's breakfast plate was empty on the table, but he wasn't in the kitchen. I looked for him in the front room and the larder. His wellington boots were still in the porch. I looked in his bedroom and the bathroom, in Robbie's bedroom and our own. When I asked Cerys if she'd seen him she said she had no idea where he was, and then resumed singing so ferociously I couldn't ask her anything else. German, definitely.

I opened Jack's bedroom curtains, and leaned over the piled books on the windowsill to look out across the garden. Up the bank, under the elder bushes that stood over Kip's grave, was what looked like a big black mushroom, with a white button at its centre. It took me a minute of peering through the rain-streaked glass to realise the mushroom was an ancient, frayed umbrella that spent most of its life ignored among the walking sticks and shepherd's crooks. I guessed Jack must be sitting under it. At least he'd taken notice of my warning to stay close to home. I put my coat and boots back on and went out into the wet garden.

The white button on top of the mushroom turned out to be an upturned yogurt pot from last night's tea. I tapped a fingernail on it. "Hello? What's this for?"

Jack's voice said from under the umbrella, "It's to stop the rain running down the handle."

"Oh, okay then." I noted that his brain seemed to be working all right. "Is it dry under there now? Can I come in?"

The umbrella rose slightly in response, so I sat down and huddled in next to my son. He was sitting on a carrier bag beside the big slate that Robbie had put on Kip's grave. His black eye had progressed from slate blue and purple to shades of yellow and green, and he'd drawn up his knees and wrapped his arms around his shins in a defensive crouch. As I arranged myself I realised his legs were longer than mine now.

"What are you doing out here, then?" I asked. Hiding under an umbrella might have been normal if Jack was four, but he wasn't.

"Cerys is making a hell of a racket."

"I think it's German."

"Whatever it is, it's doing my head in."

"You're tired, that's all," I said. He rubbed his fingers across the damp surface of the slate and I saw that his knuckles were red and angry-looking. "What have you been doing? Are you still worrying about that dream last night?"

"No." There was a pause, with the rain pattering on the old umbrella and trickling off the end of each rib. Below its edge swallows flipped in and out of view, hunting low as they sieved midges out of the wet, honeysuckle-scented air. Five nestlings had fledged and were squatting on the wall top, with their navy suit-tails outspread and their beaks outlined in white, like sad-clown makeup.

I let the silence stretch and eventually Jack said, "Things keep dying."

"Yes," I said, without stressing it. "But you've lived on a farm all your life. You know that."

"Someone killed Kip."

"It was an accident, though."

Another little stretch of silence. Last night's bad dreams had not been about the dog.

He went on rubbing the wet surface of the slate. "Iwan said the police might take away Da's rifle and the shotgun. Does Robbie know? He's going to be steaming mad at me."

"He'll live."

"I didn't mean to get Da into trouble."

"You didn't."

He gave the slate a couple of despondent, half hearted punches. "I didn't get anything right, either."

"Life's full of what-ifs," I said. Last night he'd branded himself a coward for not daring to face Gwylim when he'd been hit. I'd fretted over that myself, and through the dark sleepless hours a crazy idea had emerged and survived into daylight. I decided to try it. "Listen. I'm going to tell you a story."

He sighed. "If you have to."

"Once upon a time..." I began. He made a scornful noise but I went on, "in a land not all that far from here... there was a girl who worked in a racing stable. The trainer's son was a grand handsome boy with yellow hair and blue eyes. When he invited her out she was flattered, so she said Yes."

I didn't know whether he was listening, but he hadn't shown any impatience either, so I continued.

"She was very happy at first. But she began to notice that the handsome boy was rough with the horses she looked after. He was mean to the other lasses who worked there, but if anybody complained he said it was just a bit of fun."

"Mm," he said, studying his trainers with his chin between his knees. "Why didn't she tell him to stop it?"

My pulse had begun to race. The girl had been me, and it hadn't been a fairytale. I had never told this story to anyone, other than Madoc, and Jack wasn't in a fit state for anything but distant, impersonal facts, so I must make a fairytale out of them to keep us all under control, Jack, myself, and the words.

"The other people working at the stables had got used to it, as if it was normal. After all, his father was the boss, and the horses and the people had to do what he said. If she complained, they laughed at her. She didn't tell the trainer because he would have laughed too. The handsome boy went out with another girl, and he didn't care if she got upset. She tried telling him he was unkind. She tried being nice to him. But nothing worked. So the horses kept on being hurt, and she kept on being hurt, and she thought she was a failure. She felt horrible all the time, like her head was full of broken glass."

Jack lifted his head and looked at me.

"Did you know her?" I realised he had seen through the fairytale. Before I had time to panic about what else he might guess, he went on, "I'd have jacked-in a job like that."

"I – she – she was fond of the horses." I had stayed because of Double Jump – King Coel's grandmother. "The owner moved her favourite filly to another racing yard, so she asked if she could go with it and work there. They happened to be nice people so they said Yes. They treated her fairly. They were kind to her."

"Is she all right now?"

Was I all right? The young swallows erupted off the wall and the whole family swooped past, twittering to each other.

I said, "Yes. She wasn't to blame for other people being bastards. It took her a long while to stop feeling guilty, but you have to stop blaming yourself, if you're going to go on living."

"Did she manage it?"

"Yes," I said.

"You weren't going to tell me she didn't, though, were you!" He picked at an incipient hole in the knee of his jeans. "It's a story,

335

after all! I suppose she married a handsome prince who turned the broken glass into diamonds."

"Don't be cynical," I said. I resisted the urge to tell him how I'd fallen in love with Madoc, because at Jack's age romance wasn't going to look like a cure. "The thing is, you can't change what's happened. Sometimes you don't know till a long time afterwards what you could have done differently, and perhaps, after all, there wasn't anything you could have done."

He abandoned the hole and went back to the original problem. "I always thought Uncle Gwylim liked me."

"People can like you and still do shitty things. I don't think he wanted to hurt you."

"I know, Iwan told me he must have been in trouble. But he still hit me, didn't he! Iwan won't tell me what happened to him. I think he doesn't want to scare me. But I want to know. Whoever killed Gwylim, they meant to hurt him, they wanted him to die. I'm not scared – I'm angry. I can't do anything about him being dead and makes me want to beat them." He made a fist again and pounded on the slate. "I want to get a rock and smash them."

"Shh," I said, capturing his hand.

He gulped. "I didn't tell any of this to Iwan. I s-said I wanted them put in prison, so they can't hurt anybody else."

"You want justice," I said. "We all do."

The rain tip-tapped on the umbrella. The soaked fabric had begun to diffuse a fine mist over us, and damp was seeping coldly out of the ground through my jeans. I went on holding his hand.

After a while he asked, "How do you manage stuff like this? You and Da?"

"I don't know," I said, with a small laugh. "We're still learning."

"Well, what did you do when Da's stallion died? Robbie calls him the skeleton in the closet – the family what-if."

"I know he does." Cymru wasn't the only skeleton in that closet, and today I'd already opened the door as far as I could bear to. "We just had to get on with it."

"Did you sweep up the broken glass, or smash it some more?"

"We swept it under the carpet. Your Da had to give up a lot of dreams."

The umbrella swayed as Jack sat up. He pulled his hand from mine and the yogurt pot rattled and fell onto the grass. "Why didn't he just buy another stallion? I thought he'd made a lot of money."

"Oh, no. He did win a bit, but not hundreds of thousands of pounds." I didn't want to complicate the story with property prices and economic recession, so I said, "A jockey only gets a percentage of the prize money."

"Wasn't he Champion Jockey, then?"

"No. I think he liked horses too much."

"What d'you mean?"

"He's kind to them, like you are. He's curious about how they tick, and so he's patient. That's why he made such a success out of Cymru, being willing to carry on when other people said the horse was useless. And then, your Da would never race any horse to exhaustion, no matter who its owner was. He'd pull up and walk it home. I know some of the old-style trainers wouldn't book him to ride their horses. They thought he wouldn't ride hard enough."

"So he didn't ride hundreds of winners?" He sounded disappointed.

"D'you know, I never asked him? I think he won quite a bit the year we met, but you know how tall he is, he was always starving himself to 'make the weight'. He loved riding your Great-uncle Dava's horses, but he was getting too heavy for the ones at the bottom of the handicap. He knew he'd have to retire quite soon. And that's why Cymru was so important to him."

"Oh. He wanted to breed horses because he couldn't race them any more."

"Pretty much. But we didn't have the money to buy another stallion when Cymru died – and your Da couldn't go back into racing, so we ended up farming and pre-training instead."

Jack said thoughtfully, "I hope I won't be tall, then."

I glanced at him. "I didn't know you wanted to be a jockey."

"It's up there with a few other ideas," he said, examining his knuckles.

"Hm. You're as tall as Robbie was at your age." I let that sink in. The swallows had flown away. I could hear them twittering in the yard now, on the other side of the house. I wondered how Jack would cope if he got onto the emotional roller-coaster of working with racehorses. He would make each one his friend yet he would never be sure when it went down to the starting post whether it would come back as a winner or an also-ran, or crippled, or perhaps never come back at all.

He was quiet for longer than I expected so I added, "Robbie's six foot now, and I bet he weighs twelve stone."

"Oh. Well, that's that then." He made a fist again, but this time he bumped it casually off the stone, as though dismissing that ambition as just one of many possibilities. "I wondered about being a vet."

"There's a lot of death involved in being a vet," I reminded him, still aware of his emotions. "It isn't all bunnies and bottle-fed lambs. You might not like it as much as you think."

"Mam! I'm not a babby any more! But if I was a vet I could stop animals suffering. Some of them, anyway. Give the what-ifs a fighting chance." His blue eyes, with the fading bruises, met mine in a flashing challenge. "I'll help you do Zilla's dressings."

"Will you!" I glanced at him, and as quickly away again. "Right, I'll get you up in good time to go to school tomorrow. You'll need top exam results to get into vet college."

He groaned. "Do you have to be so practical!"

"Yes! This umbrella's leaking, and if your bum's as wet as mine we're going to have to change our clothes. Let's go in."

Chapter 42.

Linda phoned us the following day.

"I'm at my wits' end," she said. "How are we going to organise Gwyl's funeral? The police can't tell me how long it will be until the inquest, and I can't do anything till I know."

"The Liaison Officer told me it can be three weeks," I said.

"Our woman told us the same. She says I should talk to the Council here. I can claim costs back from some compensation scheme."

"Criminal Injuries," I said. "The Liaison Officer told us about that."

"But I have to pay up front! I can't claim unless they catch whoever killed him, and I won't get anything if he isn't convicted."

"I know. The Liaison Officer told us that, too."

Iwan Bradley had been the gift that kept on giving: explaining the developments in police enquiries, the implications of what had happened, why the demands of the investigations were necessary. He focused us on the world of the living, instead of dwelling on the horrors around Gwylim's death. I wondered if Linda's Officer was not so good at her job.

"The joint bank account's overdrawn," Linda said, "and I haven't got anything to spare in my own account. Rent and food is about all I can manage."

I asked, "Could you give up the flat and move back into the house? It's standing empty, isn't it?"

"Obviously," she said, with acid in her voice, "but I don't want to. I lived with him there, remember? Anyway it's mortgaged. Suppose the bank repossessed it after we moved in?" Her tone moderated a little as she admitted, "I wouldn't feel safe there. I'm scared of that rat Humphrey. I mean, really scared. I have to hope he doesn't know where this flat is. Look, Siân – I'm sorry to harp on about the funeral – but you said Gwyl lent you money..."

I'd heard that one coming. "He did, and we gave him a great chunk of it back."

"Did you? Then where's it gone?" There was a note of desperation in her voice.

"I bet Charles Humphrey's got it by now," I said. I knew she wanted me to say we'd pay for the funeral, but I couldn't because I had no idea how we could manage it. "Look – I'll have to talk to Madoc about it. It isn't going to be simple."

"Nothing Gwyl did was ever simple," she said.

"I'll phone you back."

Even the ever-helpful Iwan was unable to give us an answer. He said, "Talk to the local Council, wherever you want to hold the funeral."

"I hope the funeral director will take payment in legs of lamb."

I understood why there had to be a delay, and I knew we needed to wait for the post-mortem and the coroner's inquest and a death certificate, but I wanted everything to be over. We'd had enough of the sorrows and – as Jack had observed – the what-ifs. Perhaps Madoc could wait patiently for justice to be done, but I wanted the misdeeds and their outcomes swept into a box and, literally, buried.

~~~

The weather was still wet next day and I couldn't get out of the house. People kept calling or phoning, wanting information that I didn't have or didn't want to give. I reacted to my imprisonment with furious cleaning of the kitchen. I did the floor and the worktops and the Rayburn, and by mid-afternoon I was reduced to de-cluttering cupboards and wiping shelves and plates and tea mugs.

When the phone rang again I was scrubbing stains out of the teapot with the blue iris pattern. I launched profanities before I picked up the handset.

"Siân?" Linda said. Her voice sounded shaky. "What's this envelope you've sent me?"

"What envelope?" I asked. I wasn't in the mood for guessing games.

"It was on the doormat just now when I came in from work. Someone must have pushed it through the door. Did you send it?"

"Sorry, I've no idea what you're talking about."

"It's wrapped up in sellotape like a mummy. I had to take the scissors to it. It's got your name and address on it and it's full of fifty-pound notes." There was a quiver in her voice that suggested she was close to tears.

"Good lord," I said. "That's the money we gave to Gwylim."

"I can't believe it. It would solve all sorts of problems," she said, "if it's really ours."

I gritted my teeth. "Yes, it would, wouldn't it."

~~~

To track the movements of the envelope between us and Linda was a puzzle.

I said to Madoc, "How on earth did that money get to her? She's no idea."

"I don't know," he said. "I can only guess. We know Gwyl had decided Humphrey wasn't having it – that's what the shooting was about, wasn't it? But when he heard Humphrey wasn't dead he must have known the musclemen would come to get him. What if he handed the money on to someone he could trust – someone Humphrey didn't know – and told him, if the worst happened, to take it to Linda."

"D'you really think he'd risk that?" I said. Gwylim's world was one I had learned not to trust. I was still afraid Humphrey might send people like Jamie or Henry to have a "little chat" with us.

The rain trickled down the windows and blurred the green light from the garden.

"Gwyl must have had *some* friends who aren't crooks!" he said. "He couldn't risk taking that money to Linda in person, in case he led Humphrey's goons to her – and the girls. At least he made sure it got there in the end. That's more like the brother I grew up with. The man he used to be."

"A pity he didn't think of that when he was knocking our Jack about," I said. "I wish the money had come back to us."

Madoc shook his head. "At least Charles Humphrey didn't get his hands on it. If it has to go to anyone, why not Linda and the girls? I want to see Gwyl's funeral done properly."

"And if Humphrey sends his bouncers here again? What then?"

"I can't spend my life worrying something that might never happen," said Madoc. "Even your best mate Iwan says – "

"He isn't," I began crossly.

"There are times it looks like it! But when someone like him tells me that witnesses worry more than they need to, I believe him. Look, Mouse – those tattooed knuckle-draggers aren't going to risk coming here. They must know the police might drop in any minute. So stop worrying about them."

~~~

I was in Zilla's stable, with the mare head-collared and pulling grumpily at her morning hay-net while I dealt with her wound.

I took the coverings off a fresh dressing and pressed it gently into place. By now Zilla's stamp of the foot and flick of the tail were merely recognition that I'd reached the final stage and would stop annoying her.

"Job done," I said.

Madoc went limping past the door with his sheep crook, the exercise saddle over his other arm. Zilla carried on eating as though her life depended on it. I took her head-collar off, gathered the used dressing and the papers and left her to it.

Madoc was saddling King Coel, chatting to him in a low voice, and when I looked in at the door the colt pricked his long ears and whickered at me.

Madoc said, "I thought I'd have a last spin round the fields with this lad before he goes off to Dava." He ran his fingers down the inside of the girth, making sure the tender skin under the colt's ribcage was not being pinched. "We may as well enjoy ourselves, isn't that right, boyo?"

I leaned on the stable door, enjoying the play of light on the young horse's summer coat – not just black and brown but oily refractions of blue, silver and purple. The sun flickered in his cairngorm eyes and made mysteries of their dark, oblong pupils.

"He looks a picture," I said. "I'll be sorry to see him go."

"You always are," said Madoc, slipping the bridle over Coel's head.

"Yes, but this one's special, isn't he? How about I take some photographs of him?"

He paused, considering. "I'd like that."

"Then I'll just pop this rubbish on the fire," I said, "and I'll see you up the field."

The grass had jumped six inches since the rain. The views across the fells were crystal clear and a fleet of little clouds was floating over, rounded, white and flat bottomed like newly baked meringues. In the trees at the far side of Sweet Holme a cuckoo called, again and again. The day was perfect.

I didn't care that the hems of my jeans were soaked. I forgot all the strain and anguish of the past few weeks. Madoc was riding King Coel again. He was riding, and the young horse was full of promise. I got out my phone and hoped its camera could do it all justice.

The colt was fresh and inclined to spook for sheer joy. Madoc was amused, but patient. I knew his ankle wasn't yet fit to carry him in a racing position and though that frustrated him, much as not being able to ride Zilla frustrated me, he kept Coel to that walk for almost an hour, on the long track around the farm, worn to a darker green with the regular passage of hooves. I photographed him walking up the field; I photographed him walking down. I photographed him coming towards me; I photographed him going away. Then towards the end of the session, Madoc took Coel to the bottom of the gallop and quietly slipped his feet from the stirrups and let his legs wrap round the horse's belly. And then he put Coel into a trot up the hill.

"You eejit," I said, as I realised what he was doing. He was facing the young horse towards five flights of hurdles, without the security of stirrups. "You tell me I take risks..."

But if I tried to stop him, I might provoke the very fall I was worrying about. Coel broke into a canter.

"Oh what the hell." I steadied myself against the wall and set the phone to video mode.

The colt rose to the first jump, and Madoc sat him in easy balance, folding at the hip as though he was part of the horse. They came on up the jumping lane and, with each jump, Madoc gave Coel a little more freedom until as they flew over the last hurdle, he dropped the reins completely and spread his arms like an aeroplane. I couldn't help but laugh. As a display of skill it was impressive; as evidence of a reckless streak in my normally sober husband, it was totally unexpected. I recognised it all the same, his way of letting off steam after the frustrations of the past few weeks. The colt cantered towards the top of the gallop and Madoc picked up control again and slowed him to a gentle trot.

I stopped videoing and went to meet them.

"Did you get that?" Madoc was wearing the biggest grin I'd seen for months.

"Yes! But for God's sake," I said, "don't do it again!" I reached up and rubbed the colt's forehead. "You're a grand lad, aren't you! Got more sense than some I could name!"

"He's much more straightforward than Cymru ever was. I don't think I'd have risked doing that with him!"

"Coel," I said, "you've got big boots to fill."

The colt moved his head out of my hands and rubbed his sweaty nose on his knee. Madoc said, "All right, boyo. Let's go in and get you washed down."

We began to walk down the fields towards the farm. Madoc sat relaxed in the saddle, with his long legs moulding to the colt's ribs.

"I'm going to be stiff tomorrow," he said, with a chuckle. "I haven't ridden like that in years. Did you get plenty of photographs?"

"I got a video of you being a lunatic! I dread to think what Helen would say – "

"Just don't tell her!"

"You needn't worry about that! How's your ankle?"

"It'll be fine."

"Sounds as though you aren't sure."

He laughed. "My shoe feels tight. My foot's swollen a bit, but it's not painful." I guessed that meant it hurt but he wasn't going to admit it. "I'll put the moon boot back on and have a quiet walk-about before Paul comes with the horsebox."

"And don't be too proud to use your stick." I had to jog to keep up with Coel's effortless walk over the growing grass. "What time's Paul supposed to be here?"

"Any time after twelve."

I said, trying to keep my tone light, "I'll be sorry to see this boy go."

"I will, too." He pulled a face. "But I'll live. I miss racing and missing it hasn't killed me."

I reached up and put my hand on his thigh, feeling the muscles move with the horse's eager stride. "That much? Still?"

"Yep. Every day. If I was still working for Dava I'd beg to ride this fellow through his career. But I haven't got any race-riding left in me, and I'd need three or four years to do justice to him."

"Is he that good?"

Madoc looked down at me and smiled. The habitual air of reserve had gone. His eyes were alive and confident, the way he'd looked on the day the photographer had captured us, Cymru and Madoc and me, coming into the winner's enclosure after that last race at Aintree.

"You can never be certain. But that's what we're going to find out."

Chapter 43.

With King Coel loaded up and gone, and Zilla still recovering, Madoc and I were back to our position of six months before. We had no horses mature enough to ride.

On Friday morning I was driven by boredom to attack the grime on the pickup, and I was still halfway through the job when Iwan Bradley came bouncing into the yard in his little grey Golf. His smile seemed to have gained in cheerfulness in the two days since we'd last seen him.

Madoc came out of the house to meet him, and I put down the wash-brush and crossed the yard to turn off the hosepipe.

"Good news?" asked Madoc.

"Yep. I'm here to tell you officially, Charles Humphrey's been arrested."

I shook the water off my hands and said, "Thank God for that!"

"So have James Walker, Henry Heseldine and several other rather nasty characters." It took me a moment to realise that Walker and Heseldine must be the two henchmen.

"What have they been charged with?" asked Madoc.

"You name it – threatening and abusive behaviour, assault, criminal damage, cocaine trafficking, conspiracy to murder. The best thing from your point of view is that they've all been remanded in custody."

"In prison?" I said.

"That's right. You can stop worrying they're going to walk in on you. Their solicitors applied for bail but with a list of charges like those, they had no chance. They'll be on remand till the case comes to court. And once the court sees the evidence we've got, they won't walk anywhere in public for a very long time to come."

I leaned back against the pickup and shut my eyes. The relief was indescribable.

Madoc said, "Perhaps now we can get back to normal."

"As normal as we can ever be," I said, opening my eyes again. "We'll have visitors in the holiday cottage before tea-time."

~~~

On Saturday evening Robbie brought Beth to visit. He ushered her into the kitchen with an unexpected flourish, hiding his left hand behind his back in way that reminded me of Jack when he was feeling puckish. The flourish became understandable when he lifted Beth's hand and showed us a sapphire and diamonds on her ring-finger.

"Aha," I said, "so that's what you've really been doing at The Ghyll."

I got up and kissed both of them. Robbie smelled of aftershave and Beth of hospital hand gel, and there was no trace of the shrill scent she'd worn at the show.

"Well done," said Madoc. "You've picked a good one."

Beth slipped her arm through Robbie's in a gesture that was both possessive and protective. "We meant to tell you sooner but with Gran's funeral, and all the police business you've had going on, we didn't dare."

Robbie said, "Now, as you won't have had time to stock up with bubbly..." His awkward posture resolved as he produced a bottle from behind his back and gave it to me.

"Champagne! You little devil!" I passed it on to Madoc to open. "I'm out of practice with that stuff. I don't want to knock anyone unconscious."

"Don't open it yet!" Robbie exclaimed, as Madoc crunched the foil off the cork. "Do we actually possess any wine glasses?"

I said, "There's a set upstairs, you cheeky bugger."

"Is there? Where?"

"In a box in our bedroom. I haven't unpacked them since we moved."

"A full set?"

"Well, at least five of them are the same."

"Cor! I thought we'd have to drink it out of mugs!"

Beth was watching the exchange with a growing smile. I said, "Does he talk like this to your Mam and Dad?"

"Not yet, but he's working on it."

I brought the glasses down from the bedroom and gave them a wipe with a tea towel. Beth and Robbie sat at the table next to each other. Madoc opened the bottle. Robbie, a glass in each hand, managed to catch most of the eruption, and the tea towel and I dealt with the overflow.

"Here's to a happy life together..." Madoc added with a wink to Robbie, "And long may you be under her thumb!"

The bubbles in the wine were fresh and tickled my mouth and nose. I couldn't remember when I'd last drunk champagne. It had been such a long time since we'd had any event worthy of it.

After a few moments Robbie suggested to Beth, "Shall we tell them the rest?"

"I think we'd better."

"You do it, then. It's your news."

She looked from Madoc to me. For a moment, as she gathered herself, I thought, *She's pregnant*. I was quite unprepared for her to say, "Gran has left me her share of the farm."

"Good heavens," I said, and, as an afterthought, "That's wonderful."

Perhaps Robbie guessed what I'd been thinking, because he said airily, "Of course, the land's the only reason I'm marrying her. And the herd of Shorthorns and the fact she's got no brothers to beat me up."

"Of course," Beth said in the same tone, "and that would also be the only reason why Dad's offered you a job. Obviously."

"So you'll be independent at last," Madoc said.

"That's what he thinks." Beth tickled Robbie and he had to put down his champagne to fight her off.

Madoc said to me under the chaos, "Well, that's one less child to worry about – just Cerys and Jack to go!"

"Don't be so mean!" I said. When Beth allowed Robbie to sit up again I asked, "Have you set a date?"

"Some time in the autumn," said Robbie, "September probably. We' need to find a house to rent."

"If we don't find somewhere handy, Mam and Dad have said we can stay with them," said Beth. "Mam keeps telling me the farmhouse is big enough."

Her expression was ambiguous, but I could read from Robbie's face that the idea wasn't entirely to his liking so I guessed she wasn't keen either. I said to Madoc, "What about the holiday cottage?"

"What about it?" he asked.

I nudged him. "Don't be dim. Can't they rent it off us? We could easily take it off the holiday agency's books."

"I see," said Madoc, with an air of surprise. "Well! Why not?"

Beth got up, marched round the table and bent to kiss him.

"I take it you like the idea," he said drily. "Renting, I mean."

"Yes, thank you very much. We'd love to."

I said, "I promise not to step over the threshold without being invited." Beth laid a hand on my shoulder as she went back to her place, and I added, "Anyway, I've cleaned the place so often, I'll be really happy to leave it to someone else!"

Robbie leaned back and stretched his long legs. "Do I get any say in this?"

"No," we replied together.

"Then can I make a suggestion?"

"Go on," said Madoc, with reservations in his voice.

"Well, Andy's said more than once that he'd like to buy a couple of meadows off us. Wouldn't that help you out with the loans? I know you were trying to hang onto the land for my sake, but now that I'm going off to farm at Tebay..." I half expected him to say, 'this place will be more than you old ones can cope with' but he didn't. Perhaps he was beginning to learn tact. "Wouldn't you rather concentrate on the horses? Cut back on the sheep, let Andy have the fell right that goes with Syke Side and Sweet Holme. You can always buy hay off him if you need it."

Madoc sat back, his eyebrows high with astonishment, and I said to Beth, "If you're still giving away kisses, give that boy a couple from me. I think it's a bloody wonderful idea."

Chapter 44.

Andy and Hazel called one evening in the week after Robbie's engagement. I was sitting in the kitchen and heard the car pull into the yard, and when I didn't recognise the engine note I got up, but Hazel had already knocked at the kitchen door and, as usual, walked straight in.

"Hello, stranger!" I said.

"Evening! I tried phoning you – but is your phone not working?"

"Oh – no, sorry! We've pulled the plug on it."

"Why? What's the problem?"

"People kept phoning us! – well, not 'people' so much as the newspapers and the magazines." Everybody who wanted to talk to us had an angle. It was their work. The police wanted to make arrests. Reporters and journalists wanted to sell news: there was one very persistent woman who wanted to do a profile about us and the farm and the horses and wouldn't take no for an answer. Madoc had got cross then and unplugged the land line. Even Iwan had a professional interest in our sanity. We were deleting texts and leaving e-mails unanswered.

"Robbie and Cerys are pretty calm about it all, but I have to keep reminding Jack that if strangers ask personal questions, we shut our mouths."

"Aye. Tell them to do one."

"Oh, we have! It all kicked off when the police made the arrests. The Family Liaison Officer, he put out a statement that we didn't want to be bothered, but the media are still trying."

"Well, I'm not the media." Andy dumped a six-pack of beer on the draining board and shut the door, and at the sound of his voice Madoc limped in from the front room.

"Eh, man! Are you going somewhere, with your clean shirt and tie?"

"I thought I'd better dress him up a bit," Hazel said, "you know, give him the edge in negotiations."

"Aha," Madoc said. "You've come to talk about Syke Side and Sweet Holme."

Andy nodded. "Robbie told me you were thinking of selling, so here we are."

Hazel said, "Well, you two go into the garden with the beer, and we'll stop here in the kitchen. Go on, out!"

The two men looked at one another, then Madoc hooked a finger into the beer cans and led the way through the front room into the garden, collecting his sheep crook on the way.

I was satisfied for once that the state of the kitchen was up to Hazel's standards. In the last few days I'd cleaned an awful lot more than came naturally. The long-suffering blue and white teapot had survived having its innards scrubbed and sat, slightly startled, on a dust-free, uncluttered worktop. The table and chairs had been polished till nobody could sit down without squeaking.

"Tea? Coffee? Or would you rather have white wine?"

"Thought you'd never ask."

I poured two glasses of cheap Lambrini, and we squeaked into seats at the table.

Hazel said, "We saw Jack on the way up the lonnin, with your bay pony. He looks to be very fond of her."

"Yes. She can't graze on High Field with the other two because they'll rip those dressings off, so he's been leading her out to trim the verges."

"Remind him about our bitch having pups. He can take his pick, remember."

"I don't think he's forgotten, but thanks." We both drank. "You know, it's quite peaceful with the phone permanently off."

"Looks like you need it. Where are your other kids?"

"Cerys is working a shift at the services, and Robbie's out with Beth. You'll have heard that they're engaged?"

"Aye, our Katie told me."

"I can't believe he's that grown up, but there it is. I must be nearly old enough to be a granny."

"Get away." Hazel considered me. "You're looking well on it. Younger, if anything."

"Do I?" I was surprised.

"Aye. You've put a bit of weight on. It suits you."

"It must be the wine," I said, joking.

"Steady on! Next thing you'll be knocking back Prosecco, and then Pimms, and who knows where you'll end up."

"Don't worry, I have another addiction that's much more dangerous. It's called horses." I watched the wine tilt and sway as I rotated my glass.

Hazel let me have a minute of silence before she urged, "Come on! Andy and me have been dying of curiosity. You've had the police buzzing in and out of your place for days on end. You can't sit there just swigging wine and saying nothing!"

"It's quite a relief to sit and say nothing. It does muck up your life having policemen around all the time."

"Well, I want to know all about it, so come on."

I chuckled. "Are you sure?"

"Ooh yes. Murder and mayhem are right up my street."

One of the things Iwan had said frequently was that people would often go a long way to help us – and I knew Hazel was one of them. She was interested us as people, without calculating how to turn a profit, tick boxes or make an arrest. It would be even more of a relief than making a victim statement, to talk things over with her.

I said, "The law itself gets more and more like a game of chess."

"Oh? I was never any good at that kind of thing."

"I'm not either."

She waited, her eyes thoughtful, while I refilled her glass and mine.

"Go on then."

So I went back to the beginning, about us owing money to Gwylim, how he'd slid into debt himself through the shady side of Humphrey's night clubs, and about Humphrey threatening us and Gwylim trying to shoot him.

Hazel said, "It doesn't bear thinking about."

"No. I thought what happened here was bad, then with Gwylim being killed it's all gone up a gear. But it's shifted away to Manchester, thank goodness. They've arrested Humphrey and the two muscle-men. I can't tell you what a relief it is to know that none of them got bail."

"Eh," she sighed. "What a bunch of bastards."

"Charles Humphrey's at the bottom of it all, every single thing." I found myself telling her about the Ninja and King Coel coming to us for pre-training, and Charles Humphrey and his wife staying in the cottage to see the horses working. By the end of the second glass I'd told her about taking my father's will to Chester and how I'd met Humphrey again at the races.

"D'you know," I said, gulping more wine, "would you believe, he tried to make a deal – if I'd let him sleep with me, he wouldn't push Gwylim for our money."

"Oh! My word, that's creepy."

"Yes. He tried to make out it was some sort of compliment."

"Oh, I'm not saying you aren't attractive!" Hazel was half shocked, half curious; exactly the kind of emotion that sold the "real life" magazines who'd been sounding us out. "But blackmail's hardly a chat-up line, is it! You can't have been tempted."

"Good God, no – but I keep thinking it was my fault. Isn't that weird? I mean, suppose I *had* said Yes? Perhaps we wouldn't have had to go through all this awfulness."

She said briskly, "Oh don't be so soft! Bastards like that don't stick to bargains! They flatter you till they get what they want, then it would have been, 'Wham, Bam, Thank-you Mam." Then he'd have wanted the money as well!"

"Very likely." I realised that Hazel was saying exactly the same as I'd said to Jack – but it was far harder for me to believe I'd done the right things. "Well, I'm looking forward to Humphrey standing in the dock, and with a bit of luck a judge will sentence him – I know it won't be for *that*, but it'll be good enough for me."

"I can understand that," she said. "What did Madoc have to say?"

I thought of Madoc's warm voice murmuring, "I'm not going to share you. Ever," and I smiled at her and shook my head.

She broke into a chuckle, her eyes twinkling with enjoyment. "All right then. Did you tell the police about it? You ought to."

"I wasn't going to tell anybody. I almost didn't tell Madoc."

"Wow. Then I'm flattered you told me."

I emptied my glass. "Well, but I'm pissed," I said.

She laughed. "Nowhere near, not by our Katie's standards."

Madoc came in from the garden with Andy. The crook went back into the corner, and the unopened cans of beer clunked onto the table.

"Them midges is getting serious out there," Andy said.

"Ah, stop moaning," said Hazel. "When they bite you, they fall off dead."

"I wish!"

Madoc sat down beside me. Andy slid onto the other chair and halfway off again. "By heck, lass," he said as he righted himself. "You've been short of summat to do, haven't you?" He opened another can of beer. "Anyway, your man and me, we've agreed about the land."

"That was quick," I said.

"Quick?" Madoc studied the level of wine in the bottle. "Well they do say alcohol affects your perception."

I brushed a hand at him. "Oh, hush."

"You see," Hazel said to me, "there's method in my madness. Shove the men out there with the midgies and they have to crack on wi't job."

"I'll talk to a solicitor tomorrow," Andy said. "Seventeen acres at two thousand nine hundred an acre, yes?" The wine prevented my brain from doing the necessary multiplication, but it seemed the total would clear a fair chunk of our debts. "And then we'll need a valuation of the fell right. Will you have time to do it, with all this police business going on?"

Madoc drew a deep breath, considering. "Yes, I think so. I can drive again now – it makes a lot of difference being able to get into

Penrith without needing a lift. There's still Gwylim's funeral to sort out, of course, but we can't do much with that until there's been an inquest. Linda – my sister-in-law – she's looking after it for the moment. Then there's that police chap, Iwan – "

"He keeps us sane," I added. "Jack, in particular." Hazel patted my hand comfortingly, and I smiled at her.

"He's here that often, I keep thinking he's going to run off with my wife, but she tells me otherwise."

"No such luck," I said, laughing at him. "I'm staying."

Andy chuckled. "Aye, you women know when you're on to a good thing."

"Mind you," said Madoc, "it isn't all plain sailing even now. The firearms officer is not happy that Jack could get at the rifle, so the police have revoked our certificate. They've pushed us to surrender the guns too."

"Nay! They've never tooken them off you!"

"Not quite," I said. "Iwan suggested we should give the guns up voluntarily."

Andy glanced at me. "Him again!"

Madoc said, "The police were twitchy on account of Gwylim, so I could see he had a point. I took them to the dealer in Penrith who's got specialised storage. We'll probably get them back sooner that way than if the police had confiscated them."

"What! I wouldn't have let them go in the first place," said Andy. "You'll have to appeal to get your certificate back, you know that, don't you? That'll cost you summat, not to mention a lot of bother."

"It's all going to be a lot of bother," I said.

Madoc agreed. "There'll be at least one trial at Manchester Crown Court. We don't know yet how many we'll have to go to, but once they start the firearms certificate will be the least of our worries."

Jack arrived at the back door, and I made a silencing expression at Madoc.

"Now then, young man," said Hazel, scanning Jack's face. "How's your eye?"

"It's better, thank you." He was rubbing his neck and arms. "Mam, have you got anything for midge bites? I had to bring Zilla back indoors because they were eating us alive."

"Did you put some spray on her?"

"Yes."

"Right. Good. You'd better fetch the first aid box out of the larder."

"Aye well," said Andy to Madoc, as Jack went out of the room. "Just let us know if you need owt."

"Thanks."

There was a pause. Jack came back with the box and set it on the table and began to rummage in it.

"You need the tube of anti-histamine," I told him.

When he'd found it he dug in his pocket and offered me a letter in a dog-eared white envelope. "Is this yours, Mam? I think it's from Grandad? You haven't opened it."

"Heavens, where did you find that?"

"In the larder behind the box."

He dotted cream over his freckled skin and began to rub it in.

Hazel said to him, "I was telling your Mam just now, our bitch is definitely going to have pups."

"Is she? That'll be cool."

I opened the letter with a feeling of resignation, not wanting to be dragged into my father's usual litany of aches and pains and complaints about Simon his assistant. But the opening paragraph of the letter brought me up short.

> I've got a buyer for the shop. I thought I'd better let you know that we'll exchange contracts some time in the next couple of months. After the last time you called, I went to look at the new sheltered housing on the road to Port Sunlight. They're not much bigger than rabbit hutches but there's a warden on duty 24 hours a day.
>
> I'm going to move there as soon as I can, so I need to get rid of all the furniture that won't fit the rabbit hutch. Do you want any of it? Come and have a look before I send it to the sale room...

Jack cleaned his fingers and put the lid back on the tube. "Mam, can I have some juice?"

"What?"

"Can I have a drink?"

"Yes. Yes, of course."

He made himself a drink and wandered into the front room. The television began to play music.

I tucked the letter back into its envelope and laid it ceremoniously on top of the first aid box. "It's from my Dad. I'll write back to him in the morning."

"Is everything all right?" asked Madoc, watching me.

"Yes," I said. "Funnily enough, I think it is."

I shared the last of the wine with Hazel, and Madoc and Andy's conversation turned to cattle and sheep and neighbouring farmers. Hazel speculated about what kind of outfit the Mother of the Groom ought to wear at Robbie and Beth's wedding, and where I might go to buy it. We giggled a lot. We didn't discuss the letter, or say any more about the investigation.

At last Andy pushed back his chair and said, "We'd best be off, I suppose."

We got up and stretched. "Oh, will you listen to us groaning," Hazel said. "We sound like a lot of old grannies."

"I can offer you a drop of oil," Madoc suggested.

Andy said with a half laugh, "I need a bloody grease-gun, me."

"I don't care what you use," she said, "if it'll stop you grumbling. How's your ankle, Madoc?"

"It's all right. I'm doing the exercises. Bending and stretching." He grinned. "Chasing the wife."

"Sometimes I even let him catch me." I leaned my shoulder against him, and chuckled when he put his arm round me.

Hazel said, "Oh, get a room, you two... We can't have this sort of carry-on, you'll corrupt the youth of the neighbourhood. If you're that short of summat to do, how about coming to choir next Monday?"

"Oh, I can't sing," said Madoc.

"You bloody can," I said. "Where d'you think Cerys gets it from?"

"Both of you," said Hazel firmly.

We all went out into the yard together. The shadowed evening air was fresh and calm and the honeysuckle was pumping out scent, and the swallow family chittered and swooped in the light above the barn roofs. I felt light-headed from the wine and Madoc, attempting to walk without his stick, was hardly any better, so when we bumped against each other we linked arms for want of better support.

Zilla came to the stable door and whickered at us.

"Is that the pony that got hurt?" asked Andy.

"Yes," I said.

"It wants a medal, if what our Daniel says is right."

We strolled across to see her. She put up with us stroking her for a minute or two, then when she found we had no food she shook her ears, turned her backside to us and went back to eating hay. The wound and its blue adhesive dressing, and the swelling under her skin, were all much smaller than they had been.

"She's healing nicely," I said, "thank goodness."

"You won't can sell her for showing, though, with a scar that size."

"It doesn't matter. Zilla," I said, "is family."

His eyebrows went up at the firmness of my reply. "Oh! Well, I daresay she's earned it. You've got nothing in the other stables now? No racehorses?"

"Not just at the minute," said Madoc. "The colt went off to training last week." There was the briefest of pauses in which I guessed he might have begun to tell Andy about Helen Rogers' plans for King Coel, but he decided not to. "There are two young ones coming at the start of next month, so by the time this ankle's properly mended, we'll be back into full work."

"By," said Hazel, "if you're not careful there'll be nowt left to twine about."

"Except these bloody midges," said Andy. "Come on, Missis, let's be-garn."

They got into the battered little van and drove away.

Madoc leaned his back against the stone wall while I refilled Zilla's water bucket, and when I'd bolted the door for the night he asked, "Well, Danger Mouse. Everything all right?"

"I'm a bit squiffy. Not used to that much wine in one go! I couldn't work out how much Andy is offering for Sweet Holme."

"About fifty thousand, by the time we've added in the fell right. He's getting a good bargain."

"It sounds huge to me."

"Well, we set the price per acre by comparing some land down the Lune Gorge that was sold in February – that was sour stuff, not good limestone like this. The thing is, we're both happy with the deal, and that goodwill is worth a lot."

"Do you mind?" I asked. "Selling it?"

"Well... no, if I'm honest. Robbie's hit the ground running at The Ghyll, and it will probably make our lives easier to have a bit less land."

"I can't believe we're going to have money in the bank at last. I thought we'd have to spend the rest of our lives fighting."

He laughed, softly. "You've done enough of that in the last couple of weeks to last you a lifetime. D'you think you got what you were fighting for?"

"I wasn't fighting to *get* anything. I was fighting to keep *this* – you. The family. The things I love."

He put his arms round me and kissed my forehead. "But there will be changes, no matter how much you fight. Robbie will have his own household. Cerys will be at college."

"We'll still have Jack," I said.

"He's growing up fast, though."

"Yes." I sighed. "I know he's got to fly at some point. He's thinking of being a vet, did he tell you?"

"Jack, handling drugs and scalpels? Wow. Mind you, he'll fit right in with vet students. They're a wild bunch."

"Mm."

"Don't sound so down about it. I'm looking forward to letting them all go. We'll be Madoc-and-Siân again, instead of That-Lot's-Parents." His hands slid warm under my tee-shirt. "If you were a bird, you'd be moulting your worn-out breeding feathers and growing a new set. Or maybe courting all over again. That would be fun."

"I'd quite like a bit of courtship," I said, as his arms tightened round me. "But I can do without gifts of worms, and let's skip the second brood, shall we!"

He chuckled.

We heard a vehicle pull up at the road-end, then drive away. It was about the time when the service station minibus would drop Cerys on her way home from the early evening shift. Footsteps came running up the track. Light, quick. She didn't usually feel like running at the end of a shift. I lifted my head from Madoc's shoulder.

"No peace for the wicked. I wonder what's happened."

She came through the gateway skipping with excitement and waving her phone. "Look! Look! It's an e-mail from Open Mike! They want me to audition!"

Madoc murmured in my ear, "Two down, one to go."

The End

Other books by Sue Millard

Against the Odds

(Prequel to SCRATCH)

Leaving home to work in a racing stable, Siân finds that the long hours and hard work are more than she bargained for. The only compensation is her responsibility for her favourite filly, Double Jump.

Siân is badly treated by her boyfriend, the trainer's arrogant son, Justin. When Double Jump's owner moves the filly to another yard, Siân decides to follow so she can escape him.

At the new yard she meets stable jockey Madoc Owen, who is determined to make a National Hunt winner out of Cymru, a bored flat-race stallion. Siân and Madoc may have a future together but there will be more than steeplechase fences in their way – Justin will see to that.

GENRE: Fiction, romance, sporting, equestrian. First published by J A Allen, 1995.

ISBN 978-0-85131-630-1 (Paperback is Remaindered – available as Author's own stock.) £5.00

Kindle ASIN: B00BGBIGNU

Coachman

Good-looking and ambitious George Davenport travels to London with his bride Lucy, determined to make the most of his skill in driving a four-in-hand of horses. It's 1838. Queen Victoria is crowned and England is at peace, but it isn't a good time to be a coachman.

As George finds employment with William Chaplin, the "Napoleon of coaching", the first railways are about to open across the country. Their competition will kill off the road-coaching trade. George has a lot to come to terms with... even before the boss's daughter starts to stalk him.

GENRE: Historical fiction, romance, sporting, equestrian, transport.

Published: 2012.

ISBN: 978-0-9573612-5-6 (Paperback) £9.99

Kindle ASIN: B009DORFOI.

Hoofprints in Eden

Winner of the Saint and Company Prize at the Lake District Book of the Year Awards, 20 June 2006. Based on a 2-year-long series of interviews with established breeders, this book explores the Fell pony breed and its traditions at the start of the new millennium.

Read about the Fell pony's Cumbrian background, the events of a typical year, its life on the fell, its traditional keeping and its links with hill farming, its characteristics and the work it can do.

Fully illustrated, and complete with a dictionary of Cumbrian farming expressions.

GENRE: Non-fiction, equestrian, history, farm & working animals

Published by Hayloft, 2005. ISBN 978-1-9045243-4-2. £17.00

Hoofprints in Eden

4-part digital edition for Kindle

The 2005 text is revised and additional photographs are included. Each part is roughly 25% of the whole book, though because some chapters are longer or shorter the number of chapters does vary.

Parts 1, 2, 3 and 4 (November-December 2013) are available on Kindle.

Kindle ASINs:

B00GB84MWC

B00GFW78L6

B00GWPCTD8

B00H8XMYMY

One Fell Swoop

This is where it all started, with humour, history and horses.

Norman Thelwell was Sue's hero (they both hailed from the Wirral) so when Sue moved to Cumbria and bought a Fell pony this "fellwell" book was the inevitable result.

A series of affectionate cartoons, poking gentle fun at the Fell breed and its history.

GENRE: Cartoon humour, farm & working animals.
ISBN 978-0-9573612-7-0 (Paperback) £5.00
Kindle ASIN B008ZBPB14

The Forthright Saga

Nothing ever happens in a small country town ... does it?

Nora Forthright and her grandson Wayne stumble through the fictional Cumbrian towns of Dangleby and Pullet St Mary, putting things right entirely by accident.

GENRE: Comedy thriller / cosy crime.
Published: 2012.
ISBN: 978-0-9573612-3-2 £6.99
Kindle ASIN: B0099RQNLU

For Children

Dragon Bait

Princess Andra volunteers to act as bait for the dragon ravaging her father's lands, on condition that she is released from an arrangement to marry a foreign prince.

Unfortunately the Knight Rescuer who turns up is not the trusty old retainer she expects, but an unknown conservationist who wants the dragon, not the lady. After that very little goes according to plan.

GENRE: Comic fantasy (age 9-12).

Published: 2012.

ISBN: 978-0-9573612-1-8 (paperback) £6.99

Kindle ASIN: B008K8SDWG

Fell Fun and Fell Facts

Two activity books for children relating to ponies, and Fell ponies in particular.

Fell Fun

for ages 4 to 7 years

Puzzles, counting, colouring, spot the difference, spot the same, matching, rhyming, starting letters, mazes and dot to dot, cutting and sticking – all about ponies.

GENRE: Activity book. 20 pages. £2.00

Fell Facts

for 7 years and upwards

Description of the Fell pony breed, what the ponies can do, where they live, crosswords, wordsearches, picture quiz, a story and lots of pictures, plus a list of other books and DVDs about Fell ponies.

GENRE: Activity book. 20 pages. £2.00

Both books can go in one mailing for the same postage cost.

Fell Fun and **Fell Facts** were produced at the request of the Fell Pony Society and may also be purchased from the FPS office in Appleby, Cumbria, and at shows and events run by the Society.

JACKDAW E BOOKS
Daw Bank, Greenholme, Tebay, Penrith, Cumbria
CA10 3TA
England
http://www.jackdawebooks.co.uk